MW00904912

SQL Architecture
Basics
Joes 2 Pros

Beginning Architecture Concepts for
Microsoft SQL Server 2008

(SQL Exam Prep Series 70-433 Volume 3 of 5)

By
Rick A. Morelan
MCDBA, MCTS, MCITP, MCAD, MOE, MCSE, MCSE+I

ISBN: 1451579462
EAN-13: 978-145-157-9468
Rick A. Morelan
Rick@Joes2Pros.com

Table of Contents

About the Author

In 1994, you could find Rick Morelan braving the frigid waters of the Bering Sea as an Alaska commercial fisherman. His computer skills were non-existent at the time, so you might figure such beginnings seemed unlikely to lead him down the path to SQL Server expertise at Microsoft. However, every computer expert in the world today woke up at some point in their life knowing nothing about computers. They say luck is what happens when preparation meets opportunity. In the case of Rick Morelan, people were a big part of his good luck.

Making the change from fisherman seemed scary and took daily schooling at Catapult Software Training Institute. Rick got his lucky break in August 1995, working his first database job at Microsoft. Since that time, Rick has worked more than 10 years at Microsoft and has attained over 30 Microsoft technical certifications in applications, networking, databases and .NET development.

Acknowledgements

As a book with a supporting web site, illustrations, media content and software scripts, it takes more than the usual author, illustrator and editor to put everything together into a great learning experience. Since my publisher has the more traditional contributor list available, I'd like to recognize the core team members:

Editor: Jessica Brown, Joel Heidal
Cover Illustration: Jungim Jang
Technical Review: Tom Ekberg, Joel Heidal
Software Design Testing: Irina Berger
Index: Denise Driscoll
User Acceptance Testing: Michael McLean
Website & Digital Marketing: Gaurav Singhal

Thank you to all the teachers at Catapult Software Training Institute in the mid-1990s. What a great start to open my eyes. It landed me my first job at Microsoft by August of that year.

A giant second wind came from Koenig-Solutions, which gives twice the training and attention for half the price of most other schools. Mr. Rohit Aggarwal is the visionary founder of this company based in New Delhi, India. Rohit's business model sits students down one-on-one with experts. Each expert dedicates weeks to help each new IT student succeed. The numerous twelve-hour flights I took to

India to attend those classes were pivotal to my success. Whenever a new generation of software was released, I got years ahead of the learning curve by spending one or two months at Koenig.

Dr. James D. McCaffrey at Volt Technical Resources in Bellevue, Wash., taught me how to improve my own learning by teaching others. You'll frequently see me in his classroom because he makes learning fun. McCaffrey's unique style boosts the self-confidence of his students, and his tutelage has been essential to my own professional development. His philosophy inspires the *Joes 2 Pros* curriculum.

Introduction

Sure I wrote great queries and was always able to deliver precisely the data that everyone wanted. But a "wake up call" occasion on December 26, 2006 forced me to get better acquainted with the internals of SQL Server. That challenge was a turning point for me and my knowledge of SQL Server performance and architecture. Almost everyone from the workplace was out of town or taking time off for the holidays, and I was in the office for what I expected would be a very quiet day. I received a call that a query which had been working fine for years was suddenly crippling the system. The ask was not for me to write one of my brilliant queries but to troubleshoot the existing query and get it back to running well. Until that moment, I hadn't spent any time tuning SQL Server – that was always done by another team member. To me, tuning seemed like a "black box" feat accomplished by unknown formulas that I would never understand. On my own on that Boxing Day, I learned the mysteries behind tuning SQL Server. In truth, it's really just like driving a car. By simply turning the key and becoming acquainted with a few levers and buttons, you can drive anywhere you want. With SQL Server, there are just a few key rules and tools which will put you in control of how things run on your system.

Skills Needed for this Book

If you have no SQL coding knowledge, then I recommend you first get into the groove of the *Beginning SQL 2008 Joes 2 Pros* book (ISBN 978-1-4392-5317-5). If you already have basic SQL skills and want to get really good at writing queries, then I recommend *SQL Queries Joes 2 Pros* (ISBN 978-1-4392-5318-2) as your best starting point before tackling the architecture and programming topics.

About this Book

As companies grow and do more business, the data they store in databases similarly grows. If you want to be a go-to person on the inner workings of SQL Server, then this book will be your partner in achieving that goal. If you have completed the *SQL Queries Joes 2 Pros* book, you already have written some advanced queries. This book builds on that knowledge and will show you more about the parts of SQL Server at work behind the scenes when you are running queries and creating new database objects. Most importantly, you will learn how to make the essential queries for your business run most efficiently and at the fastest speed possible.

It is time for books and schools to compete on quality and effectiveness and not a mass marketing push. The more this book succeeds, the more we will get their attention and what people really need and are demanding. To put it simply, there is a recipe for success – you are empowered to choose your own ingredients. Just learn the lesson, do the lab, study the Points to Ponder, and play the review game at the end of each chapter.

Most of the exercises in this book are designed around proper database practices in the workplace. The workplace also offers common challenges and process changes over time. For example, it is good practice to use numeric data for IDs. If you have ever seen a Canadian postal code (zip code), you see the need for character data in relational information. You will occasionally see an off-the-beaten-path strategy demonstrated so you know how to approach a topic in a job interview or workplace assignment.

I'm often asked about the Points to Ponder feature, which is popular with both beginners and experienced developers. Some have asked why I don't simply call it a "Summary Page." While it's true that the Points to Ponder page generally captures key points from each section, I frequently include options or technical insights not contained in the chapter. Often these are points which I or my students have found helpful and which I believe will enhance your understanding of SQL Server.

The *Joes 2 Pros* series began in the summer of 2006. The project started as a few easy-to-view labs to transform the old, dry text reading into easier and fun lessons for the classroom. The labs grew into stories. The stories grew into chapters. In 2008, many people whose lives and careers had been improved through my classes convinced me to write a book to reach out to more people. In 2009 the first book began in full gear until its completion (*Beginning SQL Joes 2 Pros*, ISBN 978-1-4392-5317-5).

How to Use the Downloadable Companion Files

Clear content and high-resolution multimedia videos coupled with code samples will take you on this journey. To give you all this and save printing costs, all supporting files are available with a free download from www.Joes2Pros.com. The breakdown of the offerings from these supporting files is listed below:

Training videos: To get you started, the first three chapters are in video format for free downloading. Videos show labs, demonstrate concepts, and review Points to Ponder along with tips from the appendix. Ranging from 3-15 minutes in length, they use special effects to highlight key points. There is even a "Setup" video that shows you how to download and use all other files. You can go at your own pace and pause or replay within lessons as needed.

Answer Keys: The downloadable files also include an Answer Key for you to verify your completed work. Another helpful use for independent students is that these coding answers are available for peeking if you get really stuck.

Resource files: Located in the resources sub-folder from the download site are your practice lab resource files. These files hold the few non-SQL script files needed for some labs. You will be prompted by the text each time you need to download and utilize a resource file.

Lab setup files: SQL Server is a database engine and we need to practice on a database. The Joes 2 Pros Practice Company database is a fictitious travel booking company whose name is shortened to the database name of JProCo. The scripts to set up the JProCo database can be found here.

Chapter review files: Ready to take your new skills out for a test drive? We have the ever popular Bug Catcher game located here.

AdventureWorks: The JProCo database will be used more often but this is the first *Joes 2 Pros* book which requires that you have AdventureWorks installed in order to do some of the lessons. Be aware there are many versions of AdventureWorks, and the file you need to locate and download is the AdventureworksDBCI.msi.

AdventureworksDBCI.msi. Once you download and run this file, you may find that it is installed but not visible in Management Studio. You first need to attach the database. In Management Studio's Object Explorer, simply right-click the Databases folder, click Attach, then click Add, and then navigate to locate the filepath for this mdf file (listed at the top of page 13). You will find it in your Program Files folder:

\Microsoft SQLServer\MSSQL.1\MSSQL\Data\AdventureWorks_Data.mdf.
Once you attach the file, you may need to right-click and refresh the Databases
folder in order to see the AdventureWorks database in Object Explorer.

What This Book is Not

This is not a memorization book. Rather, this is a skills book to make preparing
for the certification test a familiarization process. This book prepares you to apply
what you've learned to answer SQL questions in the job setting. The highest
hopes are that your progress and level of SQL knowledge will soon have business
managers seeking your expertise to provide the reporting and information vital to
their decision making. It's a good feeling to achieve and to help at the same time.
Many students comment that the training method used in *Joes 2 Pros* was what
finally helped them achieve their goal of certification.

When you go through the *Joes 2 Pros* series and really know this material, you
deserve a fair shot at SQL certification. Use only authentic testing engines
drawing on your skill. Show you know it for real. At the time of this writing,
MeasureUp® at http://www.measureup.com provides a good test preparation
simulator. The company's test pass guarantee makes it a very appealing option.

Chapter 1.   Database File Structures

In *Beginning SQL Joes 2 Pros*, we compared data to cargo and database objects to containers for our mission-critical data. The curriculum for that book included the core keywords for each of the four components of the SQL language: DML, DDL, DCL, and TCL.

To put it plainly, this book is about what is under the hood of SQL Server: the engine and parts which process all your data. This book will utilize a great deal of **DDL** (Data Definition Language), since we will be addressing the design and programming of database objects – those vital containers of our business data. However, we will see a fair amount of DML working hand-in-glove with DDL in this book. In the first two books, we built stored procedures using DDL statements which encapsulated the DML statements needed to handle our data tasks. When we build objects like views and functions in this book, we similarly will see statements which define the objects executed simultaneously with the data-centric statements needed to carry out the object's purpose. This is the principal reason it is better for students to gain extensive exposure to queries before launching into the Architecture class.

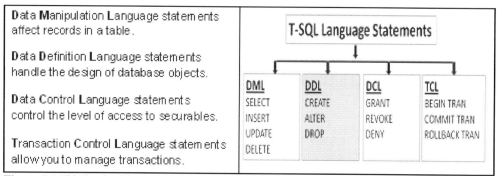

Figure 1.1 This book will emphasize DDL statements, as well as DDL combined with DML.

Each chapter will include instructions for the setup scripts you need to run in order to follow along with the chapter examples. The setup scripts give you the freedom to practice any code you like, including changing or deleting data – or even dropping entire tables or databases. Afterwards you can rerun the setup script (or run the setup script when you reach the next section) and all needed objects and data will be restored. This process is also good practice – these are typical tasks done frequently when working with SQL Server, particularly in a software development and testing environment.

READER NOTE: *In order to follow along with the examples in the first section of Chapter 1, please install SQL Server and run the first setup script SQLArchChapter1.0Setup.sql. The setup scripts for this book are posted at Joes2Pros.com.*

Database File Structures

In the first two *Joes 2 Pros* books, we used the default settings provided by SQL Server whenever we created a database. Our first topic examines database file structures and how we can customize those available structures and settings to best fit our data traffic and system performance needs.

SQL Server databases consist of files which are stored on a hard drive. Actually, I should qualify that – at least 80% of readers are probably like me and the "server" which their instance of SQL Server runs on is their local hard drive. (There may be a few developers who have a network set up and who are already running SQL Server on a separate machine or disk drive.) I have several machines, but I have one dedicated laptop I use for my *Joes 2 Pros* work.

Let's begin with a database we are familiar with, JProCo. I'll begin by dropping this database to see what my server (i.e., my hard drive) looks like without the JProCo database. Before and after I re-create this database, we will look at my hard drive to see the net impact of the JProCo database on my system.

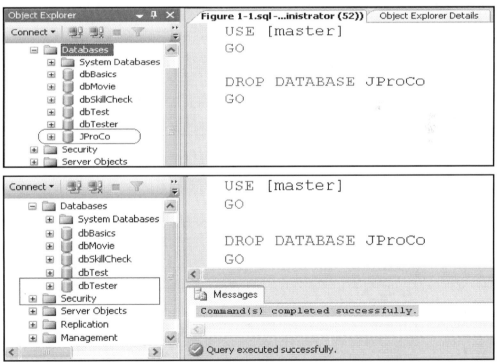

Figure 1.2 *Upper figure:* The JProCo database before I remove it from SQL Server shown alongside the code I will run to drop it. *Lower figure:* I have removed JProCo and double-checked the Object Explorer to confirm that it is gone.

Now that JProCo has been removed, let's look at my hard drive and its current capacity.

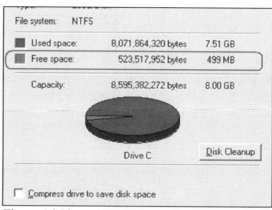

To find capacity details on your own machine, open Windows Explorer (Start+E) > right-click the C drive > Properties.

It appears that I have 499 MB free on my hard drive without the JProCo database (see Figure 1.3).

Figure 1.3 I have 499 MB free without the JProCo db.

I'll now rerun the first setup script for this chapter in order to bring back the JProCo database. The setup script (**SQLArchChapter1.0Setup.sql**) will load the JProCo database onto my system fully populated (Figure 1.4, Panel A). Once the script has executed successfully, I'll go to SQL Server's Object Explorer > right-click the Databases folder > and choose **Refresh** (Figure 1.4, Panel B). After the refresh, the JProCo folder becomes visible in my Object Explorer (Figure 1.4, Panel C).

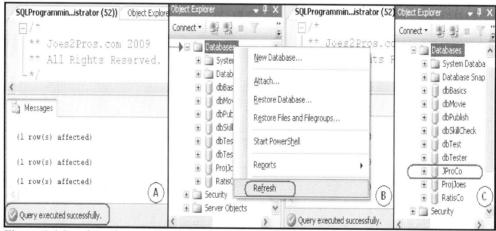

Figure 1.4 *Panel A* – the setup script has run successfully. *Panel B* – the Databases folder is refreshed. *Panel C* – the JProCo database becomes visible in Object Explorer.

Be aware that the Object Explorer tree does *not* dynamically update a database object after it is added or dropped. *Expect to run this same refresh process each time you check Object Explorer and wish to see your updated changes in the list.*

Now I'll return to my hard drive. Recall it showed 499 MB of free space prior to reloading the JProCo database onto my system. With JProCo now reloaded on my system, my hard drive shows just 305 MB of free space (see Figure 1.5). *So it appears JProCo is occupying roughly 200 MB someplace on my local drive.*

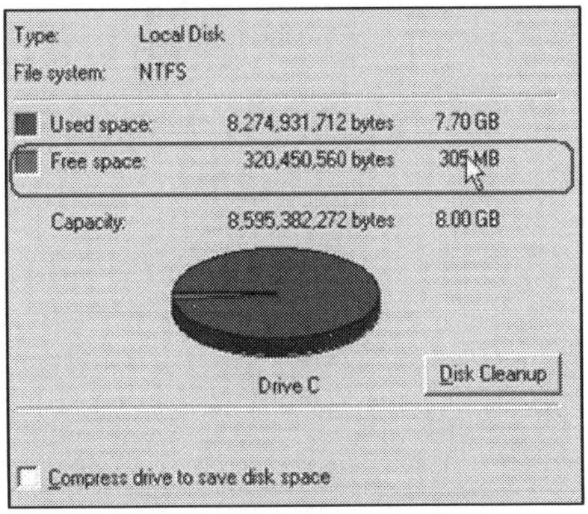

SQL Server chooses a default location to store databases whenever an alternate location is not specified. The filepath shown here (and in Figure 1.6) is the default location for SQL Server 2008:

Figure 1.5 Just 305 MB of space is now free.

C:\Program Files\Microsoft SQL Server\MSSQL10.MSSQLSERVER\MSSQL\DATA

This is the default location for SQL Server 2005:
C:\Program Files\Microsoft SQL Server\MSSQL9.MSSQLSERVER\MSSQL\DATA

This screen capture of my **MSSQL\DATA** folder shows the two files which comprise the JProCo database. When I ran the setup script, SQL Server loaded these two files onto my system.

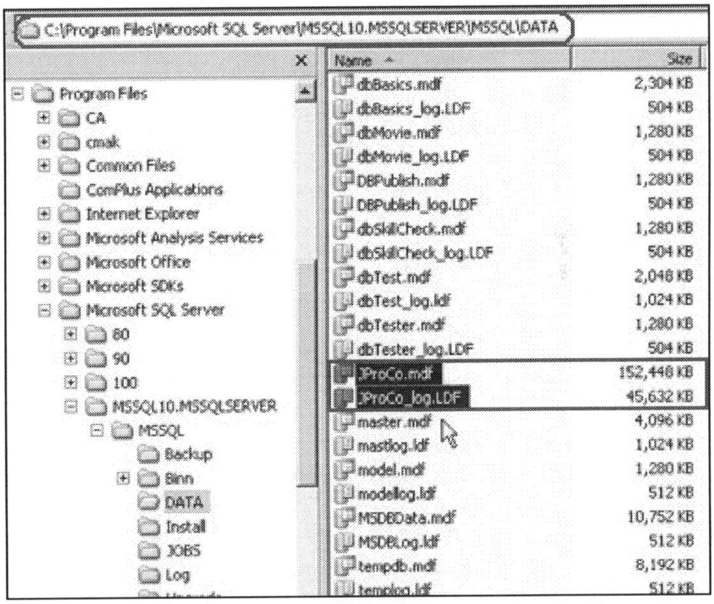

Notice that one file is roughly 152 MB in size *(JProCo.mdf)*. The other file is roughly 45 MB *(JProCo_log.ldf)*.

Figure 1.6 My MSSQL\DATA folder shows two JProCo files.

Together they total roughly 200 MB – the same amount which we estimated JProCo occupies on my hard drive. These two files stored on the hard drive contain all of the data and all of the logging activity for the JProCo database.

DataFiles and LogFiles

In my experience, many students do not find the concept of datafile and logfile activity an intuitive one. So we will ease into it with an example that I've found helps students grasp this topic more quickly. But first we need a little explanation as to why SQL Server uses logfiles.

We know that SQL Server stores its data much like other applications – in files which are saved to a persistent drive. But a distinguishing feature of SQL Server is its robust ability to keep track of things. ***The security and safety of your data and reliability of your system are SQL Server's top priorities.*** Therefore, you can imagine that logging activity – which tracks every transaction made in your database – is a pretty big deal. Examples where logging saves the day generally involve some type of database restore or recovery need. Once a database backs itself up, you're generally assured a reliable mechanism you can use to restore the system in case something unfavorable happens. Suppose you notice bad data has come into your system through one of your periodic feeds. In fact, this data is so problematic that your team decides you must restore the database back to the point a week ago before the bad data began entering the system. *Your periodic database backup is built using information provided by the logfile.* Logfiles keep track of your database transactions and help ensure data and system integrity, in case a system recovery is ever necessary.

Ok, now we're ready to tackle datafiles and logfiles. A datafile is fairly straightforward – it contains all your current data. Suppose you've been making changes to JProCo's Employee table. If you could peek into the datafile, you would find data identical with the result of **SELECT * FROM Employee**. However, it wouldn't tell you that an hour ago, you deleted an employee record, or that today at 9:45 a.m. your manager added a new employee record to the table.

I sometimes compare the datafile to getting information from my ATM. Usually I'm happy with the data my ATM shows me (i.e., my current balance), and it always provides my data rapidly. But if I need to look back and see deposit or withdrawal information, the ATM can't help me. To see the transaction detail which has led to my current account balance, I need to look elsewhere. Logfiles are just like the transaction history shown in my bank statements, where I can find a separate transaction entry for every purchase, deposit, or withdrawal made. The two identically structured WordPad files shown here (Figure 1.7 and 1.8) are going to help us visualize the transaction activity retained by the logfile.

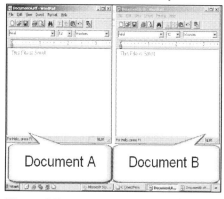

Figure 1.7 Two identically structured files.

These are pretty small files, just 1 KB each. In the lesson video for this section (Lab1.1_DatabaseFileStructures.wmv), you will see me make some significant edits to Document A, which I won't make to Document B. Not only will the documents differ visually, but when we see that the changes cause Document A's size to expand to 6 KB, it's clear that Document A and Document B are no longer identical files.

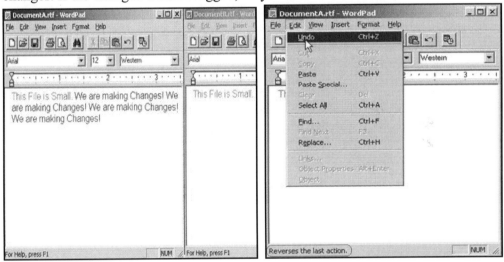

Figure 1.8 Documents A & B begin as identical files.

Where my classes tend to find the "ah-ha" moment is when we actually see the changes in Document A being removed one by one as I use Edit > Undo to backtrack and see the edits disappear. Similarly, if I delete a few words one by one, the Undo operation will backtrack and make each word reappear one by one. What the application is doing is traversing through the log of changes and accessing memory to find all of those changes. If the changes weren't logged, they wouldn't be available.

Figure 1.9 Our demonstration with two WordPad files helps conceptualize logfile activity.

At the end of the video demonstration, Document A has been returned to its beginning state – it contains the identical information as Document B and I've saved the file in order to clear the logged changes from memory. Thus, Document A and B each are 1 KB in size at the end. But just prior to saving Document A, we make another interesting "ah-ha" observation. On the surface, both documents appear identical (as shown in Figure 1.10). However, when we compare the size of the two files, Document A is many times larger than Document B. In my classroom demos, the file grows to 250 KB with relatively few clicks. The log tracks changes made to the document from the last time it was saved up until the current moment.

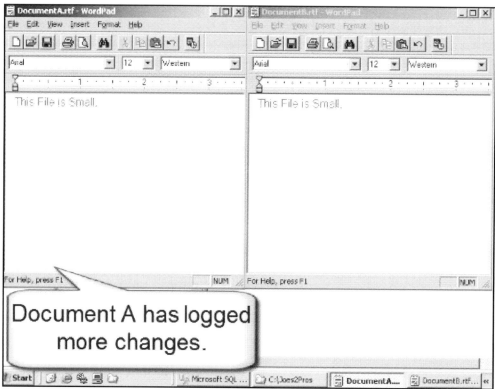

Figure 1.10 The log tracks all the changes from the last document backup (save) until now.

At this point, an expert database admin (DBA) would understandably be bored silly with this demo. However, over the years I've found this the fastest way to ramp up students new to the abstract concept of the work done by logfiles. When the document save operation clears out the log, we also get a nice reference point to regular server backups, which truncate (empty) the logfile. Document A's condition at the beginning and end of the demo (i.e., 1 KB and reflecting the data "This File is Small.") serves as a comparison to the datafile. Because the file was saved at the beginning of the demo and then again at the end, the document showed just the current state of the data – nothing to do with tracking data which was added or deleted along the way. The datafile's purpose is to reflect the current state of your database.

For student readers still trying to get their heads around this idea of datafiles and logfiles, have no fear – the video demonstrations contain many examples, as well as a practice or challenge at the end of the video to give you plenty of practice with datafiles and logfiles. And the next four pages include a step by step tutorial following data through the datafile and logfile as it enters a new database.

Step 1. Pretend you have a brand new database with one table (Employee) which contains zero records. There are no records in your JProCo database, so there are no records in your datafile. And since you haven't made any changes to the database, there are zero records in your logfile.

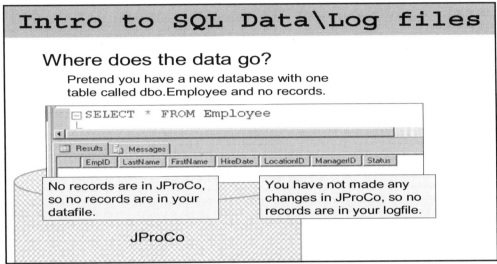

Figure 1.11 The brand new database contains zero records.

Step 2. Now data starts coming into the JProCo database. You add one new record for Alex Adams to the Employee table. So now you have one record in your datafile and one record in your logfile.

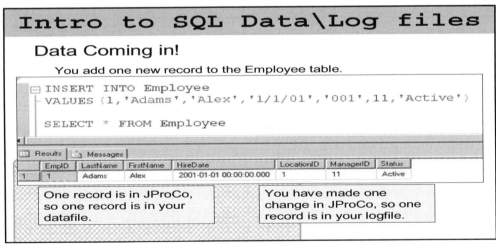

Figure 1.12 One record now appears in the database.

Step 3. You then add another record (Barry Brown). Two records are now in JProCo, so two records are in the datafile and two records in the logfile. So you have two pieces of data and two entries in the logfile reflecting those changes.

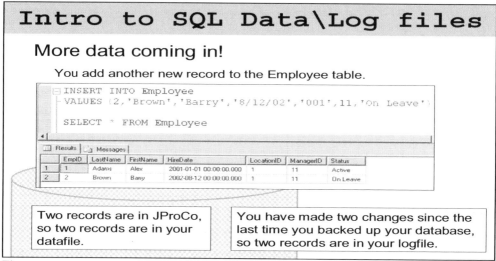

Figure 1.13 A total of two records are now in the database.

Step 4. Your next step updates an existing record. Employee 2 is coming back from leave, so you're going to change his status from "On Leave" to "Active." There will still be two records in the database, so the datafile will contain two records. But there will be three records in your logfile, since you made three changes since the last time you backed up your database.

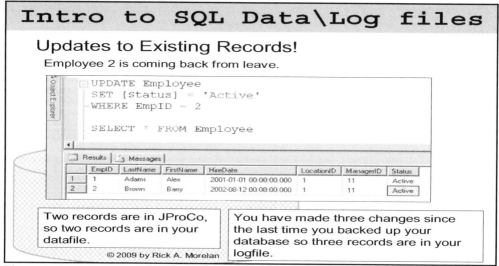

Figure 1.14 An existing record is updated; 2 records in the database but 3 records in the LDF.

Impact of the Database Backup Process

Step 5. The database is backed up nightly at midnight. After the three earlier changes happen, suppose it's after midnight and the database backup has just finished running. At 12:05AM, there would still be two records in the JProCo database, so you would have two records in your datafile. During most backup processes, the changes contained in the logfile are sent to the backup file. The logfile is truncated as part of the backup process, so zero records remain in the logfile immediately after each backup.

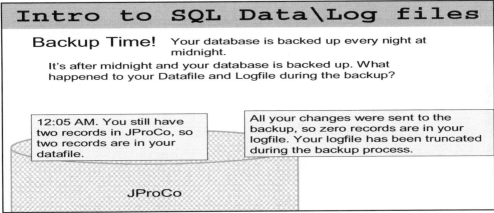

Figure 1.15 The database backup runs. The logfile is truncated, so it contains no records.

Step 6. On Day 2, you insert Lee Osako's record (the third record added to Employee). At this point you have three records in your datafile. The logfile has been empty since the backup, and this change now adds one record to the logfile.

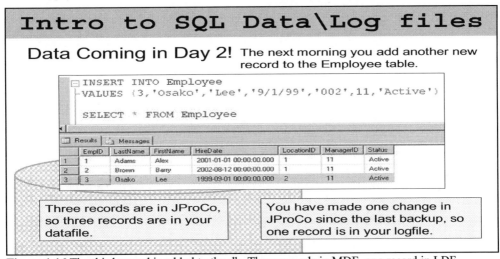

Figure 1.16 The third record is added to the db. Three records in MDF, one record in LDF.

Step 7. On the same day (Day 2), you delete Barry Brown from the table. Removing one record leaves two records in the datafile. The logfile now contains two records, one for the INSERT (Lee) and one for the DELETE (Barry).

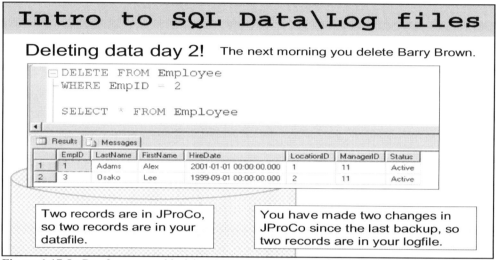

Figure 1.17 On Day 2 one record is deleted. Two records remain in MDF, two in LDF.

Recall Figure 1.6 where we saw the default data and log files which SQL Server originated when we created the JProCo database. It named the datafile JProCo.MDF and the logfile JProCo_log.LDF.

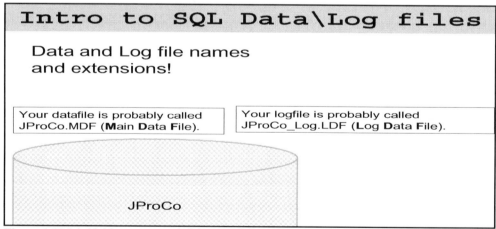

Figure 1.18 It is highly recommended that you follow the naming convention shown here.

This convention for naming files and the extensions reflect best practice recommendations (see Figure 1.18). *SQL Server does not enforce the .mdf/.ldf extensions, but following this standard is highly recommended.*

Creating Databases

If you were to execute this statement, you would create a database called "TSQLTestDB," and all the defaults for name, size, and location of the datafile and logfile would be chosen for you. Up until now, we have accepted SQL Server's defaults for these items each time we have created a database.

```
CREATE DATABASE TSQLTestDB
GO
```

Figure 1.19 This code would create a db using defaults for name-size-location of MDF & LDF.

But you can actually choose your own options. For our examples in this chapter, we won't store any of our files in the default location (MSSQL10.MSSQLSERVER\ DATA folder). Create a folder titled **SQL** on your hard drive (C:\SQL). The MDF and LDF files for our new test database will be stored there.

In addition to specifying the location, we will also choose the name and size for TSQLTestDB's datafile and logfile. As a rule of thumb, it's generally a good idea to make the size of your LDF 25% of the MDF. Now run all of this code together.

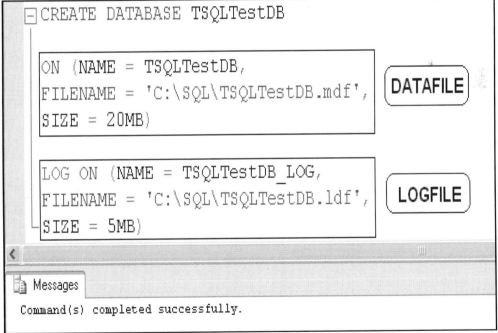

Figure 1.20 You can choose the name, size, and location for your datafiles.

Let's check the C:\SQL folder and confirm we can see the newly created files TSQLTestDB.mdf (20 MB) and TSQLTestDB.ldf (5 MB).

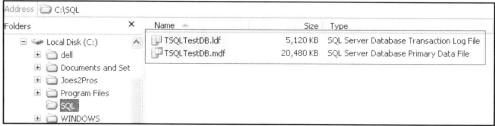

Figure 1.21 We specified the name, size, and location for TSQLTestDB, its MDF, and its LDF.

Now let's see how to locate metadata for this test database using SQL Server's Object Explorer. Remember to first refresh the Databases folder in the Object Explorer, since we know that SQL Server does not change its contents automatically (Object Explorer > right-click Databases > Refresh, as shown earlier in Figure 1.4).

Navigate to TSQLTestDB (Object Explorer > Databases > TSQLTestDB). Then open the Database Properties dialog by right-clicking the TSQLTestDB folder > Properties.

In the left-hand "Select a page" nav menu, click the Files page. This will show you the name for the database, the MDF, and the LDF. You can see the custom specifications we included in our CREATE DATABASE statement (see prior page, Figure 1.19) for the logical and physical name, size, and location (C:\SQL) for each file.

Figure 1.22 TSQLTestDB > Properties.

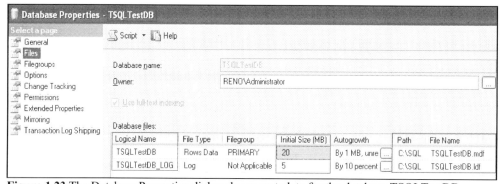

Figure 1.23 The Database Properties dialog shows metadata for the database TSQLTestDB.

Lab 1.1: Database File Structures

Lab Prep: Each lab has one or more Skill Checks. Start with Skill Check 1 and proceed until you reach the Points to Ponder section. Before you can begin the lab, you must have SQL Server installed and have run the current setup script (SQLArchChapter1.1Setup.sql). Since this is your first lab, please make sure you have viewed the video on how to set up a typical lab called SQLArchSetupLabSteps.wmv. This video shows you the steps involved in setting up all the labs in this book. View the lab video instructions for this specific lab named Lab1.1_DatabaseFileStructures.wmv.

Skill Check 1: Create a database named after your fictitious company, **RatisCo**. Using what you've learned, create RatisCo with the following properties.

    a. **50MB** file named **RatisCo_Data.mdf**.

    b. A **20MB** log file name **RatisCo_Log.ldf**.

    c. The file should be located at **C:\SQL\RatisCo_Data.mdf**

    d. The logfile location should be **C:\SQL\RatisCo_Log.ldf**

When complete, your result should resemble the figure below (Figure 1.24).

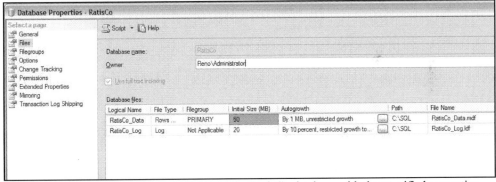

Figure 1.24 In Skill Check 1, you will create the RatisCo database with the specified properties.

Answer Code: The T-SQL code to this lab can be found in the downloadable files in a file named Lab1.1_DatabaseFileStructures.sql.

Database File Structures - Points to Ponder

1. Transact-SQL (T-SQL) statements are a common way to interact with SQL Server, view and modify data, or change the configuration of the server.

2. A new database can be built through the graphical UI (user interface) in SQL Server Management Studio or by using a CREATE DATABASE script.

3. Even when a graphical management tool is used to create or modify a database, the actions are translated into T-SQL statements and then executed.

4. SQL Server stores data in one or more datafiles.

5. A file is the physical allocation of space on disk. Each database has two or more files.

6. Datafiles hold the actual database objects and the data.

7. If only one datafile exists, it will have an .MDF extension by default.

8. Regardless of how a database is created, T-SQL can be used to perform the following tasks:
   - Create and modify tables and indexes in a database.
   - Query objects by using the SELECT statement.
   - Insert and delete rows in a table.
   - Modify existing data in a table.
   - Repair a database.
   - Create a database.
   - Manage and connect to other databases.

DataFile Planning and Implementation

From the last section, we know that SQL Server stores all the objects and data for a database in a datafile. Think back to our analogy of database objects as containers for data. If the containers of our mission-critical data are important, then the file responsible for physically housing all of the objects and all of the data on your disk drive merits special attention. It's wise to take extra care with design and capacity considerations for your datafiles, which is what the remainder of this chapter covers.

When you create a database, you must create at least one datafile.
If SQL Server needs data, we know it looks to datafiles for all of its objects. At a minimum, each database must have at least one datafile – multiple datafiles are also possible. Every datafile must have a storage location (e.g., C:\SQL\JProCo.mdf) whether you define the filepath or have SQL Server choose the default location behind the scenes. Below is the default filepath.
C:\Program Files\Microsoft SQL Server\MSSQL10.MSSQLSERVER\MSSQL\DATA *(SQL 2008)*
C:\Program Files\Microsoft SQL Server\MSSQL9.MSSQLSERVER\MSSQL\DATA *(SQL 2005)*

Make the datafile large enough to hold all of your expected data.
It's a good idea to make sure the MDF is adequately large, even when your database starts out empty. If you estimate your data will likely grow to 5 GB of data, then create your MDF from the outset to be at least 5 GB.

Your datafile size is only limited by the size of your hard drive.
The minimum size for a datafile is 3 MB and 1 MB for a logfile. These are also the default file sizes when you create a database without specifying the size. The upper limit for your datafile's size is essentially the amount of available space on your available hard drives. If your datafile fills up, then SQL Server can't process additional data. One solution is you can adjust the size property of your datafile. When you increase the size property, the datafile will procure more space on the drive. You can also adjust the filegrowth property to allow the datafile to grow. You can specify the incremental rate at which you want your datafile to grow once the current size specification has been reached. This rate is known as filegrowth and is controlled by the MDF's filegrowth property. For example, assume your hard drive has 100 MB available and your MDF is approaching 30 MB, which is the maximum size you specified when you created your database. You can set the MDF to grow and occupy additional hard drive space (up to roughly 70MB more). However, if your hard drive runs out of space, then you either need a larger drive or a separate drive. That's where **Alternate Datafile Placement** can be the solution. You have the option of placing your datafile on a separate drive, or even

on its own dedicated drive. (e.g., if you have the D drive available, you could dedicate it just to your data D:\SQL\JProCo.mdf).

Your data activity may overwhelm the throughput of one drive.
In your SQL Server work, you will occasionally encounter scenarios where your business moves so quickly that the throughput of your data traffic exceeds the throughput capacity of the drive. For example, since the C drive can become very busy with operating system (OS) activity and several services running on it, you might want to reserve the throughput of the C drive for the day to day operations. Also, the main use of the database is one giant data table which receives billions of hits per hour. The activity of that table could overwhelm the throughput of any single drive. You can use **Multiple Datafiles Placement** to spread the entire database workload evenly across several datafiles (see Figure 1.24). In addition to your MDF (main datafile), you can create secondary datafiles and split where the storage takes place. (Note: SQL Server allows just one file per database to use the .MDF extension. Any additional datafile(s) must use the .NDF extension (for secoNdary DataFile, e.g., E:\SQL\JProCo.ndf).) A table (or any single database object) may be assigned to just one filegroup. However, you can associate a filegroup with as many datafiles as you need. Thus, when you wish to spread a giant table's workload across many drives, you will use multiple datafiles but place them all in the same filegroup.

SOLUTION #1: Adjust the Size of Your Datafile
You can adjust the size property of your datafile. When you increase the size property, the datafile will procure more space on the drive.

You can also adjust the filegrowth property to allow the datafile to grow. If your datafile fills up, then SQL Server can't process additional data. You can specify the incremental rate at which you want your datafile to grow once the current size specification has been reached. This rate is known as filegrowth and is controlled by the MDF's filegrowth property.

SOLUTION #2: Alternate Datafile Placement
You may choose to place your datafile on its own dedicated drive. Since the C drive can become very busy with operating system (OS) activity and several services running on it, you might want to reserve the throughput of the C drive for the day to day operations. You have the option of placing your datafile on a separate drive, or even on its own dedicated drive. (e.g., if you have the D drive available, you could dedicate it just to your data D:\SQL\JProCo.mdf)

SOLUTION #3: Multiple Datafiles for Data Placement
Suppose you have already placed your datafile on a dedicated drive (e.g., the D drive, D:\SQL\JProCo.mdf), but you soon see that this drive will not be big enough for your growing database. Or perhaps it's not fast enough. In addition to your MDF (main datafile), you can create a secondary datafile and split where the storage takes place. (**Note**: SQL Server allows just one file per database to use the .MDF extension. Any additional datafile(s) must use the .NDF extension (for secoNdary DataFile, e.g., E:\SQL\JProCo.ndf).)

Suppose your database contains multiple tables and you figure out that your production tables comprise about half of the workload of your entire SQL Server database infrastructure. The other tables combined use the rest of the available workload. You can elect to have your secondary datafile dedicated to your production tables, and the remaining tables (e.g., reporting tables, lookup tables) can reside in your MDF on another drive.

SOLUTION #4: Multiple Datafiles for Automatic Load Balancing
Suppose the main use of your database is one giant data table which receives billions of hits per hour. The activity of that table could overwhelm the throughput of any single drive. You can spread the entire database workload evenly across several datafiles (see Figure 1.25). Note that a table (or any single database object) may be assigned to just one filegroup. However, you can associate a filegroup with as many datafiles as you need. Thus, when you wish to spread a giant table's workload across many drives, you will use multiple datafiles but place them all in the same filegroup.

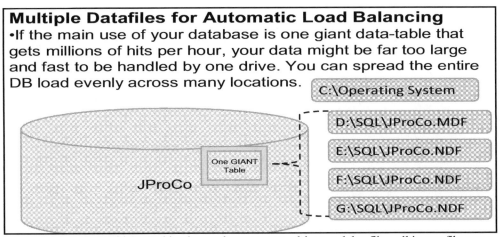

Figure 1.25 A giant table's workload spread across many drives and datafiles, all in one filegroup.

Using Filegroups

There are many advantages to using filegroups to manage the database workload. A filegroup may contain many datafiles, and the properties of all the datafiles can be managed simultaneously with a filegroup (see Figure 1.26).

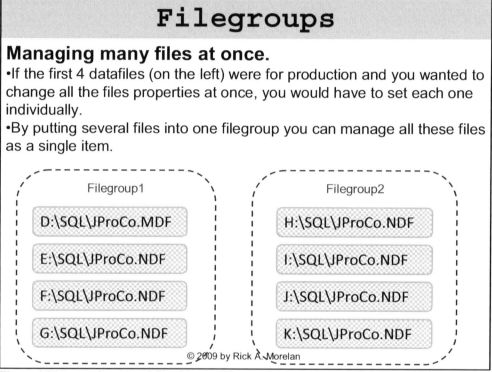

Figure 1.26 By putting several files into one filegroup, you can manage them as a single item.

Primary and Secondary Filegroups

A *primary filegroup* contains the primary datafile (MDF) and possibly secondary datafiles (NDF). All system tables are allocated to the primary filegroup.

A *secondary filegroup* (also called a *user-defined filegroup*) contains secondary datafiles (NDF) and database objects.

The default filegroup contains objects which were created without an assigned filegroup. The primary filegroup is the default filegroup unless another filegroup is specified.

Logfiles are never part of a filegroup. We learned about log files at the beginning of the chapter. The log datafile tracks all the changes that have taken place since the last database backup. Whereas datafiles have the file extension .mdf or .ndf, log datafiles always have the .ldf extension.

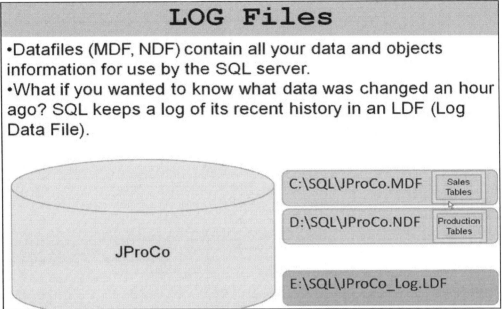

Figure 1.27 The Log Data File (LDF) must exist but can't be part of a filegroup.

When we completed Lab 1.1, we created one datafile called RatisCo_Data.mdf in the SQL folder of the C drive (C:\SQL\RatisCo_Data.mdf). Since we didn't specify any filegroups, SQL Server automatically placed it in the primary filegroup for us. We also created a log file in the same location (C:\SQL\RatisCo_Log.ldf). That file was not placed inside a filegroup, since log files are never part of a filegroup.

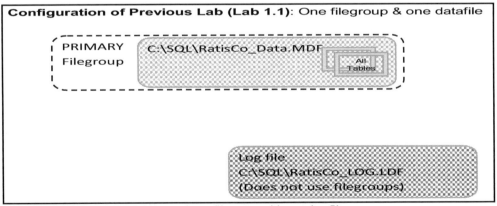

Figure 1.28 Our previous lab created one filegroup with one datafile.

Our next lab will create one datafile in the primary filegroup and two datafiles in the secondary filegroup (also known as the user-defined filegroup).

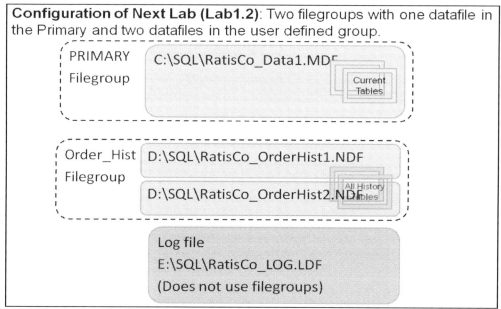

Figure 1.29 Our next lab will create one MDF in the primary filegroup, 2 NDFs in the secondary.

You will accomplish Part 1 of the Lab 1.2 by following along hands-on with the demonstration. Later you will accomplish Part 2 independently. As shown in Figure 1.29 (previous page), the goal of Part 1 will be the following:

1) Create one MDF (main datafile) in the primary filegroup;

2) Create two NDFs (secondary datafiles) in a user-defined filegroup called Order_Hist located on a separate drive;

3) Create the LDF (log datafile) on a separate drive.

Note: For at least 80% of readers, it's unlikely that the machine you are practicing on has several drives you can write to. It's important to practice sending datafiles to different drives upon database creation and writing our code as such. Thus, we will improvise by creating separate folders, which we will treat as drives in order to simulate workplace conditions.

Let's create the following three folders on our hard drives to stand in for the C, D, and E drives, respectively:

C:\C_SQL

C:\D_SQL

C:\E_SQL

Let's also make sure the RatisCo database has been dropped from our server:

```
USE master
GO

DROP DATABASE RatisCo
GO
```

The CREATE DATABASE statement we will write for RatisCo will contain all the specifications for the datafiles and filegroups. The ON clause specifies which datafile(s) to store the database on and also accepts arguments to specify which filegroup the datafile(s) should belong to. The usual practice is to place the .MDF file in the PRIMARY filegroup. All other filegroups must be explicitly defined within the FILEGROUP argument.

```
CREATE DATABASE RatisCo
ON PRIMARY ( ), --Primary Filegroup (will reside on our "C drive" (C:\C_SQL)).
          --The next line represents a secondary filegroup, which we must name.
FILEGROUP [Order_Hist]
( ), ( )  --These NDFs will be placed in our makeshift "D drive" (C:\D_SQL).

LOG ON( )--Our log will go in the folder representing our "E drive" (C:\E_SQL).
```
Figure 1.30 Our next lab will create one MDF in the primary filegroup, 2 NDFs in the secondary.

Run the code in Figure 1.31 to create the RatisCo database.

```
CREATE DATABASE RatisCo
ON PRIMARY
(NAME = RatisCo_Data1,
FILENAME = 'C:\C_SQL\RatisCo_Data1.MDF'),

FILEGROUP [Order_Hist]
(NAME = RatisCo_OrderHist1,
FILENAME = 'C:\D_SQL\RatisCo_OrderHist1.NDF'),
(NAME = RatisCo_OrderHist2,
FILENAME = 'C:\D_SQL\RatisCo_OrderHist2.NDF')

LOG ON(NAME = RatisCo_LOG,
FILENAME = 'C:\E_SQL\RatisCo_LOG.LDF')
GO
```
Messages
Command(s) completed successfully.

Figure 1.31 Our code successfully executes and creates RatisCo per our specifications.

Below is the **Files** page from the Database Properties dialog for RatisCo (Figure
1.32, lower frame). We see RatisCo and all its files were created as we specified.
The **Filegroups** page from the Database Properties dialog (Figure 1.32, upper
frame) shows one primary filegroup containing one file and an Order_Hist filegroup
containing two files.

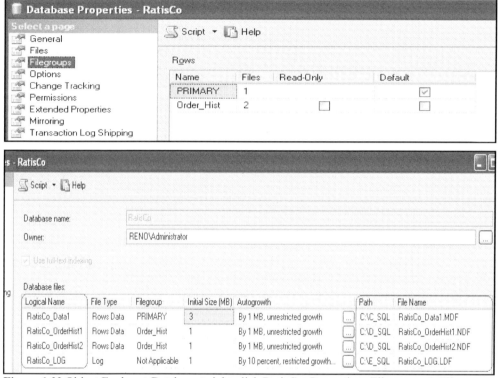

Figure 1.32 Object Explorer>Databases>right-click RatisCo>Properties> Filegroups & Files.

Notice the default size and growth properties ("Initial Size (MB)" and "Autogrowth")
showing for RatisCo (Figure 1.32, previous page). SQL Server assigned the default
settings for these properties, since we did not specify otherwise.

Here we see each RatisCo file as it appears in Windows Explorer (Start+E).
RatisCo and all its files appear as we created them in our code (see Figure 1.31
on the previous page for the syntax of the CREATE DATABASE statement).

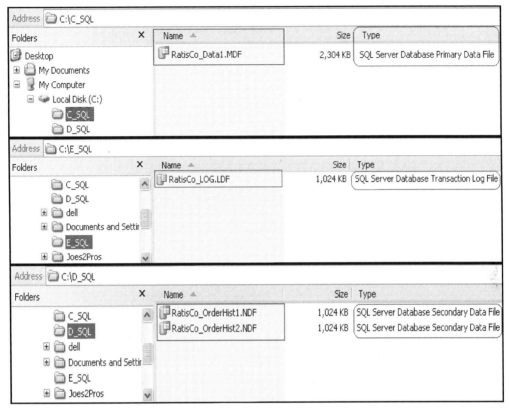

Figure 1.33 We find the MDF, two NDFs, and the LDF have all been created as we specified.

In the second part of the lab, you will drop RatisCo and then create it with two files (the MDF and an NDF) in the primary filegroup, three NDF files in the Order_Hist filegroup, and one log datafile (LDF). In the final section of this chapter, we will make these types of file structure changes (add datafiles, add filegroups) to existing databases without having to first drop and re-create the database.

The model for Lab 1.2 Part 2 is shown on the next page (Figure 1.34). The primary filegroup contains the current tables, and the historical tables are housed in the Order_Hist filegroup.

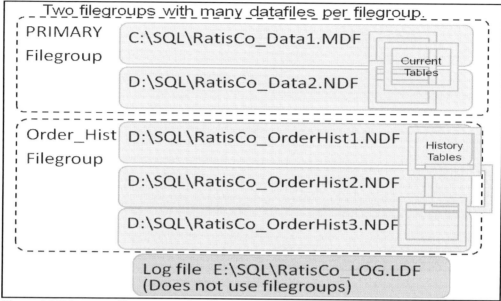

Figure 1.34 Next we will create two datafiles in the primary filegroup, 3 NDFs in the secondary.

Please note, in this chapter we frequently capitalize the extensions of datafiles in filenames (as .MDF, .NDF, .LDF) for illustrative purposes. As you can see, SQL Server gives you the freedom to capitalize filenames as you wish, including your file extensions. Where our code capitalized the datafile extensions, SQL Server created the file precisely as we specified. We saw the uppercase lettering reflected in both the Object Explorer and the Windows Explorer views of the files (Figures 1.31 through 1.33). Similarly, where we coded lowercase lettering for the file extensions, we saw that SQL Server again created the file precisely as we specified (Figures 1.20 through 1.23).

**NOTE: This book includes references and code samples for capabilities such as Autogrowth, Filegrowth, and Auto Shrink, which you need to be aware of as a SQL Pro. However, the rule of thumb for homes and buildings, "it's more expensive to remodel than to build it right the first time", also applies to constructing databases. Ideally, you want each database file to be physically located in one place and not fragmented in various locations on a drive. Each time you upsize your database in small increments, SQL Server grabs any available hard drive space. The additional space procured most likely won't be adjacent to the location on the hard drive where your datafile currently sits. More Input/Output (I/O) resources are needed when SQL Server must search for information which is scattered across a drive. Also, most SQL Pros would recommend you avoid the use of "automatic" settings (e.g., Autogrowth, Filegrowth, Auto Shrink, Auto Close). Not only does the frequent monitoring utilize additional CPU and system resources, but shrinking a datafile invariably results in file and index fragmentation. Instead, SQL Pros prefer to have SQL Server alert them when the database is nearing its maximum size. In cases where you do need to upsize or downsize a database, the best practice is generally to perform these tasks manually.

Lab 1.2: Using Filegroups

Lab Prep: Before you can begin the lab, you must have SQL Server installed and run the SQLArchChapter1.2Setup.sql script. View the lab video instructions in Lab1.2_UsingFilegroups.wmv.

Skill Check 1 (Part 1): You should have already accomplished Part 1 of this Skill Check during the hands-on demonstration in the last section ("Using Filegroups"). See Figure 1.28 detailing the database file structures we created during the demonstration. Our code syntax appears in Figure 1.30, and screenshots of the created file structures appear in Figures 1.31-1.33.

Skill Check 1 (Part 2): Drop the RatisCo database and re-create it with the datafiles and filegroups shown on the previous page (Figure 1.33). When complete, your Database Properties dialog (Filegroups page and Files page) should resemble the screenshots below in Figure 1.35). **Object Explorer > Databases > right-click RatisCo > Properties**

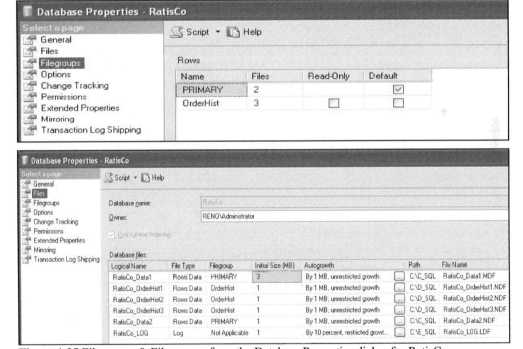

Figure 1.35 Filegroups & Files pages from the Database Properties dialog for RatisCo.

Answer Code: The T-SQL code to this lab can be found in the downloadable files in a file named Lab1.2_UsingFileGroups.sql.

Skill Check 2: Create the database GrowthCo using the name, size, filegrowth, and location specifications below:

1) One MDF (main datafile) in the primary filegroup and in the C:\SQL directory.
2) Initial db size is 50MB, db can grow up to 80MB max, increase by 15MB increments.
3) One LDF (log datafile) in the C:\SQL directory.
4) Initial log size is 20MB, log can grow up to 100MB max, increase by 25% increments.
5) Use the recommended naming convention.

After creating this database, confirm your result matches the Database Properties dialog shown below (see Figure 1.36).

Object Explorer > Databases > GrowthCo > right-click Properties > Files (page)

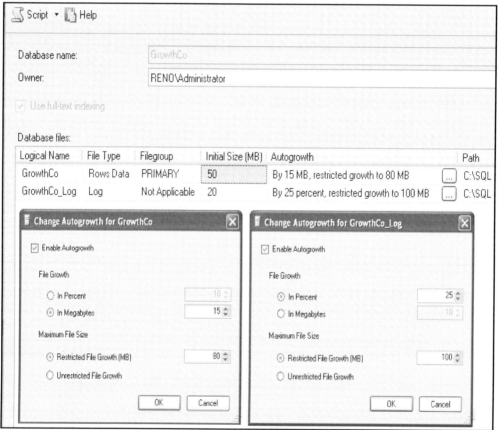

Figure 1.36 The Database Properties dialog for GrowthCo confirms the properties you created.

Skill Check 3: There will be times when you don't want to your database to grow automatically. You want SQL Server to notify you when the MDF or log file is full, so you can manage the upsizing process yourself. Create the database No_Growth using the name, size, filegrowth, and location specifications below:

1) One MDF (main datafile) in the primary filegroup and in the C:\SQL directory.
2) Initial db size is 40MB, db cannot grow.
3) One LDF (log datafile) in the C:\SQL directory.
4) Initial log size is 10MB, log cannot grow.

Use the recommended naming convention.

After creating the No_Growth database, confirm your result matches the Database Properties dialog shown below (see Figure 1.37).

Object Explorer > Databases > No_Growth > right-click Properties > Files (page)

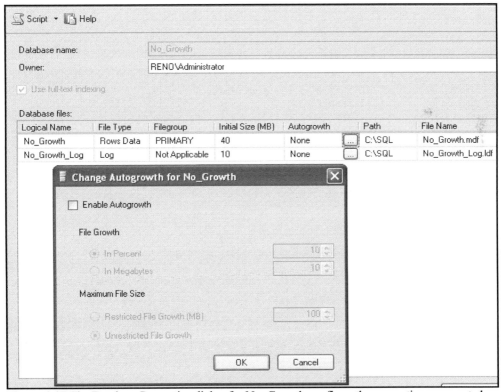

Figure 1.37 The Database Properties dialog for No_Growth confirms the properties you created.

Using Filegroups - Points to Ponder

1. A filegroup is a collection of datafiles which are managed as a single unit.

2. SQL Server databases have a primary filegroup and may also have user defined secondary filegroups (like OrderHist).

3. If no filegroups are defined when the database is created then the only filegroup that exists will be the PRIMARY filegroup, which is the default.

4. The primary filegroup contains the MDF file and as many NDF files as specified.

5. A secondary datafile is optional and will carry an .NDF extension. A database can contain a maximum of 32,766 secondary datafiles.

6. By putting several files into one filegroup, all these files can be managed as a single item.

7. A good use of files and filegroups is to separate files which are heavily queried (OLAP) from files which are heavily changed (OLTP). Example:
    a. Products, Customers, and Sales are in one file
    b. Order History tables could be in another.

8. The two main reasons for using filegroups are to improve performance and to control the physical placement of the data.

9. Log files have a structure different from datafiles and cannot be placed into filegroups.

10. When a database is created, at least one datafile (.MDF) must be created.

11. It's a good idea to make the datafile large enough to hold all of the expected data.

12. The datafile size is only limited by the size of the hard drive.

13. A datafile can be placed on its own dedicated drive.

14. Production tables might be so critical and have such a large workload that they need their own storage location.

15. The FILEGROWTH property can be used to expand a datafile when it grows beyond its initial size.

16. Setting a database datafile or logfile to "no-growth" is considered best for performance, but that increases the risk of a growing database running out of available SQL datafile space.

17.   If filegrowth is set to zero, then the datafile will never grow automatically. But the file can manually be resized at any time.

18.   If a filesize or filegrowth or any other database property is not specified then the database properties will be modeled after the model database.

19.   If you don't choose a filesize or filegrowth or any other database property then your database properties will be modeled after the model database.

Altering Database Filegroups

Our earlier examples created datafiles and filegroup(s) at the same time we created a database. It is also possible to add or change file structures within an existing database.

To prepare for our demonstration, make sure the RatisCo database has been dropped from our server:

```
USE master
GO

DROP DATABASE RatisCo
GO
```

We will now create a simplified version of RatisCo:

```
CREATE DATABASE RatisCo
ON PRIMARY (NAME = RatisCo_Data1,
FILENAME = 'C:\C_SQL\RatisCo_Data1.MDF')
LOG ON (NAME = RatisCo_LOG,
FILENAME = 'C:\E_SQL\RatisCo_LOG.LDF')
```

Figure 1.38 The code used to create the RatisCo database.

Suppose we had intended to create an NDF file (secondary datafile) on the D drive but forgot this step when we created the database. We can add this file without having to rebuild the database. We will do this by using an ALTER DATABASE statement.

Find RatisCo in the Object Explorer, right-click it, and select "Properties" to open the Database Properties dialog. Then click Files in the left nav menu ("Select a page") and notice the files we have created are present. The MDF has been created on our virtual C drive, and the LDF (log) is on our virtual E drive.

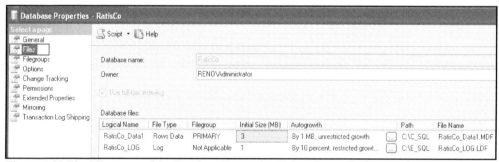

Figure 1.39 The **Files** page of the Database Properties dialog shows the files we just created.

Now switch to the **Filegroups** page (left nav menu) and see we have just one filegroup, the Primary. Inside this filegroup we see one file, which is the MDF. We want to add a user-defined filegroup called RatisCo_OrderHist. We will then put two NDF files inside of that group.

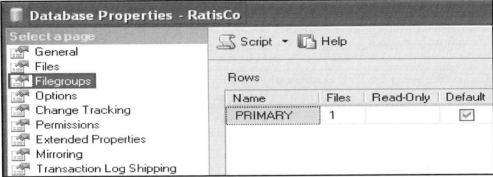

Figure 1.40 The **Filegroups** page of the Database Properties dialog shows just the default filegroup.

First, add the secondary filegroup, RatisCo_OrderHist:

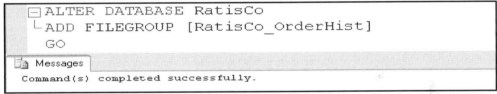

Figure 1.41 We can add a secondary filegroup (RatisCo_OrderHist) to an existing database.

Now let's re-check the **Filegroups** page of the Database Properties dialog to see the result of our code. *If your dialog is still open (i.e., from Figure 1.40), then you must first close and re-open the dialog.* We now see the new filegroup, RatisCo_OrderHist, which contains no files.

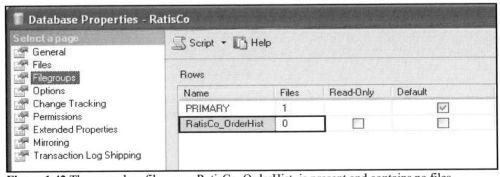

Figure 1.42 The secondary filegroup, RatisCo_OrderHist, is present and contains no files.

Now let's create an NDF file, RatisCo_Hist1, and add it to the new filegroup.

```
ALTER DATABASE RatisCo
  ADD FILE(NAME = RatisCo_Hist1,
      FILENAME = 'C:\D_SQL\RatisCo_Hist1.NDF')
  TO FILEGROUP [RatisCo_OrderHist]
```

Messages
Command(s) completed successfully.

Figure 1.43 Create the secondary datafile, RatisCo_Hist1, and add it to RatisCo_OrderHist.

Notice in Figure 1.43 we put the filegroup in square brackets even though it was not required. When you add to a filegroup like PRIMARY that is also a keyword, you may need to delimit in square brackets. Now let's re-open the Database Properties dialog and check the **Filegroups** page to see the changes. One file should show in RatisCo_OrderHist.

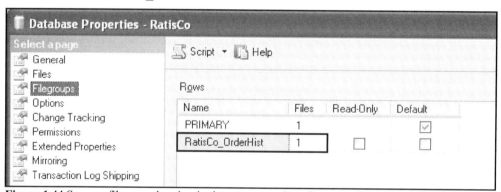

Figure 1.44 See one file now showing in the new secondary filegroup (RatisCo_OrderHist).

Now switch to the Files page and look at all the files. We can see the newly created NDF file showing on the D drive.

Logical Name	File Type	Filegroup	Initial Size (MB)	Autogrowth	Path	File Name
RatisCo_Data1	Rows Data	PRIMARY	3	By 1 MB, un...	C:\C_SQL	RatisCo_Data1.MDF
RatisCo_Hist1	Rows Data	RatisCo_OrderHist	1	By 1 MB, un...	C:\D_SQL	RatisCo_Hist1.NDF
RatisCo_LOG	Log	Not Applicable	1	By 10 perce...	C:\E_SQL	RatisCo_LOG.LDF

Figure 1.45 The new NDF file now shows in our secondary filegroup, RatisCo_OrderHist.

Finally, we will add an additional NDF into the new filegroup, (RatisCo_OrderHist). We will name this file RatisCo_Hist2. However, we will use SQL Server Management Studio's user interface (UI) to add this file, instead of running code which appears in Figure 1.46.

First, let's look at the code statement which would accomplish this task. *Do not run this code.*

```
ALTER DATABASE RatisCo
ADD FILE(NAME = RatisCo_Hist2,
    FILENAME = 'C:\D_SQL\RatisCo_Hist2.NDF')
TO FILEGROUP [RatisCo_OrderHist]
```

Figure 1.46 We will add the file RatisCo_Hist2 using the SSMS UI, not running code.

Step 1. From the **Files** page of the Database Properties dialog for RatisCo, click the Add button in the lower right corner of the dialog.

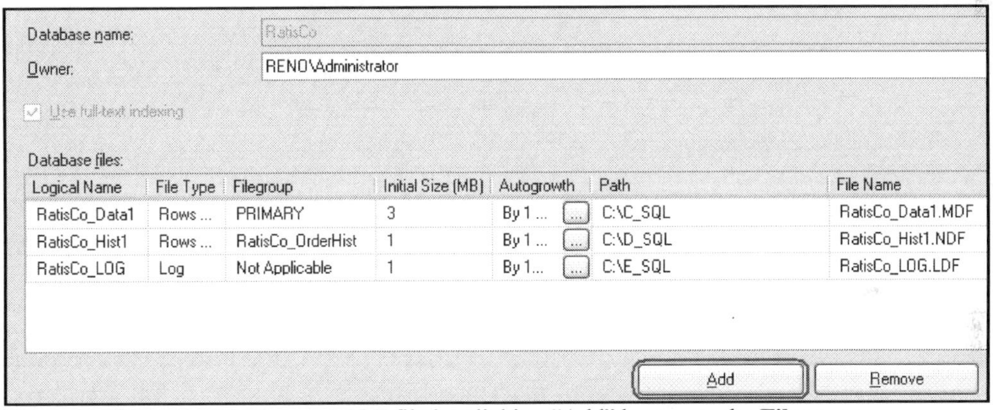

Database name: RatisCo
Owner: RENO\Administrator

☑ Use full-text indexing

Database files:

Logical Name	File Type	Filegroup	Initial Size (MB)	Autogrowth	Path	File Name
RatisCo_Data1	Rows ...	PRIMARY	3	By 1 ...	C:\C_SQL	RatisCo_Data1.MDF
RatisCo_Hist1	Rows ...	RatisCo_OrderHist	1	By 1 ...	C:\D_SQL	RatisCo_Hist1.NDF
RatisCo_LOG	Log	Not Applicable	1	By 1...	C:\E_SQL	RatisCo_LOG.LDF

Add   Remove

Figure 1.47 Step 1. Add the new NDF file by clicking "Add" button on the **Files** page.

Step 2. Notice that SQL Server has automatically populated five fields in the new row. These fields (File Type, Filegroup, Initial size (MB), Autogrowth, and Path) contain SQL Server's default values but can be customized to our specifications. The filepath shown on the next page (Figure 1.48, upper frame) is SQL Server's default location for storing data (as discussed in Figure 1.6). The default filegroup is Primary, and the initial size defaults to 3 MB and is allowed to grow by 1MB. Rows Data is the default value for File Type, but we can choose Log if we are adding a log datafile. The two fields which do not automatically populate are Logical Name and File Name.

Now change the filegroup to the secondary filegroup, RatisCo_OrderHist.

File Type	Filegroup	Initial Size (MB)	Autogrowth		Path
Rows Data	PRIMARY	3	By 1 MB, unrestricted growth		C:\C_SQL
Rows Data	RatisCo_OrderHist	1	By 1 MB, unrestricted growth		C:\D_SQL
Log	Not Applicable	1	By 10 percent, restricted growth t...		C:\E_SQL
Rows Data	PRIMARY ▾	3	By 1 MB, unrestricted growth		C:\Program Files\Microsoft SQL Server\MSSQL10.MSSQLSERVER\MSSQL\DATA

🗒 Script ▾ 📖 Help

Database name: RatisCo

Owner: RENO\Administrator

☑ Use full-text indexing

Database files:

Logical Name	File Type	Filegroup	Initial Size (MB)	Autogrowth		Path	File Name
RatisCo_Data1	Rows ...	PRIMARY	3	By 1 ...		C:\C_SQL	RatisCo_Data1.MDF
RatisCo_Hist1	Rows ...	RatisCo_OrderHist	1	By 1 ...		C:\D_SQL	RatisCo_Hist1.NDF
RatisCo_LOG	Log	Not Applicable	1	By 1...		C:\E_SQL	RatisCo_LOG.LDF
	Rows ...	PRIMARY ▾	3	By 1 ...		C:\Program Files\Microsoft...	
		PRIMARY					
		RatisCo_OrderHist					
		<new filegroup>					

[Add]   [Remove]

Figure 1.48 Step 2. Notice the 4 default field values. Change the filegroup to RatisCo_OrderHist.

Step 3. Change the filepath to C:\D_SQL by clicking the white ellipsis button to launch the "Locate Folder" dialog, which opens to the MSSQL\DATA folder.

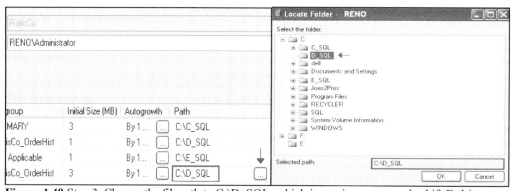

Figure 1.49 Step 3. Change the filepath to C:\D_SQL, which is serving as our makeshift D drive.

Step 4. Manually enter the two file names in the two blank fields (Logical Name, File Name). The logical name for this secondary datafile (NDF) is RatisCo_Hist2. The full file name is RatisCo_Hist2.NDF

Database name:	RatisCo						
Owner:	RENO\Administrator						

☑ Use full-text indexing

Database files:

Logical Name	File Type	Filegroup	Initial Size (MB)	Autogrowth		Path	File Name
RatisCo_Data1	Rows ...	PRIMARY	3	By 1 ...	[...]	C:\C_SQL	RatisCo_Data1.MDF
RatisCo_Hist1	Rows ...	RatisCo_OrderHist	1	By 1 ...	[...]	C:\D_SQL	RatisCo_Hist1.NDF
RatisCo_LOG	Log	Not Applicable	1	By 1...	[...]	C:\E_SQL	RatisCo_LOG.LDF
RatisCo_Hist2	Rows ...	RatisCo_OrderHist	3	By 1 ...	[...]	C:\D_SQL	[...] RatisCo_Hist2.NDF

Figure 1.50 Step 4. Manually enter the Logical Name and the full File Name.

Step 5. Change the size to 1 MB ("Initial Size (MB)" property). Then click OK to save all the changes we've made to the new NDF file, RatisCo_Hist2. *Be aware that, whenever we click OK in the Database Properties dialog, it snaps shut.*

Database files:

Logical Name	File Type	Filegroup	Initial Size (MB)	Autogrowth		Path	File Name
RatisCo_Data1	Rows ...	PRIMARY	3	By 1 MB, unrestricted growth	[...]	C:\C_SQL	RatisCo_Data1.MDF
RatisCo_Hist1	Rows ...	RatisCo_OrderHist	1	By 1 MB, unrestricted growth	[...]	C:\D_SQL	RatisCo_Hist1.NDF
RatisCo_Hist2	Rows ...	RatisCo_OrderHist	1	By 1 MB, unrestricted growth	[...]	C:\D_SQL	RatisCo_Hist2.NDF
RatisCo_LOG	Log	Not Applicable	1	By 10 percent, restricted growth t...	[...]	C:\E_SQL	RatisCo_LOG.LDF

[Add] [Remove]

[OK] [Cancel]

Figure 1.51 Step 5. Change the file size to 1MB instead of SQL Server's default 3MB. Click OK.

Recall the beginning of this section and our premise that we wanted to add a secondary filegroup and two NDF files to the existing RatisCo database. We altered the database with code to create the filegroup RatisCo_OrderHist (in Figure 1.42), added the first NDF file with code (Figure 1.43), and finally we added the second NDF file using the UI in SQL Server Management Studio. We see both NDF files appearing in our makeshift D drive (Figure 1.52).

Address	C:\D_SQL			
Folders	**Name** ▲	**Size**	**Type**	**Date Modified**
D_SQL	RatisCo_Hist1.NDF	1,024 KB	SQL Server Database Secondary Data File	9/14/2009 7:20 PM
⊞ dell	RatisCo_Hist2.NDF	1,024 KB	SQL Server Database Secondary Data File	9/14/2009 8:01 PM
⊞ Documents and Set				

Figure 1.52 Confirm that both NDF files appear in our makeshift D drive.

Now re-open the Database Properties dialog to see the change reflected in the **Filegroups** page.

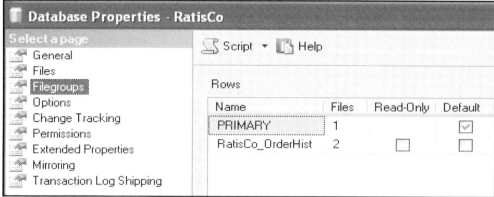

Figure 1.53 Reopen the Database Properties dialog to see all our changes reflected.

In the first two *Joes 2 Pros* books, we emphasized robust and reusable code as the preferred method of writing queries and creating database objects. That approach is still the best practice and is the one we hope to use most frequently in our SQL Server career. When we click through an interface to add or modify database objects, we aren't creating an automatic trail to check our code (in case of error) and we aren't able to easily repeat or rerun those steps the way we can with a script. However, there are helpful tools in the SQL Server Management Studio, which we should be able to navigate as part of our journey to becoming a SQL Pro. For example, we can generate the T-SQL needed to recreate the RatisCo database by navigating through Databases > RatisCo > Script Database as > CREATE To > New Query Editor Window. This can then be saved to reconstruct the database in case it is dropped. We covered a number of these tools in the first two books, and we will continue to demonstrate them in this book, as well.

Lab 1.3: Altering Database Filegroups

Lab Prep: Before you can begin the lab, you must have SQL Server installed and run the SQLArchChapter1.3Setup.sql script. View the lab video instructions in Lab1.3_AlteringDatabases.wmv.

Skill Check 1: In our last example, we added two secondary datafiles to our secondary filegroup, RatisCo_OrderHist. Add a third datafile to this filegroup using code. In Figure 1.56 you can see the logical name should be **RatisCo_Hist3**. The file location is **C:\D_SQL\RatisCo_Hist3.NDF**.

When complete, your result should resemble the Filegroups page (Figure 1.54) and the Files page (Figure 1.55) of the Database Properties dialog.

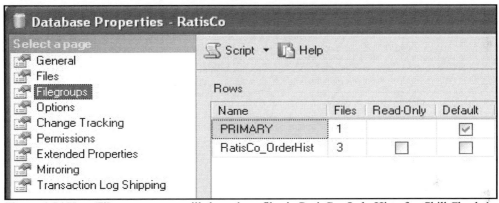

Figure 1.54 Your **Filegroups** page will show three files in RatisCo_OrderHist after Skill Check 1.

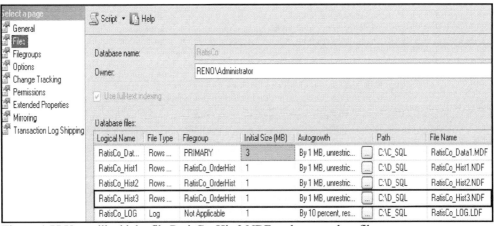

Figure 1.55 You will add the file RatisCo_Hist3.NDF to the secondary filegroup.

Skill Check 2: After Skill Check 1, the RatisCo database contains one MDF (main datafile), three NDFs (secondary datafiles), and one LDF (log datafile). Add another file to the RatisCo database. Place this file in the primary filegroup. *Note*: since PRIMARY is a keyword use square brackets in your code [PRIMARY] when specifying the filegroup.

The screenshot below is taken from the **Files** page of the Database Properties dialog for RatisCo. Your file's logical name should be RatisCo_Data2, and the full file name will be C:\C_SQL\RatisCo_Data2.ndf (as shown in Figure 1.56).

It is recommended that you write the code for this Skill Check, even if you elect to also try adding the file using the UI. When complete, your Files page should match that shown below (Figure 1.56).

Database files:

Logical Name	File Type	Filegroup	Initial Size (MB)	Autogrowth	Path		File Name
RatisCo_Data1	Rows ...	PRIMARY	3	By 1 MB, ...	...	C:\C_SQL	RatisCo_Data1.MDF
RatisCo_Data2	Rows ...	PRIMARY	1	By 1 MB, ...	...	C:\C_SQL	RatisCo_Data2.ndf
RatisCo_Hist1	Rows ...	RatisCo_OrderHist	1	By 1 MB, ...	...	C:\D_SQL	RatisCo_Hist1.NDF
RatisCo_Hist2	Rows ...	RatisCo_OrderHist	1	By 1 MB, ...	...	C:\D_SQL	RatisCo_Hist2.NDF
RatisCo_Hist3	Rows ...	RatisCo_OrderHist	1	By 1 MB, ...	...	C:\D_SQL	RatisCo_Hist3.ndf
RatisCo_LOG	Log	Not Applicable	1	By 10 per...	...	C:\E_SQL	RatisCo_LOG.LDF

Figure 1.56 You will add the file RatisCo_Data2.ndf to the primary filegroup.

Altering Database Filegroups - Points to Ponder

1.   File structures within an existing database can be added or changed using the ALTER DATABASE command.

2.   File structures within an existing database can be added or changed using SQL Server Management Studio's UI (user interface).

3.   Recall that one can generate the SQL that is executed to create the RatisCo database by navigating through Databases > RatisCo > Script Database as > CREATE To > New Query Editor Window. This can then be saved to reconstruct the database in case it is dropped.

Chapter Glossary

Alternate Datafile Placement: Placing your datafile on a separate drive that you select.

Autogrowth: The property in SQL that can be set up to determine the rate of file growth.

Auto Shrink: A database setting that automatically check a database size and return unused space back to the hard drive.

CREATE Database: A SQL statement that is used to create new databases and can determine specifications for the datafiles and filegroups within it.

DCL: Data Control Language. A statement that affects the permissions a principal has to a securable.

DDL: Data Definition Language. A statement that creates, drops or alters databases or database objects.

DML: Data Manipulation language. DML statements handle the structure or design of database objects.

Datafile: A file that contains your current data and whose purpose is to reflect the current state of your database.

Filegroup: A collection of datafiles which are managed as a single unit.

Filegrowth: A property that can be used to expand a datafile when it grows beyond its initial size.

Filegrowth property: A property that can be used to expand a datafile when it grows beyond its initial size.

Graphical UI: User interface.

Logfile: Logfiles keep track of your database transactions and help ensure data and system integrity.

Metadata: Data about data.

Multiple Datafiles Placement: A process that is used to spread the entire database workload evenly across several datafiles.

Primary filegroup: Contains the primary datafile (MDF) and possibly secondary datafiles (NDF). All system tables are allocated to the primary filegroup.

Secondary Datafile: A secondary datafile is optional and will carry an .NDF extension.

Secondary filegroup: Also called a user-defined filegroup; these contain secondary datafiles (NDF) and database objects.

T-SQL: Transact Structured Query Language is the computer programming language based on the SQL standard and used by Microsoft SQL Server to create databases, populate tables and retrieve data.

TCL: Transaction Control Language, or TCL, provides options to control transactions.

Chapter One - Review Quiz

1.) What is the extension given to the Main datafile?

   O a. MDF
   O b. Main
   O c. MData

2.) Which files do not automatically get truncated after a backup?

   O a. Datafile(s)
   O b. Logfile(s)

3.) What type of action will cause the logfile to grow but not the datafile?

   O a. SELECT
   O b. INSERT
   O c. UPDATE
   O d. TRUNCATE

4.) What type of action will cause the logfile and the data file to increase their size?

   O a. SELECT
   O b. INSERT
   O c. UPDATE
   O d. DELETE

5.) How many primary filegroups can you have?
   O a. None
   O b. One
   O c. Two
   O d. Eight
   O e. As many as you want

6.) How many user defined filegroups can you have?
   O a. None
   O b. One
   O c. Two
   O d. Eight
   O e. As many as you want

7.) What are two main reasons for using multiple filegroups? (Choose Two)
O a. User defined filegroups use compression to save space.
O b. To improve performance.
O c. To control the physical placement of the data.
O d. To open up more keyword usage.

8.) How many files can go into the primary filegroup?
O a. None
O b. One
O c. Two
O d. Eight
O e. As many as you want.

9.) If you have two files in the same filegroup can they be on different drives?
O a. Yes
O b. No

10.) Can you place an .NDF file into the primary filegroup?
O a. Yes
O b. No

11.) Can you place a .LDF file (log file) into the primary filegroup?
O a. Yes
O b. No

Answer Key

1.) a   2.) a   3.) c   4.) b   5.) b   6.) e   7.) b, c 8.) e   9.) a   10.) a   11.) b

Bug Catcher Game

To play the Bug Catcher game run the
BugCatcher_Chapter01DatabaseFileStructures.pps from the BugCatcher folder of
the companion files. You can obtain these files from www.Joes2Pros.com or by
ordering the Companion CD.

Chapter 2. Database Schemas, Snapshots & Properties

Back in 2005, I heard there was some fancy invention called schemas coming later that year in the new SQL Server 2005 release. My initial reaction was, "Yikes, I'm already too busy and schemas must mean some fancy code design that will take many hours of serious late night studying to get a handle on." *As it turned out, schemas weren't difficult at all!* In fact, SQL Server's use of schemas resembles a simple categorization and naming convention used from prehistoric times when humans began organizing themselves into clans. And centuries later, names progressed to the system we have now where we each have our individual name (like Bob or Paul) along with our family name (like Paul *Johnson*). If we were SQL Server objects, we might say our two-part naming convention was *FamilyName.FirstName*. Our two-part name ensures easier identification and also classification. Paul *Johnson* and Krista *Johnson* are more likely to be in the same immediate family than *Paul* Johnson and *Paul* Kriegel.

In .NET programming languages, the names Johnson and Kriegel would be called Namespaces. In SQL Server we might create two tables called Employee and PayRates which belong to the HR department. We can refer to them as HR.Employee and HR.Payrates if we first set up the HR schema. All HR tables would then be created in the HR schema. You could say that the schema is SQL Server's answer to the Namespace used in .NET languages.

READER NOTE: *In order to follow along with the examples in the first section of Chapter 2, please run the setup script SQLArchChapter2.0Setup.sql. The setup scripts for this book are posted at Joes2Pros.com.*

Schemas

We know that data contained and tracked in SQL Server most likely relates to an organization. The database we frequently use in the *Joes 2 Pros* series is JProCo, which contains all the data for this small fictitious company. No matter how small an organization, certain tables will be more important to one group than to others. For example, even in JProCo, employee and pay data would be controlled by a Human Resources group. Customer data usually is managed by the Sales and Marketing team, whether that team consists of five or 15,000 people.

Shown here is the list of JProCo's tables. Notice that all tables show the default "dbo" ("database owner") prefix. There isn't any category to help indicate whether a table is managed by the Sales team or by HR.

Prior to SQL Server 2005, the syntax for fully qualified names in SQL Server was [server].[databasename].[owner].[object name], and the idea of "dbo" pertained to [owner] or which database user created and/or was allowed to access the object. Since SQL Server 2005, the owner identity has been replaced by the schema name. This eliminates the need for a namespace to be tied to the user who created the object. You have the freedom to pick meaningful category names.

In SQL Server 2005, the new **schemas** capability was introduced. Let's look at a sample from the AdventureWorks database to see how schemas can help organize objects within databases.

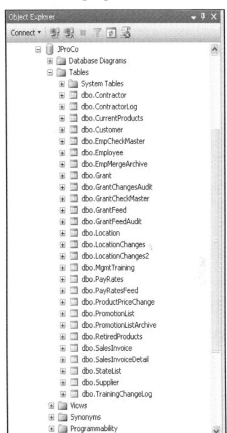

Figure 2.1 The tables in the JProCo database.

In the two screenshots here, most of the AdventureWorks schemas are visible: *dbo, HumanResources, Person, Production, Purchasing, and Sales.*

The figure to the right shows there are 71 tables contained in AdventureWorks sorted in order of table name (Figure 2.2).

Below, the Object Explorer Details window shows there are 71 tables contained in AdventureWorks sorted in order of schema (Figure 2.3).

Figure 2.2 You can sort by table name.

Instead of creating all tables in the general dbo schema, AdventureWorks has defined a separate category for the tables used by each of its key departments (e.g., Sales, HR).

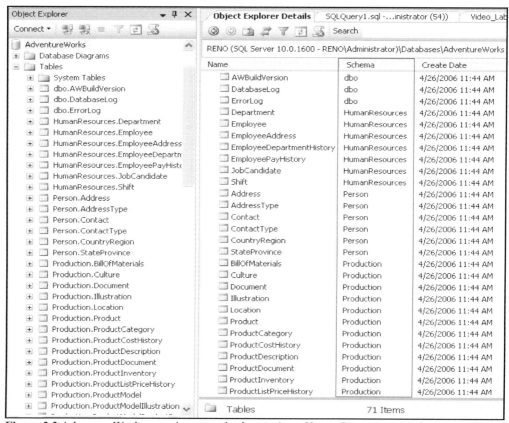

Figure 2.3 AdventureWorks contains several schemas (e.g., HumanResources, Production, Sales).

We can easily see that the Department, Employee, EmployeeAddress, EmployeeDepartmentHistory, EmployeePayHistory, JobCandidate, and Shift tables all belong to the HumanResources department. Tables such as CreditCard, Customer, and CurrencyRate all belong to the Sales group.

The introduction of schemas *(SchemaName.ObjectName)* has provided more freedom for DBAs to use meaningful names to categorize tables and other database objects. Schemas and principals can also have a "One-to-Many" relationship, meaning that a principal may own many differently named schemas.

Prior to SQL Server's 2005 release, it was not uncommon for DBAs to house each department's tables in a separate database. Now DBAs have more choices and can simply manage access to schemas, rather than managing separate databases just to be able to distinguish tables belonging to separate categories.

Below we can see the five custom schemas the AdventureWorks DBA defined to manage each of the five departments' tables (Figure 2.4). Notice the many other system-defined schemas which SQL Server has created for its own management and tracking of the database (db_accessadmin, db_backupoperator, etc.).

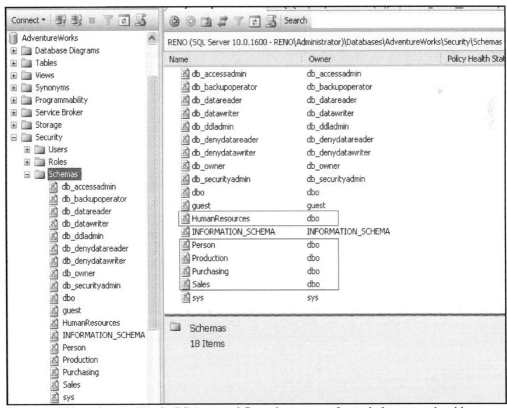

Figure 2.4 The AdventureWorks DBA created five schemas, one for each department's tables.

Creating Schemas With Code

Now we will define several schemas of our own and then create tables within those schemas. Later we will add schemas to the JProCo database, but first we'll run a few practice examples inside RatisCo. The RatisCo database currently contains no tables.

Before we make any changes to RatisCo, let's first check Object Explorer and confirm what schemas we find. From Management Studio, use F8 or the following path:
Management Studio > View > Object Explorer > Databases > RatisCo > Security > Schemas

To display the Object Explorer Details window, hit the F7 key or this path:
Management Studio > View > Object Explorer Details

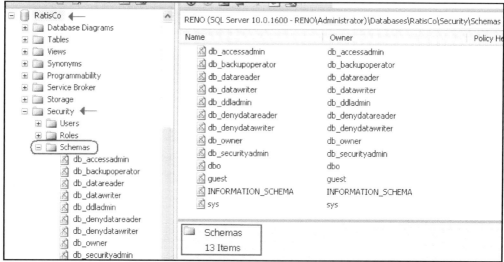

Figure 2.5 RatisCo contains no user-defined schemas. These 13 schemas are all system-defined.

There should be just the 13 system-defined schemas – no user-defined schemas are there yet, such as the Sales, Purchasing, or HumanResources schemas we're now going to create.

First let's make sure we are in the RatisCo database context by doing either of these items:

　　1) Toggling the dropdown list (as shown in Figure 2.6).

　　OR

　　2) Beginning our code with a "USE RatisCo" statement. (Recall that GO delimits the end of a batch statement and must appear on the line below the last DDL statement.)

Now let's run this code to create the Sales schema and the Sales.Customer table.

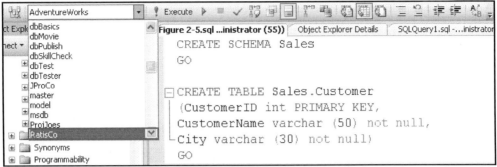

Figure 2.6 When you are in the RatisCo db context, you will create the Sales schema and one table.

Suppose we ran the code in Figure 2.6 but forgot to first check the Object Explorer and see the 13 system-defined schemas by themselves. We would want to go back and remove the Sales schema, so we could see just the system-defined schemas. To do this, we would first need to remove Sales.Customer (DROP TABLE Sales.Customer GO) before SQL Server would allow us to remove the Sales schema (DROP SCHEMA Sales GO). *SQL Server will not allow a schema to be removed, if database objects which are dependent on that schema still exist.*

Now let's run the code below to create two additional schemas (Figure 2.7).

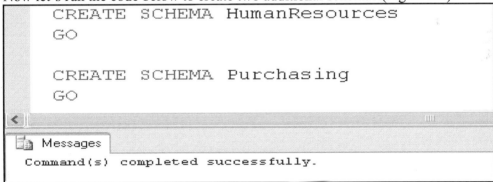

Figure 2.7 These two statements create two new schemas in the RatisCo database.

Now let's check the Schemas folder to see that the newly created schemas are present (Sales, HumanResources, and Purchasing). In Figure 2.5, we saw 13 system defined schemas. We should now see a total of 16 schemas:

Management Studio > View > Object Explorer > Databases > RatisCo > Security > Schemas

Creating Schemas with Management Studio

Next we will create two more schemas (People and Production) using SQL Server Management Studio's UI:

Object Explorer > Databases > RatisCo > Security > right-click Schemas > New Schema > Schema Name: People > OK

Figure 2.8 shows the creation steps for the first schema, People. *After creating the People schema, repeat the process and create the **Production** schema.*

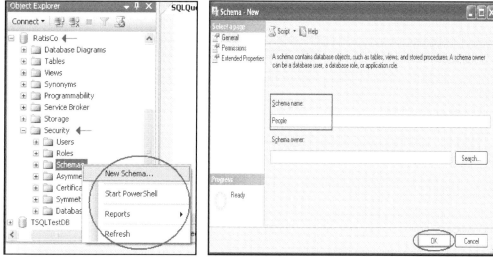

Figure 2.8 Create two new schemas (People and Production) in the RatisCo database.

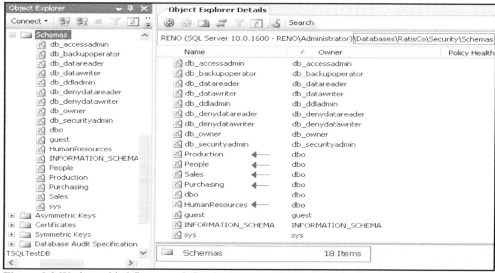

Figure 2.9 We just added five user-defined schemas to the RatisCo database.

We'll stay with the Management Studio interface and next add some records in the Sales.Customer table we created in the last section (see p. 60, Figure 2.6).

We begin by navigating to this table in Object Explorer:
Management Studio > View > Object Explorer > Databases > RatisCo > Tables > **Sales.Customer**

As shown in Figure 2.10, we will right-click the Sales.Customer table which expands a full menu of options. Choosing "Edit Top 200 Rows" makes the record editing interface launch in a new tab.

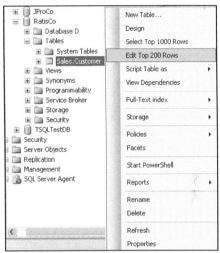

 Now we enter the two rows of data as shown below (Figure 2.11). Just by clicking and beginning to type inside the first cell containing "*NULL*", a new blank row will appear for us to populate. This interface is similar to Microsoft Access, in that there isn't an explicit "OK" or "Enter" button – once the user clicks away from a row, the data will be entered into the database. We must enter the two records precisely as we see them here. We will continue working with these records later in this chapter.

Figure 2.10 Add records using the SSMS UI.

Notice the full four-part name in the tab *(Server.Database.Schema.ObjectName)*. My server name is RENO. So the fully qualified name of this table object is RENO.RatisCo.Sales.Customer.

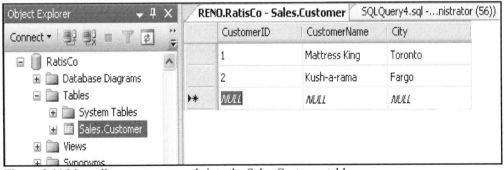

Figure 2.11 Manually enter two records into the Sales.Customer table.

We must enter the two records precisely as we see them here. We will continue working with these records later in this chapter.

Qualified Names Using Schemas

Next we'll query to see the records and confirm they are showing in our Sales.Customer table. If we queried "SELECT * FROM Customer", we would get a SQL Server error ("Invalid object name 'Customer'."). Generally speaking, once we create a table within a schema, we must explicitly use the *SchemaName.ObjectName* naming convention whenever we call upon it.

(In most cases, we will explicitly use the two part name *SchemaName.ObjectName* as a best practice and recommended guideline for objects created within a specific schema. Later in the security book in the *Joes 2 Pros* series, we will see that changing a user's security settings and selecting a default schema other than dbo is one way to mitigate the requirement to explicitly invoke an object by its two-part name, even if it was created within a schema.)

Another interesting point. Notice that, if we specify the database in the table name (*Database.Schema.ObjectName*), the query is able to locate our intended table even though the database context is set to another database (i.e., AdventureWorks).

Running this query will show the two records we entered manually (Figure 2.12).

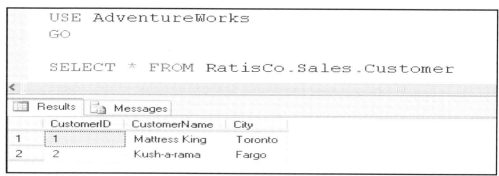

Figure 2.12 This query locates the intended table even though the context points to a different db.

When we specify (*SchemaName.ObjectName*) in our query (SELECT * FROM *SchemaName.ObjectName*), this is known as a qualified query because we are using the qualified name. Qualified queries look in the exact schema for the table.

Unqualified queries (SELECT * FROM *ObjectName*) use dbo as the default schema and consequently only check within the dbo schema. In other words, SQL Server actually interprets the query [SELECT * FROM *ObjectName*] as [SELECT * FROM dbo.*ObjectName*].

The four part name (*Server.Database.SchemaName.ObjectName*) is also referred to as the **fully-qualified name.** Later in this book, we will see that a fully-qualified name is required with linked servers.

Lab 2.1 Schemas

Lab Prep: Before you can begin the lab, you must have SQL Server installed and run the SQLArchChapter2.1Setup.sql script. View the lab video instructions in Lab2.1_Schemas.wmv.

Skill Check 1: In the JProCo database, use T-SQL code to create the following five schemas:

        HumanResources, Purchasing, Production, Person, Sales

Before you add these schemas to JProCo, open Object Explorer and notice the Owner dbo has just one schema created (dbo). After you add the five new schemas, your Object Explorer & Object Explorer Details should resemble Figure 2.13.

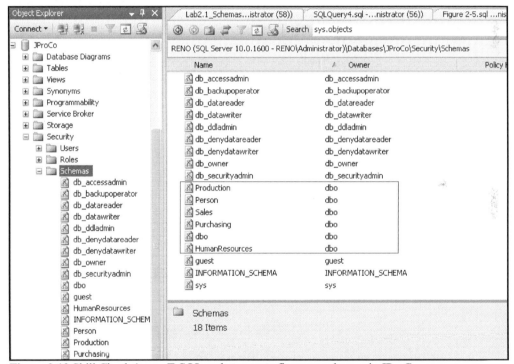

Figure 2.13 Skill Check 1 uses T-SQL code to create five new schemas in JProCo.

Answer Code: The T-SQL code to this lab can be found in the downloadable files in a file named Lab2.1_Schemas.sql

Schemas - Points to Ponder

1. A schema is a namespace for database objects.

2. In previous versions of SQL Server, database owners and schemas were conceptually the same object. Beginning in SQL Server 2005, owners and schemas are separate, and schemas serve as containers of objects.

3. Objects (tables, stored procedures, views, etc.) are created within a schema inside the database.

4. Objects can be transferred between schemas by using the following code:
   ALTER SCHEMA schema_name TRANSFER *securable_name*
   Example: ALTER SCHEMA HumanResources
   TRANSFER Person.Address

5. Each database has its own schema set.

6. Every object in a database has a fully qualified name (Server.Database.Schema.Object). A usage example would be:
   SELECT * FROM Reno.RatisCo.People.Employee.

7. To use object delimiters with the schema name it would be [People].[Employee]

8. A fully qualified name (FQN) is the complete object identifier. The FQN includes the server name, database name, schema name, and object name.

9. The first three parts (server, database, and schema names) are known as the qualifiers of the object name, as they are used to differentiate the object from any other database object.

10. Partially qualified names omit some of the qualifiers by leaving them out or by replacing them with another period. For example, since Reno.JProCo..Employee does not list the schema, it is assumed to be dbo.

11. When using fully qualified names, the object must be explicitly identified.

12. Each object must have a unique fully qualified name. Objects can have the same simple name as long as the fully qualified names are different.

    Example: With multiple schemas in place , two tables with the same name could exist. For example, two Order tables:
    a. Sales.Order
    b. Production.Order

13. Within a database the name can be shortened to *SchemaName.ObjectName*. Example: SELECT * FROM People.Employee.

14. A query with a simple name might cause some confusion if multiple schemas have an object with the same name (SELECT * FROM Order).

15. SQL attempts to search schemas for simple object names in the following order:
    a. SQL attempts to find simple names from the default schema.
    b. If no default exists (OR if the default does not contain the requested object) it attempts to find simple names from dbo.

16. A default schema can be assigned to a user in two ways.
    a. Using the UI in the properties of a Database user.
    b. Specifying the schema name in the DEFAULT_SCHEMA clause of the CREATE or ALTER user statement.

17. A default schema can be assigned to each database user.

Database Snapshots

Most database backups sit in a file store in case you ever need to restore a database to a point in the past. We can't see the data inside the backup unless we restore the database. This makes comparing the real-time database with the backup file limited or even impossible.

A new capability introduced in SQL Server 2005 is the *database snapshot*. A snapshot is an online, point-in-time reference to a database on our system. Think of it like taking a static picture of our database with references to its data. We can use SQL Server to query our database and look for all changes made since the last snapshot was taken. (We will see this done toward the end of this section in Figure 2.18.)

Snapshot Basics

Database snapshots are created from our source database (e.g., the JProCo database, the RatisCo database). Database snapshots are not really backups at all. A snapshot can help our database revert back to a point in time, but the snapshot relies upon the source database and must be able to communicate with it in order to function. In fact if the source database becomes corrupt or unavailable, the snapshot(s) of it will be useless.

The snapshot begins as an empty shell of our database file(s) and stores only changed data pages. If our database never changes after we create the snapshot, then the snapshot will always remain just an empty shell. When we make (or write) a change to the source database, the database gets updated and the old record is then copied into the snapshot. This is known as **copy on write** (COW).

If we query for changes, the snapshot shows us those records from its own datafiles. However, if we query a snapshot database for data that has never changed, SQL Server will fetch the data from the source database. When a change is made to the source database the new record is updated. The old record is then copied to the snapshot. In this way a snapshot maintains a view of the database as it existed when the snapshot was created.

Creating Database Snapshots

Database snapshots are one of the few features that can only be created using T-SQL code – there is no point-and-click method to create a snapshot using the Management Studio UI.

Before we can create a snapshot, we need to know the name of the database and where all of its data is stored. In other words, we need to know the name and storage location for the MDF, as well as any NDF files.

We want to create a snapshot of RatisCo, so let's look for the file details contained in the Files page of the Database Properties dialog for RatisCo. (Object Explorer > Databases > right-click RatisCo > Properties > **Files** page (from left nav menu).)
In Figure 2.14, we see the MDF file for the RatisCo database is named **RatisCo**.

Database name: RatisCo

Owner: RENO\Administrator

Use full-text indexing

Database files:

Logical Name	File Type	Filegroup	Initial Size (MB)	Autogrowth	Path	File Name
RatisCo	Rows ...	PRIMARY	3	By 1...	C:\Program Files\Microsoft SQL ...	RatisCo.mdf
RatisCo_log	Log	Not Applicable	1	By 1...	C:\Program Files\Microsoft SQL ...	RatisCo_log.LDF

Figure 2.14 Prepare to create a snapshot of RatisCo by locating the MDF and NDF files (if any).

Before we create the snapshot database it's a good idea to change you current query window context to the Master database. The code used to create a snapshot of a database is similar to the code we use to create a database (see Figure 2.15).

```
CREATE DATABASE RatisCo_Monday_noon
ON (NAME = ) ---Source MDF Name
AS SNAPSHOT OF RatisCo --Source Database Name
GO
```

Figure 2.15 The skeleton code used to create a snapshot of the RatisCo database.

```
CREATE DATABASE RatisCo_Monday_noon
ON (NAME = RatisCo, ---Source MDF Name
    FILENAME ='C:\SQL\RatisCo_SnapshotMonNoon.ss')
AS SNAPSHOT OF RatisCo --Source Database Name
GO
--Snapshots are not stored in MDF files, they are stored
---in SS files.
```

Messages

```
Command(s) completed successfully.
```

Figure 2.16 We have successfully created our snapshot of RatisCo database.

Check Object Explorer to confirm we can see the newly created snapshot.

Object Explorer > Database Snapshots > **RatisCo_Monday_noon**

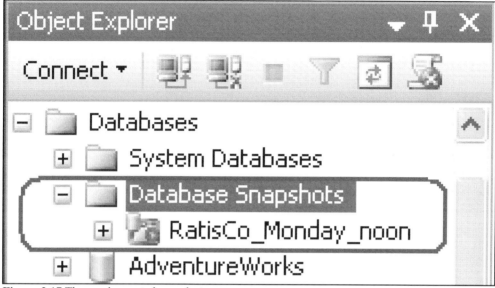

Figure 2.17 The newly created snapshot.

Querying Source and Snapshot Database Data

We can use SQL Server to query our database and look for all changes made since the last snapshot was taken.

Since we just created the snapshot, the queries below produce an identical result.

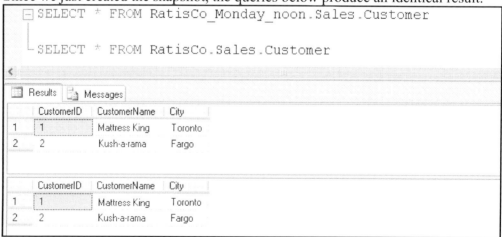

Figure 2.18 The queries of the snapshot and Sales.Customer produce an identical result.

Note that the snapshot is a static, read-only reference to the database. No matter what data or objects are added to the RatisCo database after 12:01pm Monday, the snapshot we created (RatisCo_Monday_noon) will not contain those changes. The snapshot's job is to keep track of any changes impacting the data it cares about (i.e., RatisCo and its data at the time the snapshot was taken at noon on Monday).

An EXCEPT query is a quick way to check for changes between the snapshot and the source database. Since we just created this snapshot of RatisCo (RatisCo_Monday_noon), we would expect there to be no difference between the snapshot and the source (see Figure 2.19).

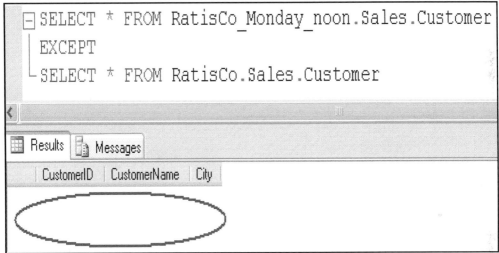

Figure 2.19 An EXCEPT query will reveal any changes between the snapshot and the source db.

Recall with multiple query operators, the top table is dominant. So in this query, if changes had been made to data which the snapshot is tracking, the result would show the old record. To see the new record, just reverse the order of these tables so that the table from the source database is dominant.

```
--The result of this query will be the new record(s).
SELECT * FROM RatisCo.Sales.Customer
EXCEPT
SELECT * FROM RatisCo_Monday_noon.Sales.Customer
```

(To read more on the multiple query operators EXCEPT, INTERSECT, UNION, and UNION ALL, please see Chapter 8 of *SQL Queries Joes 2 Pros*.)

Let's make a change to a record that was included in the Monday noon snapshot.

```
UPDATE RatisCo.Sales.Customer
  SET CustomerName = 'Cush-A-Rama'
  WHERE CustomerID = 2
```

Messages

(1 row(s) affected)

Figure 2.20 Changing a record in the Customer table.

Now let's reattempt our EXCEPT query with the snapshot as the dominant table.

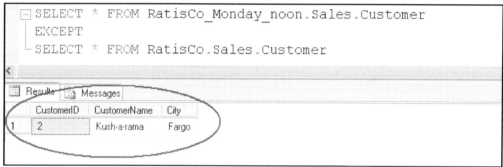

Figure 2.21 Our EXCEPT query reveals one record changed after the Monday noon snapshot.

This result provides us two pieces of information. It tells us at least one record has changed in RatisCo since we took the Monday noon snapshot. It also provides us the old record.

Let's think about the activity of the snapshot and the COW (copy on write) behavior. Prior to the moment we updated one of the records this snapshot (RatisCo_Monday_noon) is tracking, the snapshot was an empty shell. When the one record was updated in RatisCo (Figure 2.21, the CustomerName Kush-a-rama was changed to Cush-A-Rama), the source database copied the old record into the snapshot file. In other words, when RatisCo *wrote* the update to the record, the old record was *copied* into the snapshot. Afterwards, the snapshot was a shell containing exactly one record.

Lab 2.2 Database Snapshots

Lab Prep: Before you can begin the lab, you must have SQL Server installed and run the SQLArchChapter2.2Setup.sql script. View the lab video instructions in Lab2.2_DatabaseSnapshots.wmv.

Skill Check 1: Create a database snapshot from the dbBasics database called dbBasics_Monday_Noon.

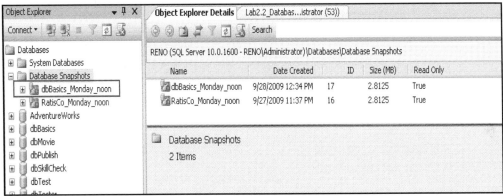

Figure 2.22 The dbBasics_Monday_Noon snapshot is created.

Skill Check 2: Change the last name of Employee 106 from Davies to Santwon. Run a query to show all the changes from the source database Employee table and the snapshot database Employee table. Use the snapshot you created in the first Skill Check (dbBasics_Monday_Noon).

	EmpNo	LastName	FirstName	Dept	Position	Salary	LocationID
1	106	Davies	Diana	Admin	Clerk	23400.00	1

Figure 2.23a The data for Employee 106's old record contained in the snapshot.

	EmpNo	LastName	FirstName	Dept	Position	Salary	LocationID
1	106	Santwon	Diana	Admin	Clerk	23400.00	1

Figure 2.23b The data for Employee 106's new record contained in the source database.

Answer Code: The T-SQL code to this lab can be found in the downloadable files in a file named Lab2.2_DatabaseSnapshots.sql

Database Snapshots - Points to Ponder

1. Database snapshots enable working with data as it appears at a point in time rather than reflecting the current status of the data.

2. Snapshots are useful for reporting, development, and testing purposes.

3. Database snapshots:
    a. Are read-only (point-in-time)
    b. Must exist on the same server as the source data

4. Snapshots are also known as a "simple copy."

5. Use the AS SNAPSHOT OF clause of the CREATE DATABASE statement to create a database snapshot.

6. Database snapshots are read-only and static from the point in time they were created.

7. The database which the snapshot is created from is referred to as the "Source Database."

8. Database snapshots CANNOT be created from Model, Master, or tempdb.

9. Snapshot databases are listed in the Object Explorer and Object Explorer Details but cannot be created through the UI.

10. Snapshot databases can only be created with the CREATE DATABASE statement with an AS SNAPSHOT OF clause appended.

11. A snapshot can be created very quickly.

12. Snapshots allow us to quickly create multiple point-in-time views of our data.

13. Not every user will have permissions to create snapshots. Any user who can create a database can create a database snapshot.

14. Database snapshots are supported by SQL Server Enterprise and are not available in every edition of SQL Server.

15. Full-text indexing is not supported by snapshots.

Setting Database Properties

So far we've worked quite a bit with the Database Properties dialog and its Files and Filegroups pages, which provide useful information for each database and its datafiles. In this section we will look at properties and settings found in the Options page of the Database Properties dialog.

Management Studio >View > Object Explorer > Databases > right-click **RatisCo** > Properties >

Once inside the Database Properties dialog, choose **Options** from the "Select a page" menu.

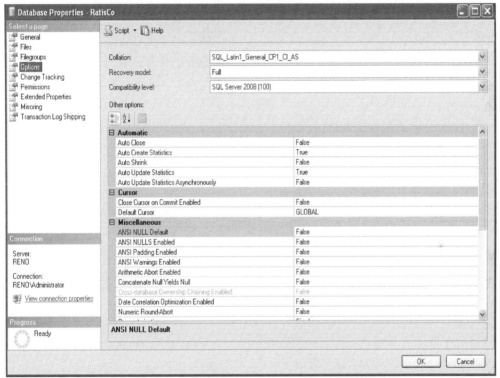

Figure 2.24 The **Options** page in the Database Properties dialog displays properties and settings.

Open this page in your own instance of SQL Server and notice the several categories of settings and properties found on the Options page (Automatic, Cursor, Miscellaneous, Recovery, Service Broker, and State). Most of these settings can be altered from this page. Later we will also change properties using T-SQL code, and we will also use the scripting tool to generate T-SQL code from the Options page.

Another interface where we can quickly view metadata for a database is the Object Explorer Details window. To get this window to appear, press the F7 key. There are two panes and most of the data we want to see is in the lower pane. The bottom area contains the "Details Pane" that displays certain details of the selected object. To see more of this lower pane drag the divider from bottom of the window (see Figure 2.25). We cannot use this interface to change settings, as might be guessed from the grey shading. However, it's a handy resource for viewing high level metadata (creation date, size (MB), space available (KB)), the physical location and name of the default filegroup, and some commonly referenced properties, such as the ANSI NULL Default setting and the Read Only property.

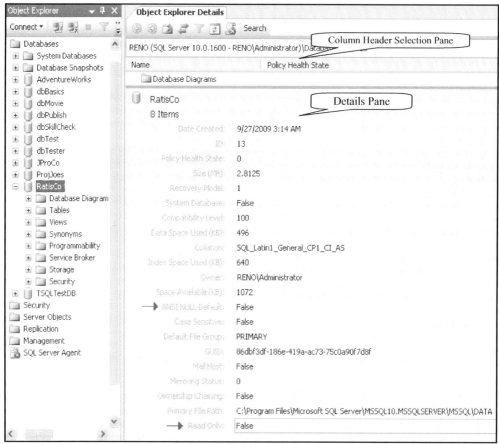

Figure 2.25 The Object Explorer Details window displays 21 points of metadata for a database.

Figure 2.25 shows RatisCo's Read Only property set to False, meaning that it is not in read-only mode. Another indication that RatisCo is not in read-only mode is that its icon displays normally in Object Explorer. A read-only database's icon will be greyed out in the Object Explorer display, and it will have a "Read-Only" label alongside its name (an example is shown in Figure 2.27).

Altering Databases Using Management Studio

Let's begin by checking our RatisCo database. If RatisCo is not already set to
Read-Only mode, then we will first reset that property before proceeding.

Navigate to the **Database Read-Only** property near the bottom of the Options page
and confirm it is set to "True."

Management Studio >View > Object Explorer > Databases > right-click **RatisCo** > Properties >

Choose **Options** from the "Select a page" menu, and then scroll nearly to the bottom of the page.

Database Read-Only > True > OK > Yes

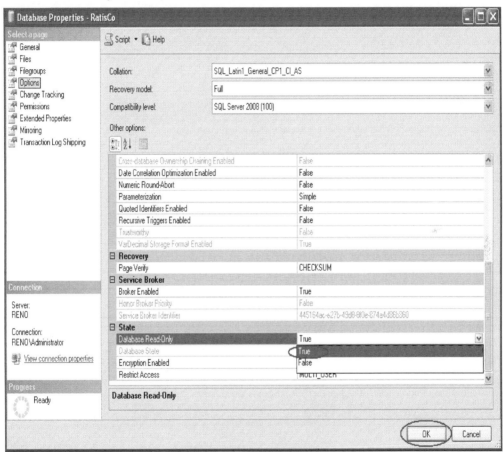

Figure 2.26 Reset the Database Read-Only property of RatisCo to "True."

Once we've confirmed the Database Read-Only property of RatisCo is set to
"True", we will recheck the Object Explorer to note the icon's changed appearance
(as shown on the next page in Figure 2.27). We may need to right-click the

Databases folder and choose the refresh option in order for the icon to be refreshed and display its newly modified status.

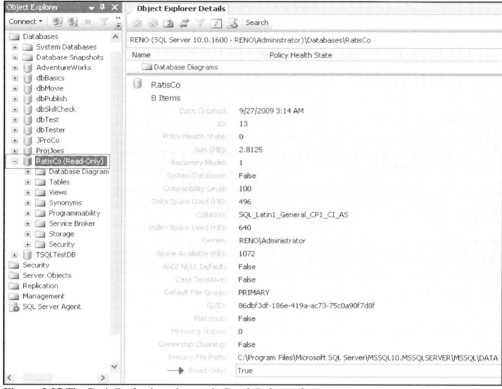

Figure 2.27 The RatisCo database is now in Read-Only mode.

Altering Databases Using T-SQL Code

Although RatisCo is in Read-Only mode, we can query the Sales.Customer table and see the two records (see Figure 2.28).

```
SELECT * FROM Sales.Customer
```

	CustomerID	CustomerName	City
1	1	Mattress King	Toronto
2	2	Cush-A-Rama	Fargo

Figure 2.28 We can query objects within the RatisCo database while it is in Read-Only mode.

Suppose we wanted to update one of these records. *We cannot run an UPDATE statement while RatisCo is in Read-Only mode (see Figure 2.29).*

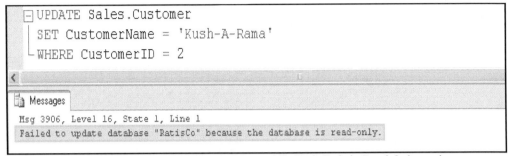

Figure 2.29 We cannot run an UPDATE statement while RatisCo is in Read-Only mode.

Let's now take the RatisCo database out of Read-Only mode – or in other words, put it back into Read-Write mode – using the T-SQL code below.

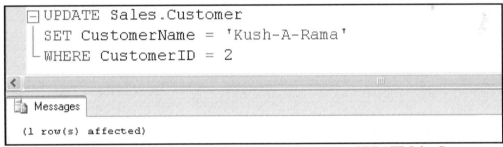

Figure 2.30 We can use T-SQL code to take the RatisCo database out of Read-Only mode.

We now reattempt our UPDATE to the Sales.Customer table.

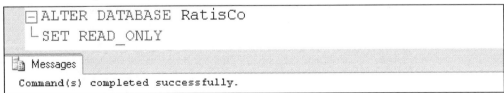

Figure 2.31 With RatisCo no longer in Read-Only mode, we can now UPDATE Sales.Customer.

Now let's change it back to Read-Only using code.

Figure 2.32 We can use T-SQL code to put RatisCo back into Read-Only mode.

Check the Management Studio interface and see that running the code has the same effect as toggling the Database Read-Only property dropdown to "True."

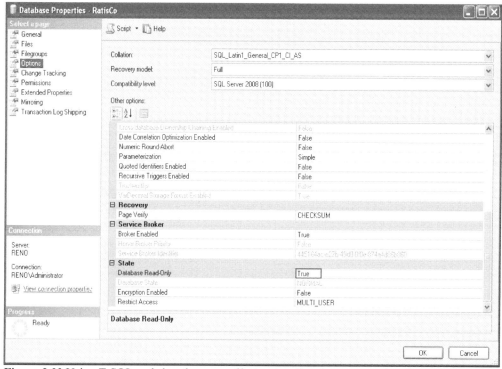

Figure 2.33 Using T-SQL code has the same effect as toggling the property dropdown.

Database Code Generators

Another database setting we will use for practice is **Auto Shrink**, which relates to your MDF and NDF files. With this setting, you can have SQL Server periodically poll your database to check its size and return unused space back to the hard drive. The default setting is False (i.e., the default for Auto Shrink is off – this feature remains in SQL Server 2005 and 2008 only for backwards compatibility), which is also what many experts recommend since shrinking and later regrowing can fragment datafiles. You may encounter a rare instance where you perform a onetime deletion of a large quantity of data and know your database will not need such a large amount of space in the future. In that case, you might consider temporarily turning on the Auto Shrink option so that your database can be downsized to its new smaller size and the excess space may be returned to the hard drive.

Currently the Auto Shrink option for RatisCo is set to "False." Let's use the Management Studio interface to change Auto Shrink to "True" and click OK. When we click OK, the properties dialog snaps shut.

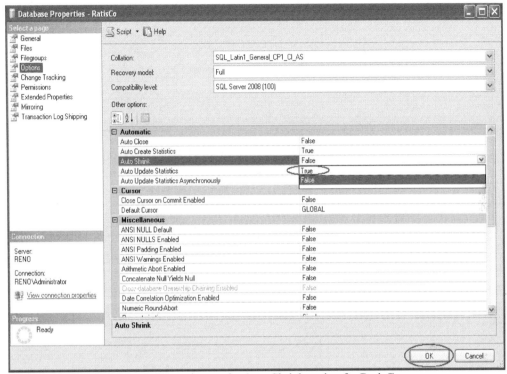

Figure 2.34 We are temporarily turning on the Auto Shrink option for RatisCo.

Now let's use T-SQL code to turn off Auto Shrink, which has the same effect as changing the dropdown to "False" in the **Options** page.

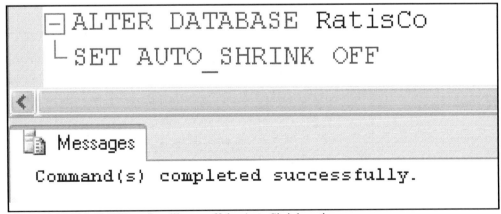

Figure 2.35 This T-SQL code will turn off the Auto Shrink option.

Suppose we need to change some properties for our database, but we aren't sure of the T-SQL code syntax. Each of the nine pages within the Database Properties dialog contains a Script menu (see Figure 2.36). For most actions we can take using these pages, we can have Management Studio generate the T-SQL code which would accomplish that action.

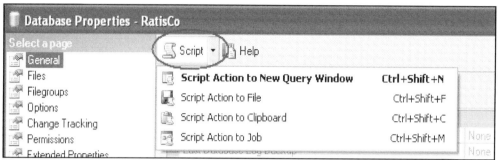

Figure 2.36 Management Studio's scripting capability provides T-SQL code upon request.

Every operation performed in SQL Server is accomplished by the execution of T-SQL code. That is to say, SQL Server requires code in order to accomplish any task, whether we accomplish the task by running code in a query window, or by clicking through the SQL Server Management Studio interface. When we write and run our own code in the query window, we are obviously providing the code. However, when we use the Management Studio interface to perform tasks (e.g., create or drop database objects, change database properties), behind the scenes SQL Server automatically generates and runs the code needed to execute our tasks.

Let's have the scripting tool generate the code for the two settings we've been practicing, Auto Shrink and Database Read-Only. Open the Options page in the Database Properties dialog for RatisCo. Change the Auto Shrink and Read-Only properties (toggling the dropdowns to true and false, respectively) BUT don't yet click OK (see Figure 2.37 on next page).

Once we have toggled the dropdowns for the two settings, we will hit the Script button and then the Cancel button to close the Options page.

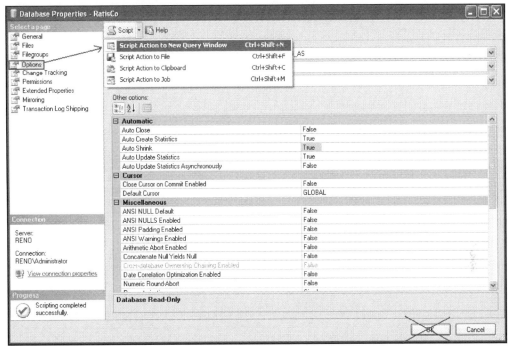

Figure 2.37 Management Studio's scripting capability provides T-SQL code upon request.

The Script button registers the changes which we've toggled in the interface and generates a script showing us the code which will affect the change(s) we are considering.

Let's run the code which Management Studio has generated for us. Make sure any query windows pointing to RatisCo are closed before running this code.

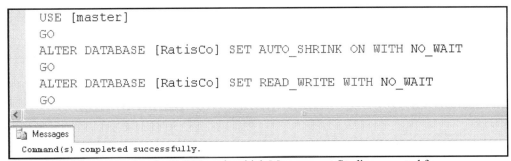

Figure 2.38 We are running the T-SQL code which Management Studio generated for us.

Notice that SQL Server automatically uses square brackets to delimit every database object name. These and other signs, such as an N appearing with Unicode characters, are often hints that a code sample was generated by a machine (i.e., SQL Server) and not written by a person.

83

After running the code, refresh the Databases folder in Object Explorer and see the RatisCo icon appearing normally (it's no longer greyed out and the Read-Only notation is gone). Return to the Options page and see that Auto Shrink is now set to "True" and Database Read-Only is set to "False."

Since most SQL Pros do not use Auto Shrink on their databases (and prefer to manually control any database resizing operations), let's be sure to reopen the Options page and generate the code to turn Auto Shrink off for RatisCo.

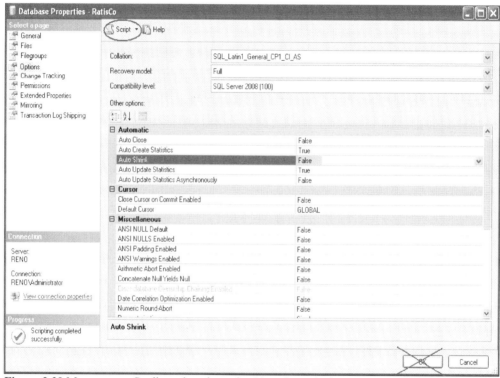

Figure 2.39 Management Studio scripts the action(s) registered when you toggle dropdown items.

Before leaving this section, run the code to turn off Auto Shrink for RatisCo.

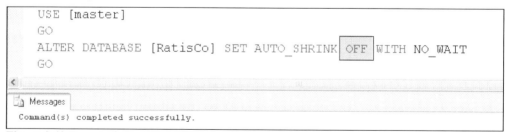

Figure 2.40 Execute the script which Management Studio generated for us.

Lab 2.3: Setting Database Properties

Lab Prep: Before you can begin the lab, you must have SQL Server installed and run the SQLArchChapter2.3Setup.sql script. View the lab video instructions in Lab2.3_SettingDatabaseOptions.wmv.

Skill Check 1: Use T-SQL code to set properties for the RatisCo database as follows:
1) ANSI NULLS Enabled to True
2) AUTO_CLOSE to True
3) Database Read-Only to False

You are encouraged to obtain your code by having SQL Server Management Studio generate it for you.

Skill Check 2: Reset each property of RatisCo as follows by using T-SQL code:
1) ANSI NULLS Enabled to False
2) AUTO_CLOSE to False
3) Database Read_Only to True

You are encouraged to obtain your code by having SQL Server Management Studio generate it for you.

Answer Code: The T-SQL code to this lab can be found in the downloadable files in a file named Lab2.3_DatabaseProperties.sql.

Setting Database Properties - Points to Ponder

1. T-SQL code can be used to manage properties and settings for the database.

2. SQL Server also allows database properties and settings to be managed using the Options page of the Database Properties dialog.

    Management Studio > View > Object Explorer > Databases >
    Right-click *DatabaseName* > Properties > **Options** page

3. SQL Server Management Studio's code generating capabilities can show the T-SQL code syntax for any database action available in the Database Properties dialog.

4. Every operation performed in SQL Server is accomplished by the execution of T-SQL code. That is to say, SQL Server requires code in order to accomplish any task, whether we accomplish the task by running code in a query window, or by clicking through the SQL Server Management Studio interface. When we write and run our own code in the query window, we are obviously providing the code. However, when we use the Management Studio interface to perform tasks (e.g., create or drop database objects, change database properties), behind the scenes SQL Server automatically generates and runs the code needed to execute our tasks.

Chapter Glossary

ANSI NULL Default property: When creating a table, you specify each column as nullable to be non-nullable. If you do nothing, then SQL Server defaults the field as nullable (ANSI NULL default = False). However, the ANSI standard says that if you don't explicitly specify nullability, then the field will NOT allow nulls. If you want SQL Server to utilize this ANSI NULL default, then you would set this property to True.

Copy on Write (COW): When we make (or write) a change to the source database, the database gets updated and the old record is then copied into the snapshot. This is known as **copy on write** (COW).

Database properties: A SQL dialog box that allows you to view and set useful information for each database and its datafiles.

Database Snapshots: Database snapshots are read-only (point-in-time) and must exist on the same server as the source data. Database snapshots begin as an empty shell of the database file(s) and stores only changed data pages.

Fully qualified names: The syntax for fully qualified names in SQL Server is [server].[databasename].[owner].[object name]. In a fully qualified name the object must be explicitly identified.

Naming convention: The convention used for naming databases and files within a system.

Objects: Tables, stored procedures, views, etc. are SQL database objects.

Partially qualified names: Partially qualified names omit some of the qualifiers by leaving them out or by replacing them with another period.

Qualified query: Qualified queries look in the exact schema for the table.

Schemas: A namespace for database objects.

Script: SQL code saved as a file. Also a control in SQL Server Management Studio which allowed you to generate the underlying code for a database or object.

Source database: The database which the snapshot is created from is referred to as the "Source Database."

System-defined schema: The schemas created by SQL Server.

User-defined schema: Schemas created by the user.

Chapter Two - Review Quiz

1.) Find the two things that are true about database snapshots (choose two).

- ☐ a. Are Read Only
- ☐ b. Are Read/Write
- ☐ c. Can be updated
- ☐ d. Are static at a point in time and cannot be updated.

2.) You have the following.

```
CREATE DATABASE dbPublish_Snap
ON (Name = dbPublish_Data, FILENAME = 'C:\SQL\dbPubMon.ss')
AS SNAPSHOT OF dbPublish
```
What is the name of the "source database"?

- O a. dbPublish
- O b. dbPublish_Snap
- O c. dbPublish_Data
- O d. dbPublish_dbPubMon

3.) You have the following code.

```
CREATE DATABASE dbPublish_Snap
ON (Name = dbPublish_Data, FILENAME = 'C:\SQL\dbPubMon.ss')
AS SNAPSHOT OF dbPublish
```
What is the name of the "source data file"?

- O a. dbPublish
- O b. dbPublish_Snap
- O c. dbPublish_Data
- O d. dbPublish_dbPubMon

4.) Database snapshots are:

- O a. Read Only
- O b. Read/Write

5.) Which statement is not true about database snapshots?

- O a. They are static point in time versions of a database.
- O b. They must be located on the same server as the source database.

O c. You can create a snapshot for any database including Master.

Answer Key

1.)a, d 2.) a   3.) c   4.) a   5.) c

Bug Catcher Game

To play the Bug Catcher game run the
BugCatcher_Chapter02DatabaseSchemasSnapshotsProperties.pps from the
BugCatcher folder of the companion files. You can obtain these files from
www.Joes2Pros.com or by ordering the Companion CD.

Chapter 3.   Data Type Usage

In the last chapter we discussed the importance of creating your database adequately large in size, in order to provide the space your data will need. While processing power, memory, and disk storage have all become cheaper and more plentiful in the last decade, the tasks of capacity planning and estimating infrastructure requirements are still important to the IT world.

It is also incumbent upon you as a SQL Pro to become intimately familiar with the data types available to SQL Server and their impacts on performance and storage consumption. The next three chapters will cover data type options and usage. In your database career you will use this knowledge in designing and implementing your own database systems, as well as troubleshooting and diagnosing performances issues with existing databases.

Factors affecting the space your data consumes are its data types, including fixed versus variable length, and whether or not the data type supports Unicode. The building blocks of database objects are fields, so our storage calculations will be based on the fields contained within a row.

READER NOTE: *In order to follow along with the examples in the first section of Chapter 3, please run the setup script SQLArchChapter3.0Setup.sql. The setup scripts for this book are posted at Joes2Pros.com.*

Data Row Space Usage

Most of a table's space is occupied by records. Indexes and other properties use a relatively small amount of known space. Suppose your company – or a hiring manager – shows you the design of the SalesInvoiceDetail table and says, "We expect this table to receive an average of 100,000 records per day during the next two years. *How much hard drive space should we purchase to handle this expected growth?"* You know how many rows will be received in a day and how many days there are in a year. The unknown in this scenario is the amount of space each row will use. If you calculate the amount of space each row needs, you can then answer this resource planning question for the new table.

100,000 rows/day * 365 days   = 36,500,000 rows

36,500,000 rows   * __ KB/row = ____ KB of storage space needed

Our calculations will similarly focus on data rows. In order to estimate a row's space consumption, we must know the amount of space each field's data will use.

There are three key components which contribute to a field's space consumption:

· The data type
· Whether the data type is fixed or variable
· Whether the field is nullable

Nullability is a substantial topic, so we will handle it in the next section. *(Note: The storage calculations in this section will ignore nullability and will be revised in the nullability section.)*

Units of Measurement

The data types and storage measurements in this chapter are denominated in bytes, since the smallest data type in SQL Server uses 1 byte.

A kilobyte (KB) consists of 1024 bytes. A megabyte (MB) consists of 1024 KB, or over a million bytes (1,048,576 bytes), and a gigabyte (GB) consists of 1024 MB.

Row Header

Every row has a 4 byte header. It contains two bytes that say what kind of record is: one byte for index records and one for the null bitmap. The null bitmap is always present whether or not the columns are nullable. (An exception to this rule of thumb would be tables comprised solely of sparse columns, which are discussed in Chapter 4.)

Common Data Types

The names and storage amounts per field for many commonly used data types are shown here. *(* denotes variable length data types)*

<u>Exact numeric data types</u>

int (integer)	4 bytes
bigint	8 bytes
smallint	2 bytes
tinyint	1 byte
money	8 bytes
smallmoney	4 bytes
decimal	5-17 bytes, depending on the number of digits
numeric	5-17 bytes, depending on the number of digits
bit	1-8 bit fields use 1 byte; 9-16 bit fields use 2 bytes; etc.

<u>Approximate numeric data types</u>

Float	4 bytes (1-24 digits); 8 bytes (25-53 digits)

<u>Character data types</u>

char (character)	1 byte per character (to a maximum of 8000 characters)
varchar*(variable size)	1 byte per character (to a maximum of 8000 characters)
text	1 byte per character (to a maximum of 2 GB)

<u>Date and time data types</u>
(sample outputs in Figure 3.1)

time	5 bytes
datetime	8 bytes
smalldatetime	4 bytes
date	3 bytes
datetime2	6-8 bytes, depending on precision

Data Type	Sample Output
datetime	2009-07-03 10:19:43.123
smalldatetime	2009-07-03 10:19:00
date	2009-07-03
datetime2	2009-07-03 10:19:43.1234567
time	10:19:43.1234567

Figure 3.1 Date and time data types.

<u>Unicode character data types</u>

nchar	2 bytes per character (to a maximum of 4000 characters)
nvarchar*	2 bytes per character (to a maximum of 4000 characters)
ntext	2 bytes per character (to a maximum of 2GB)

<u>Spatial data types</u> (new to SQL Server 2008 – see Chapter 5)
Geography data type (geodetic)
Geometry data type (planar)

<u>Other data types</u>

XML	2GB

92

Unicode Data

Unicode supports foreign language characters needed for international data (e.g., German umlauts, accents for romance language characters, Japanese characters, etc.).

With Unicode data types (e.g., nchar, nvarchar, ntext), each character occupies 2 bytes. In SQL Server, a Unicode data type is generally denoted by an "n" or "N." When SQL Server generates code involving Unicode data, you see an "N" accompanying Unicode data throughout the script. (Refer to Chapter 2 for more information on code generators.)

Just like with regular character data (char, varchar), a blank space included in Unicode data (e.g., a space in a name [Joe Smith] or an address [1234 Main Street]) is counted as a character.

Fixed Data

Fixed length data types always occupy the amount of space allotted to them. For example, an int will always use 4 bytes. A char(3) always takes up 3 bytes, even if the field contains just 1 or 2 characters. Fixed length data is predictable and the easiest type of data for SQL Server to manage. Calculations involving fixed data are straightforward. However, variable length data incurs additional overhead.

Variable Block

Every record containing variable length data includes something called a variable block. The first time you create a field with a variable length data type (e.g., varchar, nvarchar), the variable block is created. This block keeps track of the number of variable length data fields within the record and takes up 2 bytes.

The more variable length fields you have, the bigger the variable block grows. Each variable length field adds another 2 bytes to the block. (These 2 bytes keep track of where the data is positioned within the row.) For example, if you have one varchar field in your row, your variable block would contain 4 bytes. If you have two varchar fields, your variable block would contain 6 bytes (2 bytes per field plus 2 bytes to set this up).

Variable Data

Variable length data types do pretty much what the name implies – they expect the data length to vary from row to row. Fields using variable length data types, such as varchar and nvarchar, are typically name or address fields where you aren't certain how long the data will be.

The advantage these data types offer is that shorter names or addresses can take up less storage space than a fixed data type. For example, if you have a char(100) field to allow for long addresses, then that field always uses 100 bytes no matter how long the data actually is. However, if you know that most of your addresses will consist of 20 characters, you probably would choose a varchar(100) to use less storage space but retain the flexibility to accept addresses up to 100 characters in length.

In addition to the storage used by the variable block, you must count the actual number of characters in each varchar or nvarchar field. This is one difference between fixed and varying length data. With fixed data, you can calculate the storage consumption without needing to look at the actual data. For varying length data, you could estimate the maximum storage a row would need without looking at the table data. However, to precisely calculate how much storage a row or table is actually utilizing, you would need to examine the length of data in each of the variable data fields (the LEN( ) function is shown in Figure 3.2).

Varchar data consumes 1 byte per character. Nvarchar data consumes 2 bytes per character, because it is Unicode. For example a varchar(10) field containing the name "Rick" would consume 4 bytes. If it were an nvarchar, it would use 8 bytes.

```
SELECT *, LEN(RoomName) AS VarDataLength
FROM JProCo.HumanResources.RoomChart
```

	ID	Code	RoomName	VarDataLength
1	1	RLT	Renault-Langsford-Tribute	25
2	2	QTX	Quinault-Experience	19
3	3	TQW	TranquilWest	12
4	4	XW	XavierWest	10
5	5	NULL	NULL	NULL

Figure 3.2 The LEN( ) function measures the length of data for each RoomName.

Now let's bring in the design interface for the RoomChart table, which we will use to calculate the actual space consumption for rows in the RoomChart table. We will look at the table design along with our LEN( ) query result (above - Figure 3.2), so that we have handy the length measurements for the RoomName field. (See Figure 3.3 on the next page.)

To see this interface, open Object Explorer > Databases > JProCo > Tables. Then right-click HumanResources.RoomChart > **Design** (SQL Server 2005 users must click **Modify**).

RENO.JProCo-...rces.RoomChart		
Column Name	Data Type	Allow Nulls
ID	int	☐
Code	char(3)	☑
▶ RoomName	nvarchar(25)	☑

🗔 Results	🗎 Messages			
	ID	Code	RoomName	VarDataLength
1	1	RLT	Renault-Langsford-Tribute	25
2	2	QTX	Quinault-Experience	19
3	3	TQW	TranquilWest	12
4	4	XW	XavierWest	10
5	5	NULL	NULL	NULL

Figure 3.3 The design of the HumanResources.RoomChart table in the JProCo database.

Let's calculate the actual space consumption for Row 1 of the RoomChart table.

We will begin with the fixed length data. Each of the four rows contains two fixed length fields. The ID field uses 4 bytes and the field named "Code" uses 3 bytes. Each row also has a 4 byte header. Thus, without looking at the data, we already know each row uses at least 11 bytes.

Header + Fixed Length Fields (ID and Code fields)

[4 bytes + 4 bytes + 3 bytes   = **11 bytes**]

The final field (RoomName) contains variable length data, so in order to evaluate the space consumption we must: 1) calculate the variable block; and 2) look at the actual data.

Since there is one variable field per row, we must allow 2 bytes for the creation of the variable block. Then we must multiply the number of variable field(s) in the row by 2 bytes.

Variable Block

[2 bytes + (1 field * 2 bytes/field) = **4 bytes**]

Actual Data

[Renault-Langsford-Tribute, 25 unicode chars = **50 bytes**]

Header 4 │ Fixed Data 7 │ Variable Block 4 │ Variable Data 50 = 65 bytes

Thus, the total space used for Row 1 of the RoomChart table is 65 bytes.

Now let's calculate the space used by the second row of this table (JProCo.HumanResources.RoomChart).

Begin with the fixed length data.

Header + Fixed Length Fields (ID and Code fields)

[4 bytes + 4 bytes + 3 bytes   = **11 bytes**]

The variable block consumes the same amount of space in each row. We calculated Row 1's variable block to be 4 bytes. This will be the same for Row 2.

Variable Block

[2 bytes + (1 field * 2 bytes/field) = **4 bytes**]

Actual Data

[Quinault-Experience, 19 unicode chars = **38 bytes**]

Header 4 │ Fixed Data 7 │ Variable Block 4 │ Variable Data 38 = 53 bytes

Thus, the total space used for Row 2 of the RoomChart table is 53 bytes.

Note: It is recommended that you watch the lab video Lab3.1_Data rows.wmv, which recaps the data type guidelines and calculations covered in this section. It also contains additional storage calculation demonstrations. The video shows a helpful interface to reference when you need to check data type information for columns in your tables (see Figure 3.4).

This figure shows the Amount field of the Grant table (JProCo.dbo.Grant). The storage size of Amount is 4 bytes as shown in the "Size" item on the Column Properties tab of the Design interface.

Management Studio > Object Explorer > Databases > **JProCo** > Tables > Right-click **dbo.Grant** > Design

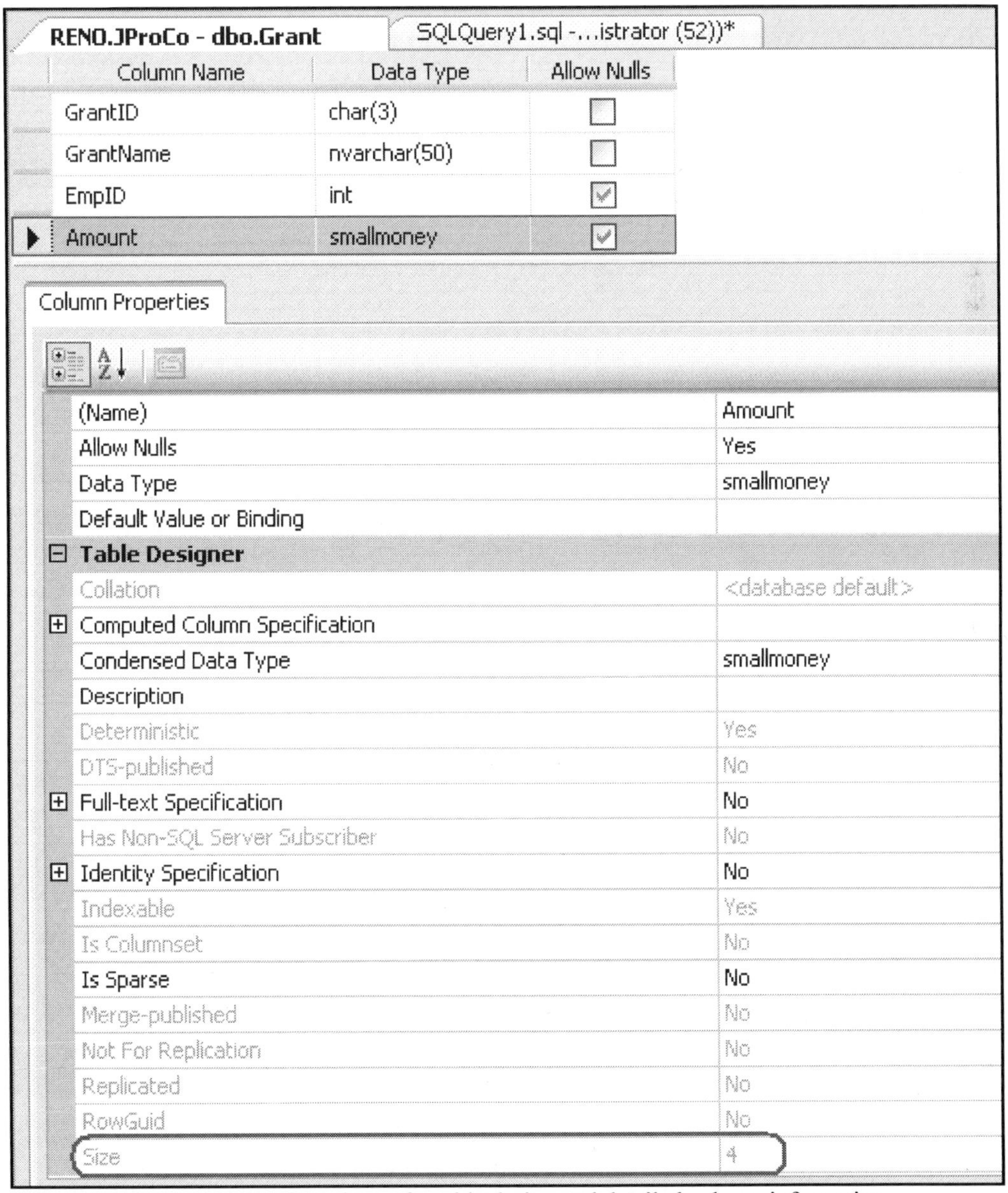

RENO.JProCo - dbo.Grant	SQLQuery1.sql -...istrator (52))*	
Column Name	Data Type	Allow Nulls
GrantID	char(3)	☐
GrantName	nvarchar(50)	☐
EmpID	int	☑
▶ Amount	smallmoney	☑

Column Properties

(Name)	Amount
Allow Nulls	Yes
Data Type	smallmoney
Default Value or Binding	
⊟ **Table Designer**	
Collation	<database default>
⊞ Computed Column Specification	
Condensed Data Type	smallmoney
Description	
Deterministic	Yes
DTS-published	No
⊞ Full-text Specification	No
Has Non-SQL Server Subscriber	No
⊞ Identity Specification	No
Indexable	Yes
Is Columnset	No
Is Sparse	No
Merge-published	No
Not For Replication	No
Replicated	No
RowGuid	No
Size	4

Figure 3.4 The design interface shows the table design and detailed column information.

Similar information may also be found in a slightly different interface (see next page – Figure 3.5). Either interface may be used to quickly look up a field's size, which can be helpful if you can't recall how much space a certain data type uses.

The "Size" property shown above in the Design interface is generally the equivalent of the "Length" property. For most unicode types (except ntext), "Size" will display the number of bytes and "Length" will show the number of characters.

Notice that the Properties interface includes a description for the behavior of each property.

Management Studio>Object Explorer>Databases>JProCo>Tables>**dbo.Grant** >Column >**Amount** >

From either Object Explorer or Object Explorer Details > right-click **Properties**.

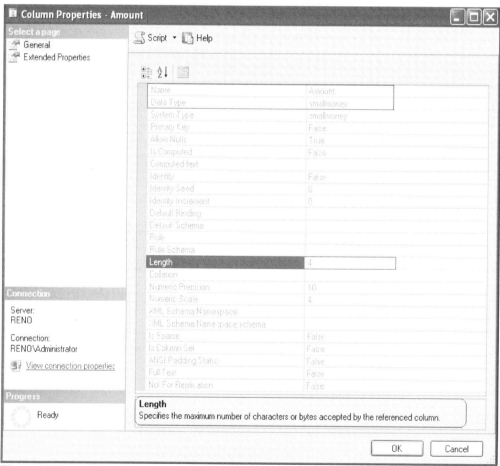

Figure 3.5 "Length" in this read-only property in this interface is the equivalent of the Size property for a specific field.

Lab 3.1 Data Row Space Usage

Lab Prep: Before you can begin the lab, you must have SQL Server installed and run the SQLArchChapter3.1Setup.sql script. View the lab video instructions in Lab3.1_Data rows.wmv.

Skill Check 1: Calculate the space consumption of Rows 3 and 4 according to the table design and data you see here.

RENO.JProCo-...rces.RoomChart		
Column Name	Data Type	Allow Nulls
ID	int	☐
Code	char(3)	☑
▶ RoomName	nvarchar(25)	☑

	ID	Code	RoomName	VarDataLength
1	1	RLT	Renault-Langsford-Tribute	25
2	2	QTX	Quinault-Experience	19
3	3	TQW	TranquilWest	12
4	4	XW	XavierWest	10
5	5	NULL	NULL	NULL

Figure 3.6 The design of the HumanResources.RoomChart table in the JProCo database.

Answer Code: The T-SQL code to this lab can be found in the downloadable files in a file named Lab3.1_Data rows.sql.

Data Row Space Usage - Points to Ponder

1. A data row consists of 1) a row header and 2) a data portion. The row header (positioning header) keeps track of where the row is in the table and the fields it contains.

2. A data row always includes a 4 byte header. The rest of the space is dedicated to holding and supporting the actual data in the data portion.

3. Fixed length data types always occupy the same amount of storage regardless of the number of characters actually present in the field. For example, a char(100) name field will take up 100 bytes in each row whether a name contains 0 (Null), 2, 52, 92, or 100 characters.

4. Fixed length data is easier for SQL Server to manage than variable length data, which incur additional overhead for SQL Server to manage. Where you expect column data to be fairly consistent, it's generally better to use a fixed length data type.

5. If a table includes any variable data types, then each row will contain a variable block. This variable block consists of 1) 2 bytes used to keep track of the number of variable fields in the row; and 2) an additional 2 bytes for each variable data type field.

6. A space in a field is considered a character and consumes the same number of bytes as any other character in the field. For example, the RoomName value 'Blue Room' consists of 9 characters. It would consume 18 bytes in a Unicode field and 9 bytes in a regular (ASCII) field.

7. The manufacturer of SQL Server (Microsoft) has indicated that the data types **ntext**, **text**, and **image** will be removed in a future version of SQL Server. (No planned release or date has yet been specified as of the publication date of this book.) Since the introduction of the max specification in SQL Server 2005, three data types (known as "the max data types") are the preferred types for handling large values (see the final section of this chapter "Large Values" for more on this topic).

Null Data

One important piece of the storage calculation we haven't yet considered is the null block. Somewhat like variable length data fields, each record in a table containing nullable field(s) uses a little extra storage space.

Null Block

In the last section, we learned that each record begins with a standard 4 byte row header. Right after the row header, the first item in the data portion of the record is the fixed data. SQL Server stores together all of the columns containing fixed width data.

If your table contains nullable data, then a null block follows the fixed data and occupies the third space in the physical structure of the record. (Without the null block, the usual order prevails - #1 Row Header, #2 Fixed Data, #3 Variable Block, and #4 Variable Data payload.)

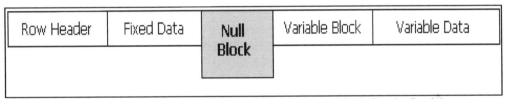

Figure 3.7 In the data portion of your row, the null block is located just after the fixed data.

The null block (also called the *null bitmap*) is created as soon as a nullable field is created in a table. The null block in each row begins as 2 bytes but may grow as you add more fields to your table.

Next you must count the total number of columns in the table. Add an additional byte to the row's null block for the first field and another byte for every 8th field. In other words, if a table has between 1-8 fields, then the null block in each row will be 3 bytes. If the table contains 9-16 fields, then the null block will be 4 bytes per row. If the table contains 17-24 fields, then the null block will be 5 bytes per row, and so forth.

These additional bytes contain an indication for each column's nullability. In other words, whether the column will allow nulls (e.g., Code, RoomName) or won't allow nulls (e.g., the ID column in the RoomChart table).

Null Block Storage Allocation

It often surprises people to know that it only takes one nullable field to cause every field in the table to take up 1 bit of extra space in the null block. These additional bits keep track of each column and whether it does or doesn't contain a null. The following diagram (Figure 3.8) illustrates two tables: one in which every column is nullable and one containing only a single nullable column.

Table T1	Row 1
	Row Data
c1 nullable	1
c2 nullable	2
c3 nullable	3
c4 nullable	4
c5 nullable	5
c6 nullable	6
c7 nullable	7
c8 nullable	8
c9 nullable	9
c10 nullable	10

Null Block

Byte 2								Byte 1							
7	6	5	4	3	2	1	0	7	6	5	4	3	2	1	0
1	1	1	1	1	1	0	0	0	0	0	0	0	0	0	0
Unused						c10	c9	c8	c7	c6	c5	c4	c3	c2	c1

Table T2	Row 1
	Row Data
c1 not null	1
c2 not null	2
c3 not null	3
c4 not null	4
c5 not null	5
c6 not null	6
c7 not null	7
c8 not null	8
c9 no nulls	9
c10 nullable	null

Null Block

Byte 2								Byte 1							
7	6	5	4	3	2	1	0	7	6	5	4	3	2	1	0
1	1	1	1	1	1	1	1	0	0	0	0	0	0	0	0
Unused						c10	c9	c8	c7	c6	c5	c4	c3	c2	c1

Figure 3.8 In the data portion of your row, the null block is located just after the fixed data.

Each table contains 10 columns, c1 through c10. Since there are 10 columns, and each table contains at least one nullable column, 10 additional bits are needed which means 2 additional bytes are needed. The null block already contains a 2 byte fixed length field, and a variable length bitmap of 1 bit per column. In this case 10 bits (c1 – c10) crosses into the next byte. The variable length bitmap takes up 2 more bytes, bringing the size to 4 bytes for both tables' null blocks.

Note that in table t1, an INSERT statement placed the integer values 1 through 10 in columns c1 through c10, respectively. Since none of these values is null, the null block bitmap contains 0's for columns c1 through c10. On the right half of this figure, you see these bits are located in byte 1 for columns c1 through c8, and byte 2 for columns c9 and c10. The additional 6 bits of byte 2 of the null block bitmap are allocated to the null block not used by any columns. In table t2 we have one null value in the last column. An INSERT statement placed the integer values 1 through 9 in columns c1 through c9, and null in column c10. Columns c1 through c9 are not null, so the null block bitmap contains 0's (zeros) for those columns. Column c10 (lower right half of Figure 3.8) does contain null, so its bit in the null block bitmap reflects a 1.

In a table that contains at least one nullable column, each row will contain a null block whose length depends on the number of columns in the table. If a row of such a table contains a null value for a nullable column, its bit in that row's null block bitmap will be set to 1. Columns which are not null have their bits in the row's null block bitmap set to 0.

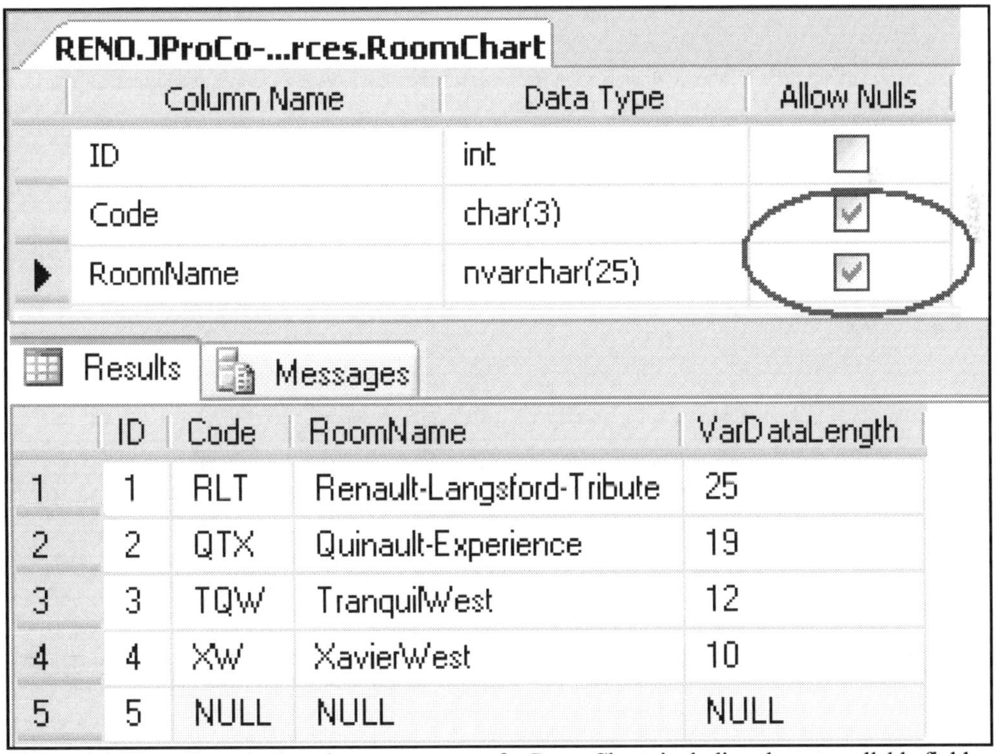
RENO.JProCo-...rces.RoomChart

Column Name	Data Type	Allow Nulls
ID	int	☐
Code	char(3)	☑
RoomName	nvarchar(25)	☑

Results | Messages

	ID	Code	RoomName	VarDataLength
1	1	RLT	Renault-Langsford-Tribute	25
2	2	QTX	Quinault-Experience	19
3	3	TQW	TranquilWest	12
4	4	XW	XavierWest	10
5	5	NULL	NULL	NULL

Figure 3.9 We will recalculate the storage space for RoomChart, including the two nullable fields.

Recall that we calculated the space consumption for Row 1 as 65 bytes.

Actual Data

[Renault-Langsford-Tribute, 25 unicode chars = **50 bytes**]

Header 4 | Fixed Data 7 | Variable Block 4 | Variable Data 50 = 65 bytes

We know a null block is needed, because there are nullable fields in the RoomChart table. There are two nullable fields, Code and RoomName (as shown in Figure 3.9).

Creating the null block uses 2 bytes. Then you must count the total number of columns in the table. Since this table contains 3 columns, 1 byte is added to the null block.

Null Block

[2 bytes + 1 byte (only 3 fields)] = **3 bytes**]

So we must add 3 bytes to our original storage calculation for Row 1:

Header 4 | Fixed Data 7 | Null Block 3 | Variable Block 4 | Variable Data 50 = 68 bytes

Thus, the full amount of space used by Row 1 of the RoomChart table is 68 bytes.

Now let's recalculate the second row's space usage including the null block.

Recall we calculated the space consumption for Row 2 as 53 bytes.

Actual Data

[Quinault-Experience, 19 unicode chars = **38 bytes**]

Header 4 | Fixed Data 7 | Variable Block 4 | Variable Data 38 = 53 bytes

Since the null block for each record in the table will be the same size, we know the null block for Row 2 will be the same as Row 1: 3 bytes.

Null Block

[2 bytes + 1 byte (only 3 fields)] = **3 bytes**]

So we must add 3 bytes to our original storage calculation for Row 2:

Header 4 | Fixed Data 7 | Null Block 3 | Variable Block 4 | Variable Data 38 = 56 bytes

Thus, the full amount of space used by Row 2 of the RoomChart table is 56 bytes.

Here are a few additional tips to keep in mind when calculating variable length data payloads:

1) Spaces count as characters. Suppose the room in the HumanResources table named "Quinault-Experience" was instead spelled "Quinault Experience". *Both versions of this name consume 38 bytes.*

2) If a variable length field contains a NULL value, then the data payload is 0 bytes.

3) A fixed lengh field will always contain the same data payload, even if the field contains a NULL value. For example, a char(20) field will always consume 20 bytes. If that field contains a NULL value, then the data payload for the field is still 20 bytes.

Note: The lab video Lab3.2_NullData.wmv recaps the data type guidelines and calculations covered in this section. It also contains additional storage calculation demonstrations from the Grant and Employee tables of the JProCo database.

Lab 3.2: Null Data

Lab Prep: The lab is theoretical and there is no need to run a reset script to fill out the form below. View the lab video instructions in Lab3.2_NullData.wmv.

Skill Check 1: Calculate the Header, Fixed Data, Null Block, Variable Block, Variable Data, and Total storage space used for each row of the HumanResources.RoomChart table. Use the table design and the data contained in the five rows below. Note: We have changed the values in some of the records to be a bit different than the examples used earlier or later in this chapter. Count what you see for Figure 3.10.

RENO.JProCo-...rces.RoomChart

Column Name	Data Type	Allow Nulls
ID	int	☐
Code	nchar(3)	☑
RoomName	nvarchar(25)	☑
RoomDescription	nvarchar(200)	☑
MaxTemp	int	☑
MinTemp	int	☑

Results | Messages

	ID	Code	RoomName	RoomDescription	MaxTemp	MinTemp
1	1	RLT	Renault-Langsford-Tribute	Customer Previews	79	66
2	2	QTX	Quinault-Experience	Party	85	50
3	3	TQW	TranquilWest	Misc	85	55
4	4	XW	XavierWest	NULL	NULL	NULL
5	5	NULL	NULL	NULL	NULL	NULL

	Row Header	Fixed Data	Null Block	Variable Block	Variable Data	TOTAL
Row 1						
Row 2						
Row 3						
Row 4						
Row 5						

Figure 3.10 Skill Check 1 calculates the storage space for each row in the RoomChart table.

Answer Code: The T-SQL code to this lab can be found in the downloadable files in a file named Lab3.2_NullData.sql.

Null Data - Points to Ponder

1. A data row consists of a row header and a data portion. The 4 byte row header contains information about the columns and the data row.

2. The data portion of a row can contain the following elements.
    a. Fixed length data
    b. Null block
    c. Variable block
    d. Variable length data

3. Data rows can hold up to a total of 8060 bytes per row.

4. Fixed length data (like int, char, nchar etc.) comes right after the row header portion of the record. It is always the first section of the data portion of the row space allocation.

5. Variable length data goes at the end of the row data, and takes up varying amounts of space, depending on its content.

6. A 2 byte null block (a.k.a., null bitmap) is created to track nullable fields in your table.

7. The null block has one bit per column in the table definition, as long as at least one column in the table is nullable. (8 bits make up 1 byte).

8. An additional byte is added to the null block for the first column in the table and every 8th column thereafter. At a minimum the null block adds 3 bytes of storage to each row in the table. (Note: only non-sparse columns are included in the one bit per column calculations. In other words, sparse data columns are excluded from the count of columns. The sparse data option is discussed in Chapter 4.)

9. A NULL value in a variable length field counts as 0 data payload.

Large Values

Thus far, the data types we've examined carry a maximum of 8000 bytes per field. However, there may be times when you need a field to hold *large values* – that is to say, values exceeding 8000 bytes.

Every day we see examples of databases containing large items. When you upload a document or an image to a SharePoint site, you're storing a large value data item in a database field. Many online shopping outlets use picture and sound files in this way. And if your company stores employee photos (e.g., to print onto employee badges), it most likely stores them as varbinary files within a database.

Prior to SQL Server 2005, large object (LOB) types were the only way to bypass the 8000 byte limit of typical data types (e.g., char, varchar, varbinary, etc.). The three LOB types are *image, text, and ntext.* Since you may encounter LOB types hanging around in legacy systems, we will examine these types in this section. However, the use of these types is discouraged since: 1) Microsoft plans to eliminate them and 2) the new types introduced in SQL Server 2005 to replace LOBs have better performance and are easier to work with.

Since SQL Server 2005, developers have been praising the new MAX specification used in combination with varchar, nvarchar, and varbinary to handle large values. In fact, the MAX specification, varchar(max), nvarchar(max), and varbinary(max) are known as *large-value data types*, which make it easier to include large items with your typical relational database data.

In this section we will explore the difference between programming with regular data types versus large-value data types, as well as SQL Server's behind-the-scenes handling of these data types.

Memory Page

Discussions of large values invariably must consider how SQL Server stores data. A *memory page* is 8 KB (8 kilobytes) of physical space set aside for rapid storage and retrieval of records. The amount 8 KB actually converts to 8192 bytes, but SQL Server can only utilize 8060 of those 8192 bytes for storage. Therefore data types which limit themselves to 8000 bytes operate very fast and efficiently, because they can fit within the organized pages of memory.

Most data types in SQL Server are known as value types because each value will be 8000 bytes, or less, and thus will fit within an 8 KB page of memory. For example, an int is just 4 bytes. An nvarchar(4000) takes up to 8000 bytes, as does a varchar(8000).

Let's evaluate HumanResources.RoomChart with respect to how SQL Server will store this table's data. First we need to calculate how much storage it consumes.

If you ran the last reset script, SQLArchChapter3.2Setup.sql, then your table and data will match Figure 3.11 (below).

RENO.JProCo-...rces.RoomChart		
Column Name	Data Type	Allow Nulls
▶ ID	int	☐
Code	nchar(3)	☑
RoomName	nvarchar(25)	☑
RoomDescription	nvarchar(200)	☑

Results   Messages

	ID	Code	RoomName	RoomDescription
1	1	RLT	Renault-Langsford-Tribute	This room is designed for Customer Previews
2	2	QTX	Quinault-Experience	Parties and Morale Events get top priority
3	3	TQW	TranquilWest	Misc
4	4	XW	XavierWest	NULL
5	5	NULL	NULL	NULL

Figure 3.11 The RoomChart table following the last setup script, SQLArchChapter3.2Setup.sql.

The safest method for performing capacity planning calculations on tables with variable length data is to assume each field will contain the maximum allowable length of data. Now let's calculate the storage requirements for this table.

1) Begin with the row header and fixed length data.

Header + Fixed Length Fields (ID field and Code field, which is Unicode)

[4 bytes + 4 bytes + 6 bytes   = **14 bytes**]

2) The null block consumes the same amount of space in each row. Two (2) bytes for the setup of the null block, 1 byte for the first column in the table and 1 byte for every 8th column thereafter.

Null Block

[2 bytes + 1 byte (only 4 fields)] = **3 bytes**]

3) The variable block also consumes the same amount of space in each row. The setup of the variable block takes 2 bytes. Add 2 more bytes for each variable length field present (RoomName, RoomDescription).

Variable Block

[2 bytes + (2 fields * 2 bytes/field) = **6 bytes**]

4) The variable data can only be calculated after you have put data in the table. If you put 1 character in an nvarchar(200) it will take up less space than if you were to put 200 characters in that field.

Variable Data Fields (estimate the maximum allowable length)

[RoomName, 25 unicode chars = **50 bytes**]
[RoomDescription, 200 unicode chars = **400 bytes**]

Header 4 | Fixed Data 10 | Null Block 3 | Variable Block 6 | Variable Data 450 = 473 bytes

Thus, each row of the RoomChart table will use up to 473 bytes.

Rows are meant to fit into a page of data (8060 bytes). Many rows can fit into a page, which is very efficient. For example, since each row of the RoomChart table will use up to 473 bytes, then 17 rows of this size will fit into one 8 KB page.

[473 bytes/row * 17 rows = 8041 bytes]

In case a table's rows become big, then the next most efficient thing is if each field can fit within an 8 KB page. This is why data types which limit themselves to 8000 bytes, or less, operate very fast and very efficiently, as mentioned earlier.

Large Object Types

Suppose you need a field to contain data beyond the typical 8000 byte limit. For example, we might be asked to add a RoomNotes field to the RoomChart table to hold lengthy notes for a few of the conference rooms which have historical anecdotes or significance. Perhaps a foreign dignitary visited this room, and we'd like to store that information in the database.

Prior to SQL Server 2005, if you needed a field to contain a string greater than 8000 bytes, you would have used a large object (LOB) type, such as a text or ntext. These act much like a varchar or an nvarchar but are stored outside of the row's normal memory space.

We will add this field to the table and make the data type ntext. We believe the field will likely contain 5000 characters (i.e., 10,000 bytes of Unicode data), but we want our users to be free to include as much data as they wish.

With the ntext data type, they will be able to include up to 2 GB of data or over 1 billion Unicode characters (1,073,741,822). The storage limit for text and image data is 2,147,483,647 characters, and bytes, respectively.

In the design interface add a RoomNotes column which has the data type ntext and is nullable.

Management Studio > Object Explorer > Databases > JProCo > Tables >
Right-click **HumanResources.RoomChart** > Design

OR

Management Studio > Object Explorer > Databases > JProCo > Tables >
HumanResources.RoomChart > Object Explorer Details > right-click Columns > **New
Column**

Column Name	Data Type	Allow Nulls
ID	int	☐
Code	nchar(3)	☑
RoomName	nvarchar(25)	☑
RoomDescription	nvarchar(200)	☑
RoomNotes	ntext	☑

Column Properties

(Name)	RoomNotes
Allow Nulls	Yes
Data Type	ntext
Default Value or Binding	(N'No notes have been recorded for this room.')
Table Designer	
Collation	<database default>
⊞ Computed Column Specification	
Condensed Data Type	ntext
Description	

Figure 3.12 In the design interface, add an ntext RoomNotes column which is nullable.

Recall that the LOB data is stored outside of the row's normal memory space.
LOBs were the first SQL Server data type allowing developers to exceed the 8000
byte constraint. However, they have to be managed by SQL Server in a separate
memory space, which costs additional processing time and degrades performance.
For each row in a table with a LOB field, SQL Server creates separate memory
pages for that field's data. If you have a 100-row table, then separate memory
pages will be created for every row, even if a row's LOB field is null or contains
just a small amount of data.

As a database developer or designer, you want to avoid LOBs. Eliminate or
convert existing LOBs where possible, and use the newer data types for any new
development work. The fact that the LOB is not stored with the rest of the row data
automatically increases processing time because SQL Server needs extra I/O
(input/output) cycles to access the other data pages – and it must repeat the process
for every row in the table. SQL Server logically links the row together when you
query or run update/insert statements for the table.

When you include a LOB field in your table, SQL Server stores a pointer to the LOB data in the row along with the regular data. This 16-byte pointer in the data row points to a root structure in another part of memory where the actual LOB data is held.

This pointer's 16-byte "Size" is shown in the Column Properties tab of the Design interface (see Figure 3.13).

Management Studio > Object Explorer > Databases > JProCo > Tables >
Right-click **HumanResources.RoomChart** > Design

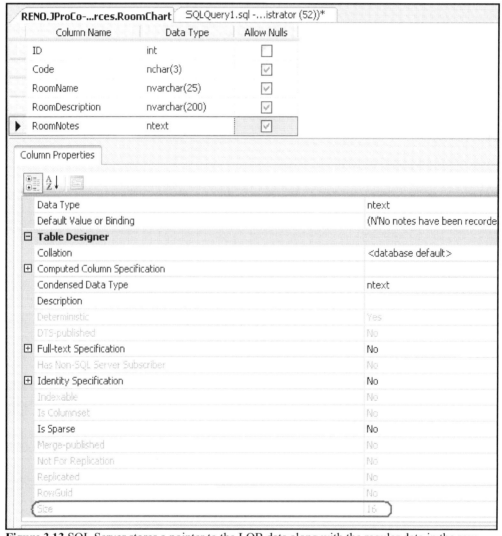

Figure 3.13 SQL Server stores a pointer to the LOB data along with the regular data in the row.

Next we'll add the RoomNotes field into our storage estimation for the RoomChart table (refer to the design shown above – see Figure 3.13).

In a capacity planning report, the net impact of adding the RoomNotes field (ntext) would be: 1) the additional 16 bytes in the fixed length portion of the row, and 2) allowing up to 2 GB in the datafile (MDF/NDF) for each LOB field. Since the data payload for LOBs is stored outside the data row, the data payload itself won't be added to the data row.

Prior to adding the RoomNotes field, recall that we estimated that each row of the RoomChart table would use up to 473 bytes and as many as 17 rows would fit into one 8 KB page.

Header 4 | Fixed Data 10 | Null Block 3 | Variable Block 6 | Variable Data 450 = 473 bytes
[473 bytes/row * 17 rows = 8041 bytes]

Now we'll add the ntext field, RoomNotes, to the row calculation. With LOBs, the 16-byte pointer for each field is stored with the fixed data. The data payload is stored outside the data row.

1) Add the pointer to the row header and fixed length data calculation.

Header + Fixed Length Fields (ID and Code fields) + External Row Pointer

[4 bytes + 4 bytes + 6 bytes + 16 bytes   = **30 bytes**]

2) The RoomNotes field is nullable. But since it only increases the number of columns in the table from 4 to 5, no additional bytes are needed for the null block.

Null Block

[2 bytes + 1 byte (only 5 fields)] = **3 bytes**]

3) LOBs never impact the variable block.

Variable Block

[2 bytes + (2 fields * 2 bytes/field) = **6 bytes**]

4) *Variable Data Fields (estimate the maximum allowable length)*

[RoomName, 25 unicode chars = **50 bytes**]
[RoomDescription, 200 unicode chars = **400 bytes**]

Header 4 | Fixed Data 26 | Null Block 3 | Variable Block 6 | Variable Data 450 = 489 bytes

Thus, each row of the RoomChart table will now use up to 489 bytes. At 489 bytes per row, one fewer row will now fit within a data page.

[489 bytes/row * 17 rows = ~~8313 bytes~~] *must be below 8060 bytes*

[489 bytes/row * 16 rows = 7824 bytes]

113

Since we would need to allow for an additional 2 GB of RoomNotes data outside of each data row, an estimate of how many rows are expected would be important. The JProCo datafile(s) (MDF/NDF) would need to have that amount of disk storage available, in addition to the 489 bytes for each record in the table.

As well, if we were calculating actual storage for this table, we would need to know the length or size of each row's ntext field. The actual data payload for each LOB is the amount of storage it uses.

In the next section, we will look at the newer data types which make handling large value data a little easier. *For large value data, the best practice is to use the newer data types and avoid using LOBs altogether*. Converting LOB type columns to a max data type is very easy and requires just a single ALTER statement:

```
ALTER TABLE HumanResources.RoomChart
ALTER COLUMN RoomNotes NVARCHAR(MAX)
GO
```

However, there may be times when you will be forced to work with a LOB (e.g., if you must work with a legacy system containing an **image** or **text/ntext** type and the cost-benefit ratio doesn't favor rebuilding the table(s)). In these cases, there are some mitigation strategies you can attempt.

In our RoomNotes column example, one mitigation strategy you might consider is using two separate columns to store notes – e.g., one called "RoomNotes" for notes which fit within the limits of a regular data type and another called "RoomNotesLrg" to store the notes which exceed 8000 bytes. The LOB data would still be stored separately, but the regular notes would be stored as regular data within the row.

Another strategy is to override the normal behavior of the LOB and force smaller data in the LOB field to be stored in the row along with the regular data types. SQL Server allows you some control over the storage location. You can instruct SQL Server to store data ranging from 24 to 7000 bytes in the regular row. For example, the code below instructs the RoomChart table to store fields containing fewer than 5001 bytes in the regular data row.

EXEC sp_TableOption 'HumanResources.RoomChart', 'Text In Row', 5000

When the "Large Value Types Out of Row" property is set to **1** for a table, The large values, like varchar(max) or nvarchar(max), that are normally stored in the row will be stored outside of the row. This setting will have no effect on LOB types like text and ntext. When this property is set to **0**, then all values small enough are stored in the row and pointers are only used if the data is too large.

EXEC sp_TableOption 'HumanResources.RoomChart', 'Large Value Types Out of Row', 0

When you change this property from 1 (on) to 0 (off), you need to update the column's values in order for the values being stored outside the data row to appear inside the data row.

```
UPDATE HumanResources.RoomChart
SET RoomNotes = RoomNotes
```

Including large data values in the main row can be helpful, if you use these fields frequently in your queries and reports. However, if the large data values are seldom queried, then there may be a performance advantage to storing that data outside the main data row. This would allow more rows of your table to be stored in the same data page – which means more rows are read with each I/O cycle – thereby improving performance.

Note: As with the LOBs, the **Text In Row** property has been deprecated and will be removed in a future version of SQL Server.

Large-Value Data Types

The large-value data types (varchar(max), nvarchar(max), and varbinary(max)) were introduced in SQL Server 2005. These are also known as **max data types** and can contain the maximum amount allowed for a field by SQL Server (which is 2 GB in SQL Server 2005 and 2008).

Therefore, a max data type column can hold up to 2 GB (i.e., 2,147,483,647 bytes). A varchar(max) or varbinary(max) can contain 2,147,483,647 characters. An nvarchar(max) can contain roughly half that number of characters (1,073,741,822), since Unicode consumes 2 bytes per character.

Suppose that, after populating many records in the HumanResources.RoomChart table, we discover our values in the RoomNotes field rarely exceed 8000 bytes. The large-value data types have the ability to handle our smaller notes as a regular data type would yet handle the large notes as a LOB type would – all within a single column.

This capability is very useful. Essentially, this data type behaves like a regular data type when the field value is ≤8000 bytes, and it stores data in the row page along with the other fields. When the field contains a large value (>8000 bytes), then the max data type behaves like a LOB type by storing the data separately and including a 16-byte pointer in the data row.

For our RoomNotes example, where the vast majority of the field values are under the 8000 byte limit, changing to an nvarchar(max) means we will see a performance gain. At the same time, we won't be limited in cases where a field value causes the row to exceed the 8 KB (8060 byte) limitation.

Please note that, if you want to make this type of a change to an existing table (i.e., change a field from an ntext to an nvarchar(max)), then SQL Server may prompt you to drop and re-create the table.

Because every row in the table has the possibility of being stored either inside or outside the data row based on its size, the Size property for a large value data type field will always display a value of -1 (see Figure 3.14).

Each field exceeding 8000 bytes behaves like a LOB. The data payload is stored outside the data row and a 16-byte pointer is stored in the data row.

Fields containing values of 8000 bytes, or fewer, behave like any variable length field. Each row requires a variable block and stores the data payload inside the row.

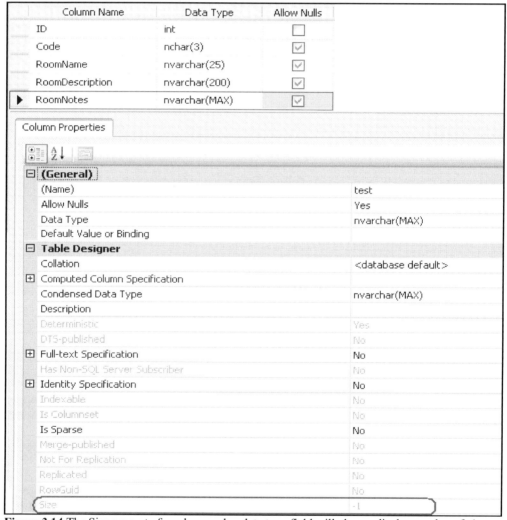

Figure 3.14 The Size property for a large value data type field will always display a value of -1.

The ability of the Large Value Data Types to automatically handle the placement of data inside or outside the data row is novel and exciting (and is made possible in part by SQL Server 2005's row-overflow data feature). However, there could be instances where you might want to set the **Large Value Types Out of Row** property to "1" (on) and force all the variable max length fields to be stored outside of the row.

With large value data types, their default setting for that property is "0", so that all values small enough to fit in the row are stored there and pointers are only used if the data is too large.

One reason you might consider this unusual step is for a table which is queried frequently and thus performance is a high visibility issue. If the large-value data field(s) is rarely queried, then there may be a performance advantage to storing that data outside the main data row. This would allow more rows of your table to be stored in the same data page – meaning more rows are read with each I/O cycle – and thus should improve performance for the tables your users query frequently.

Finally, let's update our storage estimation for the HumanResources.RoomChart table to show the RoomNotes field as an nvarchar(max) data type. (Refer to the design shown on the previous page – see Figure 3.14.)

Recall that, after the addition of the RoomNotes field as an ntext, we estimated that each row of the RoomChart table would use up to 489 bytes and as many as 16 rows would fit into one 8 KB page.

Header 4 | Fixed Data 26 | Null Block 3 | Variable Block 6 | Variable Data 450 = 489 bytes

[489 bytes/row * 16 rows = 7824 bytes]

For an actual data calculation, we would need the actual size of each value in the **nvarchar(max)** column. For each field >8000 bytes, we would: 1) add a 16-byte pointer to the data row and 2) add the data payload amount to the out of row calculation, which adds to the size of the JProCo datafile (MDF/NDF) but doesn't increase the data row. For each field ≤ 8000 bytes, we would: 1) add 2 bytes to the variable block, 2) add the data payload to the data row, and 3) add a 24-byte pointer if the data row exceeds 8060. We will discuss the 24 byte pointer later.

However, since we are updating our capacity planning report, we want to estimate the *maximum storage* that should be provided for the HumanResources.RoomChart table. At a high level, we know all rows of the RoomChart table could, at most, consume the same as we calculated for the LOB: 489 bytes in each data row and 2 GB stored outside the row. (See RoomNotes calculated as ntext – p. 110, Fig 3.13.)

In the real world, some assumptions would have to be made, in order to plan for this table. Ideally, a stakeholder familiar with the underlying business would be able to project how much data the variable length fields would actually receive.

Here we will demonstrate the mechanics for calculating the largest amount each row in the table would consume with the nvarchar(max) as: 1) >8000 bytes and 2) ≤8000 bytes (Figure 3.14).

1) The row header and fixed length data calculation is the same as the LOB estimate for each row with a RoomNote value >8000 bytes.

Header + Fixed Length Fields (ID and Code fields)

[4 bytes + 4 bytes + 6 bytes = **14 bytes**]

2) No change to the null block.

Null Block

[2 bytes + 1 byte (only 5 fields)] = **3 bytes**]

3) Just like LOBs, the >8000 byte values of an nvarchar(max) do not impact the variable block.

Variable Block

[2 bytes + (2 fields * 2 bytes/field) = **6 bytes**]

4) *Variable Data Fields (estimate the maximum allowable length) + External Row Pointer (always 16 bytes which is included with the variable data payload)*

[RoomName, 25 unicode chars = **50 bytes**]
[RoomDescription, 200 unicode chars = **400 bytes**]
[External Row Pointer = **16 bytes**]

Header 4 | Fixed Data 10 | Null Block 3 | Variable Block 6 | Variable Data 466 = 489 bytes

Thus, each row of the table with a RoomChart value >8000 bytes would store its data payload *outside* of the data row and would consume up to 489 bytes in the data row. At 489 bytes per row, 16 rows would fit within a data page.

[489 bytes/row * 16 rows = 7824 bytes]

Now we will run an estimate for those rows where RoomNote contains <= 8000 bytes.

1) There is no need for the 16-byte pointer when the data is stored in row. However, for every data row which exceeds 8060 bytes, the row-overflow data feature will move the largest individual column(s) to a different data page. Since each nvarchar(max) value can be as much as 8000 bytes, row-overflow data will move the

RoomNotes column to a different data page. A 24-byte pointer is added to the data row to keep track of that data.

Header + Fixed Length Fields (ID and Code fields)

[4 bytes + 4 bytes + 6 bytes = **14 bytes**]

2) No change to the null block.

Null Block

[2 bytes + 1 byte (only 5 fields)] = **3 bytes**]

3) Each nvarchar(max) value of 8000 bytes will add 2 more bytes to the variable block.

Variable Block

[2 bytes + (3 fields * 2 bytes/field) = **8 bytes**]

4) *Variable Data Fields (estimate the maximum allowable length) + External Row Pointer (24 bytes)*

[RoomName, 25 unicode chars = **50 bytes**]
[RoomDescription, 200 unicode chars = **400 bytes**]
[RoomNotes, 4000 unicode chars = **8000 bytes**]
[External Row Pointer = **24 bytes**]

Header 4 | Fixed Data 10 | Null Block 3 | Variable Block 8 | Variable Data 8474=8499 bytes

Thus, each row of the RoomChart table could use up to 8499 bytes where the nvarchar(max) field is <= 8000 bytes.

Since row-overflow data will move the 8000 byte field (RoomNotes) to a separate data page, each data row will contain up to 499 bytes. At 499 bytes per row, 16 rows can fit within a data page.

[499 bytes/row * 16 rows = 7984 bytes]

Be aware you will encounter SQL references which aren't 100% consistent in their naming convention for large value types. Some resources refer to all the large value types as LOBs (or BLOBs) and call text, ntext, and image types "legacy LOBs."

Lab 3.3: Large Values

Lab Prep: Before you can begin the lab, you must have SQL Server installed and run the SQLArchChapter3.3Setup.sql script. View the lab video instructions in Lab3.3_LargeObjectTypes.wmv.

Skill Check 1: Calculate the actual amount of storage consumed by the HumanResources.RoomChart table (design shown below in Figure 3.15). Each field length is also shown, as well as each field's size in bytes (Figure 3.16). For any data which would be stored outside the row, include that in the variable data payload (see "Variable Data" in worksheet below).

RENO.JProCo-...rces.RoomChart	SQLQuery1.sql -...istrator (52))*	
Column Name	Data Type	Allow Nulls
ID	int	☐
Code	nchar(3)	☑
RoomName	nvarchar(25)	☑
RoomDescription	nvarchar(200)	☑
▶ RoomNotes	ntext	☑

1		Row Header	Fixed Data	Null Block	Variable Block	Variable Data	Total in Row Storage	Out of Row Storage
2	Row 1							
3	Row 2							
4	Row 3							
5	Row 4							
6	Row 5							
7	Row 6							
8	Row 7							
9	Row 8							
10	Row 9							
11	Row 10							

Figure 3.15 The design of the RoomChart table. The data type for RoomNotes is ntext with sheet to fill out based on table design.

```
SELECT LEN(ID) AS lenID,
  LEN(Code) AS lenCode,
  LEN(RoomName) AS lenNRoomName,
  LEN(RoomDescription) AS lenNRoomDescription,
  LEN(RoomNotes) AS lenNRoomNotes
  FROM HumanResources.RoomChart
```

Results | Messages

	lenID	lenCode	lenNRoomName	lenNRoomDescription	lenNRoomNotes
1	1	3	25	43	NULL
2	1	3	19	42	NULL
3	1	3	12	4	NULL
4	1	2	10	NULL	NULL
5	1	NULL	NULL	NULL	NULL
6	1	NULL	NULL	NULL	3025
7	1	NULL	NULL	NULL	2025
8	1	NULL	NULL	NULL	125
9	1	NULL	NULL	NULL	122
10	2	NULL	NULL	NULL	100

Figure 3.16 The length of each value in the RoomChart table. N is the symbol for Unicode data. Tip: use DATALENGTH( ) for the RoomNotes field, otherwise you will get an error.

```
SELECT DATALENGTH(ID) AS ID_bytes,
  DATALENGTH(Code) AS Code_bytes,
  DATALENGTH(RoomName) AS NRoomName_bytes,
  DATALENGTH(RoomDescription) AS NRoomDescription_bytes,
  DATALENGTH(RoomNotes) AS NRoomNotes_bytes
  FROM HumanResources.RoomChart
```

Results | Messages

	ID_bytes	Code_bytes	NRoomName_bytes	NRoomDescription_bytes	NRoomNotes_bytes
1	4	6	50	86	NULL
2	4	6	38	84	NULL
3	4	6	24	8	NULL
4	4	6	20	NULL	NULL
5	4	NULL	NULL	NULL	NULL
6	4	NULL	NULL	NULL	6050
7	4	NULL	NULL	NULL	4050
8	4	NULL	NULL	NULL	250
9	4	NULL	NULL	NULL	244
10	4	NULL	NULL	NULL	200

Figure 3.17 The size (bytes) of each value in the RoomChart table. N is the symbol for Unicode data.

Skill Check 2: Calculate the actual amount of storage consumed by the HumanResources.RoomChart table (design shown below in Figure 3.18). Each field length is shown on the previous page (Figure 3.16), as well as each field's size in bytes (Figure 3.18). For any data which would be stored outside the row, include that in the variable data payload (see "Variable Data" in worksheet below).

RENO.JProCo-...rces.RoomChart	SQLQuery1.sql -...istrator (52))*	
Column Name	Data Type	Allow Nulls
ID	int	☐
Code	nchar(3)	☑
RoomName	nvarchar(25)	☑
RoomDescription	nvarchar(200)	☑
► RoomNotes	nvarchar(MAX)	☑

1		Row Header	Fixed Data	Null Block	Variable Block	Variable Data	Total in Row Storage	Out of Row Storage
2	Row 1							
3	Row 2							
4	Row 3							
5	Row 4							
6	Row 5							
7	Row 6							
8	Row 7							
9	Row 8							
10	Row 9							
11	Row 10							

Figure 3.18 The design of the RoomChart table. The data type for RoomNotes is nvarchar(max).

Answer Code: The T-SQL code to this lab can be found in the downloadable files in a file named Lab3.3_LargeObjects.sql.

Large Values - Points to Ponder

1. Data rows can hold up to a total of 8060 bytes per memory page.

2. If you try to fit more than 8060 bytes in a row, then some data will sit outside that row. Inside the row will be a pointer to the location of the data.

3. A data type can't be larger than a page, so LOBs might have to be stored somewhere else and have just a pointer from the row itself.

4. A 16-byte pointer in the data row points to a root structure in another part of memory that holds the actual LOB data. This is why you see "16" for size when you select **ntext**, **text**, and **image** in the table design.

5. With small to medium sized LOBs, SQL provides the option to store values in the row rather than pointing to the data. (Note: the pointer system in SQL uses a B-tree structure).

6. When **Large Value Types Out of Row** is on (set to 1 or 'ON') the pointer is being used, if off (set to 0 or 'OFF') then all values small enough to fit in the row are stored there and pointers are only used if the data is too large.

7. The Max specifier was introduced in SQL Server 2005 and is used with Varchar, Nvarchar, and Varbinary.

8. Max value types are stored in the row if they fit and only moved to another memory space for the rows that go over the limit.

9. Max makes it possible to store values larger than 8060 bytes the same way as a LOB without some of the limitations of Text and Ntext.

10. In SQL Server 2005 and 2008, the storage limit for max data types is 2 GB.

11. It is generally considered bad practice to put an index or constraint on any field wider than 900 bytes. (Indexes will be covered in Chapters 8-13.)

12. Since the introduction of the large-value data types (a.k.a., the max data types) in SQL Server 2005, the manufacturer of SQL Server (Microsoft) has indicated that the data types **ntext**, **text**, and **image** have been deprecated (i.e., will be removed in a future version of SQL Server).

13. These deprecated LOB types (ntext, text, image) have limited functionality in DML statements. The max data types have much greater functionality and perform more like regular data types (e.g., with queries, subqueries, joins, variables, functions, and triggers).

14. Note: the **Text In Row** property has been deprecated and will be removed in a future version of SQL Server.

Chapter Glossary

Data row space usage: The amount of space each row of data will use.

Data portion: A data row consists of the header and the data portion, which is dedicated to holding and supporting the actual data in the data portion

Fixed data: SQL data with consistent fixed size.

Fixed length data types: Fixed length data types always occupy the amount of space allotted to them. Examples of fixed length data types are INT, char(2) and money.

Large Object Types: A data type that is larger than the 8000 byte limit.

Large Value Data Types: Also known as **max data types,** they can contain the maximum amount allowed for a field by SQL Server.

Large Value Types Out of Row: When this is being used the **Large Value Types Out of Row** is on (set to 1 or 'ON') the pointer is being used, if off (set to 0 or 'OFF') then all values small enough to fit in the row are stored there and pointers are only used if the data is too large.

MAX Data Types: These 3 types (varchar(max), nvarchar(max), and varbinary(max)) were introduced in SQL Server 2005. These are also known as **max data types** and can contain the maximum amount allowed for a field by SQL Server**.**

Memory page: A memory page is 8 KB (8 kilobytes) of physical space set aside for rapid storage and retrieval of records.

NULL Bitmap: Another name for a NULL Block.

NULL Block: This is created to track nullable fields in your table. .

Row header: This is a positioning header which keeps track of where the row is placed in the table and which fields the row contains.

Unicode data: Unicode supports foreign language characters needed for international data (e.g., German umlauts, accents for romance language characters, Japanese characters, etc.).

Variable block: This block keeps track of the number of variable length data fields within the record and takes up 2 bytes.

Variable data: Data with length that varies from row to row.

Variable length data types: Variable length data types expect the data length to vary from row to row. They include varchar and nvarchar data types.

Chapter Three - Review Quiz

1.) If you have two fields in your table, one is an INT and the other is a NCHAR(3), what will be the size of your fixed length data?

  O a. 3
  O b. 4
  O c. 7
  O d. 9
  O e. 10

2.) You have three variable length data fields. What are the rules that go into the calculation of how large the variable block will be?

  □ a. You will allocate 2 bytes to the creation of the variable block
  □ b. You will allocate 3 bytes to the creation of the variable block
  □ c. You will allocate 2 more bytes for each of the three variable fields
  □ d. You will allocate 1 byte for every eight columns in the table.

3.) All your fields are set to NOT NULL for the dbo.Employee table. What will be the result for your null block?

  O a. You will not have a null block for dbo.Employee
  O b. Your null block will be 2 bytes
  O c. Your null block will be 3 bytes
  O d. Your null block will be 2 bytes + Number Of Fields/8 (rounded up) bytes.

4.) You have one row in a table called dbo.Bonus, which has two fields. The first field is called BonusID and is a NOT NULL int. The second field is called BonusAmount set to Money and is nullable. Ints are 4 bytes and Money is 8 bytes. The first record has a BonusID of 1 and a BonusAmount of Null. What is the fixed length data payload?

  O a. 4 bytes
  O b. 8 bytes
  O c. 12 bytes

5.) You have ten fixed length fields in your dbo.Employee table. How much data is dedicated to your header?

  O a. 2 bytes
  O b. 4 bytes
  O c. 6 bytes

6.) Exactly how big is a page of memory in SQL Server?

O a. 8000 Bytes
O b. 8060 bytes
O c. 8192 Bytes

7.) How many bytes of a memory page can SQL Server use for data?

O a. 8000
O b. 8060
O c. 8192

8.) Which of the following are considered Large Object (LOB) types?

☐ a. CHAR
☐ b. VARCHAR(8000)
☐ c. VARCHAR(MAX)
☐ d. TEXT
☐ e. NCHAR
☐ f. NVARCHAR(4000)
☐ g. NVARCHAR(MAX)
☐ h. NTEXT

Answer Key

1.) e   2.) a, c   3.) a   4.) c   5.) b   6.) c   7.) b   8.) d, h

Bug Catcher Game

To play the Bug Catcher game run the BugCatcher_Chapter03DataTypeUsage.pps from the BugCatcher folder of the companion files. You can obtain these files from www.Joes2Pros.com or by ordering the Companion CD.

Chapter 4.   Special Data Type Options

At the age of 12, my two main ways of making extra money were delivering papers and mowing lawns. Like most other paperboys with an 80-home coverage area, I wore a double bag. Picture a backpack that is also a "front pack." This contraption held roughly 40 rolled up papers in the front and 40 more in the back. As I began my route, the full packs, with their large loads, made my silhouette look like a pregnant bowling pin. By the end of the route, with both bags empty, it looked like little more than a gray towel loosely hanging over both shoulders. As each paper was delivered, it left more space and my bag contracted. Less room was needed in my bag and the load became smaller.

The infamous Sunday paper was a beast of a job, since each paper weighed approximately three pounds. My father took the time to build a wooden box with two 20-inch wheels from an old bicycle and two long broom handles. You might imagine a wheel barrow but, for steering ease, he crafted a rickshaw. The customers in north Tacoma would sometimes take pictures of the novelty of their paper being delivered by rickshaw. Unlike the double bag I used for weekday deliveries, the rickshaw was no smaller when all the Sunday papers were gone.

So a key question to consider is whether your data type resembles a pack whose size varies according to its payload, or alternatively, whether your data type is more like the hard box shape of the rickshaw, which is the same size at all times. In other words, if you have 500 integer (4 byte) records and most of them are null, do they always have to consume 2000 bytes of space? Many innovative, new data type options are featured in SQL Server 2008. Not only are there new types but also options to make these exciting types work more efficiently. This chapter will focus on the special things you can do with these exciting new and custom data types.

When people ask, "What is new about SQL Server 2008 compared to the relatively new SQL Server 2005?" this is the area of biggest improvement. *(So much so that it's challenging to effectively capture all of these innovations in one chapter!)*

READER NOTE: *In order to follow along with the examples in the first section of Chapter 4, please run the setup script SQLArchChapter4.0Setup.sql. The setup scripts for this book are posted at Joes2Pros.com.*

Sparse Data

The other day, I brought home a gallon of milk from the grocery store and went to the refrigerator to put it away. In my refrigerator, the only shelf tall enough to hold a gallon jug is the top shelf. However, the top shelf was already full. Shorter jars of salsa and mayonnaise were occupying that space, so naturally I moved those to a lower shelf to make space for my tall gallon of milk. I did not want to customize, remodel, or buy a second refrigerator to solve my problem. A quick and easy, innovative solution allowed me to solve a relatively easy dilemma with little expense to my time or existing systems. Many innovative, new data type options are featured in SQL Server 2008.

From our in depth look at data types in the last chapter, recall that fields with fixed length data types (e.g., int, money) always consume their allotted space irrespective of how much data the field actually contains. This is true even if the field is populated with a null.

Occasionally you will encounter a column in your database which is rarely used. For example, suppose you have a field called Violation in an Employee table but very few employees have any violations – perhaps two or three for every 1000 employees. In this case, over 99% of the Violation field values are null. This would be a *sparsely populated field*.

To demonstrate a sparsely populated field, we will create a simple table with the design shown here. Create the Bonus table by running this code (see Figure 4.1).

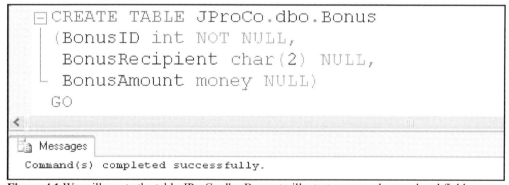

```
CREATE TABLE JProCo.dbo.Bonus
 (BonusID int NOT NULL,
  BonusRecipient char(2) NULL,
  BonusAmount money NULL)
GO
```

Messages

Command(s) completed successfully.

Figure 4.1 We will create the table JProCo.dbo.Bonus to illustrate a sparsely populated field.

Now populate the fields with these values (see Figure 4.2).

```
--In this book, we will use the new
 --SQL Server 2008 row constructors feature
INSERT INTO JProCo.dbo.Bonus VALUES (1, 'AB', NULL),
                                      (2, 'CD', NULL),
                                      (3, 'EF', NULL)

--SQL Server 2005 users must write separate
--insert statements for each row
INSERT INTO JProCo.dbo.Bonus VALUES (1, 'AB', NULL)
INSERT INTO JProCo.dbo.Bonus VALUES (2, 'CD', NULL)
INSERT INTO JProCo.dbo.Bonus VALUES (3, 'EF', NULL)
```

Figure 4.2 We will load data into a simple table to illustrate sparsely populated fields.

*Please note that INSERT statements demonstrated in this book will use **row constructors**, which debuted as a new feature in SQL Server 2008. However, readers who are running SQL Server 2005 must write their INSERT statements using the alternate syntax shown in the lower portion of Figure 4.2.*

Now look at all the records in the table. Since all fields contain fixed length data types (i.e., int, char(2), money), we could have accurately calculated the per row consumption before we even added any data to the table. With no variable data types in the table, there is no variable block or variable data payload to calculate.

```
SELECT * FROM JProCo.dbo.Bonus
```

	BonusID	BonusRecipient	BonusAmount
1	1	AB	NULL
2	2	CD	NULL
3	3	EF	NULL

Figure 4.3 At 21 bytes per row, 1000 rows of the Bonus table would require three data pages.

Each row of the Bonus table will consume 21 bytes.

Row Header – 4 bytes

Fixed Data – 14 bytes
BonusID is an int (4 bytes) and BonusAmount's data type is money (8 bytes).

Null Block (aka Null Bitmap) – 3 bytes
The table contains 3 non-sparse fields. (Sparse fields do not contribute to the null block). Creation of the null block (2 bytes) + [3 fields* (1 byte/8 non-sparse fields) rounded up to the nearest byte].

As we reviewed earlier, the nulls in the money field do not change the space consumption – *fixed length data types always use the full amount of space allocated to them.*

At 21 bytes per row, 1000 rows of the Bonus table would require 21,000 bytes and fill up about 3 data pages (1 data page = 8060 bytes).

Analyzing Space Used

When I was about 10, my big brother introduced me to a British comedy group called Monty Python. We had fun listening to their tapes and I'll never forget one sketch in particular. Michael Palin visits a university in Australia and is welcomed by several faculty members. One comic point of the sketch is that there are a lot of Australians named Bruce. "Michael, this is Bruce" was repeated over and over as Michael was introduced to each faculty member. At the time, I remember saying it would have taken a lot less airspace to just say the name Bruce once and point to everyone. Well, what if all your records for a field are null. Can you store null once and just point each field to that sparse data? If you could what are the pros and cons of doing so?

In the last chapter, we talked quite a bit about memory pages which physically contain your data. Within your database's datafiles (MDF/NDF), SQL Server organizes your data into these 8 KB memory pages (also called *data pages*). SQL Server attempts to fit the greatest number of rows from your table into a single data page, since that enables the fastest and most efficient data retrieval. If rows in your table exceed 8060 bytes, and/or contain a large value (>8000 bytes/field), then SQL Server will move the largest variable length field(s) into a separate data page.

A newly created table consumes no storage space until you begin adding data. The table we created at the beginning of this chapter (JProCo.dbo.Bonus) was empty and consumed no space until we began populating the fields. The moment we added a value to the first row, SQL Server reserved space in memory for the rows of JProCo.dbo.Bonus and began filling up the first 8 KB page.

A handy tool for checking the storage amount which an object occupies is **sp_spaceused**. The figure below (see Figure 4.4) shows the Bonus table passed into this stored procedure. We see the Bonus table contains three rows and its data has not yet exceeded its first 8 KB page. (Note: indexes are ignored at present, since those will be covered in depth in Chapters 7-11.)

```
EXEC sp_spaceused 'Bonus'
```

	name	rows	reserved	data	index_size	unused
1	Bonus	3	16 KB	8 KB	8 KB	0 KB

Figure 4.4 Having just three rows, the Bonus table is still filling its first 8 KB memory page.

If we hadn't passed in the Bonus table, this sproc (short for "stored procedure") would have shown similar detail for the current database context, which is JProCo.

USE JProCo
GO

EXEC sp_spaceused

If you're curious about the code underlying this system stored procedure, you can have SQL Server Management Studio generate the code for you:

Management Studio > Object Explorer > Databases > JProCo > Programmability > Stored Procedures > System Stored Procedures > right-click **sys.sp_spaceused** > Modify

Since we are still in the process of filling up the first data page for the Bonus table, we can add many more records before the first data page is full.

Let's run this loop to add 997 more records to the Bonus table. The first record populated will be row 4 (BonusID 4, BonusRecipient NULL, BonusAmount NULL). Our code increments each subsequent BonusID value by 1, and the loop runs as long as the BonusID value is <=1000. Once the row containing BonusID 1000 has been entered into the table, the loop will end (see Figure 4.5).

```
DECLARE @ID INT
  SET @ID = 4
WHILE @ID <= 1000
BEGIN
      INSERT INTO JProCo.dbo.Bonus VALUES (@ID, NULL, NULL)
      SET @ID = @ID + 1
  END
```

Figure 4.5 This loop helps us quickly add and populate 1000 rows in the Bonus table.

The Bonus table now contains 1000 records (see Figure 4.6).

```
SELECT * FROM JProCo.dbo.Bonus
```

Results | Messages

	BonusID	BonusRecipient	BonusAmount
1	1	AB	NULL
2	2	CD	NULL
3	3	EF	NULL
4	4	NULL	NULL
5	5	NULL	NULL
6	6	NULL	NULL
7	7	NULL	NULL
8	8	NULL	NULL
9	9	NULL	NULL
10	10	NULL	NULL
11	11	NULL	NULL
12	12	NULL	NULL

Query... JProCo 00:00:00 1000 rows

Figure 4.6 The Bonus table now contains 1000 records.

Since one row occupies 21 bytes, we know these 1000 rows will take up 21 KB of space and should fit within three data pages.

[21000 bytes/(8060 bytes/page) = 2.61 pages]

Let's rerun the **sp_spaceused** sproc and confirm the number of data pages.

```
EXEC sp_spaceused 'Bonus'
```

Results | Messages

	name	rows	reserved	data	index_size	unused
1	Bonus	1000	32 KB	24 KB	8 KB	0 KB

Figure 4.7 The Bonus table's 1000 rows (21 KB) fit within three data pages.

The information provided by **sp_spaceused** confirms what we expected – the data currently in the Bonus table fits within 24 KB (i.e., three data pages).

Now this seems a little wasteful with respect to storage space usage. Nulls are taking up 8 bytes in the money field, because it's a fixed length data type. *BonusAmount is a **sparsely populated field**.*

Using the Sparse Data Option

The sparse data option is a new SQL Server 2008 feature for fields you expect to be predominantly null. Using the sparse data option, you can instruct SQL Server to not have nulls consume space in sparsely populated fields. In this section we will demonstrate the sparse option, including how SQL Server handles the non-nulls in a sparse field.

We're going to delete the Bonus table and then re-create it using the same steps we took previously. The only difference will be that the BonusAmount field will be created using the sparse option. Recall we expect the BonusAmount field to contain very little actual data – most records will be null.

First, run the DROP TABLE command for the Bonus table.

```
DROP TABLE JProCo.dbo.Bonus
GO
```

Messages
Command(s) completed successfully.

Figure 4.8 Drop the JProCo.dbo.Bonus table, so that we can rebuild it with a sparse column.

Now repeat our previous steps (shown in Figures 4.1, 4.2, 4.5, 4.6) to create and populate the Bonus table using the sparse data option (see Figure 4.9).

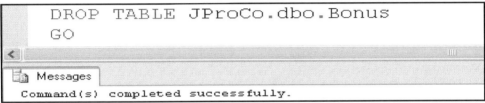

```
CREATE TABLE JProCo.dbo.Bonus
 (BonusID int NOT NULL,
  BonusRecipient char(2) NULL,
  BonusAmount money SPARSE NULL)
GO

INSERT INTO JProCo.dbo.Bonus VALUES (1, 'AB', NULL),
                                    (2, 'CD', NULL),
                                    (3, 'EF', NULL)
GO

DECLARE @ID INT
SET @ID = 4
WHILE @ID <= 1000
BEGIN
    INSERT INTO JProCo.dbo.Bonus VALUES (@ID, NULL, NULL)
    SET @ID = @ID + 1
END
GO
```

Figure 4.9 Repeat the steps to create and populate the Bonus table using the sparse data option.

Recall we expect the BonusAmount field to contain very little actual data – most records will be null. The Bonus table now contains 1000 records and looks the same as it did previously (see Figure 4.10). BonusAmount is a sparse field, but so far we don't see any difference in the appearance of the table or the data.

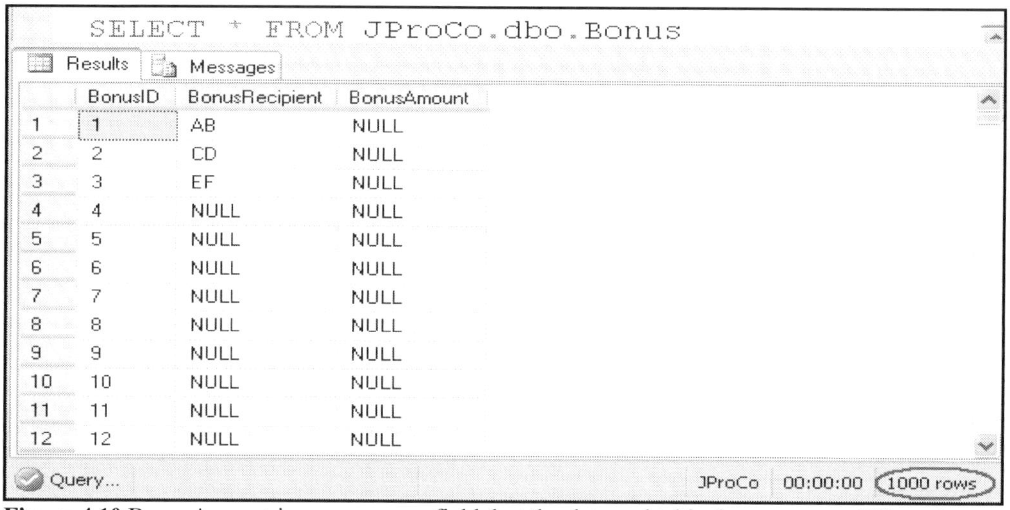

```
SELECT * FROM JProCo.dbo.Bonus
```

	BonusID	BonusRecipient	BonusAmount
1	1	AB	NULL
2	2	CD	NULL
3	3	EF	NULL
4	4	NULL	NULL
5	5	NULL	NULL
6	6	NULL	NULL
7	7	NULL	NULL
8	8	NULL	NULL
9	9	NULL	NULL
10	10	NULL	NULL
11	11	NULL	NULL
12	12	NULL	NULL

Figure 4.10 BonusAmount is now a sparse field, but the data and table do not appear differently.

Now let's review how much space the Bonus table is consuming. As originally designed (i.e., before we rebuilt the table with a sparse column), each row of the Bonus table consumed 21 bytes.

Header 4 | Fixed Data 14 | Null Block 3 = 21 bytes

[21 bytes/row * 1000 rows = 21,000 bytes]

From what we know of the sparse data option, the nulls in our sparse column (BonusAmount) should not take up any storage space. With BonusAmount as a sparse column, each row of the Bonus table will now consume 13 bytes.

Row Header – 4 bytes

Fixed Data – 6 bytes
BonusID is an int (4 bytes). BonusRecipient is a char(2) (2 bytes).
None of BonusAmount's values will consume storage space, since all values are currently null. Rows in a sparse column consume storage space only when they contain non-null values. In our example, the sparse column (BonusAmount) contains only null values.

Null Block (aka Null Bitmap) – 3 bytes
Creation of the null block (2 bytes) + [2 non-sparse fields (1 byte/8 non-sparse fields) rounded up to the nearest byte].*

At 13 bytes per row, 1000 rows of the Bonus table would require 13,000 bytes and fill up about 2 data pages (1 data page = 8060 bytes).

Header 4 | Fixed Data 6 | Null Block 3 = 13 bytes

[13 bytes/row * 1000 rows = 13,000 bytes]

Let's confirm the space usage by running sp_spaceused (see Figure 4.11).

```
EXEC sp_spaceused 'Bonus'
```

	name	rows	reserved	data	index_size	unused
1	Bonus	1000	24 KB	16 KB	8 KB	0 KB

Figure 4.11 The sparse option saved an 8 KB data page -- a significant amount of space.

As predicted – the sparse option saved a significant amount of space. Even though the data in the Bonus table is identical, it now uses just two data pages thanks to the sparse option. In large tables, this savings could be quite substantial.

Along with the benefits of the sparse option, we also need to be mindful of associated tradeoffs or limitations:

1) For any populated rows in the sparse column, the populated data consumes more space than would a regular field.

2) The sparse option cannot be used with certain data types.

In addition to the actual data payload, the sparse option adds 4 bytes to each record when the sparse field is non-null. In the case of our Bonus table, any non-null value in the BonusAmount field will consume 12 bytes (8 bytes for the smallmoney data payload + 4 bytes for the sparse vector).

Thus, you should only use the sparse option on fields you know will be sparsely populated. Consider the current state of the Bonus table (refer back to Figure 4.10). The BonusAmount value for each of the 1000 rows is Null. As a non-sparse column, BonusAmount would consume 8000 bytes. As a sparse column, however, BonusAmount consumes 0 bytes.

Suppose some rows of the sparse column, BonusAmount, were populated. If 600 of these 1000 rows contained non-null values, they would consume 7200 additional bytes. This is still less than the 8000 bytes that this field would consume, if it weren't a non-sparse column.

The sparse option works with most regular numeric and character data types in SQL Server (Int, Decimal, Char, Varchar, Nchar, Nvarchar, etc.). However, it cannot be used with several data types, such as CLR data types (e.g., Geography, Geometry) or Filestream. It also cannot be used with the old LOB types (text, ntext, image).

In order to modify an existing column and make it a sparse column, you can use the code below (see Figure 4.12). Alternatively, you can open the Design view of the table and toggle the "Is Sparse" column property to Yes.

```
ALTER TABLE JProCo.dbo.Bonus
  ALTER COLUMN BonusRecipient
      ADD SPARSE
GO
```

Messages
Command(s) completed successfully.

Figure 4.12 Adding the sparse option to a column using T-SQL code.

You can also use T-SQL code (see Figure 4.13) or the table's Design view (column properties tab) to remove the sparse option from an existing column.

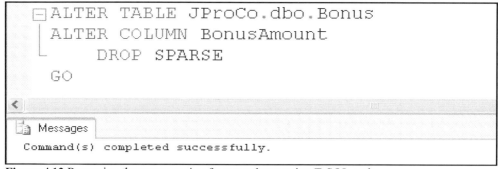

```
ALTER TABLE JProCo.dbo.Bonus
  ALTER COLUMN BonusAmount
      DROP SPARSE
GO
```

Messages
Command(s) completed successfully.

Figure 4.13 Removing the sparse option from a column using T-SQL code.

Since SQL Server's process of adding the sparse option to a column can cause the data row to temporarily exceed the row limit (8060 bytes for tables with no sparse columns, 8018 bytes for tables with a sparse column(s)), be aware that you may need to rebuild a table in order to add the sparse option to an existing column.

Lab 4.1: Sparse Data Option

Lab Prep: Before you can begin the lab, you must have SQL Server installed and run the SQLArchChapter4.1Setup.sql script.

Skill Check 1: The CompanyName field of the Customer table is sparsely populated (773 of 775 rows contain nulls). Currently this column takes up 48 KB, which consumes the equivalent of about 6 data pages.

Use T-SQL code to change the CompanyName field so that it will be optimized for sparsely populated data. When you are finished, check the Design view of the Customer table and confirm it resembles Figure 4.15.

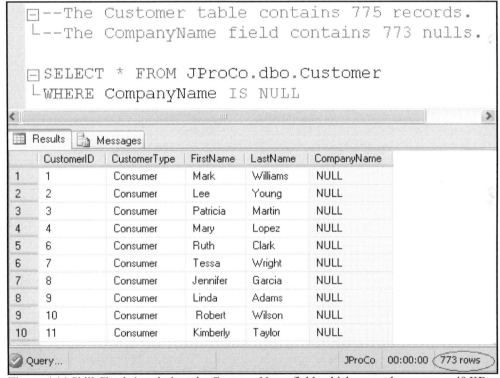

Figure 4.14 Skill Check 1 optimizes the CompanyName field, which currently consumes 48 KB.

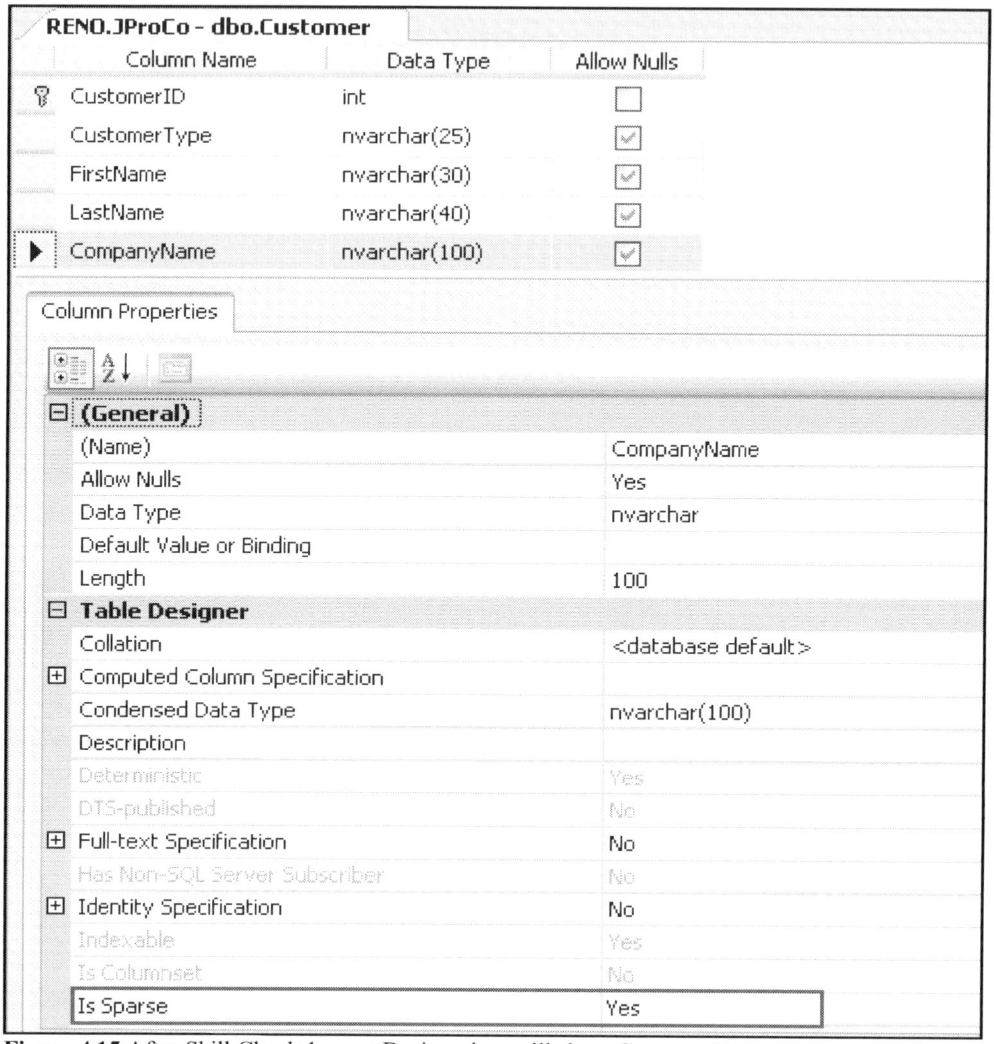

RENO.JProCo - dbo.Customer		
Column Name	Data Type	Allow Nulls
🔑 CustomerID	int	☐
CustomerType	nvarchar(25)	☑
FirstName	nvarchar(30)	☑
LastName	nvarchar(40)	☑
▶ CompanyName	nvarchar(100)	☑

Column Properties

⊟ **(General)**	
(Name)	CompanyName
Allow Nulls	Yes
Data Type	nvarchar
Default Value or Binding	
Length	100
⊟ **Table Designer**	
Collation	<database default>
⊞ Computed Column Specification	
Condensed Data Type	nvarchar(100)
Description	
Deterministic	Yes
DTS-published	No
⊞ Full-text Specification	No
Has Non-SQL Server Subscriber	No
⊞ Identity Specification	No
Indexable	Yes
Is Columnset	No
Is Sparse	Yes

Figure 4.15 After Skill Check 1, your Design view will show CompanyName as a sparse column.

Answer Code: The T-SQL code to this lab can be found in the downloadable files in a file named Lab4.1_SparseDataOption.sql

Sparse Data Option - Points to Ponder

1. A table operation with a sparse column takes a performance hit over a normal column. Sparse will save space for null values at the cost of more overhead to retrieve non-null values.

2. A numeric sparse column that contains data will take up 4 bytes more than a non-sparse column. For instance a non-sparse int will take up 4 bytes, whereas a sparse int will take up 8 bytes.

3. Sparse cannot be used for every data type. For instance sparse cannot be used with the old LOB types (text, ntext, image). You also cannot use the Sparse option with CLR (common language runtime) data types, such as Geography or Geometry.

4. For an identical block of data, a column marked as sparse will take more space. This will only save space if that column is null.

5. Sparse is best used when you are expecting to have a lot of nulls and you want to save hard drive space.

6. A sparse column cannot be a primary key.

7. A column defined as sparse cannot have a default value.

8. When a column is defined as sparse and that column is null then that column requires no storage space.

9. Sparse columns should be considered when the storage savings is at least 20 to 40 percent. (A list of "Estimated Savings by Data Type" may be found at http://msdn.microsoft.com/en-us/library/cc280604.aspx)

10. You cannot use the Sparse option with the Filestream attribute.

Custom Data Types

This spring, one of my brothers wanted to pour 3000 lbs of new concrete in his basement. This would have been a small and very costly job for a cement truck and professional crew if he wanted to spend thousands of dollars. He had access to a cement mixer but hauling buckets full of wet cement downstairs would be taxing to his friends who volunteered a few Saturday hours. He realized that he needed a chute so the mixer upstairs could simply pour down the chute to the spreaders downstairs. How much does a chute cost? Significantly more than the custom contraption my brother devised.

His long, narrow piece of plywood with 2x4s on each side looked a lot like a wooden park slide. It worked brilliantly and things went smoothly. This custom contraption was really made up of a standard wood type you can get at the hardware store. Whenever you customize something, you generally begin with standard materials. So what if you want to make your own data type?

Most data types we encounter are supplied by the system. However, SQL Server also gives users the option of defining their own types. In this section, we will demonstrate creating, using, and removing these custom types.

Let's take a look at the Location table, which is a fairly simple table consisting of five records and four fields (see Figure 4.16).

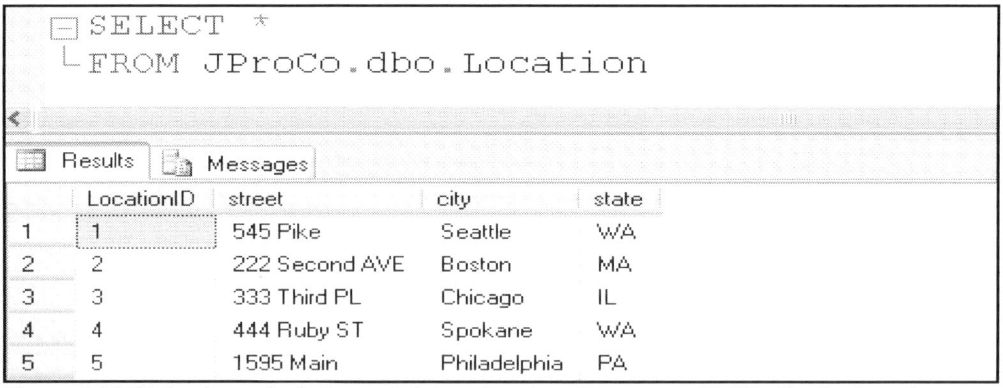

```
SELECT *
FROM JProCo.dbo.Location
```

	LocationID	street	city	state
1	1	545 Pike	Seattle	WA
2	2	222 Second AVE	Boston	MA
3	3	333 Third PL	Chicago	IL
4	4	444 Ruby ST	Spokane	WA
5	5	1595 Main	Philadelphia	PA

Figure 4.16 We begin our look at constraints and custom data types with JProCo.dbo.Location.

Let's edit some of the data in the table (Object Explorer > Databases > JProCo > Tables > right-click **Location** > Edit Top 200 Rows). Try adding a sixth location by typing "Six" instead of a "6" for the ID (see Figure 4.17).

LocationID	street	city	state
1	545 Pike	Seattle	WA
2	222 Second AVE	Boston	MA
3	333 Third PL	Chicago	IL
4	444 Ruby ST	Spokane	WA
5	1595 Main	Philadelphia	PA
Six	NULL	NULL	NULL
NU			

Microsoft SQL Server Management Studio

Invalid value for cell (row 6, column 1).

The changed value in this cell was not recognized as valid.
.Net Framework Data Type: Int32
Error Message: Input string was not in a correct format.

Type a value appropriate for the data type or press ESC to cancel the change.

OK

Figure 4.17 A column's data type serves as a constraint and protects your table's data integrity.

So here we see that a data type can serve as a safety catch, in that it won't allow you to add data which is improper according to the table design. In the database world, this is known as a *constraint*. A constraint restricts your data input to values within the limits you specify in the design of your table and its fields.

If we attempt another entry which doesn't follow the design of our Location table, we will similarly get an error. Suppose we tried to enter "Nevada" in the [State] field, which is a char(2). We would get a prompt telling us that our data input can't be committed as we've typed it in. *[Error: "String or binary data would be truncated."]* Our table design allows just two characters in that field. SQL Server enforces your data constraints whether you attempt to input values using T-SQL code or via the Design interface (as we saw previously in Figure 4.17).

Now let's look at a *custom data type* (also known as a *user-defined data type*). The data type shown here, "CountryCode", is a custom data type created from a regular value type (i.e., char(2)).

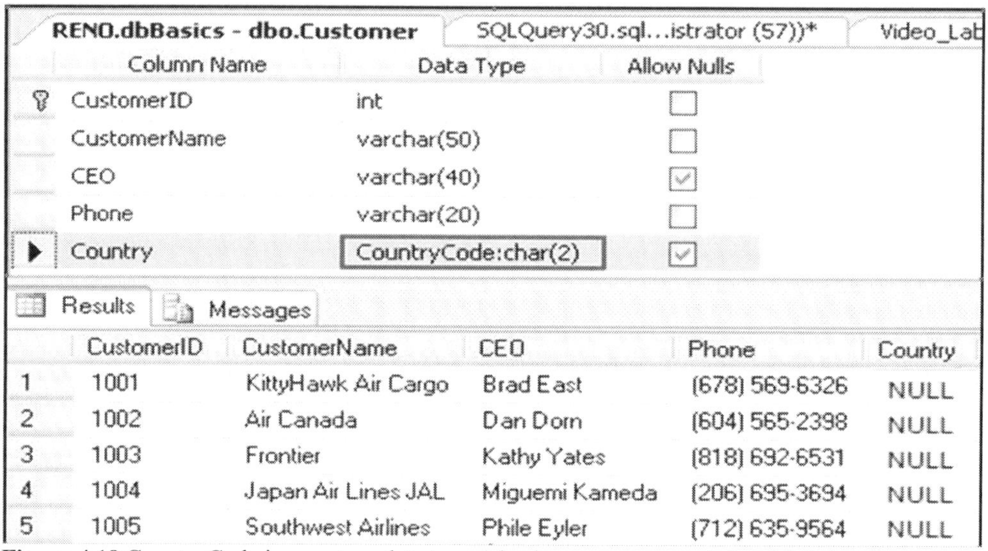

Figure 4.18 CountryCode is a custom data type (also known as a user-defined data type).

(Note: the two-letter country codes shown here are known as ISO codes. These codes are established and maintained by the International Standards Organization. www.iso.org/iso/english_country_names_and_code_elements)

When a custom data type is created, that type may be used as the data type for any field within the same database. Therefore, the custom data type CountryCode is available to every field of every table in the dbBasics database.

Here we see that, if we add a new field to another table in the dbBasics database, the custom data type appears as an option in the Data Type dropdown list.

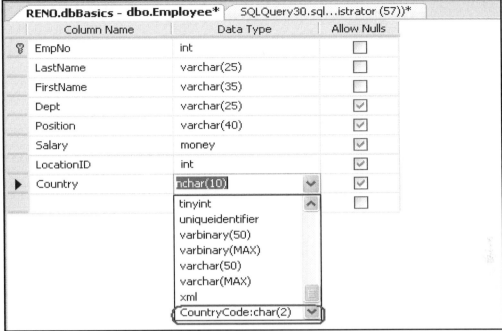

Figure 4.19 The custom data type CountryCode is available to every field in the dbBasics database.

Creating Custom Types

Let's walk through creating a custom data type. First we will demonstrate this using the Management Studio interface, and later we will use T-SQL code to create a custom data type.

We want to create the custom CountryCode data type in the JProCo database. Begin with Object Explorer > Databases > **JProCo** > Programmability > Types > right-click User-Defined Data Types > **New User-Defined Data Type**.

In the New User-Defined Data Type dialog, we will make the following selections:
1) Retain the pre-populated schema (dbo)
2) Enter **CountryCode** in the Name box
3) Select **char** in the Data Type dropdown
4) Enter a Length of **2**
5) Place a check in the Allow NULLs box
6) Then click **OK** to save the new data type and close the dialog (see Figure 4.20).

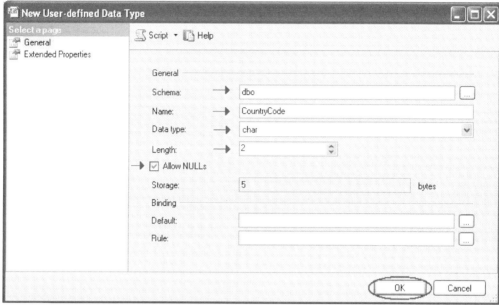

Figure 4.20 We are creating the custom data type CountryCode in another database (JProCo).

This data type is now available to every table and field in the JProCo database. For example, if we wanted to add a Country field to JProCo.dbo.Supplier or JProCo.dbo.Location, we can add the field and use CountryCode as the data type.

Now let's create a custom data type using T-SQL code. In the dbBasics context, run the following code to create **dbo.EmailType** (see Figure 4.21).

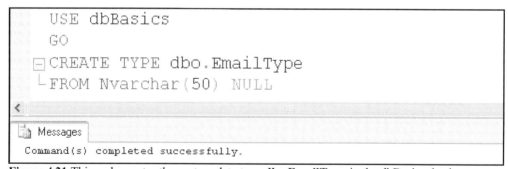

Figure 4.21 This code creates the custom data type **dbo.EmailType** in the dbBasics database.

In addition to both of these new custom data types being available to every field within their respective databases, these new data types are also visible in the Management Studio interface.

Object Explorer > Databases > **dbBasics** > Programmability > Types > User-Defined Data Types > **dbo.EmailType**

Using Custom Types

Now let's see a table actually consume this data type. Using either T-SQL code (Figure 4.22) or the Design view (Figure 4.24), add a new field called EmailAlias to the Employee table in the dbBasics database. Use dbo.EmailType as the data type for this new field.

```
ALTER TABLE dbBasics.dbo.Employee
ADD EmailAlias dbo.EmailType
GO
```

Messages

Command(s) completed successfully.

Figure 4.22 This code adds to the Employee table a new field with data type dbo.EmailType.

```
ALTER TABLE dbBasics.dbo.Employee
DROP COLUMN EmailAlias
GO
```

Messages

Command(s) completed successfully.

Figure 4.23 This code drops the EmailAlias column from the Employee table.

We've added and dropped the EmailAlias field using T-SQL code. Now we'll re-add the column using the Design interface (see Figure 4.24 on next page) and then we'll populate the EmailAlias with actual values.

Object Explorer > Databases > **dbBasics** > Tables > right-click **dbo.Employee** > Design

Now add a field called **EmailAlias** and use the data type EmailType (last one in dropdown). Save the change and close the Design interface (see Figure 4.24).

Column Name	Data Type	Allow Nulls
🔑 EmpNo	int	☐
LastName	varchar(25)	☐
FirstName	varchar(35)	☐
Dept	varchar(25)	☑
Position	varchar(40)	☑
Salary	money	☑
LocationID	int	☑
▶ EmailAlias	EmailType:nvarchar(50)	☑

Figure 4.24 We are re-adding the new EmailAlias field using the Design interface.

We can also see the EmailAlias field in the Object Explorer view of the table dbBasics.dbo.Employee:

Object Explorer > Databases > dbBasics > Tables > dbo.Employee > expand Columns > see new EmailAlias column appear in the list. EmailAlias uses the custom data type EmailType, the user-defined type we created in Figure 4.21.

Next we will populate the EmailAlias field (see Figure 4.26) and look at the first few records of dbBasics.dbo.Employee (see Figure 4.27).

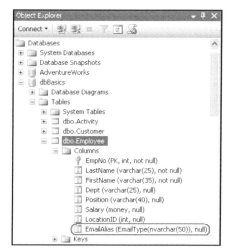

Figure 4.25 The new field EmailAlias.

```
UPDATE dbBasics.dbo.Employee
  SET EmailAlias = FirstName + LastName + '@dbBasics.com'
```
Messages

(16 row(s) affected)

Figure 4.26 This code populates the new EmailAlias field with an email address for each employee.

```
SELECT * FROM dbBasics.dbo.Employee
```

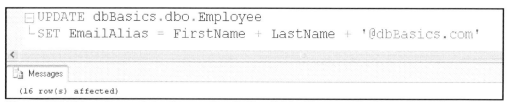

	EmpNo	LastName	FirstName	Dept	Position	Salary	LocationID	EmailAlias
1	101	Smith	Sarah	Admin	Manager	54000.00	2	SarahSmith@dbBasics.com
2	102	Brown	Bill	Sales	Clerk	25200.00	2	BillBrown@dbBasics.com
3	103	Fry	Fred	Admin	Clerk	21900.00	1	FredFry@dbBasics.com

Figure 4.27 The new EmailAlias field has been populated and shows the employee email addresses.

Dropping Custom Types

Suppose we no longer needed the new data type we created (dbo.EmailType in dbBasics). A DROP statement will remove a user-defined data type. However, you must first handle any dependencies – in other words, you must handle any table(s) which is using the custom data type.

In this case, we see the Employee table (dbBasics.dbo.Employee) is dependent upon this data type (see Figure 4.28). We encountered this same situation in Chapter 2, when we had to remove tables, or any other dependent objects, before SQL Server allowed us to delete a schema.

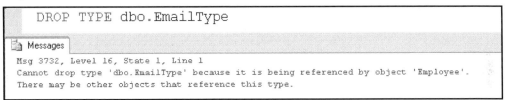

Figure 4.28 Since the Employee table is dependent upon dbo.EmailType, we cannot drop it yet.

Notice the error message names the Employee table as an object which is currently referencing dbo.EmailType. However, it's possible there are other objects within the dbBasics database which are referencing this custom data type.

Management Studio can help us find which table(s) is using this data type:

Object Explorer > Databases > **dbBasics** > Programmability > Types > User-Defined Data Types > right-click **dbo.EmailType** > View Dependencies (see Figure 4.29).

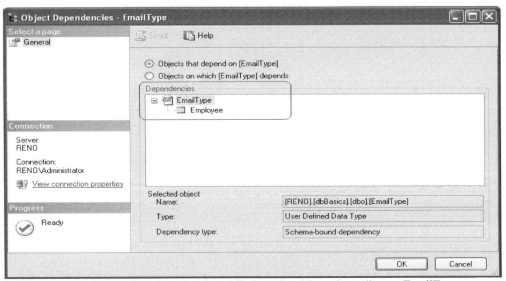

Figure 4.29 The Object Dependencies dialog displays the objects depending on EmailType.

The Object Dependencies dialog tells us the only object using the EmailType is the Employee table. To remove this dependency, we will DROP the EmailAlias column. This T-SQL code will remove the column EmailAlias and all of its data.

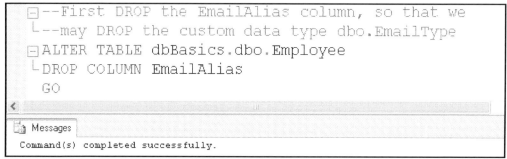

Figure 4.30 Remove the column EmailAlias and all of its data in order to drop dbo.EmailType.

We know that no tables or fields in dbBasics are referencing our user-defined data type, dbo.EmailType. If we re-check the Object Dependencies dialog, we find no table is listed there.

Now we can reattempt the DROP TYPE statement (see Figure 4.31).

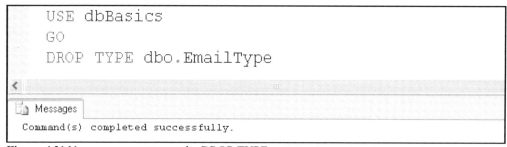

Figure 4.31 Now we can reattempt the DROP TYPE statement.

Excellent! Our user defined data type is now gone.

Lab 4.2: Custom Data Types

Lab Prep: Before you can begin the lab, you must have SQL Server installed and run the SQLArchChapter4.2Setup.sql script.

Skill Check 1: In the JProCo database, use T-SQL code to create a user-defined data type called **dbo.Email**. Use this data type in a new field, EmailAddress, which you will add to the Employee table. When complete, the design of your Employee table will resemble the figure below (Figure 4.32).

Column Name	Data Type	Allow Nulls
EmpID	int	☐
LastName	varchar(30)	☑
FirstName	varchar(20)	☑
HireDate	datetime	☑
LocationID	int	☑
ManagerID	int	☑
Status	char(12)	☑
Country	CountryCode:char(2)	☑
▶ EmailAddress	Email:varchar(50)	☑

RENO.JProCo - dbo.Employee

Figure 4.32 Skill Check 1 creates a user-defined data type and uses it in a new column added to the Employee table (JProCo.dbo.Employee).

Skill Check 2: Drop the custom data type CountryCode from the JProCo database. If any field(s) is using this data type, then first drop those field(s) from the table. When you are able to successfully run the follow code (i.e., without generating an error message), then you have completed this Skill Check.

```
DROP TYPE dbo.CountryCode
GO
```

Messages

Command(s) completed successfully.

Figure 4.33 Skill Check 2 removes the custom data type CountryCode.

Answer Code: The T-SQL code to this lab can be found in the downloadable files in a file named Lab4.2_CustomTypes.sql.

Custom Data Types - Points to Ponder

1. The data type defines the characteristic of the data that is stored in a column.

2. The data type should be chosen based on the information you wish to store. For example, you would not use an integer data type for an employee name column.

3. There are more than 30 system-supplied data types like char, int, money, etc.

4. The data length defines the size of the data string that can be held in the column. The data length is automatically defined for most data types. You may modify the data length property for binary, char, nchar, varbinary, varchar, and nvarchar data types.

5. In addition to the system-supplied data types, user-defined data types can be created for specific needs.

6. User defined data types are also called Alias types.

7. Alias types are user-defined data types based on one of the 30 supplied-system data types.

8. An Alias data type is a custom data type based on a system supplied data type; this can be handy for re-use of data types.

9. Alias data types are defined in a specific database. If you create a CountryCode in the publishing database it will only be available in that database.

10. When you create a data type you can specify its nullability, making the "Not Null" option in the CREATE TABLE statement possible.

11. If a data type is not nullable then all tables which use this data type must implement it as NOT NULL.

12. You cannot change a data type. You would first have to execute DROP TYPE and then re-create it.

13. You cannot drop a data type that is being used in a table.

14. You can determine which tables are using a User-Defined Data Type by navigating to the Object Dependencies dialog box: Programmability > Types > User-Defined Data Types > right-click *[name of the custom data type]* > View Dependencies.

15. User-defined data types are located in your database node under the Programmability > Types > User-Defined Data Types node.

Date and Time Data Types

Keeping track of date and time data points has always been a critical part of online transactional databases. For example, each sales invoice needs a date-time stamp, as do systems which track quotes and customer contacts regarding sales opportunities.

Think of how many times during your workday that you rely on a date-time stamp as helpful metadata to sort or locate the latest information in a report or data source. Global organizations, in particular, have a need for their in-house communication, reporting, and collaboration tools to appropriately convey accurate date and time information in order to keep every part of the organization in sync.

Recap of DateTime Functions

Let's review some common date and time functions. **GETDATE( )** returns the current time in your time zone.

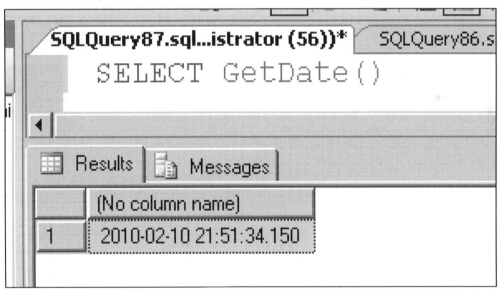

Figure 4.34 GETDATE( ) returns the current time in your time zone.

GETDATE( ) and **SELECT SYSDATETIME( )** both return the current date and time in your time zone. However, **GETDATE( )** shows fractional seconds expressed in milliseconds (.333 second), and **SYSDATETIME( )** shows fractional seconds expressed in nanoseconds (.3333333 second).

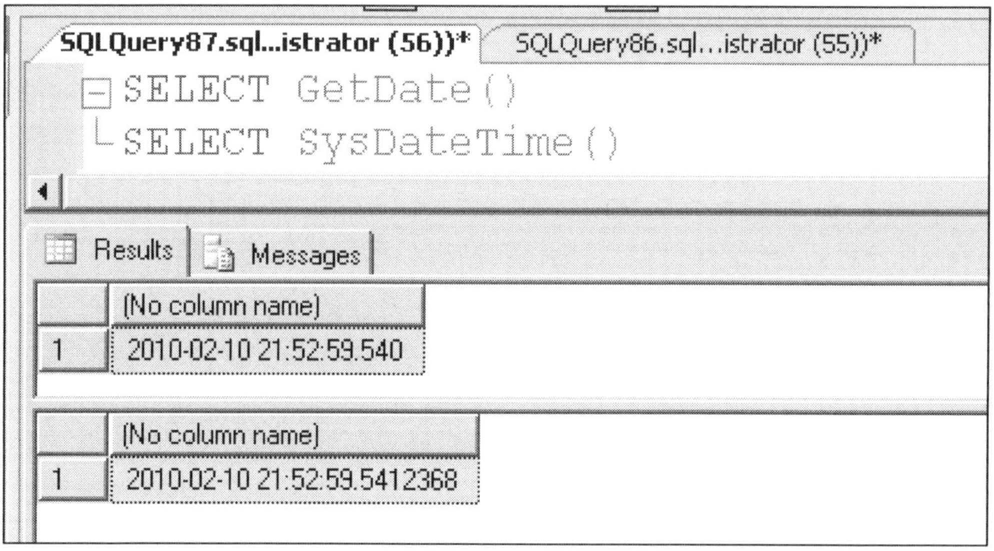

Figure 4.35 GETDATE( ) and SYSDATETIME( ) return similar results but their precisions differ.

What time is it right now in the UK? We know it's sometime in the early evening. UTC is Coordinated Universal Time, formerly known as Greenwich Mean Time (GMT). (UTC is also known by the terms zulu time, world time, and universal time.)

SELECT GETUTCDATE( ) will show the current time expressed in terms of UTC. Notice **GETUTCDATE( )** is less precise than **SYSUTCDATETIME( )**.

GETUTCDATE( ) is less precise than **SYSUTCDATETIME ( )**. However there is a UTC function that gets down to the nanoseconds, **SYSUTCDATETIME( )**. Let's run all four of these statements together. We see the two top times in the Pacific time zone and the two bottom times in UTC.

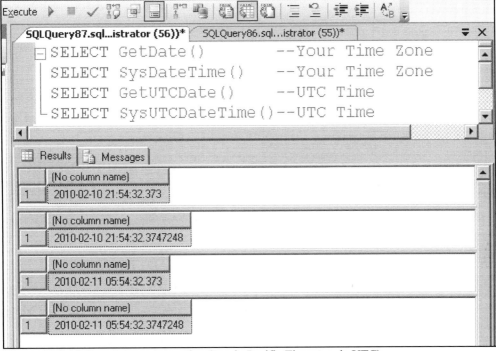

Figure 4.36 All four statements together (two in Pacific Time, two in UTC).

Standard Date and Time Data Types

In our dbBasics database, we have a dbo.Activity table which tracks the book(s) a library card number has checked out. We would like to expand the design of this table to include the date-time when each book is checked out and checked in. Let's expand the Design view of our table (dbBasics.dbo.Activity) and add the field CheckOutTime. Save the change and close the Design interface (see Figure 4.37).

RENO.dbBasics – dbo.Activity*		
Column Name	Data Type	Allow Nulls
LibraryCardNo	int	☐
Book	varchar(40)	☐
► CheckOutTime	datetime ∨	☑
		☐

Figure 4.37 Add a CheckOutTime field to the Activity table (dbBasics.dbo.Activity).

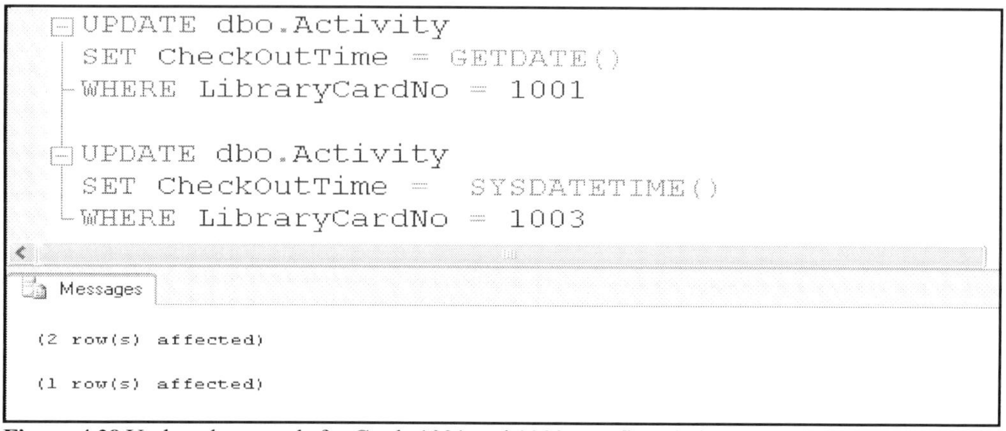

```
UPDATE dbo.Activity
 SET CheckOutTime = GETDATE()
WHERE LibraryCardNo = 1001

UPDATE dbo.Activity
 SET CheckOutTime = SYSDATETIME()
WHERE LibraryCardNo = 1003
```

Messages

```
(2 row(s) affected)

(1 row(s) affected)
```

Figure 4.38 Update the records for Cards 1001 and 1003 to reflect their CheckOutTime.

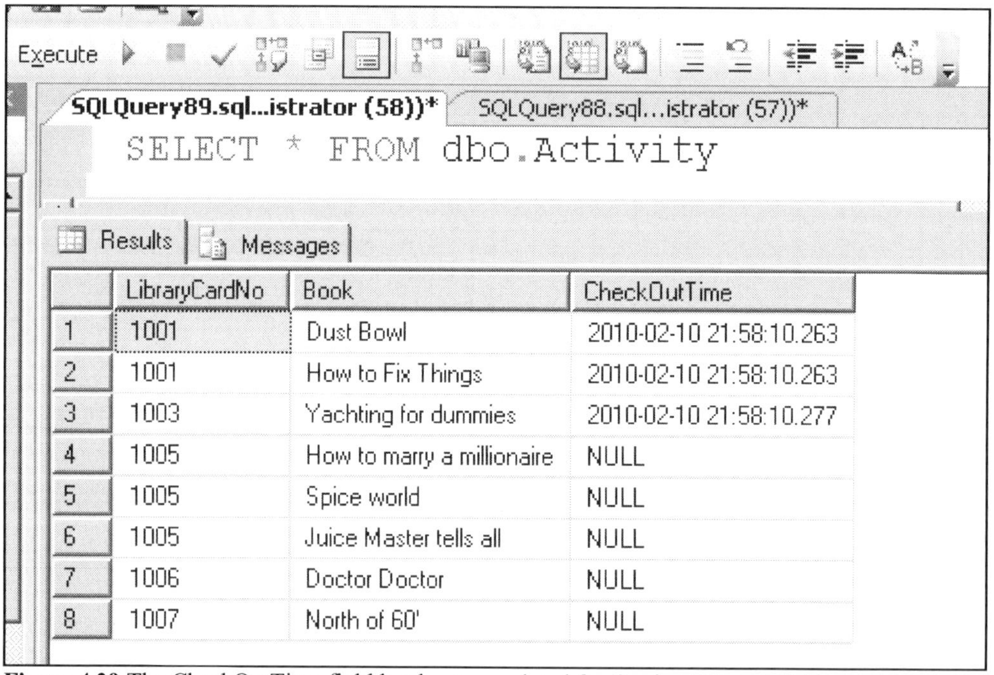

Execute

SQLQuery89.sql...istrator (58))*   SQLQuery88.sql...istrator (57))*

```
SELECT * FROM dbo.Activity
```

Results | Messages

	LibraryCardNo	Book	CheckOutTime
1	1001	Dust Bowl	2010-02-10 21:58:10.263
2	1001	How to Fix Things	2010-02-10 21:58:10.263
3	1003	Yachting for dummies	2010-02-10 21:58:10.277
4	1005	How to marry a millionaire	NULL
5	1005	Spice world	NULL
6	1005	Juice Master tells all	NULL
7	1006	Doctor Doctor	NULL
8	1007	North of 60'	NULL

Figure 4.39 The CheckOutTime field has been populated for Cards 1001 and 1003.

When we run the UPDATE statement for Card 1001, we see **GETDATE( )** captures the CheckOutTime out to the millisecond, as expected. However, Card 1003's CheckOutTime is also expressed in milliseconds – not nanoseconds – despite the fact that we used **SYSDATETIME( )** for Card 1003. The additional four digits which we know **SYSDATETIME( )** captures have been truncated by the CheckOutTime field. This is because we built the CheckOutTime field with the

datetime data type, which only stores data out to milliseconds even if you provide it more precise data (e.g., nanoseconds).

However, **datetime2** is a new SQL Server 2008 data type and it is capable of storing nanosecond data. Let's add a new field, CheckInTime, to the Activity table and have it utilize this new **datetime2** data type.

RENO.dbBasics - dbo.Activity*		
Column Name	Data Type	Allow Nulls
LibraryCardNo	int	☐
Book	varchar(40)	☐
CheckOutTime	datetime	☑
▶ CheckInTime	datetime2(7)	☑

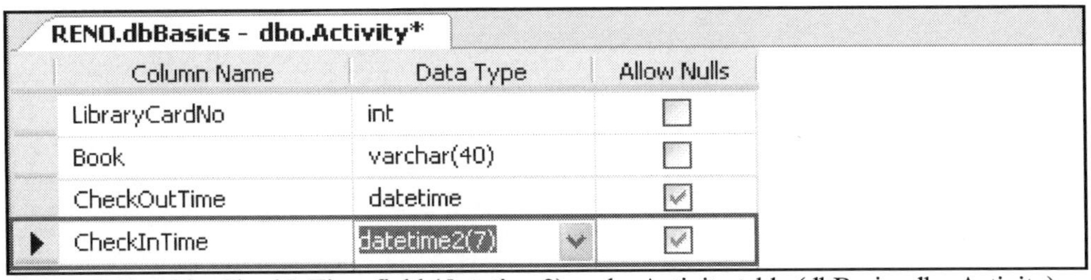

Figure 4.40 Add a CheckInTime field (**datetime2**) to the Activity table (dbBasics.dbo.Activity).

Now let's run the UPDATE statements to populate CheckInTime for Card 1001 and Card 1003 (see Figure 4.41).

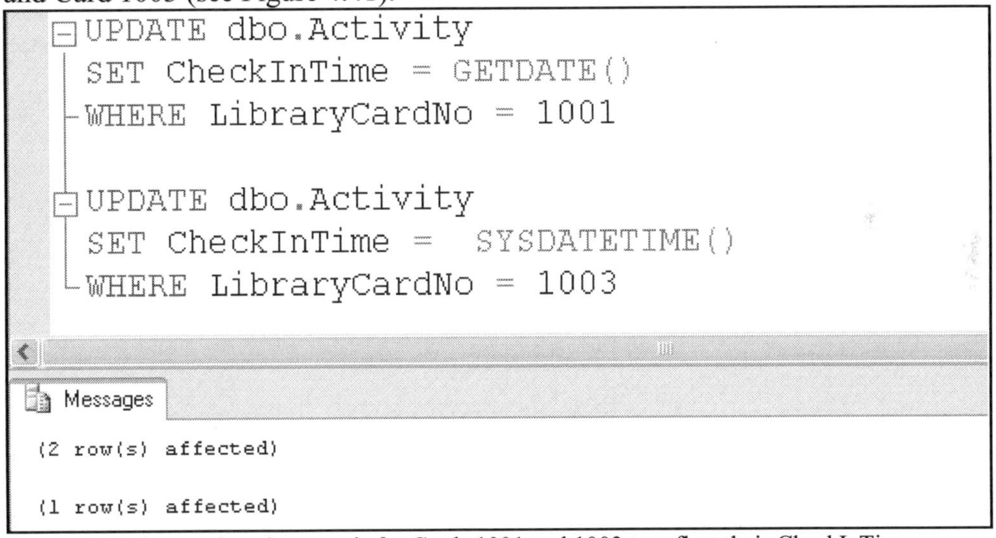

```
UPDATE dbo.Activity
  SET CheckInTime = GETDATE()
  WHERE LibraryCardNo = 1001


UPDATE dbo.Activity
  SET CheckInTime = SYSDATETIME()
  WHERE LibraryCardNo = 1003
```

Messages

(2 row(s) affected)

(1 row(s) affected)

Figure 4.41 Now update the records for Cards 1001 and 1003 to reflect their CheckInTime.

Thanks to the new **datetime2** data type, we now see all time values in the CheckInTime field carried out to nanoseconds (see Figure 4.42 – next page).

```
SELECT * FROM dbo.Activity
```

	LibraryCardNo	Book	CheckOutTime	CheckInTime
1	1001	Dust Bowl	2010-02-10 21:58:10.263	2010-02-10 22:00:26.6300000
2	1001	How to Fix Things	2010-02-10 21:58:10.263	2010-02-10 22:00:26.6300000
3	1003	Yachting for dummies	2010-02-10 21:58:10.277	2010-02-10 22:00:26.6508736
4	1005	How to marry a millionaire	NULL	NULL
5	1005	Spice world	NULL	NULL
6	1005	Juice Master tells all	NULL	NULL
7	1006	Doctor Doctor	NULL	NULL
8	1007	North of 60'	NULL	NULL

Figure 4.42 Now all time values in the CheckInTime field are carried out to nanoseconds.

But what are all the 0's in Card 1001's CheckInTime records? Since the **GETDATE( )** function only provides a time value expressed in milliseconds, the **datetime2** data type padded any unused precision spaces with a 0, so that all data in the CheckInTime field conform to the field format. In other words, all values in the CheckInTime field will be the same length, regardless of the number of significant digits. Any remaining spaces will be padded with a 0.

Notice that Card 1003's CheckInTime is more precise, because the **SYSDATETIME( )** function expresses time down to the nanosecond.

Date and Time Zone Types

(DateTimeOffset type, ToDateTimeoffset function, SwitchOffset function)

Let's take a trip back to the JProCo database and look at all the records of the CurrentProducts table. Notice we have an OriginationDate field, which is a **datetime** data type. It captured the date and time JProCo originated each product record, but this field does not show the time zone information (see Figure 4.43).

```
SELECT *
FROM JProCo.dbo.CurrentProducts
```

	ProductID	ProductName	RetailPrice	OriginationDate	ToBeDeleted	Category
1	1	Underwater Tour 1 Day West Coast	61.483	2006-08-11 13:33:09.957	0	No-Stay
2	2	Underwater Tour 2 Days West Coast	110.6694	2007-10-03 23:43:22.813	0	Overnight-Stay
3	3	Underwater Tour 3 Days West Coast	184.449	2009-05-09 16:07:49.900	0	Medium-Stay
4	4	Underwater Tour 5 Days West Coast	245.932	2006-03-04 04:59:06.600	0	Medium-Stay
5	5	Underwater Tour 1 Week West Coast	307.415	2001-07-18 19:20:11.400	0	LongTerm-Stay

Figure 4.43 OriginationDate captures the time we originated the product but not the time zone.

Suppose you needed to know what time it was in the U.K. when Product 2 was originated, or what time was it in India when the record for Product 3 was created. You would need to know what time zone the existing data was stored in, but this date field (OriginationDate) did not store that information.

So what we can do is add the time zone alongside each time value. If we do that, then when we need to move or query our data to adjust for a particular timezone (e.g., the U.K., India, Japan), it becomes an easy process.

We want to alter the CurrentProducts table to add an OriginationOffset field. This field will use another data type new to SQL Server 2008 called **DateTimeOffset**.

```
ALTER TABLE dbo.CurrentProducts
  ADD OriginationOffset DateTimeOffset NULL
```

Messages

Command(s) completed successfully.

Figure 4.44 We are adding a new field, OriginationOffset, to the CurrentProducts table.

Now we see our original OriginationDate, and we have a new field which is ready to hold the OriginationDate value plus the time zone (Figure 4.45). Next we'll populate the new field with all the values from OriginationDate (Figure 4.46).

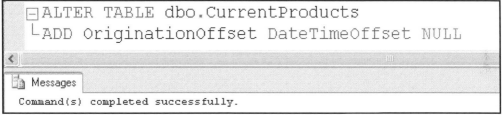

```
SELECT ProductID, ProductName,
  OriginationDate, OriginationOffset
  FROM dbo.CurrentProducts
```

Results | Messages

	ProductID	ProductName	OriginationDate	OriginationOffset
1	1	Underwater Tour 1 Day West Coast	2006-08-11 13:33:09.957	NULL
2	2	Underwater Tour 2 Days West Coast	2007-10-03 23:43:22.813	NULL
3	3	Underwater Tour 3 Days West Coast	2009-05-09 16:07:49.900	NULL

Figure 4.45 OriginationOffset will hold the original time value and its corresponding time zone.

```
UPDATE JProCo.dbo.CurrentProducts
  SET OriginationOffset = OriginationDate
```

Messages

(485 row(s) affected)

Figure 4.46 Populate the new field with the OriginationDate values.

This helps us because we now have all the OriginationDate values in the new field. However, our OriginationOffset field wants two pieces of information: 1) the date and time and 2) the time zone. Thus, we can't achieve our goal unless we add meaningful time zone information.

The genius of the **DateTimeOffset** date type is that it stores time zone information, which is the component we'll next supply to our new field. Notice that OriginationOffset shows a '+00:00' for the time zone, which indicates either: 1) the UTC time zone or 2) no time zone information has yet been supplied.

```
SELECT ProductID, ProductName,
OriginationDate, OriginationOffset
FROM dbo.CurrentProducts
```
table JProCo.dbo.CurrentProducts

Results | Messages

	ProductID	ProductName	OriginationDate	OriginationOffset	
1	1	Underwater Tour 1 Day West Coast	2006-08-11 13:33:09.957	2006-08-11 13:33:09.9570000	+00:00
2	2	Underwater Tour 2 Days West Coast	2007-10-03 23:43:22.813	2007-10-03 23:43:22.8130000	+00:00
3	3	Underwater Tour 3 Days West Coast	2009-05-09 16:07:49.900	2009-05-09 16:07:49.9000000	+00:00
4	4	Underwater Tour 5 Days West Coast	2006-03-04 04:59:06.600	2006-03-04 04:59:06.6000000	+00:00
5	5	Underwater Tour 1 Week West Coast	2001-07-18 19:20:11.400	2001-07-18 19:20:11.4000000	+00:00

Figure 4.47 We haven't yet supplied any meaningful time zone information to OriginationOffset.

We can supply the time zone info by modifying our UPDATE statement. Add the function **ToDateTimeOffset** to indicate which time zone we are in. Since each OriginationDate was recorded in Seattle, which is JProCo's main headquarters, those times all are Pacific Time. (Pacific Time is -08:00 of GMT.)

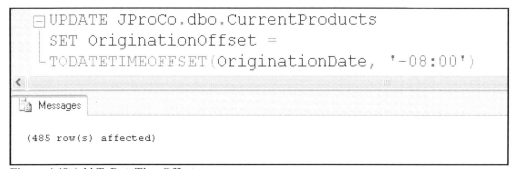

```
UPDATE JProCo.dbo.CurrentProducts
 SET OriginationOffset =
 TODATETIMEOFFSET(OriginationDate, '-08:00')
```

Messages

(485 row(s) affected)

Figure 4.48 Add **ToDateTimeOffset**.

Now let's look at the data again. Notice the offset field now shows the time zone, which is Pacific (-08:00). Also notice that this field is a **datetime2** data type with a time zone in it (see Figure 4.49).

```
SELECT ProductID, ProductName,
  OriginationDate, OriginationOffset
FROM JProCo.dbo.CurrentProducts
```

	ProductID	ProductName	OriginationDate	OriginationOffset
1	1	Underwater Tour 1 Day West Coast	2006-08-11 13:33:09.957	2006-08-11 13:33:09.9570000 -08:00
2	2	Underwater Tour 2 Days West Coast	2007-10-03 23:43:22.813	2007-10-03 23:43:22.8130000 -08:00
3	3	Underwater Tour 3 Days West Coast	2009-05-09 16:07:49.900	2009-05-09 16:07:49.9000000 -08:00
4	4	Underwater Tour 5 Days West Coast	2006-03-04 04:59:06.600	2006-03-04 04:59:06.6000000 -08:00

Figure 4.49 The offset field now shows the correct time zone for our CurrentProducts data.

Let's think about why this would be a useful tool in our global organization. You can use **ToDateTimeOffset** to translate a list of date-time event values into equivalent values for another time zone. For example, imagine that JProCo is a global organization with its Asia operations headquartered in Hyderabad. If you work in JProCo's corporate headquarters (in Seattle), you might want to take Hyderabad's list of weekly conference calls for 2009-2010 and transpose it into a list of Seattle times. You may even need to do this to provide managers in multiple regions and time zones with the India call schedule. You would want to include each manager's local time alongside the India time, so each manager knows when to dial in.

A **ToDateTimeOffset** query is a handy way to see an equivalent date-time for another time zone. If you've ever received an email thread including colleagues from differing time zones, then you're probably familiar with mentally calculating what time it was in your time zone by looking at the timestamps on the various responses. Perhaps you need to cross-reference documents your colleagues posted on a team sharepoint, which displays timestamps in your time zone.

Let's see another **ToDateTimeOffset** example using the CurrentProducts table. Imagine the India regional team handled the setup of all these products, but most of this data was input a few years ago – before we had SQL Server 2008 and added our nifty **DateTimeOffset** field to the CurrentProducts table to capture the time zone. Until now, all data in CurrentProducts has reflected the time zone of corporate headquarters in Seattle. The legal department has asked us when Product 1 (Underwater 1 Day West Coast Tour) was created, and the information must be expressed in India time. *So when Product 1 was originated, what time would it have been in India?* India is UTC +05:30.

In order to answer this question, we'll run a select statement similar to the update statement that we ran before. Namely, we will add **ToDateTimeOffset** and tell it which time zone we are in. Since each OriginationDate was recorded in Seattle, all those times are Pacific Time. (Pacific Time is -08:00 of GMT.)

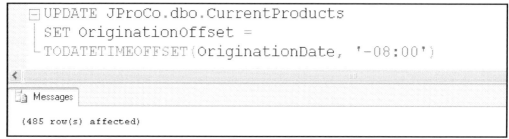

```
UPDATE JProCo.dbo.CurrentProducts
 SET OriginationOffset =
  TODATETIMEOFFSET(OriginationDate, '-08:00')
```

Messages

(485 row(s) affected)

Figure 4.50 The update statement we ran earlier to populate the OriginationOffset field.

Now we're going to take the OriginationOffset and put a switch on it to show us what the time would have been in India (i.e., when OriginationDate was input). When you have a **DateTimeOffset** field, you can use the **SWITCHOFFSET** function to see the equivalent time in another time zone.

```
SELECT ProductID, ProductName,
 OriginationDate,
 SWITCHOFFSET(OriginationOffset,'+05:30')
 AS [OriginationOffset_INDIA TEAM]
 FROM JProCo.dbo.CurrentProducts
```

Results | Messages

	ProductID	ProductName	OriginationDate	OriginationOffset_INDIA TEAM
1	1	Underwater Tour 1 Day West Coast	2006-08-11 13:33:09.957	2006-08-12 03:03:09.9570000 +05:30
2	2	Underwater Tour 2 Days West Coast	2007-10-03 23:43:22.813	2007-10-04 13:13:22.8130000 +05:30
3	3	Underwater Tour 3 Days West Coast	2009-05-09 16:07:49.900	2009-05-10 05:37:49.9000000 +05:30
4	4	Underwater Tour 5 Days West Coast	2006-03-04 04:59:06.600	2006-03-04 18:29:06.6000000 +05:30
5	5	Underwater Tour 1 Week West Coast	2001-07-18 19:20:11.400	2001-07-19 08:50:11.4000000 +05:30
6	6	Underwater Tour 2 Weeks West Coast	2008-06-30 20:40:38.760	2008-07-01 10:10:38.7600000 +05:30

Figure 4.51 Use SWITCHOFFSET to display times using a different time zone.

Now we can see it was 1:33 p.m. on the 11th (8/11/2006) Seattle time when Product 1 was originated, and at that same moment in India it was 3:03 a.m. on the 12th. For Product 2, it was originated at Oct 3rd at 11:43pm Seattle time, which corresponds to 1:13pm on the 4th in India.

Lab 4.3: Date and Time Data Types

Lab Prep: Before you can begin the lab, you must have SQL Server installed and run the SQLArchChapter4.3Setup.sql script.

Skill Check 1: Add two new fields to the Employee table (JProCo.dbo.Employee).
    1) Add a nullable field called HiredOffset that stores a **DatetimeOffset**.
    2) Add a nullable **char(6)** field called TimeZone.

Populate all Seattle and Spokane employee TimeZone fields with '-08:00'. Populate all Chicago and mobile employees with '-06:00'. Populate all Boston employees with '-05:00'. After these steps, your Employee table should resemble Figure 4.52.

```
SELECT * FROM JProCo.dbo.Employee
```

	EmpID	LastName	FirstName	HireDate	LocationID	ManagerID	Status	HiredOffset	TimeZone
1	1	Adams	Alex	2001-01-01 00:00:00.000	1	11	Active	NULL	-08:00
2	2	Brown	Barry	2002-08-12 00:00:00.000	1	11	Active	NULL	-08:00
3	3	Osako	Lee	1999-09-01 00:00:00.000	2	11	Active	NULL	-05:00
4	4	Kennson	David	1996-03-16 00:00:00.000	1	11	Has Tenure	NULL	-08:00
5	5	Bender	Eric	2007-05-17 00:00:00.000	1	11	Active	NULL	-08:00
6	6	Kendall	Lisa	2001-11-15 00:00:00.000	4	4	Active	NULL	-08:00
7	7	Lonning	David	2000-01-01 00:00:00.000	1	11	On Leave	NULL	-08:00
8	8	Marshbank	John	2001-11-15 00:00:00.000	NULL	4	Active	NULL	-06:00
9	9	Newton	James	2003-09-30 00:00:00.000	2	3	Active	NULL	-05:00
10	10	O'Haire	Terry	2004-10-04 00:00:00.000	2	3	Active	NULL	-05:00

Figure 4.52 Skill Check 1 adds two fields and includes each employee's time zone information.

Skill Check 2: Use **ToDateTimeOffset** to populate HiredOffset from the HireDate and TimeZone fields. Afterwards, your Employee table should resemble the figure below (see Figure 4.53).

```
SELECT * FROM Employee
```
table JProCo.dbo.Employee

	EmpID	LastName	FirstName	HireDate	LocationID	ManagerID	Status	HiredOffset	TimeZone
1	1	Adams	Alex	2001-01-01 00:00:00.000	1	11	Active	2001-01-01 00:00:00.0000000 -08:00	-08:00
2	2	Brown	Barry	2002-08-12 00:00:00.000	1	11	Active	2002-08-12 00:00:00.0000000 -08:00	-08:00
3	3	Osako	Lee	1999-09-01 00:00:00.000	2	11	Active	1999-09-01 00:00:00.0000000 -05:00	-05:00
4	4	Kennson	David	1996-03-16 00:00:00.000	1	11	Has Tenure	1996-03-16 00:00:00.0000000 -08:00	-08:00
5	5	Bender	Eric	2007-05-17 00:00:00.000	1	11	Active	2007-05-17 00:00:00.0000000 -08:00	-08:00
6	6	Kendall	Lisa	2001-11-15 00:00:00.000	4	4	Active	2001-11-15 00:00:00.0000000 -08:00	-08:00
7	7	Lonning	David	2000-01-01 00:00:00.000	1	11	On Leave	2000-01-01 00:00:00.0000000 -08:00	-08:00
8	8	Marshbank	John	2001-11-15 00:00:00.000	NULL	4	Active	2001-11-15 00:00:00.0000000 -06:00	-06:00
9	9	Newton	James	2003-09-30 00:00:00.000	2	3	Active	2003-09-30 00:00:00.0000000 -05:00	-05:00
10	10	O'Haire	Terry	2004-10-04 00:00:00.000	2	3	Active	2004-10-04 00:00:00.0000000 -05:00	-05:00

Figure 4.53 Skill Check 2 populates HiredOffset from the HireDate and TimeZone fields.

Skill Check 3: Show the HireDate for all employees in Alaska Time '-09:00'. Afterwards, your Employee table should resemble the figure below (see Figure 4.54).

	AlaskaHireTime	EmplD	LastN...	FirstNa...	HireDate	LocationID	ManagerID	Status	HiredOffset	TimeZone
1	2000-12-31 23:00:00.0000000 -09:00	1	Adams	Alex	2001-01-01 00:00:00.000	1	11	Active	2001-01-01 00:00:00.0000000 -08:00	-08:00
2	2002-08-11 23:00:00.0000000 -09:00	2	Brown	Barry	2002-08-12 00:00:00.000	1	11	Active	2002-08-12 00:00:00.0000000 -08:00	-08:00
3	1999-08-31 20:00:00.0000000 -09:00	3	Osako	Lee	1999-09-01 00:00:00.000	2	11	Active	1999-09-01 00:00:00.0000000 -05:00	-05:00
4	1996-03-15 23:00:00.0000000 -09:00	4	Kenns...	David	1996-03-16 00:00:00.000	1	11	Has ...	1996-03-16 00:00:00.0000000 -08:00	-08:00
5	2007-05-16 23:00:00.0000000 -09:00	5	Bender	Eric	2007-05-17 00:00:00.000	1	11	Active	2007-05-17 00:00:00.0000000 -08:00	-08:00
6	2001-11-14 23:00:00.0000000 -09:00	6	Kendall	Lisa	2001-11-15 00:00:00.000	4	4	Active	2001-11-15 00:00:00.0000000 -08:00	-08:00
7	1999-12-31 23:00:00.0000000 -09:00	7	Lonning	David	2000-01-01 00:00:00.000	1	11	On ...	2000-01-01 00:00:00.0000000 -08:00	-08:00
8	2001-11-14 21:00:00.0000000 -09:00	8	Marsh...	John	2001-11-15 00:00:00.000	NULL	4	Active	2001-11-15 00:00:00.0000000 -06:00	-06:00
9	2003-09-29 20:00:00.0000000 -09:00	9	Newton	James	2003-09-30 00:00:00.000	2	3	Active	2003-09-30 00:00:00.0000000 -05:00	-05:00
10	2004-10-03 20:00:00.0000000 -09:00	10	O'Haire	Terry	2004-10-04 00:00:00.000	2	3	Active	2004-10-04 00:00:00.0000000 -05:00	-05:00
11	1989-03-31 23:00:00.0000000 -09:00	11	Smith	Sally	1989-04-01 00:00:00.000	1	NULL	Active	1989-04-01 00:00:00.0000000 -08:00	-08:00
12	1995-05-25 23:00:00.0000000 -09:00	12	O'Neil	Barbara	1995-05-26 00:00:00.000	4	4	Has ...	1995-05-26 00:00:00.0000000 -08:00	-08:00
13	2009-06-10 23:00:00.0000000 -09:00	13	Wilco...	Phil	2009-06-11 00:00:00.000	1	11	Active	2009-06-11 00:00:00.0000000 -08:00	-08:00
14	2009-10-17 23:00:00.0000000 -09:00	14	Smith	Janis	2009-10-18 00:00:00.000	1	4	Active	2009-10-18 00:00:00.0000000 -08:00	-08:00

Figure 4.54 Skill Check 3 expresses each employee's hire date in Alaska Time.

Answer Code: The T-SQL code to this lab can be found in the downloadable files in a file named Lab4.3_DateAndTimeTypes.sql.

Date and Time Data Types - Points to Ponder

1. If you have a date time offset field, you can use the SWITCHOFFSET function to see the equivalent time in another time zone.

2. The **DateTimeOffset** data type requires 2 pieces of information: a Datetime2 + a TimeZone (in single quotes).

Chapter Glossary

Alias data types: A custom data type based on a system-supplied data type.

CLR data types: Common language runtime data types, such as Geography or Geometry.

Constraint: A constraint restricts your data input to values within the limits you specify in the design of your table and its fields.

Custom data type: This user defined data type defines the characteristic of the data that is stored in a column.

Data pages: Another name for memory pages.

Datetime: This data type only stores data out to milliseconds.

Datetime2: A new SQL Server 2008 data type that is capable of storing nanosecond data.

DatetimeOffset type: This date type stores time zone information. .

DROP TYPE: Data types cannot be changed. They first have to be dropped via a DROP TYPE statement and then recreated.

GETDATE( ): A property whose value is the time in your time zone. This is the Microsoft version. CURRENT_TIMESTAMP is the ANSI version.

GETUTCDATE( ): This shows the current time expressed in terms of UTC.

SPARSE DATA: A feature new to SQL Server 2008 for fields you expect to be predominantly null.

Sparsely populated field: A field containing mostly NULL values.

SPROC: Short for Stored Procedure; a set of defined, precompiled SQL statements stored on a SQL Server.

SWITCH OFFSET FUNCTION: If you have a date time offset field, you can use the SWITCHOFFSET function to see the equivalent time in another time zone.

SYSDATETIME ( ): This function returns the current date and time in your time zone and shows fractional seconds expressed in nanoseconds (.3333333 second).

SYSUTCDATETIME ( ): A UTC function that gets down to the nanoseconds.

TODATETIMEOFFSET: This function is used to translate a list of date-time event values into equivalent values for another time zone.

Chapter Four - Review Quiz

1.) You have two fields in your Bonus table of INT and MONEY. You have 1000 records and all instances of the money column are null. When you set up the money field, you used the Sparse option. How much space are the 1000 rows of the money field using?
 O a. None
 O b. 4000 bytes
 O c. 8000 bytes

2.) You are expecting to have some sparsely populated data in your table and need to know what types of data can use the Sparse option. Which of the following below can use the Sparse option? (choose three)

 ☐ a. INT
 ☐ b. CHAR(10)
 ☐ c. TEXT
 ☐ d. MONEY
 ☐ e. GEOMETRY
 ☐ f. NTEXT
 ☐ g. GEOGRAPHY

3.) You have a table with three fields of Varchar(max), text, and Geometry. Which is the only field that can use the sparse option?

 O a. Varchar(max)
 O b. Text
 O c. Geometry

4.) You have one row in a table called dbo.Bonus, which has two fields. The first field is called BonusID and it is a NOT NULL integer. The second field is BonusAmount, which is set to money and is nullable. Integers are 4 bytes and money is 8 bytes. The first record has an Id of 1 and an amount set to null. What is the fixed length data payload?

 O a. 4 bytes
 O b. 8 bytes
 O c. 12 bytes

5.) You have a custom data type called CountryCode and have been instructed by your manager to delete it. What must you do first?

  O a. Delete all system-supplied data types which CountryCode is based on.

  O b. Remove all fields which are using that CountryCode.

  O c. Set all rows to null for any field using the CountryCode type.

6.) Which of the following functions will return the date and time in the current time zone to a precision of milliseconds?

  O a. GETDATE( )

  O b. SYSDATETIME( )

  O c. GETUTCDATE( )

  O d. SYSUTCDATETIME( )

7.) Which of the following functions will return the current time in Coordinated Universal Time format to a precision of nanoseconds?

  O a. GETDATE( )

  O b. SYSDATETIME( )

  O c. GETUTCDATE( )

  O d. SYSUTCDATETIME( )

8.) You have an enterprise level database storing information from all over the world. You have been using a column to contain the local time and a column to contain the difference between local time and UTC time. You now have SQL Server 2008 and want to store this in one column. Which data type should you use?

  O a. Time

  O b. Date

  O c. Datetime

  O d. Datetime2

  O e. Datetimeoffset

9.) You have a datetime2 and want to turn it into a DateTimeOffset data type for the Alaska Time zone -09:00. What method will achieve this result?

  O a. SWITCHOFFSET

  O b. TODATETIMEOFFSET

10.) You work for an online ordering company that processes web purchases from all over the world. You work at the Headquarters in Vancouver BC. At the exact moment an order is accepted, it is entered as a value into an OrderDate field which uses the DateTimeOffset data type. A user in Hawaii wants to know the exact time of their last order. You recorded the transaction in Vancouver BC time and want to show the results in Hawaii time. Which Function will change the time zone while preserving the UTC stored time?

O a. DATEADD
O b. DATEDIFF
O c. TODATETIMEOFFSET
O d. SWITCHOFFSET

11.) You have an enterprise level database storing information from all over the world. You have been using a column to contain the local time as a Datetime2 and another column to contain the difference between local time and UTC time. You now have SQL Server 2008 and want to store this in one column. Which function will create a datetimeoffset from a datetime2 if you give it the time zone?

O a. DATEADD
O b. DATEDIFF
O c. TODATETIMEOFFSET
O d. SWITCHOFFSET

Answer Key

1.) a   2.) a, b, d 3.) a 4.) c   5.) b   6.) a   7.) d   8.) e   9.) b   10.) d   11.) c

Bug Catcher Game

To play the Bug Catcher game run the BugCatcher_Chapter04SpecialDataTypeOptions.pps from the BugCatcher folder of the companion files. You can obtain these files from www.Joes2Pros.com or by ordering the Companion CD.

Chapter 5.   Spatial Data Types

Maps have played an important role for navigators and cultures down the centuries. A map can chart a journey, or it can depict a place on the earth or even an entire country. Maps can also be non-geographical, like the map of all the shops in a mall. All maps have one thing in common: they show how each item in the map relates to the other items in terms of position. Most maps combine several types of items. For example, think of a treasure map where X marks the spot. If this map contains an island with the treasure mark in the middle, then the island is a shape which contains the point indicating the treasure's location.

Have you ever noticed that on our round shaped world, almost every piece of property sold is either rectangular or a polygon-shaped lot? Occasionally, you might see a round lawn design but generally, it will still be contained within a rectangular plot having decorative accents (e.g., flower gardens) in each corner.

To represent land, we need to use a flat map. To represent points on the earth we need a spherical, or ball-shaped, map. For this reason you have two spatial data types to pick from called Geography or Geometry. One is better for measuring parcels of land, while the other is better for GPS or other global type measures.

Spatial data types in SQL Server 2008 are probably the most anticipated new feature and with good reason. Entire books are now written on the subject and this chapter will show you the basics.

READER NOTE: *In order to follow along with the examples in the first section of Chapter 5, please run the setup script SQLArchChapter5.0Setup.sql. The setup scripts for this book are posted at Joes2Pros.com.*

Geography Data Type

New to SQL Server 2008 are the spatial data types called **Geography** and **Geometry**. The **Geography** data type can store information for areas and points on the earth. It also provides a built-in function to calculate distance and overlaps with other locations. This data type stores and handles calculations based on round-earth (or *ellipsoidal*) data, which relates to coordinate systems such as GPS and longitude-latitude.

Databases have been storing positional data for years, like the sample data below where we see two dedicated fields to store longitude and latitude for each JProCo location (see Figure 5.1). Please note that your Location table does not currently have the latitude and longitude fields. This is a figure of what your table will look like after you follow the next few steps in the chapter.

	LocationID	street	city	state	Latitude	Longitude
1	1	545 Pike	Seattle	WA	47.455	-122.31
2	2	222 Second AVE	Boston	MA	42.372	-71.0298
3	3	333 Third PL	Chicago	IL	41.953	-87.643
4	4	444 Ruby ST	Spokane	WA	47.668	-117.529
5	5	1595 Main	Philadelphia	PA	39.888	-75.251

SELECT * FROM JProCo.dbo.Location

Results | Messages

Figure 5.1 The true nature of geographical data could not be stored in the database prior to SQL Server 2008. Developers had to extract the data points into a custom application.

If you were to ask this database what the longitude-latitude difference between Seattle and Boston is, it would have no idea. To the database, these are just arbitrary flat data values. In order to turn each pair of numbers into a meaningful geographical point, we would have to extract this data into a custom application outside of SQL Server (e.g., into a C# application) and then run calculations using the customized app.

In other words, the true ellipsoidal nature of this geographical data wasn't stored in the database prior to SQL Server 2008. The database couldn't have differentiated our sample longitude-latitude data above (see Figure 5.1) from any other kind of information in the database. Now, thanks to SQL Server 2008, you no longer need a separate custom application, because both of these pieces of data can be stored in one **Geography** field. As well, the **Geography** type makes available all the built-in functionality, to perform calculations involving round-earth data, which would have been contained in a custom app.

Storing Latitude and Longitude

Prior to SQL Server 2008, two float or decimal fields would be used to house latitude and longitude. Now you can store these, as well as other geospatial data, in one **Geography** field.

Let's begin by looking at all the records in our Location table, as well as its design. We see typical location data – city, state, street – and the five JProCo office locations (Seattle, Spokane, Chicago, Boston, and Philadelphia). Into this table we will add fields for latitude and longitude, and then we'll see how to combine those into one **Geography** field.

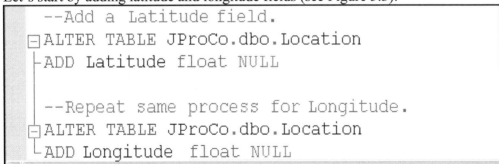

Figure 5.2 The design and data of the Location table (JProCo.dbo.Location).

Let's start by adding latitude and longitude fields (see Figure 5.3).

```
--Add a Latitude field.
ALTER TABLE JProCo.dbo.Location
ADD Latitude float NULL


--Repeat same process for Longitude.
ALTER TABLE JProCo.dbo.Location
ADD Longitude  float NULL
```

Figure 5.3 Add latitude and longitude fields to the Location table.

Now populate these fields using the values you see here (see Figure 5.4).

```
UPDATE JProCo.dbo.Location --Seattle
 SET Latitude = 47.455, Longitude = -122.31
WHERE LocationID = 1

UPDATE JProCo.dbo.Location --Boston
 SET Latitude = 42.372, Longitude = -71.0298
WHERE LocationID = 2

UPDATE JProCo.dbo.Location --Chicago
 SET Latitude = 41.953, Longitude = -87.643
WHERE LocationID = 3

UPDATE JProCo.dbo.Location --Spokane
 SET Latitude = 47.668, Longitude = -117.529
WHERE LocationID = 4

UPDATE JProCo.dbo.Location --Philadelphia
 SET Latitude = 39.888, Longitude = -75.251
WHERE LocationID = 5
```

Figure 5.4 Populate the latitude and longitude fields with these values.

> **1 Geography field replaces these 2 numeric fields.**

	LocationID	street	city	state	Latitude	Longitude
1	1	545 Pike	Seattle	WA	47.455	-122.231
2	2	222 Second AVE	Boston	MA	42.372	-71.0298
3	3	333 Third PL	Chicago	IL	41.953	-87.643
4	4	444 Ruby ST	Spokane	WA	47.668	-117.529
5	5	1595 Main	Philade...	PA	39.888	-75.251

Figure 5.5 One geography field can do more than two latitude/longitude fields.

Creating Geography as a Field in a Table

We're now going to add another field called GeoLoc (short for geographical location), which will use the new **Geography** data type.

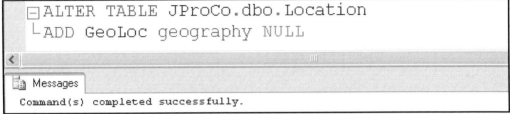

```
ALTER TABLE JProCo.dbo.Location
ADD GeoLoc geography NULL
```

Messages

Command(s) completed successfully.

Figure 5.6 Add the GeoLoc field to the Location table. GeoLoc is a **Geography** field.

We now have the latitude and longitude fields populated with values for each JProCo location. The **Geography** field GeoLoc has also been added to the table.

```
SELECT * FROM JProCo.dbo.Location
```

Results | Spatial results | Messages

	LocationID	street	city	state	Latitude	Longitude	GeoLoc
1	1	545 Pike	Seattle	WA	47.455	-122.31	NULL
2	2	222 Second AVE	Boston	MA	42.372	-71.0298	NULL
3	3	333 Third PL	Chicago	IL	41.953	-87.643	NULL
4	4	444 Ruby ST	Spokane	WA	47.668	-117.529	NULL
5	5	1595 Main	Philadelphia	PA	39.888	-75.251	NULL

Figure 5.7 The latitude and longitude values and GeoLoc field are now in place.

Populating a Geography Data Type

Based on the two data points, latitude and longitude, we can generate the geospatial locations for the GeoLoc field. Use the Point-static function to pass in the latitude and longitude values along with a style specifier value (4326 is the standard which is used the most).

```
UPDATE JProCo.dbo.Location
SET GeoLoc = GEOGRAPHY::Point(47.455, -122.31, 4326)
WHERE LocationID = 1  --Seattle
```

Figure 5.8 T-SQL code for entering one set of location values into the **Geography** field, GeoLoc for LocationID 1.

```
UPDATE JProCo.dbo.Location
 SET GeoLoc = GEOGRAPHY::Point(Latitude, Longitude, 4326)
 --passes in Latitude & Longitude values for all locations
```

Messages

```
(5 row(s) affected)
```

Figure 5.9 T-SQL code for entering all location values into the Geography field, GeoLoc.

```
SELECT * FROM JProCo.dbo.Location
```

Results | Spatial results | Messages

	LocationID	street	city	state	Latitude	Longitude	GeoLoc
1	1	545 Pike	Seattle	WA	47.455	-122.31	0xE6100000010C0AD7A3703DBA4740A4703D0AD7935EC0
2	2	222 Second AVE	Boston	MA	42.372	-71.0298	0xE6100000010C560E2DB29D2F4540EE5A423EE8C151C0
3	3	333 Third PL	Chicago	IL	41.953	-87.643	0xE6100000010C448B6CE7FBF94440FED478E926E955C0
4	4	444 Ruby ST	Spokane	WA	47.668	-117.529	0xE6100000010C2FDD240681D5474060E5D022DB615DC0
5	5	1595 Main	Philadelphia	PA	39.888	-75.251	0xE6100000010C8B6CE7FBA9F14340F2D24D6210D052C0

Figure 5.10 We have successfully combined latitude and longitude into **Geography** data.

The style specifier we used to format our Geography value is also known as a *spatial reference identifier* or *SRID* and identifies which spatial reference system the coordinates belong to. The SRID 4326 represents WGS 84, which is the most commonly used system and is used by GPS systems.

The table *sys.spatial_reference_systems* contains the list of all systems currently supported in SQL Server 2008. Below is the information contained for SRID 4326.

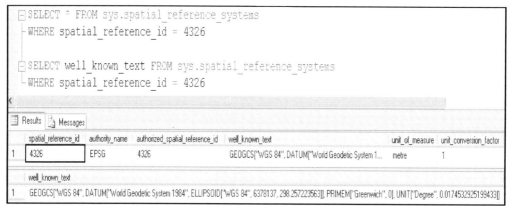

Figure 5.11 Information shown in sys.spatial_reference_systems for SRID 4326.

The string value in the well_known_text field contains the definition of the spatial reference:

Coordinate System	GEOGCS	WGS 84
Datum	DATUM	World Geodetic System 1984
	ELLIPSOID	WGS 84
		6378137
		298.257223563
Prime Meridian	PRIMEM	"Greenwich", 0 (longitude 0)
Unit of Measurement	UNIT	"Degree", 0.0174532925199433

In Chapter 4, we saw that data types can serve as *constraints* on data input to ensure that values entered will be within the limits specified in your field and table design. If you know that values in a field will all belong to one SRID, you can add a field constraint to enforce that. This T-SQL code will ensure that all values entered into the GeoLoc field will have an SRID of 4326 (see Figure 5.12).

```
ALTER TABLE JProCo.dbo.Location
ADD CONSTRAINT [enforce_srid_geographycolumn]
CHECK (GeoLoc.STSrid = 4326)
GO
```

Figure 5.12 This constraint ensures all values in the GeoLoc field will have an SRID of 4326.

Geography Functions

We just used the Point function. There are other functions and methods available for use with the **Geography** data type. Two we will use in this section, STAsText( ) and STDistance( ), are examples of *Geography instance methods*. You can reference the term *Geography instance methods* in SQL Server 2008 documentation resources (e.g., MSDN, Microsoft SQL Server Books Online 2008) to locate other available methods you can utilize with the **Geography** type.

We have successfully combined latitude and longitude into GeoLoc. However, since the values in the GeoLoc column are a little tricky to read, we can create a variable and capture each city's GeoLoc value into its respective variable.

```
DECLARE @Seattle GEOGRAPHY;
DECLARE @Boston GEOGRAPHY;


SELECT @Seattle = GeoLoc FROM JProCo.dbo.Location WHERE LocationID = 1
SELECT @Boston =  GeoLoc FROM JProCo.dbo.Location WHERE LocationID = 2


SELECT @Seattle.STAsText() AS Seattle, @Boston.STAsText() AS Boston
```

	Seattle	Boston
1	POINT (-122.31 47.455)	POINT (-71.0298 42.372)

Figure 5.13 STAsText( ) is one of the Spatial Type methods you can use with the Geography type.

The STDistance( ) method calculates the shortest distance (in meters) between two **Geography** data points. To have STDistance( ) return the distance from Seattle to Boston in kilometers (KM), we have divided by 1000 (see 5.14). Without this step, the result is just over 4 million meters (4,014,163 meters).

```
DECLARE @Seattle GEOGRAPHY;
DECLARE @Boston GEOGRAPHY;

SELECT @Seattle = GeoLoc FROM JProCo.dbo.Location WHERE LocationID = 1
SELECT @Boston =  GeoLoc FROM JProCo.dbo.Location WHERE LocationID = 2

SELECT @Seattle.STDistance(@Boston) AS [Distance in Meters],
       @Seattle.STDistance(@Boston)/1000 AS [Distance in KM]
```

	Distance in Meters	Distance in KM
1	4014162.77025097	4014.16277025097

Figure 5.14 Calculating the distance from Seattle to Boston, which is just over 4,014 KM.

Finally, let's change the distance calculation to show the same distance in miles. There are 1609 meters in a mile. It is just over 2491 miles from Seattle to Boston.

```
DECLARE @Seattle GEOGRAPHY;
DECLARE @Boston GEOGRAPHY;

SELECT @Seattle = GeoLoc FROM JProCo.dbo.Location WHERE LocationID = 1
SELECT @Boston =  GeoLoc FROM JProCo.dbo.Location WHERE LocationID = 2

SELECT @Seattle.STDistance(@Boston)/1609 AS [Distance in Miles]
```

	Distance in Miles
1	2491.18784811214

Figure 5.15 It is just over 2491 miles from Seattle to Boston.

Geography Polygon

As a young child I just loved it when my mother gave me a workbook full of connect-the-dots games. Starting with dot-1 and drawing a line in order, it was fun to see the picture it made when the task was complete. By connecting several points in a row and closing it back up at the end, you can actually make your geography type hold a polygon. This is great for when you want to represent a landmass, like the United States, instead of just a point on the map. If you connect enough dots together, you can draw any land mass.

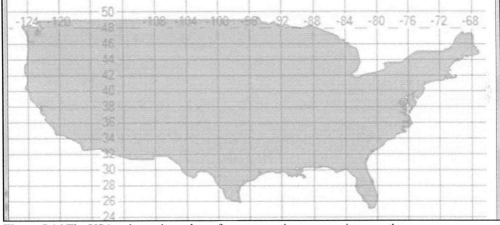

Figure 5.16 The USA polygon is made up from connecting many points together.

So then, what connect-the-dots sequence will draw a rough sketch of the United States? Let's look at this example, which begins where I live (in the northwest corner). Let's call this the upper left corner. Looking at an atlas with latitude and longitude, it's about 124 degrees west longitude and 49 degrees north latitude (see Figure 5.17).

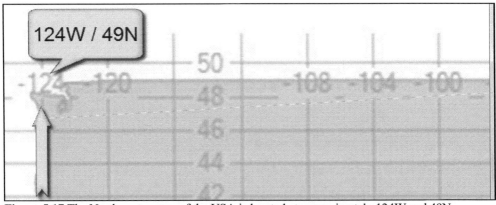

Figure 5.17 The Northwest corner of the USA is located at approximately 124W and 49N.

Looking at the lower right corner of the USA, we see that it is located at 80 degrees west longitude and 25 degrees north latitude (see Figure 5.18).

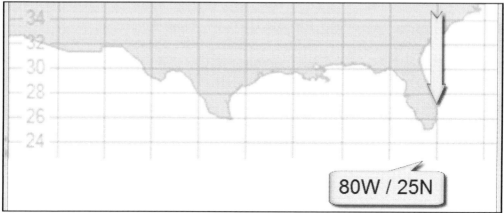

Figure 5.18 The southeast corner of the USA is located at approximately 80W and 25N.

You can keep drawing points that mark the edges of the United States. Now, if you draw enough points, then you can make a very fine version of the United States. Let's mark several points of known coordinates to make a rough drawing of the United States. We will store all these points as a Geograpy type and then view the results.

We are going to mark 16 points to get a geographical shape which resembles the map of the United States (see Figure 5.19).

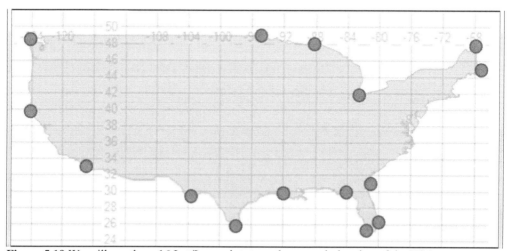

Figure 5.19 We will use these 16 Lat/Lon points to make a rough drawing of the USA.

We are going to treat this like a "Connect-the-Dots" game where we will start and end at the same point while drawing each point in order (see Figure 5.20). We will

176

come full circle by ending at the same point we started at in the upper left corner. Note: we could have picked any point as our starting and stopping point.

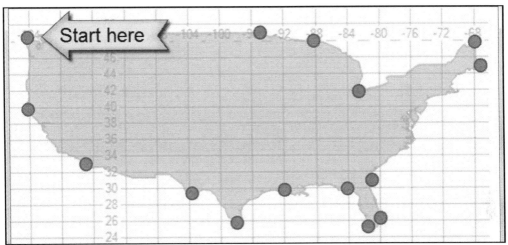

Figure 5.20 Geography polygons must start and stop on the same point.

It is important that we go in a counter-clockwise manner (see Figure 5.21). If you attempt to draw in a clockwise manner, SQL Server will give you a confusing error message about hemispheres.

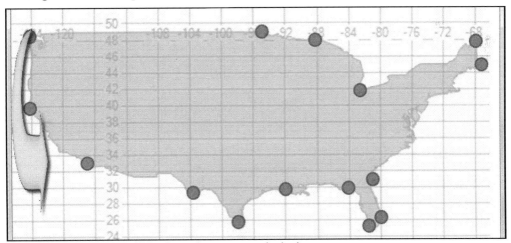

Figure 5.21 The points will be drawn in a counter-clockwise manner.

Please note that for these earth-friendly numbers, it won't matter whether we use the Geography or Geometry data type.

Declare a Geography data type and get ready to set it to our 16 point values (see Figure 5.22). The 16 points will go in the parentheses of the STGeomFromText( ) Function. Be sure to end this statement with a semi-colon.

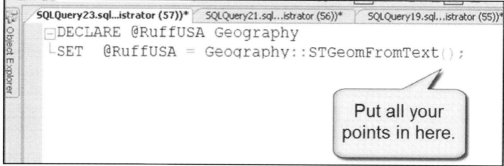

Figure 5.22 Declare and set a Geography variable.

All 16 points will go inside single quotes as the first parameter to the STGeomFromText function. The second parameter, with a value of 4326, is the WSG84 specification standard. The WSG84 and other standards are beyond the scope of this book, so we just encourage you to use the most common standard for this example.

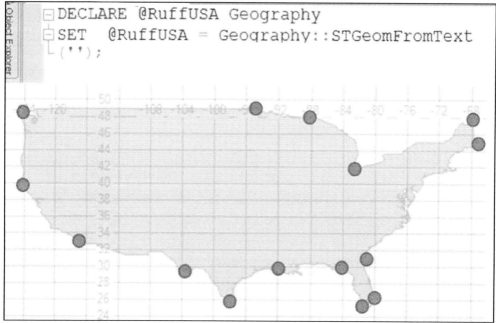

Figure 5.23 The 16 points are character parameters in the STGeomFromText function. In the next figure, we will see we are using the WSG84 standard (4326).

Since the United States is one enclosed shape, we will only need one set of parentheses inside our first parameter. If you wanted to draw Hawaii, then that would be several enclosed shapes.

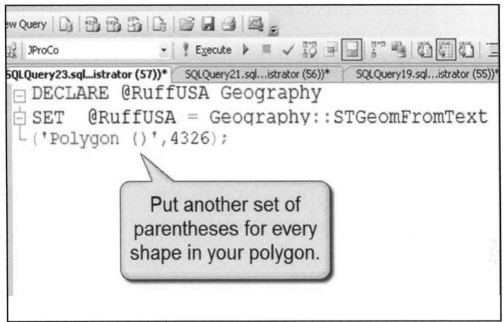

Figure 5.24 You will need one set of Parentheses for every enclosed shape in your type.

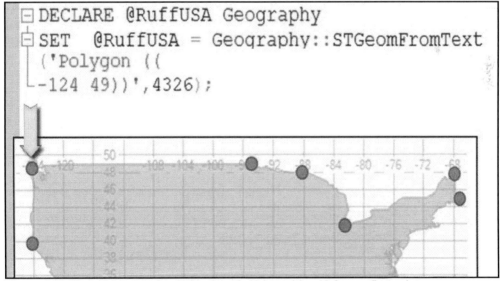

Figure 5.25 West 124 is negative 124 and north 49 is positive 49 for our first point.

Let's draw our first point. Since west longitude is a negative number, we will enter -124. Since north latitude is a positive number, we will enter 49. These two numbers are separated by a space.

The next point is at -124 west and 40 degrees north. The second set of numbers is separated from the first set of numbers by a comma (See Figure 5.26).

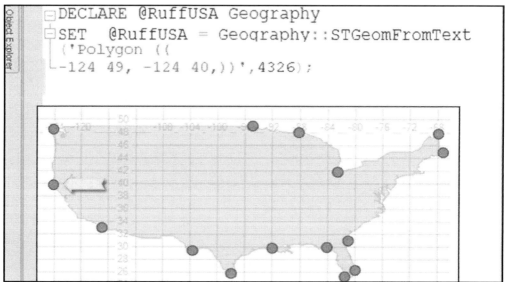

Figure 5.26 The second point is -124 40

If you keep entering numbers all the way to the lower tip of Florida, your results will contain 9 points and will resemble Figure 5.27.

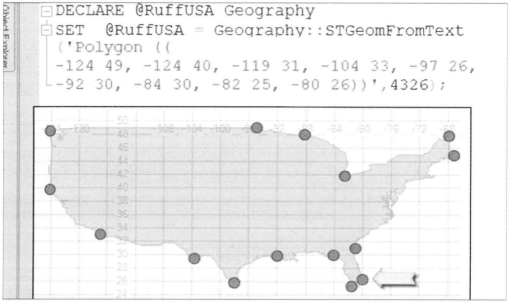

Figure 5.27 After entering 9 of the 16 points, your code has 9 sets of numbers separated by 8 commas.

Once you enter 15 of the points, you are almost done (see Figure 5.28). To finish any good "Connect the Dots" game you need to end where you began (see Figure 5.29).

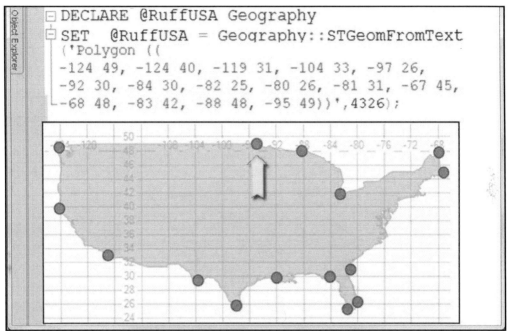

Figure 5.28 After entering 15 of the points, you're almost done.

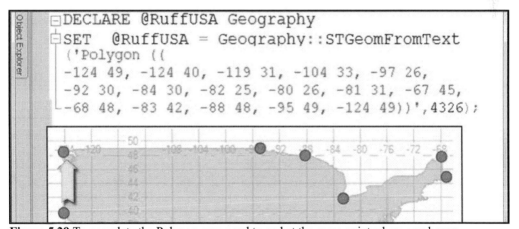

Figure 5.29 To complete the Polygon, you need to end at the same point where you began.

Run a Select statement to show the value of your data type (see Figure 5.30). Then click the Spatial Results tab to see the graphic view of your data.

```
DECLARE @RuffUSA Geography
SET  @RuffUSA = Geography::STGeomFromText
('Polygon ((
-124 49, -124 40, -119 31, -104 33, -97 26,
-92 30, -84 30, -82 25, -80 26, -81 31, -67 45,
-68 48, -83 42, -88 48, -95 49, -124 49
))',4326);

SELECT @RuffUSA
```

Results	Spatial results	Messages

	[No column name]
1	0xE6100000010410000000000000000000005FC00000000000...

Figure 5.30 The value of your Geography data type is shown.

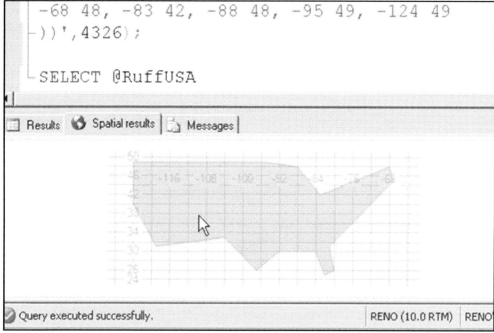

Figure 5.31 The Spatial results table shows the visual representation of your drawing.

Lab 5.1: Geography Data Type

Lab Prep: Before you can begin the lab, you must have SQL Server installed and run the SQLArchChapter5.1Setup.sql script.

Skill Check 1: Add a sixth location to the Location table (JProCo.dbo.Location) using the values shown below. Calculate the latitude and longitude values into the GeoLoc field.

LocationID:	6	*Latitude:*	-33.876
Street:	915 Wallaby Drive	*Longitude:*	151.315
City:	Sydney		
State:	Null		

[*Hint:* you will need to use the Point-static function to populate the GeoLoc while doing the INSERT statement.]

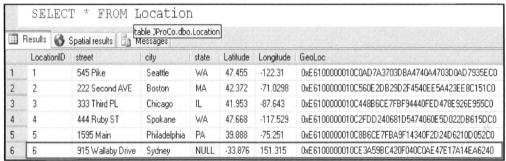

Figure 5.32 Skill Check 1 adds a sixth record to the Location table and calculates its GeoLoc value.

Skill Check 2: In order to perform this skill check, you must have completed Skill Check 1 and have six records in your JProCo.dbo.Location table.

Run a SELECT statement to show all fields and records from the Location table. Click the "Spatial Results" tab and choose the "Bonne" option from the "Select projection" dropdown. Each of the six locations will appear as a small black dot. Find all six locations and their mouseover tags by holding your mouse over each dot. (Note: the figure below has been edited to make all mouseover tags appear simultaneously, but SQL Server's normal behavior is for just one tag to appear at a time.)

Finally, click anywhere inside the grid and drag the map around. Observe that both the longitude and latitude axis labels adjust dynamically.

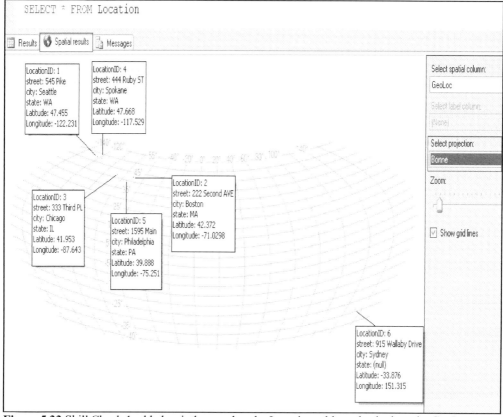

Figure 5.33 Skill Check 1 added a sixth record to the Location table and calculates its GeoLoc value. The result from Skill Check 2 shows graphical presentation of all points we added to the Location table.

Note: you cannot save or export results from the Spatial Results tab. Currently it serves as a handy tool for you to be able to view your spatial data.

Skill Check 3: Cross Join the Location table with itself to find all the cities in JProCo and their respective distances. Order your result so the greatest MilesApart values appear at the top of the list and the least MilesApart values appear at the bottom of the list. Your result should resemble Figure 5.34.

	city	City	MilesApart
1	Sydney	Boston	10088.9933868984
2	Boston	Sydney	10088.9933868984
3	Sydney	Philadelphia	9861.02737887156
4	Philadelphia	Sydney	9861.02737887156
5	Chicago	Sydney	9237.63404167734
6	Sydney	Chicago	9237.63404167734
7	Sydney	Spokane	7941.11228552353
8	Spokane	Sydney	7941.11228552353
9	Seattle	Sydney	7735.50037304043
10	Sydney	Seattle	7735.50037304043
11	Seattle	Boston	2491.18784811214
12	Boston	Seattle	2491.18784811214
13	Philadelphia	Seattle	2374.05194206331
14	Seattle	Philadelphia	2374.05194206331
15	Boston	Spokane	2272.00185407678
16	Spokane	Boston	2272.00185407678
17	Spokane	Philadelphia	2153.68858275482
18	Philadelphia	Spokane	2153.68858275482
19	Seattle	Chicago	1730.27663653008
20	Chicago	Seattle	1730.27663653008
21	Chicago	Spokane	1511.00595099965
22	Spokane	Chicago	1511.00595099965
23	Chicago	Boston	852.400343693845
24	Boston	Chicago	852.400343693845
25	Philadelphia	Chicago	663.588179044341
26	Chicago	Philadelphia	663.588179044341
27	Boston	Philadelphia	279.088117931742
28	Philadelphia	Boston	279.088117931742
29	Spokane	Seattle	220.37798803349
30	Seattle	Spokane	220.37798803349

Figure 5.34 These 30 records comprise the result for Skill Check 3.

Answer Code: The T-SQL code to this lab can be found in the downloadable files in a file named Lab5.1_GeographyDataType.sql.

Geography Data Type - Points to Ponder

1. The **Geography** data type stores round-earth latitude and longitude earth coordinates that represent points, lines, and polygons.

2. Only the **Geography** data type can store GPS data that has been defined by the OGC ().

3. A method can calculate the distance between two **Geography** coordinates.

4. STDistance( ) is an instance method which returns the closest path between two **Geography** points in meters.

5. We know points on the earth can be referenced by latitude and longitude which are two spatial numbers which intersect at one point. Representing latitude and longitude with two readable numbers (like 47.5 -122.57) is called Well-Known Text (WKT).

6. The SQL Geography type combines both these numbers into one larger binary number which appears as an encoded number that is not easy for a human to read.

7. It's very easy to get the Well-Known Text from the SQL spatial data type by calling the StAsText() method of the Geography data type.

8. WKT stands for **well-known text** for your position. If you live at 124 degrees west longitude and 40 degrees north latitude, your WKT coordinate would be (-124 40).

9. West latitudes are negative numbers while east latitude numbers are positive. North latitude numbers are positive while south latitude numbers are negative.

10. The WKT most used to source SQL Geography types are by putting longitude first, latitude second with a space between them. For example, (-119 30) is 119 west longitudes and 30 north latitude.

11. Many of the instance methods which SQL Server 2008 uses are based on methods defined by the OGC (Open Geospatial Consortium) standard. In the OGC standard, the ST prefix stands for "Spatial-Temporal" (space-time).

    SQL Server follows the ST naming convention for most methods, despite the fact that SQL Server's spatial types don't yet include a time aspect. On the job, you may encounter SQL Server developers who refer to the ST as denoting a **ST**andard method (e.g., Reduce( ) and MakeValid( ) are examples of methods which do not use an ST prefix). Other developers may explain it as standing for **S**ome **T**ype of Geography/Geometry object.

Geometry Data Type

In SQL Server 2008, you have the choice of two spatial data types, **Geography** or **Geometry**. One is better for measuring your own space and creating maps, while the other is better for GPS or other global type measures.

In the last section, we looked at the **Geography** type, which works with GPS and other global-type measurements representing points on the earth and that tend to work with a spherical (globe-shaped) map. However, we need to use a *flat map* to represent land measurement. **Geometry** is the planar spatial data type and the one with which you want to measure smaller areas (i.e., which do not need to factor in the curvature of the earth).

Geometry allows you to make your own custom maps. Perhaps you are interested in plotting out the area included within your property and seeing where items (e.g., landmarks, structures, boundaries, etc.) are in relation to everything else rather than places around the globe. Suppose you have a small industrial plot 28 meters in length and 21 meters in width. Not all of the land is used for a building. There's a parking lot, a woodpile, a warehouse, and a yard around all of it. You want to break your plot down into one square meter increments to map out where everything goes and to keep it in your database for good organization. The **Geometry** data type will help you break down and add a number grid to your new custom map.

Figure 5.35 You have a small industrial plot 28 meters in length and 21 meters in width.

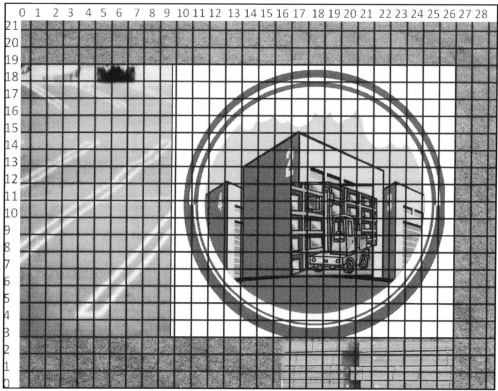

Figure 5.36 The Geometry data type breaks down your new custom map and adds a number grid.

Polygons

The term *polygon* refers to a many-sided object. Squares, rectangles, and triangles are all *polygons*. Making a polygon is like connecting the dots.

Our plot is a perfect rectangle shape, although at times you could have a triangular shaped plot, a hexagon shape, or a perfectly square shaped lot. Since we don't know the shape of it, we're going to call this our polygon, which can mean any enclosed shape. If you draw out the perimeter of your polygon using the **Geometry** data type, it will fill in all the squares for you, so you can plot it out. Our polygon begins at (0, 0), goes all the way to (28, 0), then to (28, 21), to (0, 21), and finally back to (0,0). Creating a rectangular polygon in code is as simple as connecting the 4 dots.

```
--the Yard Polygon code
POLYGON ((0 0, 28 0, 28 21, 0 21, 0 0))
```
This polygon would make a triangle: (0 0, 9 0, 0 5, 0 0).

Now notice that in a polygon, you always start with the same exact coordinates at which you end. Also notice that each coordinate pair is separated with a space and each set of coordinates that helps draw the polygon is separated by a comma. The warehouse (see Figure 5.36) is also a polygon whose dots are at 10 3, 26 3, 26 19, 10 19, 10 3. The **Geometry** data type allows you to go clockwise or counter clockwise (here we went counter clockwise).

Lastly our wood pile is located at (16 0, 26 0, 26 2, 16 2, 16 0).
(Note: we'll handle the parking lot in the Lab at the end of this section.)

Looking at the graph, we can easily answer a few questions.
#1 Is the warehouse inside the coordinates of the yard?
Yes. Result = 1 (yes)
#2 Is the Lumber Area inside the coordinates of the yard?
Yes. Result = 1 (yes)
#3 Is the Lumber Area inside the coordinates of the warehouse?
No. Result = 0 (no)

Creating Geometry as a Field in a Table

Let's take a look at our old familiar HumanResources.RoomChart table (from the JProCo database) and the records it contains. It looks like we have four rooms that are populated. We have a Room ID 5 but we've never put anything in there.

At this time the HumanResources.RoomChart does not hold any mapping or geography type information.

We want to make our own maps to show where these rooms are located, so we're going to add a sixth field, which will be a **Geometry** type.

Run this code. Notice every record now has the ability to store a RoomLocation.

```
ALTER TABLE HumanResources.RoomChart
ADD RoomLocation GEOMETRY NULL
```

Figure 5.37 Every record now has the ability to store a RoomLocation (data type Geometry).

```
SELECT * FROM JProCo.HumanResources.RoomChart
```

	ID	Code	RoomName	RoomDescription	RoomNotes	RoomLocation
1	1	RLT	Renault-Langsford-Tribute	This room is designed for Customer Previews	NULL	NULL
2	2	QTX	Quinault-Experience	Parties and Morale events get top priority	NULL	NULL
3	3	TQW	TranquilWest	misc	NULL	NULL
4	4	XW	XavierWest	NULL	NULL	NULL
5	5	NULL	NULL	NULL	NULL	NULL

Figure 5.38 All records and fields in the JProCo.HumanResources.RoomChart table.

Record 5 is pretty plain - no room name, no code name, etc. So let's catch that record up with the other four records in the table.

```
UPDATE JProCo.HumanResources.RoomChart
  SET Code = 'YRD', RoomName = 'Industrial Yard',
  RoomDescription = 'Holds Lumber and Stocking Warehouse'
  WHERE ID = 5
```

Messages

(1 row(s) affected)

Figure 5.39 This code updates Record 5.

```
SELECT * FROM JProCo.HumanResources.RoomChart
```

	ID	Code	RoomName	RoomDescription	RoomNotes	RoomLocation
1	1	RLT	Renault-Langsford-Tribute	This room is designed for Customer Previews	NULL	NULL
2	2	QTX	Quinault-Experience	Parties and Morale events get top priority	NULL	NULL
3	3	TQW	TranquilWest	misc	NULL	NULL
4	4	XW	XavierWest	NULL	NULL	NULL
5	5	YRD	Industrial Yard	Holds Lumber and Stocking Warehouse	NULL	NULL

Figure 5.40 Record 5 has been updated.

Populating a Geometry Data Type

The function STPolyFromText( ) is a *Geometry instance method* which creates a **Geometry** object. We will use this function to create **Geometry** objects in the RoomChart table.

With the five RoomChart (JProCo.HumanResources.RoomChart) records in place, let's start populating some of the room locations.

Let's begin with the Yard, Record 5. Inside the parentheses, we need to specify the polygon code. The 0 at the very end of the sequence is the SRID (spatial reference identifier) for the **Geometry** type. Just like the **Geography** type, planar **Geometry** data can have many SRIDs to choose from. We must be specific about the spatial area ID (which in this case is 0), since we might have different spatial areas. Think of the SRID as a map number. Imagine a 3-story building where we may want to compare Map-0 (the main floor) versus Map-1 or Map-2 (the upper floors)? Whenever we compare two instances of spatial data, they both must have the same SRID.

```
UPDATE JProCo.HumanResources.RoomChart
SET RoomLocation =
GEOMETRY::STPolyFromText('Polygon ((0 0, 28 0, 28 21, 0 21, 0 0))',0)
WHERE ID = 5
```

Figure 5.41 Inside the parentheses, we need to specify the polygon code.

Looks like we have populated some sort of **Geometry** type. The first digit contains the SRID. Now, the next thing is to make some sense of this.

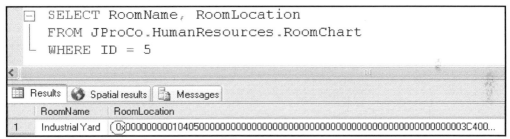

Figure 5.42 Record 5 contains some sort of Geometry type

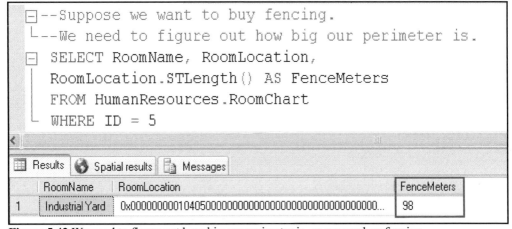

Figure 5.43 We need to figure out how big our perimeter is, so we can buy fencing.

And we see it is 98 meters around the property (see Figure 5.43).

Now what is the area of this property which we own? 588 square meters, which is 28 meters * 21 meters (see Figure 5.44).

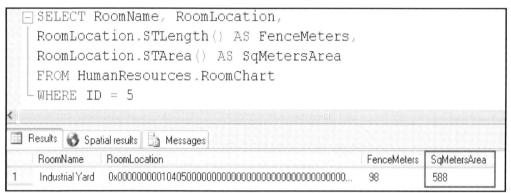

Figure 5.44 The area of the property we own is 588 square meters (28 length * 21 width).

Be aware that some instance method functions, such as STPolyFromText, are case-sensitive. This is noteworthy, since SQL Server is generally case *insensitive* and does not behave differently whether you input code as upper or lower case. The P in Poly should be capitalized. If you make a mistake and include "STpolyFromText" in your code, SQL Server will generate the error shown below (see Figure 5.45).

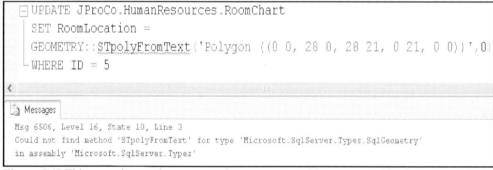

Figure 5.45 This error shows when you use the wrong case with a case-sensitive instance method.

Geometry Functions

You already learned about the STPolyFromText( ) function. There are many more, and an entire book could be dedicated to Spatial Data theory and functions. We are going to talk about STLength( ), STArea( ), and STContains( ).

STLength() and STArea( ) are two of the built-in functions of the **Geometry** data type. Now we're going to add the Warehouse (which sits inside the industrial yard) as the sixth room/record in our table.

Let's put in our switch of 0, which says the Warehouse is in the same space as the Industrial Yard.

```
INSERT INTO JProCo.HumanResources.RoomChart
VALUES (6, 'WRS', 'Warehouse', 'Holds Supplies',null,
GEOMETRY::STPolyFromText('Polygon ((10 3, 26 3, 26 19, 10 19, 10 3))',0))
```
Messages
(1 row(s) affected)

5.46 Add the Warehouse (which sits inside the industrial yard) as Record 6 in our table.

Now we have two records with populated Geometry types in our RoomChart table. Let's repeat the process and make the RoomNumber 7 be the area for the lumber or the wood pile. Include the same area ID as the others (0).

```
INSERT INTO HumanResources.RoomChart
VALUES (7, 'WOD', 'Lumber Area',null,null,
GEOMETRY::STPolyFromText('Polygon ((16 0, 26 0, 26 2, 16 2 ,16 0))',0))
```
Messages
(1 row(s) affected)

Figure 5.47 Make the Room Number 7 be the area for the lumber or the wood pile.

Now we have three different areas: (1) a yard with (2) a warehouse and (3) a lumber area. Let's capture all three areas and then run some built-in comparisons. Ok, we see the values in the table – they're not really readable to the human eye, but at least we see the values are there.

```
DECLARE @Yard GEOMETRY
DECLARE @Warehouse GEOMETRY
DECLARE @Lumber GEOMETRY

SELECT @Yard = RoomLocation
FROM HumanResources.RoomChart
WHERE ID = 5

SELECT @Warehouse = RoomLocation
FROM HumanResources.RoomChart
WHERE ID = 6

SELECT @Lumber = RoomLocation
FROM HumanResources.RoomChart
WHERE ID = 7

SELECT @Yard AS Yard, @Warehouse AS Warehouse, @Lumber AS Lumber
```

| | Results | Spatial results | Messages |

	Yard	Warehouse	Lumber
1	0x0000000001040500000000000...	0x0000000001040500000000000000000002440...	0x0000000001040500000000000000000000003040...

Figure 5.48 We would like to run some built-in comparisons, but these values aren't user-friendly.

Now let's do a more meaningful comparison. I want to look at the Yard and ask myself, *"Does the yard contain a warehouse?"*

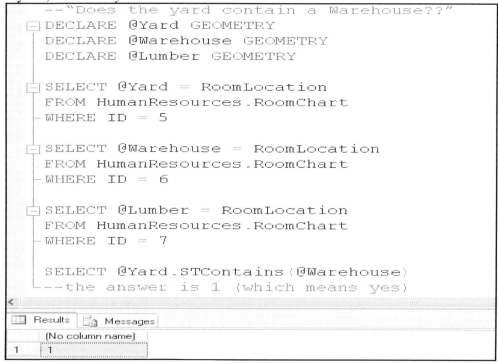

Figure 5.49 "Yes, the yard contains a warehouse."

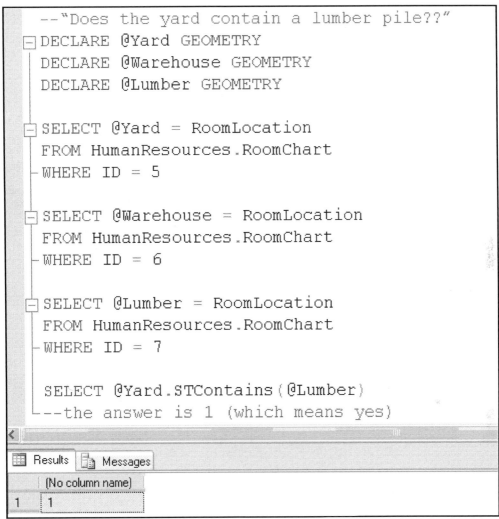

```
--"Does the yard contain a lumber pile??"
DECLARE @Yard GEOMETRY
DECLARE @Warehouse GEOMETRY
DECLARE @Lumber GEOMETRY

SELECT @Yard = RoomLocation
FROM HumanResources.RoomChart
WHERE ID = 5

SELECT @Warehouse = RoomLocation
FROM HumanResources.RoomChart
WHERE ID = 6

SELECT @Lumber = RoomLocation
FROM HumanResources.RoomChart
WHERE ID = 7

SELECT @Yard.STContains(@Lumber)
--the answer is 1 (which means yes)
```

	(No column name)
1	1

Figure 5.50 "Yes, the yard contains a lumber pile."

Finally, let's ask one where we know the answer is No.

```
SELECT @Warehouse.STContains(@Lumber)
--the answer is 0 (which means no)
```

	(No column name)
1	0

Figure 5.51 We know the answer is no. "No, the Warehouse does not contain a lumber pile."

Let's take a look at the RoomChart data as shown in the Spatial Results tab (see Figure 5.52 below). While we cannot save or export results from the Spatial Results tab, it's a handy tool for visualizing our spatial data.

Here we see the tab accompanying a simple query of the RoomChart table with the RoomName field chosen as the label. Any of the table's five fields can serve as the label (e.g., ID, Code, RoomDescription), or you can choose no label.

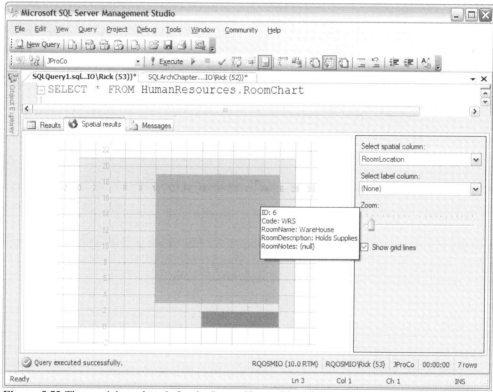

Figure 5.52 The spatial results tab for the RoomChart table using RoomName values as labels.

In the next figure (see Figure 5.53 – next page), we have chosen "None" in the "Select label column" dropdown list. Each of the mouseover tags shows the available label options we can use, which are the fields of the RoomChart table (i.e., ID, Code, RoomName, RoomDescription, and RoomNotes).

For illustrative purposes we've altered this graphic, so that you are able to see all the mouseover tags simultaneously. We have chosen "Code" in the "Select label column" dropdown list. However, SQL Server's normal behavior displays just one tag at a time per mouse over.

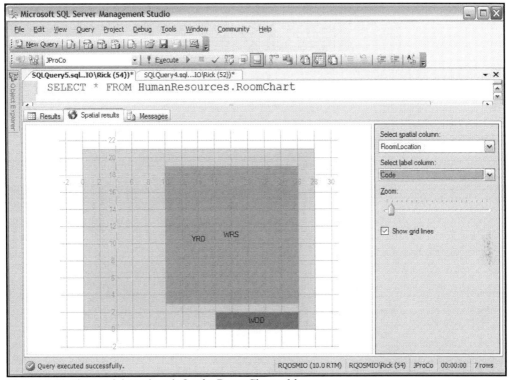

Figure 5.53 The spatial results tab for the RoomChart table.

Lab 5.2: Geometry Data Type

Lab Prep: Before you can begin the lab, you must have SQL Server installed and run the SQLArchChapter5.2Setup.sql script.

Skill Check 1: Add an eighth record to the RoomChart table for the Parking Lot of the Yard Area and populate the correct Geometry coordinates.
Take the parking lot area from the grid you see here and populate an 8th record in the RoomChart with the proper Geometry type.

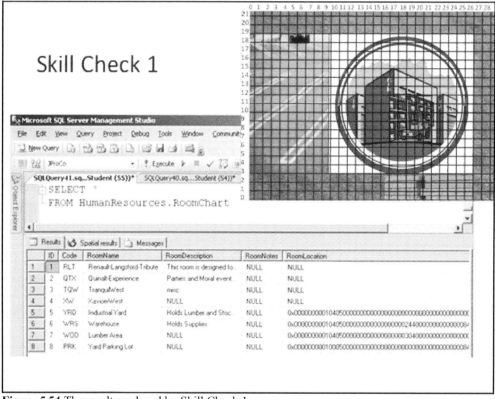

Figure 5.54 The result produced by Skill Check 1.

Skill Check 2: Check to see if the Yard contains the Parking lot. (Should be yes 1.) Also check to see that the Warehouse contains the Parking lot. (Should be no 0.)

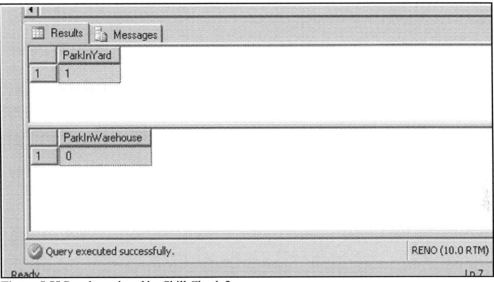

Figure 5.55 Result produced by Skill Check 2.

Answer Code: The T-SQL code to this lab can be found in the downloadable files in a file named Lab5.2_GeometryDataType.sql.

Geometry Data Type - Points to Ponder

1. SQL Server 2008 has two specific spatial data types **Geometry** and **Geography**.

2. The **Geometry** data type stores flat XY grid coordinates for points, lines, and polygons.

3. The **Geography** data type stores round-earth latitude and longitude earth coordinates that represent points, lines, and polygons.

4. The default SRID (spatial reference identifier) for the **Geometry** type is 0.

5. Some instance method functions work with both **Geometry** and **Geography** data. For example, the instance method STDistance can calculate the distance between two **Geometry** or **Geography** coordinates. However, some instance methods work only with Geometry data (e.g., STTouches, STOverlaps, STPointOnSurface, etc.).

6. Be aware that some instance method functions are case-sensitive (e.g., STPolyFromText). This is noteworthy, since SQL Server is generally *case insensitive* and does not behave differently whether you input code as upper or lower case. If you make a mistake and include "STpolyFromText" in your code, SQL Server will generate an error (*Could not find method 'STpolyFromText' for type 'Microsoft.SqlServer.Types.SqlGeometry' in assembly 'Microsoft.SqlServer.Types'*).

7. You can check to see whether two spatial objects have overlapping territory (STOverlaps).

8. Areas of any shape are called polygons.

9. Many of the instance methods which SQL Server 2008 uses are based on methods defined by the OGC (Open Geospatial Consortium) standard. In the OGC standard, the ST prefix stands for "**S**patial-**T**emporal" (space-time).

    SQL Server follows the ST naming convention for most methods, despite the fact that SQL Server's spatial types don't yet include a time aspect. On the job, you may encounter SQL Server developers who refer to the ST as denoting a **ST**andard method (e.g., Reduce( ) and MakeValid( ) are examples of methods which do not use an ST prefix). Other developers may explain it as standing for **S**ome **T**ype of Geography/Geometry object.

Chapter Glossary

Geography: A special data type that can store information for areas and points on the earth.

Geometry: The planar spatial data type and the one with which you want to measure smaller areas (i.e., which do not need to factor in the curvature of the earth).

Geometry instance method: A type of function that creates Geometry objects.

Geospatial data: Types of data, such as latitude and longitude, used in Geography functions.

OGC: An acronym that stands for Open Geospatial Consortium.

Point-static function: A function used in Geography functions.

Polygon: A many-sided object.

Spatial data type: New to 2008, the Geometry and Geography types are both examples of spatial data type.

Spatial reference identifier: A style specifier, also known as SRID, this identifies which spatial reference system the coordinates belong to.

Spatial-temporal: The ST prefix in functions stands for "Spatial-Temporal" (space-time).

SRID: A geography value is also known as a spatial reference identifier, SRID.

Standard method: Some developers refer to the ST as denoting a **ST**andard method while other developers may explain it as standing for **S**ome **T**ype of Geography/Geometry object.

STArea ( ): One of the two built-in functions of the **Geometry** data type**.**

STContains ( ): A SQL function to locate items contained in a Geography function.

STDistance ( ): STDistance( ) is an instance method which returns the closest path between two **Geography** points in meters.

STGeomFromText: ( ): A SQL function that converts text to spatial points. .

STLength ( ): One of the two built-in functions of the **Geometry** data type.

STPolyFromText ( ): This is a Geometry instance method which creates a **Geometry** object.

WKT: WKT stands for **w**ell-**k**nown **t**ext for your position. Representing latitude and longitude with two readable numbers (like 47.5 -122.57) is called Well-Known Text (WKT).

Chapter Five - Review Quiz

1.) You know that SQL Server 2008 has two new special data types. Which data type has a built in method for determining the distance between two points on the earth in meters?

  O a. Geometry
  O b. Geography

2.) You know that SQL Server 2008 has two new special data types. One uses Round-Earth calculation and the other uses planar grid calculation. Which data type uses Round-Earth data for determining the distance between two points on the earth in meters?

  O a. Geometry
  O b. Geography

3.) Which data type is ideal for you to create your own custom maps (e.g., maps of warehouse storage or a sports playing field)?

  O a. Geometry
  O b. Geography

4.) The STDistance function of the Geography Data type calculates the distance between two points in …

  O a. Feet
  O b. Meters
  O c. Kilometers
  O d. Miles
  O e. Units

5.) The Geometry Data type calculates the distance between two points in…

  O a. Feet
  O b. Meters
  O c. Kilometers
  O d. Miles
  O e. Units

6.) Your growing company is dividing areas of the country into sales territories. Your database already has every customer's GPS location stored. You plan to set up sales boundaries and set up a process between for determining the distance between your customers and your nearest store. What is the best data type for this operation?

O a. Geometry
O b. Geography
O c. XML

Answer Key

1.) b   2.) b   3.) a   4.) b   5.) e   6.) b

Bug Catcher Game

To play the Bug Catcher game run the BugCatcher_Chapter05SpatialDatatypes.pps from the BugCatcher folder of the companion files. You can obtain these files from www.Joes2Pros.com or by ordering the Companion CD.

Chapter 6.   Partitioned Tables

Recently I attended a busy SQL Saturday *(www.sqlsaturday.com)* convention in Redmond. Knowing that the lineup of attendees checking in would overwhelm the speed that registration folks could process them, the organizers set up seven check-in desks, much like bank tellers or will-call windows for tickets at a box office.

Each registered person's name was physically stored by last name in a printed list at the registration desk. The volunteer at each desk crossed off the attendee names from the list and handed the attendees their name tags. Instead of having one giant registration table they partitioned it into seven. People still called it the registration desk even though physically it was seven desks.

At the bank, any teller can access my account but at SQL Saturday I had to stand in a particular line. The first line was for people whose last name started with the letters A-D. Since my last name begins with an M, I stood in the L-N line. Logically this was one giant registration desk with seven different storage locations. Each smaller desk had just its own portion of the list (i.e., A-D, E-G, H-K, L-N, O-R, S-U, and V-Z), which made the name lookup faster. Each volunteer only scanned a narrow segment of the list instead of having to flip through all pages of the entire A-Z list each time.

This is pretty much how partitioned tables work where a dataset in a table can be stored across many filegroups. *Logically* the dataset is a single, unified list – like a long list of names A-Z or a large set of records dated between 1977 and 2009 – yet the data is *physically* stored in separate locations.

While the commands CREATE PARTITION FUNCTION and CREATE PARTITION SCHEME (which were introduced in SQL Server 2005) help us to easily define and manage table partitions, the same idea behind datafiles (which we studied in Chapter 1 of this book) is actually the key capability which enables partitioning. In this chapter, we will see that using filegroups and datafiles to control the physical placement of a table's data is at the heart of table partitioning.

READER NOTE: *In order to follow along with the examples in the first section of Chapter 6, please run the setup script SQLArchChapter6.0Setup.sql. The setup scripts for this book are posted at Joes2Pros.com.*

Giant Tables

In your database career, you will encounter tables which always remain small (e.g., lookup tables and mapping tables). Activity tables, however, can grow to contain millions or billions of transaction records. These are known as *giant tables*. Oftentimes government organizations and businesses that do extensive analyses rely on historical data and need it to reside with the current data. In fact, data warehouses typically include large, denormalized tables for this reason.

As a database professional, you must be aware of the space and processing needs of your tables. Your familiarity with each table's expected workload and space requirements will guide your decision whether to allow it to be stored in the default filegroup or whether it should be located in a separate filegroup.

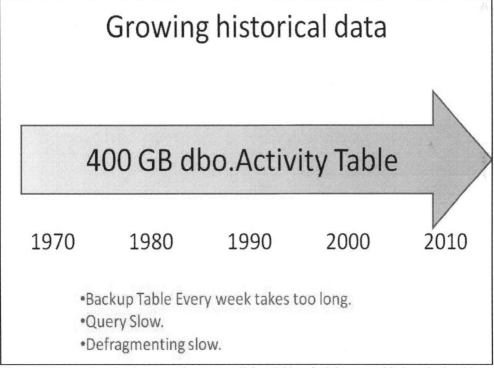

Figure 6.1 Sometimes business requirements call for all historical data to reside in a single table.

For readers unfamiliar with large tables, let's consider how an Activity table might get to be so large. Imagine a small, locally owned supermarket which features organic and locally produced foods. This store is popular and very busy but is able to manage the demand with just one store location from the time it opens in 1977 until 1991. The owners decide to add a second location in 1992 when demand outgrows the first location.

The data for both stores is kept in a single database, which the office operations manager maintains weekly. This manager also programs the cash registers and spends most of his time working with suppliers, so he and the rest of the management team have decided they want the database to be a very simple, low maintenance item. The office operations manager runs one simple sales report from the Activity table (dbo.Activity) and backs up the database to tape each Friday.

Even with two store locations, the amount of data remains fairly low. The employee table is fairly small; besides the centralized management team, each store has just 15 employees. The supplier data also is relatively small, since the same 650 suppliers provide all the stock for both locations. The sales activity data comprises the largest volume of data in the database. Despite the addition of thousands of records per day (one for each purchase receipt), the volume of data in dbo.Activity remains fairly manageable. Since the second store was added, they've needed to upgrade the hard drive every three years, or so, to accommodate the growing database and give it more storage space. The weekly report and backup process used to take less than an hour, but over the years the time needed for this cycle has steadily increased. By 2003, the weekly report query takes 90 minutes to run. The office operations manager runs the weekly database backup overnight, since it takes about eight hours to complete. For some time, he's been concerned about the size of dbo.Activity and the growing length of time required for querying and backups.

Why are backups and queries against this giant table taking longer? Each time the office operations manager performs a task involving dbo.Activity, he essentially is touching over 25 years of data. The database has to scan decades worth of data in order to pull a report for the last seven days. Defragmenting maintenance on this table would take several days instead of a few minutes.

What if the routine maintenance tasks and queries could be run again just the most recent year of data? By physically segmenting this data, many of the problems with the dbo.Activity table could be solved.

Creating Separate Tables

What if you created two separate tables, dbo.PastActivity and dbo.CurrentActivity? This would really speed up the weekly reporting and table maintenance routine (see Figure 6.2 – next page).

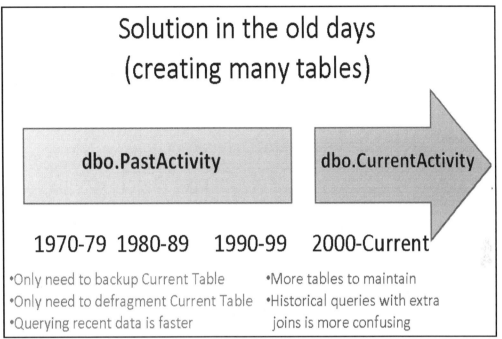

Figure 6.2 There are pros and cons to the outdated solution of creating separate tables.

Since the dbo.PastActivity table would not change at all, it would not need routine maintenance. The weekly defrag (short for defragmentation) jobs on the dbo.CurrentActivity table would only take a fraction of the time versus processing decades worth of data. The downside is that you now have two tables to UNION in historical reporting queries. Query time for historical queries is very slow, and more complex code adds to development time and/or expense.

Creating separate tables to ease the workload of a giant table is now an outdated solution, given the new ability in SQL Server 2005 to easily partition large tables.

Overview of Partitioned Tables

Suppose you could have a table that stores its data across multiple filegroups. This way you could have a single dbo.Activity table for all data to make writing queries easy. You could also store the 2010 data on an fgActivity2010 filegroup. All other data could be stored on another filegroup. Your backup and maintenance plans will just run against the 2010 data, which is physically stored in its own area. This is what partitioned tables offer: many physically stored table areas rolling up to one table name.

The concept of partitioning is not new to SQL Server. In fact, some form of partitioning has been possible in every release of the product. However, partitioning has traditionally been cumbersome and thus underutilized by DBAs as a strategy. Because of the significant performance gains inherent in the concept, SQL Server 7.0 began improving the feature by enabling forms of partitioning through partitioned views (but not tables).

While the improvements in SQL Server 7.0 and SQL Server 2000 significantly enhanced performance when using partitioned views, they did not simplify the administration, design, or development of a partitioned dataset. When using partitioned views, all of the base tables (on which the view is defined) must be created and managed individually.

With SQL Server 2005 came a much more accessible and workable process, and SQL Server 2008 now offers the most advanced method for partitioning large datasets through partitioned tables (see Figure 6.3).

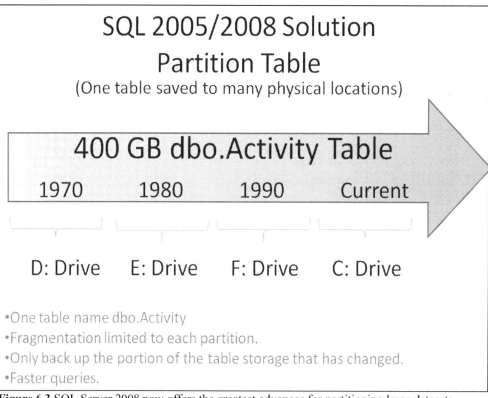

Figure 6.3 SQL Server 2008 now offers the greatest advances for partitioning large datasets.

Partitioning

Partitioning is the dividing of an object, such as a table, into parts.

1 cut = 2 partitions.
1 boundary value yields 2 boundary ranges.

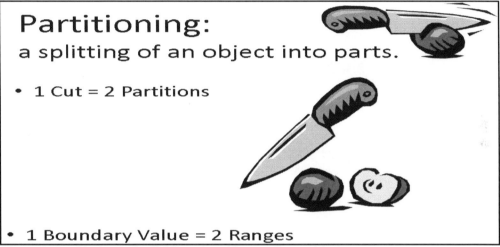

Figure 6.4 Partitioning is the dividing of an object, such as a table, into parts.

My MCTS prep students find the apple cutting analogy a helpful visual when we first approach the concept of partitioning. We refer to each *boundary value* as a "cut" throughout the lesson and to *partition functions* as the knife-like tool which creates these "cuts" (boundary values).

However, the nature of partitioning a table is slightly different from slicing apart an apple into sections which are then permanently separated. After you partition a table, it remains a single, unified object with its underlying data contained in separate filegroups. This allows the table to function logically as a single object, while its data is physically stored in separate locations.

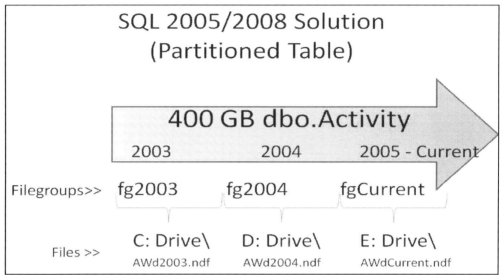

Figure 6.5 A partitioned table is a single object with its data contained in separate filegroups.

Thus, you might say partitioning a table is more like partitioning a room than slicing an apple. Adding one room divider creates two smaller rooms; two room dividers create three smaller rooms; and so forth. In the next section of this chapter, we'll also see that these partitions can be revised or even removed altogether.

First we will examine each component of the partitioning process (the partition function, the partition scheme, the filegroups, and the datafiles), and then we will create an actual partition using the SalesInvoice table of the JProCo database.

[Note – if you haven't already read Chapter 1 on Database File Structures, it is highly recommended you review that chapter, particularly the section on filegroups.]

Partition Functions

The first new tool we will encounter is the partition function, which is the tool we use to create the boundary "cuts." The number of n cuts will create $n + 1$ partitions.

- One cut divides an apple into two halves.
- Two room dividers create three smaller rooms.
- Two "cuts" divide the table in Figure 6.5 into three partitions.
- Six "cuts" would be needed to divide the conference list into seven segments A-D, E-G, H-K, L-N, O-R, S-U, and V-Z (one boundary between D and E, one between G and H, between K and L, between N and O, between R and S, and finally between U and V).

The partition function simply marks the dividing line(s) for the data. Four items are needed in order to partition a table: A) one or more boundary values created by a partition function, B) two or more data ranges defined by a partition scheme, C) one filegroup for each range, and D) one datafile for each range.

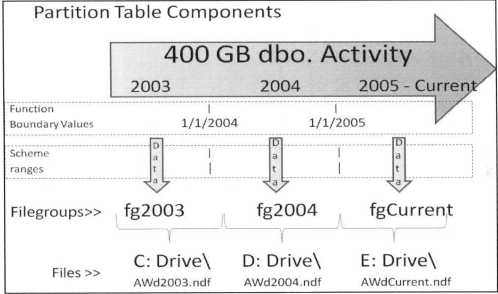

Figure 6.6 The sample table and the four main items needed to partition a table.

Let's look at our sample Activity table (see Figure 6.6), which contains three partitions (2003, 2004, and 2005 to current). Three partitions means there must be two boundary value "cuts" (i.e., one cut at 1/1/2004 and one cut at 1/1/2005). Everything to the left of the first boundary (1/1/2004) will be 2003 data, and the 2004 data will fall to the right of that boundary.

We will also have another boundary value at 1/1/2005. The 2004 data will fall to the left of this boundary, and to the right will be data from 2005, or later.

When we step through the demonstration, we will see the T-SQL keywords RANGE RIGHT and RANGE LEFT handle the placement of edge data which would land on the boundaries (e.g., records on 1/1/2004 or 1/1/2005).

Partition Schemes

At the SQL Saturday convention, I needed to follow the signs and evaluate which sign-in desk I should go to. Since my last name begins with the letter M, I recognized the L-N desk as the appropriate line to stand in. If attendees got confused, there was a helper standing by asking attendees their last name and directing them to the right group.

This person was aware of the name divisions (i.e., the boundary values) set up by the function and based on a last name pointed each attendee to the right group. This is what the *partition scheme* does. Based on its knowledge of how the data is divided up by the partition function, the partition scheme guides the data into the proper filegroup.

The partition scheme derives the boundary ranges from the partition function. The T-SQL code for the partition scheme shows it mapping the data into the filegroups based upon the boundary values contained in the partition function (see Figure 6.7).

The following pseudo code is based upon our sample table, dbo.Activity (see Figures 6.5 and 6.6). ***This code is for illustrative purposes only and will not run.***

```
--Pseudocode to create the Partition Function
--for our sample Transaction table (Figures 6.5 and 6.6)
CREATE PARTITION FUNCTION pf_TransactionDate (datetime)
AS RANGE RIGHT -->edge data falls to the right of the boundary
FOR VALUES ('1/1/2004', '1/1/2005')
-->2 boundaries, therefore 3 partitions.


--Pseudocode to create the Partition Scheme
CREATE PARTITION SCHEME ps_TransactionDate
AS PARTITION pf_TransactionDate
TO (fg2003, fg2004, fgCurrent)
-->3 partitions = 3 filegroups
```

Figure 6.7 Pseudo code creating a partition function & partition scheme based on our sample table.

Data Storage Areas

The partition scheme is going to expect that, since you made *n* cuts, you will have *n + 1* partitions. Therefore, it's going to require *n + 1* filegroups, which you must create before you run the partition scheme code.

Each filegroup is associated with a secondary datafile (NDF), which you place on the drive where you want it stored. As you can see from the pseudo code in Figure 6.7, the partition scheme maps the data into the filegroups. The filegroups then direct the data into the proper physical storage location.

While our "Overview of Partition Tables" discussion ends by talking about filegroups and storage locations, our demonstration in the next section will create each item in sequence to partition the table JProCo.dbo.SalesInvoice. SQL Server won't allow you to create the partition scheme without first creating the filegroups, so our best practice recommendation is to create the filegroups and storage areas first. Since we know the partition scheme maps data between the partition function and the filegroups, SQL Server won't let us write the partition scheme without the partition function. Step (A) of Figure 6.8 is the getting the datafiles and groups ready. Step (B) is where you decide the boundary values. Step (C) directs the data into the storage areas you set up in Step (A).

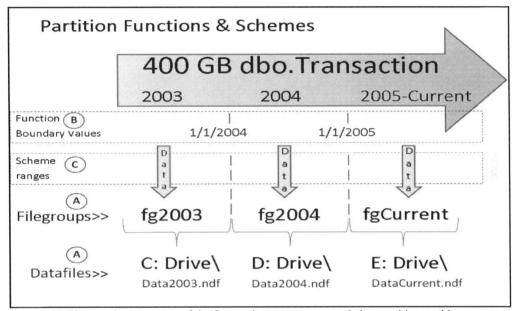

Figure 6.8 The creation sequence of the four main components needed to partition a table.

Creating Partitioned Tables

Note: this demonstration utilizes a D, E, F, G, and H drive. For nearly all readers, it's unlikely you have these drives available. To approximate the effect of having multiple storage drives, we will use folders on the C drive to represent each "drive." In order to follow along with the demonstration, create these five folders on your hard drive: C:\D_SQL, C:\E_SQL, C:\F_SQL, C:\G_SQL, C:\H_SQL.

Creating Filegroups

Let's look at our JProCo SalesInvoice table. It has 1885 records – not a giant table by any means. For our demonstration purposes, we'll suppose SalesInvoice is on the order of a 200 million record table, which we need to divide to improve its performance.

Figure 6.9 shows approximately how many records SalesInvoice currently contains and how we ought to divide this table. Your results for 2009 and 2010 might differ a little because the SQLArchChapter6.0Setup.sql reset script generates dates dynamically.

```
SELECT * FROM JProCo.dbo.SalesInvoice

SELECT DATEPART(yy,OrderDate), COUNT(*)
FROM JProCo.dbo.SalesInvoice
GROUP BY DATEPART(yy,OrderDate)
ORDER BY DATEPART(yy,OrderDate)
```

	InvoiceID	OrderDate	PaidDate	CustomerID	Comment
1	1	2006-01-03 00:00:00.000	2006-01-11 03:22:44.587	472	NULL
2	2	2006-01-04 02:22:41.473	2006-02-01 04:15:34.590	388	NULL
3	3	2006-01-04 05:33:01.150	2006-02-14 13:45:02.580	279	NULL
4	4	2006-01-04 22:06:58.657	2006-02-08 22:06:14.247	309	NULL
5	5	2006-01-05 11:37:45.597	2006-02-10 20:01:26.540	757	NULL
6	6	2006-01-06 23:53:14.320	2006-01-28 22:48:05.997	493	NULL

	(No column name)	(No column name)
1	2006	438
2	2007	455
3	2008	469
4	2009	456
5	2010	67

Figure 6.9 Review the number of SalesInvoice records and how we might divide this table.

Since there are approximately the same number of records for each previous year in the table, we will create one filegroup/datafile pair for each year (2006, 2007, 2008, 2009, and 2010) on its own drive.

Note: it would be rare (and generally not a good practice) to find filegroups with non-specific names in a live database (i.e., "Old", "Current", "ThisYear", "LastYear"). However, for illustrative purposes in this chapter we refer to the filegroup and datafile containing the newest data as "Current."

Since we want to store our data by year, we're going to create filegroups called fg2006, fg2007, fg2008, fg2009, and fg2010 (see Figure 6.10).

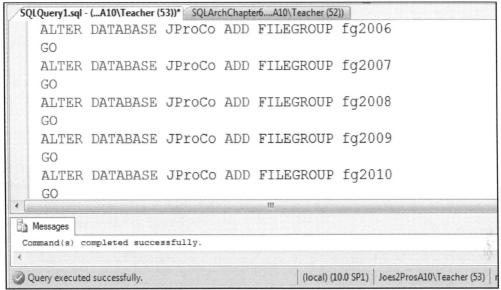

Figure 6.10 We're going to create a filegroup for each year of our data.

Let's look at the filegroups we've created.
Object Explorer > Databases > right-click **JProCo** > Properties > Filegroups (page)

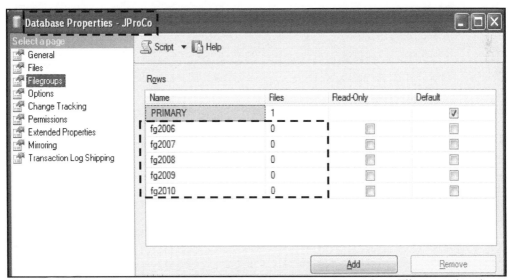

Figure 6.11 Object Explorer > Databases > right-click **JProCo** > Properties > Filegroups (page)

We see all five new filegroups we just created, yet they currently hold no files. *The new filegroups aren't yet capable of storing data until we create the datafiles.*

Creating Datafiles for the Filegroups

Let's first create the 2006 NDF file and store it on the D drive. Any data sent to the fg2006 filegroup will be stored in this NDF file on the D drive (logical name "Data2006", filepath C:\D_SQL\D2006.ndf).

```
ALTER DATABASE JProCo
ADD FILE
(NAME = Data2006, FILENAME = 'C:\D_SQL\D2006.ndf')
TO FILEGROUP fg2006
```

```
Messages
Command(s) completed successfully.
```

Figure 6.12 Let's first create the 2006 NDF file and store it on the D drive.

We see one file in this filegroup (see Figure 6.13) in the Filegroups page of the Database Properties.

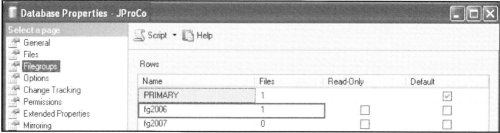

Figure 6.13 We now see one file in this filegroup.

The Files page in Figure 6.14 shows this file Data2006 is located on the D drive.

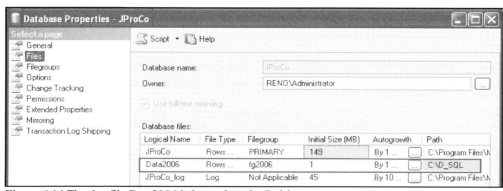

Figure 6.14 The datafile Data2006 is located on the D drive.

Now let's repeat this process to create the remainder of the secondary files we need. *Be sure you have created all the "drive" folders on your C drive, or else SQL Server will generate an error when you attempt the following code.*

```
ALTER DATABASE JProCo
ADD FILE (NAME = data2006, FILENAME = 'C:\D_SQL\D2006.ndf')
TO FILEGROUP fg2006
GO

ALTER DATABASE JProCo
ADD FILE (NAME = data2007, FILENAME = 'C:\E_SQL\D2007.ndf')
TO FILEGROUP fg2007
GO

ALTER DATABASE JProCo
ADD FILE (NAME = Data2008, FILENAME = 'C:\F_SQL\D2008.ndf')
TO FILEGROUP fg2008
GO

ALTER DATABASE JProCo
ADD FILE (NAME = Data2009, FILENAME = 'C:\G_SQL\D2009.ndf')
TO FILEGROUP fg2009
GO

ALTER DATABASE JProCo
ADD FILE (NAME = Data2010, FILENAME = 'C:\H_SQL\D2010.ndf')
TO FILEGROUP fg2010
GO
```

Messages
Command(s) completed successfully.

Query executed successfully.   (local) (10.0 SP1) Joes2ProsA10\Teacher (53) master 00:00:0
                                                    Ln 29   Col 1   Ch 1

Figure 6.15 Create the remaining four secondary files we need.

Creating Partitioned Functions

Now that we've created the filegroups and the underlying datafiles to contain our data, we're ready to define the boundaries. Since we have five partitions, we know there will be four boundary values. We want to use the OrderDate field (see Figure 6.9) to determine the partition into which each record in the SalesInvoice table should go.

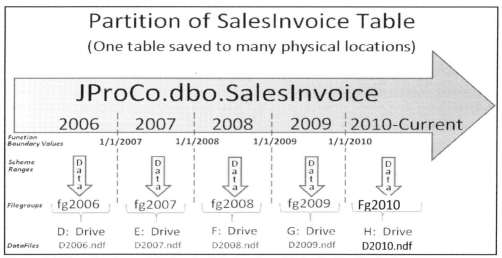

Figure 6.16 Our plan for partitioning the SalesInvoice table in the JProCo database.

The following code creates the four boundary values using the partition function. The boundary values are driven by the OrderDate field (see Figure 6.17).

```
CREATE PARTITION FUNCTION pf_OrderDate (datetime)
AS RANGE RIGHT
FOR VALUES ('1/1/2007', '1/1/2008', '1/1/2009', '1/1/2010')
```

```
Messages
Command(s) completed successfully.
```

Figure 6.17 Create the partition function pf_OrderDate using the RANGE RIGHT option.

Note the RANGE RIGHT code. This is an instruction that any data which ties with a boundary value should fall to the right of the boundary. For example, a record in the SalesInvoice table with an OrderDate of 1/1/2007 should fall into the 2007 partition. If the code had been written RANGE LEFT, then in this case the record with an OrderDate of 1/1/2007 would fall into the 2006 partition.

Creating Partitioned Schemes

Now we are ready to create the **partition scheme**. Since the partition scheme can't be created until after the filegroups and partition function are in place, the partition scheme is the last new item to be created in sequence. The partition scheme must reference the partition function and the filegroups (see Figure 6.18).

```
USE JProCo
GO

CREATE PARTITION SCHEME ps_OrderDate
 AS PARTITION pf_OrderDate
 TO (fg2006, fg2007, fg2008, fg2009, fg2010)
```

Messages

Command(s) completed successfully.

Figure 6.18 The partition scheme must reference the partition function and the filegroups.

None of the steps we've taken so far, or objects we've created, has altered the original SalesInvoice table. Our final step which brings everything together is to create a copy of the SalesInvoice table utilizing the partition scheme.

```
SQLQuery1.sql - (...A10\Teacher (53))*   SQLArchChapter6...0\Teacher (52))*
CREATE TABLE dbo.SalesInvoiceHorizontal
  (   [InvoiceID] [int] NOT NULL,
      [OrderDate] [datetime] NOT NULL,
      [PaidDate] [datetime] NOT NULL,
      [CustomerID] [int] NOT NULL,
      [Comment] [ntext] NULL,)
ON ps_OrderDate(OrderDate)
GO
```

Messages

Command(s) completed successfully.

Query executed successfully.   (local) (10.0 SP1)   Joes2Pro

Figure 6.19 Create the table **SalesInvoiceHorizontal** which has the same metadata as SalesInvoice.

This table is very similar to the original table, SalesInvoice, except it doesn't yet contain any data. SalesInvoiceHorizontal is identically structured with the same field names and data types. The only differences are: 1) the new table name, 2) the specification of the partition scheme in the table definition, and 3.) The new table cannot have an identity key or a primary key.

We will insert all the records from the SalesInvoice table into this new, partitioned table. **SalesInvoiceHorizontal** will store all existing and new records according to the partition scheme ps_OrderDate (OrderDate) and route each record to the correct filegroup. (The SalesInvoice table can then be retired or archived.)

When we insert all the records from SalesInvoice into the new table (see Figures 6.20 and 6.21), any new sales invoice records will be added to the SalesInvoiceHorizontal table. If we had wanted to retain the same SalesInvoice name for the final partitioned table, we could have done that by adding a step to rename the original table. We could have either renamed it (or a copy of it) SalesInvoice_copy and then our insert step (see Figure 6.20) would have inserted the records into JProCo.dbo.SalesInvoice.

```
INSERT INTO JProCo.dbo.SalesInvoiceHorizontal
SELECT * FROM JProCo.dbo.SalesInvoice
```

Messages

(1885 row(s) affected)

Figure 6.20 Insert all the records from SalesInvoice into the new **SalesInvoiceHorizontal** table.

```
SELECT * FROM JProCo.dbo.SalesInvoiceHorizontal
```

Results | Messages

	InvoiceID	OrderDate	PaidDate	CustomerID	Comment
1	1	2006-01-03 00:00:00.000	2006-01-11 03:22:44.587	472	NULL
2	2	2006-01-04 02:22:41.473	2006-02-01 04:15:34.590	388	NULL
3	3	2006-01-04 05:33:01.150	2006-02-14 13:45:02.580	279	NULL
4	4	2006-01-04 22:06:58.657	2006-02-08 22:06:14.247	309	NULL
5	5	2006-01-05 11:37:45.597	2006-02-10 20:01:26.540	757	NULL
6	6	2006-01-06 23:53:14.320	2006-01-28 22:48:05.997	493	NULL
7	7	2006-01-08 08:06:33.210	2006-02-05 08:41:58.453	209	NULL
8	8	2006-01-08 13:04:13.613	2006-02-17 06:43:18.010	649	NULL
9	9	2006-01-08 21:46:03.093	2006-01-27 04:05:01.967	597	NULL
10	10	2006-01-09 20:33:07.380	2006-02-20 15:50:04.133	736	NULL

Query executed successfully.   JProCo   00:00:00   1885 rows

Figure 6.21 All 1885 records now appear in the new **SalesInvoiceHorizontal** table.

Viewing Partitioned Table Information

The SalesInvoiceHorizontal table is now populated with all the records from the SalesInvoice table. The 2006 data is stored in the 2006 filegroup, and the same is true for the 2007 data, the 2008 data, and so forth. How do we prove this?

The **$Partition** function allows us to see exactly which partition each record is stored on (see Figure 6.22).

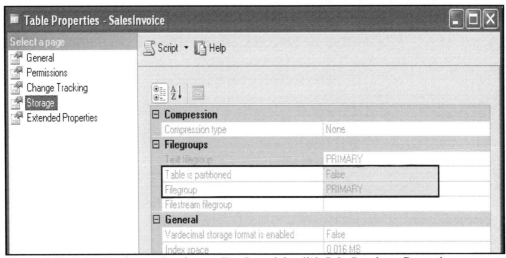

```
SELECT $Partition.Pf_OrderDate(OrderDate), *
 FROM dbo.SalesInvoiceHorizontal
```

	(No column name)	InvoiceID	OrderDate	PaidDate	CustomerID	Comment
1	1	1	2006-01-03 00:00:00.000	2006-01-11 03:22:44.587	472	NULL
2	1	2	2006-01-04 02:22:41.473	2006-02-01 04:15:34.590	388	NULL
3	1	3	2006-01-04 05:33:01.150	2006-02-14 13:45:02.580	279	NULL
4	1	4	2006-01-04 22:06:58.657	2006-02-08 22:06:14.247	309	NULL
5	1	5	2006-01-05 11:37:45.597	2006-02-10 20:01:26.540	757	NULL
6	1	6	2006-01-06 23:53:14.320	2006-01-28 22:48:05.997	493	NULL
7	1	7	2006-01-08 08:06:33.210	2006-02-05 08:41:58.453	209	NULL

Figure 6.22 With $Partition we can see which partition each record is stored on.

Let's compare the properties of the original SalesInvoice table versus the new partitioned table. The Storage page of the Table Properties dialog shows the SalesInvoice table is stored in the PRIMARY filegroup and is not partitioned.

Figure 6.23 Object Explorer > Database > JProCo > right-click **SalesInvoice** > Properties

The Storage page of the Table Properties dialog shows SalesInvoiceHorizontal is a partitioned table, has five partitions, and uses the partition scheme ps_OrderDate on the partition column, OrderDate (see Figure 6.24).

Object Explorer > Database > JProCo > right-click **SalesInvoiceHorizontal** > Properties

Figure 6.24 SalesInvoiceHorizontal is partitioned using ps_OrderDate and has five partitions.

We can also use the **$Partition** function to filter our results. In Figure 6.25 on the next page, we see **$Partition** used to filter just the 469 records in the third partition (the 2008 data) of SalesInvoiceHorizontal.

In Figure 6.26 (next page), we similarly see just the records from the third partition (the 2008 data) of SalesInvoiceHorizontal. To this query, we have also added a column (PartitionNum) to show the partition number for each record and a DateYear field to parse just the year from the OrderDate field.

```
SELECT *
  FROM dbo.SalesInvoiceHorizontal
  WHERE $Partition.Pf_OrderDate(OrderDate) = 3
```

	InvoiceID	OrderDate	PaidDate	CustomerID	Comment
1	894	2008-01-01 08:11:26.203	2008-02-03 22:03:23.883	674	NULL
2	895	2008-01-02 01:30:15.273	2008-02-09 14:35:00.270	484	NULL
3	896	2008-01-03 10:41:02.690	2008-01-21 07:47:15.330	566	NULL
4	897	2008-01-03 14:39:27.380	2008-02-04 17:14:19.083	57	NULL
5	898	2008-01-04 16:26:31.203	2008-02-08 17:00:52.660	426	NULL
6	899	2008-01-05 23:18:32.030	2008-02-10 20:40:26.757	141	NULL
7	900	2008-01-07 11:37:55.883	2008-02-02 13:57:50.617	26	NULL
8	901	2008-01-08 04:44:23.323	2008-02-13 23:51:07.247	134	NULL

Q...   JProCo 00:00:00 469 rows

Figure 6.25 Show only records from Partition 3 in the SalesInvoiceHorizontal table.

```
SELECT $Partition.Pf_OrderDate(OrderDate)
  AS PartitionNum, DATEPART (yy, OrderDate) AS DateYear, *
  FROM dbo.SalesInvoiceHorizontal
  WHERE $Partition.Pf_OrderDate(OrderDate) = 3
```

	PartitionNum	DateYear	InvoiceID	OrderDate	PaidDate	CustomerID	Comment
1	3	2008	894	2008-01-01 08:11:26.203	2008-02-03 22:03:23.883	674	NULL
2	3	2008	895	2008-01-02 01:30:15.273	2008-02-09 14:35:00.270	484	NULL
3	3	2008	896	2008-01-03 10:41:02.690	2008-01-21 07:47:15.330	566	NULL
4	3	2008	897	2008-01-03 14:39:27.380	2008-02-04 17:14:19.083	57	NULL
5	3	2008	898	2008-01-04 16:26:31.203	2008-02-08 17:00:52.660	426	NULL
6	3	2008	899	2008-01-05 23:18:32.030	2008-02-10 20:40:26.757	141	NULL
7	3	2008	900	2008-01-07 11:37:55.883	2008-02-02 13:57:50.617	26	NULL
8	3	2008	901	2008-01-08 04:44:23.323	2008-02-13 23:51:07.247	134	NULL
9	3	2008	902	2008-01-08 13:30:42.900	2008-02-07 20:44:34.513	55	NULL
10	3	2008	903	2008-01-09 22:05:20.340	2008-01-26 03:23:43.530	674	NULL

Query executed successfully.   JProCo 00:00:00 469 rows

Figure 6.26 Verify that Partition 3 of the SalesInvoiceHorizontal table contains records from 2008.

Lab 6.1: Creating Partitioned Tables

Lab Prep: Before you can begin the lab, you must have SQL Server installed and run the SQLArchChapter6.1Setup.sql script.

Skill Check 1: This skill check assumes you have created the folders C:\D_SQL and C:\E_SQL (i.e., in place of an available D:\ and E:\ drives). Achieve the following tasks.
1. Create a partitioned table name dbo.CurrentProductsHorizontal (no IDENTITY field – see note below)
2. Partition the table on the OriginationDate field
3. Store all data from 2000 to the end of 2005 on the D:\ drive in ProdThru2005.ndf
4. Store all data after Dec 31, 2005 in the E:\ drive in Prod2010.ndf
5. Create two new filegroups, fgProdThru2005 and fgProdThru2010
6. Pump all existing records from CurrentProducts into the new table, CurrentProductsHorizontal

Hint: these six requirements do not necessarily appear in order of your creation sequence. As mentioned in the chapter lesson and demonstration, certain items must be in place before you can create the partition function and/or the partition scheme.

Create the new field without the IDENTITY property. Notice that the ProductID field of CurrentProducts is an IDENTITY field. Your ProductID field in the new table, CurrentProductsHorizontal, should not be an IDENTITY field.

When you've completed all the requirements, your database properties dialog will resemble the following two figures (see Figures 6.27 and 6.28 (next page)).

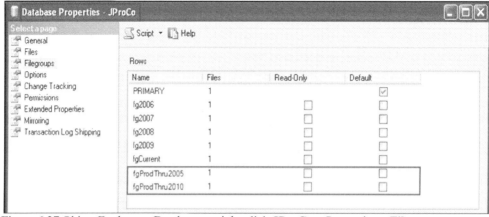

Figure 6.27 Object Explorer > Databases > right-click **JProCo** > Properties > **Filegroups** page.

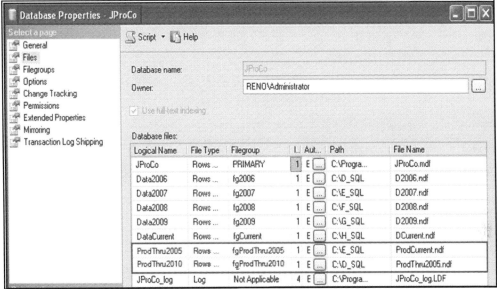

Figure 6.28 Object Explorer > Databases > right-click **JProCo** > Properties > **Files** page.

When you've completed all the requirements, the JProCo Storage folder in Object Explorer will display a new partition scheme and partition function (see Figure 6.29).

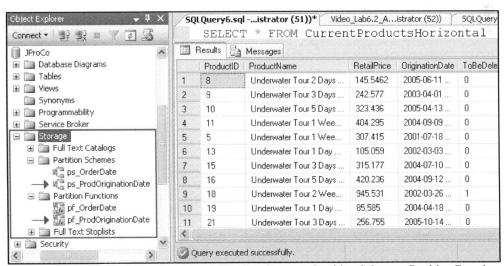

Figure 6.29 Object Explorer> Databases>JProCo> Storage> Partition Schemes, Partition Functions.

Skill Check 2: Using your result from Skill Check 1, write a query showing all fields and all records from your new table, CurrentProductsHorizontal. Add two new fields to your query, as shown below (Figure 6.30).

	PartitionNum	DateYear	ProductID	ProductName	RetailPrice	OriginationDate	ToBeDeleted	Category	SupplierID	OriginationOffset
1	1	2001	5	Underwater Tour 1 Week...	307.415	2001-07-18 ...	0	LongTerm-Stay	0	2001-07-18 19:...
2	1	2001	22	Underwater Tour 5 Days ...	342.34	2001-08-16 ...	0	Medium-Stay	2	2001-08-16 05:...
3	1	2001	96	Fruit Tasting Tour 2 Wee...	773.397	2001-07-24 ...	1	LongTerm-Stay	0	2001-07-24 10:...
4	1	2001	122	Mountain Lodge 2 Days ...	161.1018	2001-09-03 ...	0	Overnight-Stay	0	2001-09-03 15:...
5	1	2001	189	Horseback Tour 3 Days E...	125.937	2001-09-22 ...	0	Medium-Stay	1	2001-09-22 11:...
6	1	2001	196	Horseback Tour 5 Days ...	393.324	2001-08-25 ...	0	Medium-Stay	3	2001-08-25 16:...
7	1	2001	272	Acting Lessons Tour 2 Da...	200.4588	2001-09-05 ...	0	Overnight-Stay	0	2001-09-05 19:...
8	1	2001	262	Winter Tour 5 Days Canada	362.78	2001-11-10 ...	0	Medium-Stay	2	2001-11-10 01:...
9	1	2001	290	Acting Lessons Tour 2 Da...	142.11	2001-12-27 ...	0	Overnight-Stay	2	2001-12-27 21:...
10	1	2001	292	Acting Lessons Tour 5 Da...	315.80	2001-07-06 ...	0	Medium-Stay	2	2001-07-06 12:...
11	1	2001	303	Cherry Festival Tour 3 Da...	205.656	2001-11-03 ...	0	Medium-Stay	0	2001-11-03 10:...

Query executed successfully.　　　　　　　　　　　　　　JProCo　00:00:00　485 rows

Figure 6.30 Show all records and add two new fields to the CurrentProducts Horizontal query.

Skill Check 3: Modify your previous query (Skill Check 2) to show just the 239 records from Partition #1, as shown below (Figure 6.31).

	PartitionNum	ProductID	ProductName	RetailPri...	OriginationDate	ToBeDeleted	Category	SupplierID	OriginationOffset
1	1	8	Underwater Tour 2 Days Eas...	145.5462	2005-06-11 ...	0	Overnight-S...	1	2005-06-11 09:...
2	1	9	Underwater Tour 3 Days Eas...	242.577	2003-04-01 ...	0	Medium-Stay	1	2003-04-01 04:...
3	1	10	Underwater Tour 5 Days Eas...	323.436	2005-04-13 ...	0	Medium-Stay	1	2005-04-13 04:...
4	1	11	Underwater Tour 1 Week Ea...	404.295	2004-09-09 ...	0	LongTerm-...	1	2004-09-09 13:...
5	1	5	Underwater Tour 1 Week W...	307.415	2001-07-18 ...	0	LongTerm-...	0	2001-07-18 19:...
6	1	13	Underwater Tour 1 Day Mexi...	105.059	2002-03-03 ...	0	No-Stay	3	2002-03-03 01:...
7	1	15	Underwater Tour 3 Days Me...	315.177	2004-07-10 ...	0	Medium-Stay	3	2004-07-10 05:...
8	1	16	Underwater Tour 5 Days Me...	420.236	2004-09-12 ...	0	Medium-Stay	3	2004-09-12 09:...
9	1	18	Underwater Tour 2 Weeks M...	945.531	2002-03-26 ...	1	LongTerm-...	3	2002-03-26 14:...
10	1	19	Underwater Tour 1 Day Can...	85.585	2004-04-18 ...	0	No-Stay	2	2004-04-18 16:...
11	1	21	Underwater Tour 3 Days Can...	256.755	2005-10-14 ...	0	Medium-Stay	2	2005-10-14 21:...

Query executed successfully.　　　　　　　　　　　　　　JProCo　00:00:00　239 rows

Figure 6.31 Show the records for first partition of the CurrentProductsHorizontal table.

Answer Code: The T-SQL code to this lab can be found in the downloadable files in a file named Lab6.1_CreatingPartitionedTables.sql.

Creating Partitioned Tables - Points to Ponder

1. You can partition a logical set of data into multiple physical storage locations for manageability and performance.

2. Partitions were introduced in SQL Server 2005. Both SQL Server 2005 and SQL Server 2008 allow up to 1000 partitions.

3. Partition functions define boundaries for your tables. One partition function boundary value means two table partitions.

4. The filegroups are the physical locations for these partitions.

5. The main reason for partitioning a table is to get reasonable performance when executing DML on a large table.

6. Partition functions are configured as LEFT or RIGHT depending on where you want matching data boundary values to go.

    a. LEFT means exact matches go the left partition.

    b. RIGHT means exact matches go to the right partition.

7. The T-SQL syntax to create a partition function starts with CREATE PARTITION FUNCTION.

8. A partition scheme maps the partitions to the filegroups.

9. The partition scheme is used to create a partitioned table.

10. Partition Function – Sets data type and range values.

11. Partition Scheme – Maps the partitions to the filegroups.

12. To create partition tables do your steps in this order:
    - Create the files and filegroups.
    - Create the partition function
    - Create the partition scheme
    - Create the table
    - Populate the table

13. $PARTITION returns an integer value between 1 and the number of partitions of the partition function.

14. If you have two tables you want to partition at the same boundaries, they can share the same partition function.

15. Partitioning tables replaces horizontal partitioning. (Horizontal partitioning is the strategy where you separate your data into separate tables in separate storage locations.)

Chapter Glossary

Base tables: The tables on which a view is based.
Boundary values: These determine where data will go in a partition table.
Defrag: Short for defragmentation; an operation performed to clean up fragmented data.
Defragmentation: An operation performed to clean up fragmented data,
Giant tables: Activity tables which can grow to millions or billions of records.
$Partition: This function allows us to see exactly which partition each record is stored on.
Partition function: Partition functions define boundaries for your tables.
Partition scheme: This indicates which filegroup(s) data should go into.
Partition tables: When many physically stored table areas rolling up to one table name.
Partitioned views: When using partitioned views, all of the base tables (on which the view is defined) must be created and managed individually.

Chapter Six - Review Quiz

1.) Your company is going to deploy a new database. Your table will only hold the last two weeks' worth of data at any given time. You have set up two filegroups named fgInvoicePastWeek and fgInvoiceCurrentWeek and the datafiles they use are up and running. You will be implementing a partitioned table for your SalesInvoice table. What task do you implement to complete creating the partition table?

O a. Create the partition function
       Create the partition scheme
       Create the table
       Populate the table

O b. Create the table
       Create the partition scheme
       Create the partition function
       Populate the table

O c. Create the partition function
       Create the table
       Create the partition scheme
       Populate the table

2.) The partition scheme maps the boundary values of the partition function to:
(choose the correct answer)

   O a.   Table
   O b.   Function
   O c.   Filegroup
   O d.   DataFile

3.) You work for a bank that has 50,000 transactions per day. Your database has horizontal partitioning already implemented and you want to use Partitioned Tables. You have created the partition function pf_OrderDate by the OrderDate field. You need to create an efficient reporting solution to query the records from one logical table. What else must you do to achieve this solution?

   O a.   Map each partition from pf_OrderDate to a filegroup on a different physical drive.
   O b.   Create a partition scheme to replace the pf_OrderDate that partitions the data by OrderDate.

4.) You have a partition function with only one boundary value. If you specify RANGE RIGHT 1000 for field name Price in a table name dbo.Product what does this mean?

   O a.   Records with a Price of 1000 go into the default filegroup.
   O b.   Records with a Price of 1000 go into the first partition.
   O c.   Records with a Price of 1000 go into the second partition.

5.) Your SQL Server 2008 Enterprise database contains a table with 800 million rows of data. You need to partition the data physically in different locations but have the data accessed by one table name. Your goal is to increase performance and optimize maintenance. What should you do?

   O a.   Implement horizontal partitioning
   O b.   Implement vertical partitioning

Answer Key

1.) a   2.) c   3.) a   4.) c   5.) a

Bug Catcher Game

To play the Bug Catcher game run the
BugCatcher_Chapter06PartitionedTables.pps from the BugCatcher folder of the

companion files. You can obtain these files from www.Joes2Pros.com or by ordering the Companion CD.

Chapter 7.   Altering Partitioned Tables

When you segment items by time, it's a good practice to plan ahead and take into consideration that time is constantly moving forward. If the most recent year is 2010 and everything newer than January 1, 2011 is going into the current filegroup, then what do you do when 2011 rolls around? A new year should mean a new partition, along with a place to store the new data.

If you only wanted to store the last three years in your table, then in 2011 you would only want to retain 2009, 2010, and 2011. To properly ring in the New Year, you need to be able to split the newest partitions and retire (switch out) the older years no longer needed. In other words, you will need to create a place for your 2011 data and move the 2008 data out of the table.

This chapter shows you how to move with the times by altering your partitioned tables.

READER NOTE: *In order to follow along with the examples in the first section of Chapter 7, please run the setup script SQLArchChapter7.0Setup.sql. The setup scripts for this book are posted at Joes2Pros.com.*

Preparing for New Data

In the last chapter, we took all the SalesInvoice records and pumped them into a partitioned table named SalesInvoiceHorizontal based on boundary values defined in the OrderDate field.

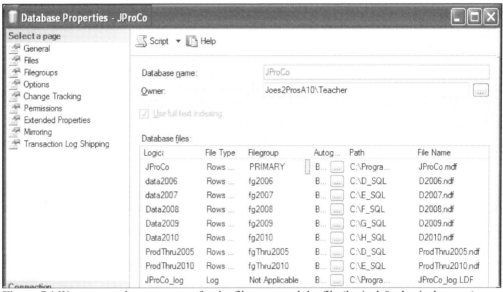

Figure 7.1 We now see the new names for the filegroup and the file (logical & physical names).

We now see the names for the filegroup and the datafile it points to. None of the data or structure of the partition scheme has changed. Our five partition ranges have specific names which map to the data they contain.

Splitting New Partitions

The fg2010 filegroup is ready to hold any data newer than January 1, 2010. What about inserting data from 2011? If a record containing 2011 data were added to the SalesInvoiceHorizontal table, it would flow into the fg2010 (H drive). This is great for now, since it's what our partition design calls for (see Figure 7.2) and currently we're still receiving 2010 invoice data. But suppose we are planning ahead and would like to build out our partitions for the upcoming year. Or perhaps we've been asked to prepare this partitioned table for the next several years' worth of invoices (i.e., 2011, 2012, 2013, etc.).

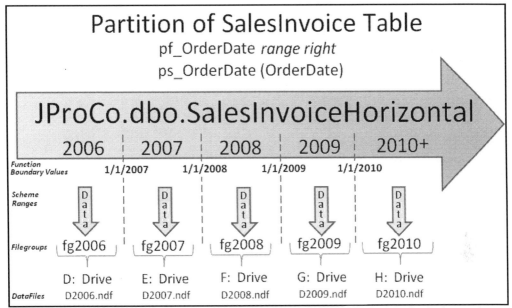

Figure 7.2 We now see the new names for the filegroup and the file (logical & physical names).

These are easy tasks, since SQL Server 2005/2008 makes administering partitions a breeze. For this demonstration, we will prepare the table for the next two years' worth of invoices. This will involve splitting our fifth partition (2010+) to accommodate the year 2011 and 2012. We won't need to do anything with the first four partitions (2006-2009), since none of those records will be changing.

We are free to add 2011 and 2012 data to the table at anytime. Doing so at this point would mean that the fg2010 filegroup (being the most recent) would hold this data. Let's test this out and see for ourselves.

Before we begin working with the table storage, partition function, or partition scheme, we first will add a couple of test records to the table so we can see the before and after effect of the new partitions (see Figure 7.3).

```
INSERT INTO JProCo.dbo.SalesInvoiceHorizontal
VALUES  (1886,'2/1/2011','2/18/2011',15,'This is a test record'),
        (1887,'4/7/2012','4/30/2012',703,'This is a test record')
```

Messages

(2 row(s) affected)

Figure 7.3 Add two test records to SalesInvoiceHorizontal prior to adding the new partitions.

Since their OrderDate values are both after (i.e., "range right") of 1/1/2010, both of our test records land in Partition 5 (see Figure 7.4). Remember Partition 5 points to the fg2010 filegroup.

```
    SELECT $Partition.Pf_OrderDate(OrderDate)
   AS PartitionNum, *
   FROM dbo.SalesInvoiceHorizontal
```

Results | Messages

	PartitionNum	InvoiceID	OrderDate	PaidDate	CustomerID	Comment
1879	5	1871	2010-02-19 ...	2010-04-02 ...	627	NULL
1880	5	1872	2010-02-20 ...	2010-03-12 ...	49	NULL
1881	5	1873	2010-02-20 ...	2010-02-22 ...	534	NULL
1882	5	1874	2010-02-21 ...	2010-02-27 ...	707	NULL
1883	5	1875	2010-02-21 ...	2010-02-28 ...	155	NULL
1884	5	1876	2010-02-23 ...	2010-03-29 ...	584	NULL
1885	5	1877	2010-02-24 ...	2010-03-29 ...	530	NULL
1886	5	1886	2011-02-01 ...	2011-02-18 ...	15	This is a test record
1887	5	1887	2012-04-07 ...	2012-04-30 ...	703	This is a test record

Query e... | | | | JProCo | 00:00:00 | 1887 rows

Figure 7.4 Our test records land in Partition 5, since their order dates are range right of 1/1/2010.

Now we will get ready to split the fifth partition to add 2011 and 2012. Our essential steps will be these:
1) Add storage areas for 2011 and 2012 (filegroups, datafiles, and two more "disk drive" folders to stand in for Drives I and J).
2) Update the partition scheme, so it recognizes the new filegroups and can identify which filegroup is "next used."
3) Add two new boundaries (1/1/2011, 1/1/2012) to the partition function. This is also known as "splitting the partition."

Step 1. *Update all needed storage areas.*
- Add the two folders representing the I and J drives (C:\I_SQL, C:\J_SQL).
- Add the two new filegroups, fg2011 and fg2012 (see Figure 7.5).
- Add the two new datafiles, Data2011 and Data2012 (see Figure 7.6).

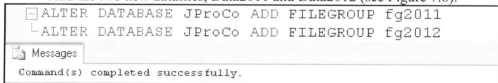

```
ALTER DATABASE JProCo ADD FILEGROUP fg2011
ALTER DATABASE JProCo ADD FILEGROUP fg2012
```

Messages

Command(s) completed successfully.

Figure 7.5 Add the two new filegroups, fg2011 and fg2012.

```
ALTER DATABASE JProCo
 ADD FILE
 (NAME = Data2011, FILENAME = 'C:\I_SQL\D2011.ndf')
 TO FILEGROUP fg2011

ALTER DATABASE JProCo
 ADD FILE
 (NAME = Data2012, FILENAME = 'C:\J_SQL\D2012.ndf')
 TO FILEGROUP fg2012
```

Messages

Command(s) completed successfully.

Figure 7.6 Add the two new datafiles, Data2011 and Data2012 located on the I and J drives.

Step 2. *Update the partition scheme with one of the new filegroups and identify which filegroup is "next used."*

In Step 1, we added all the needed storage areas (added two "drives", added two new filegroups, and added two new datafiles). However, the partition scheme **ps_OrderDate** doesn't know which of these new filegroups to use next. Think of this as if you'd just set two new dinner plates because you found out two more guests were on their way. All your other guests are sitting down and when your new guests come, you just tell each of them to use the next available seat.

Besides informing our partition scheme about the new filegroups, understanding the "next used" concept is the other key task for Step 2.

Recall when we created the partition function and partition scheme earlier in the chapter, we defined four "cuts" which created five ranges. We then included exactly five filegroups in our partition scheme. The partition scheme paired each filegroup with its corresponding range, as defined by boundary "cuts" listed in the partition function (see Figure 7.7). You can see the fg2010 will hold any data after the beginning of 2010.

```
CREATE PARTITION FUNCTION pf_OrderDate (datetime)
 AS RANGE RIGHT
 FOR VALUES ('1/1/2007', '1/1/2008', '1/1/2009', '1/1/2010')

CREATE PARTITION SCHEME ps_OrderDate
 AS PARTITION pf_OrderDate
 TO (fg2006, fg2007, fg2008, fg2009, fg2010)
```

Figure 7.7 The partition scheme mapped one filegroup to each of the five ranges.

You have 4 range values which needs 5 filegroups to hold the data. The world is perfect right now. If you were to create a fifth range value, you would need a sixth filegroup on standby ready to hold any data that falls to the right of the last value.

235

In other words, you need to have a storage place set aside and ready before you can direct data to that storage area.

The key understanding here is that our original partition scheme mapped exactly one filegroup to one range. There was no ambiguity (e.g., extra filegroup(s)) to confuse the partition scheme.

In Figure 7.7, recognize that SQL Server reads left to right and takes the first filegroup you list and connects it with the range defined by the first "cut" in the values list. The first boundary "cut" at 1/1/2007 means the first range includes OrderDate values prior to 1/1/2007.

In other words, SQL Server isn't interpreting our filegroup name fg2006 as a date value which belongs with the datetime value 1/1/2007. *If the first filegroup in our list had been named Purple, SQL Server would connect it with whatever boundary value appeared in the first position in the Values list!*
fg2006   OrderDate values prior to 1/1/2007
fg2007   OrderDate values 1/1/2007-12/31/2007
fg2008   OrderDate values 1/1/2008-12/31/2008
fg2009   OrderDate values 1/1/2009-12/31/2009
fg2010   OrderDate values 1/1/2010 or greater

NextUsedFileGroup is a property of the Partition Scheme object. Until now, a value for this property has not been required by ps_OrderDate (see Figure 7.8).

Object Explorer>Databases>JProCo>Storage>Partition Schemes >right-click ps_OrderDate>Facets

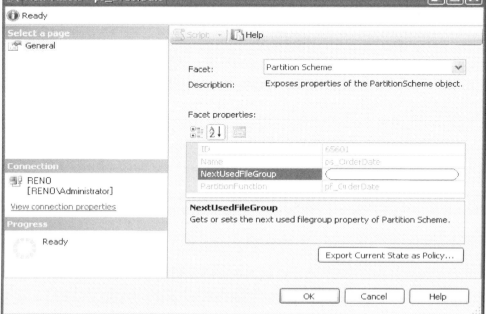

Figure 7.8 NextUsedFileGroup is a property of the Partition Scheme object.

236

At first glance it may seem silly to have 4 boundaries and 6 storage areas, since the sixth one would go unused. But this works perfectly -- when you add a new boundary value, then the new data "knows" exactly where to go. A value for the **NextUsedFileGroup** property will be required by our partition scheme the moment we attempt to add the fg2011 filegroup to the ps_OrderDate partition scheme.

A partition scheme requires you to name the "Next Used" filegroup whenever you write an ALTER PARTITION SCHEME statement (e.g., to add a new filegroup(s), to add a partition, to split an existing partition) AND/OR when you have an extra filegroup. In other words, when there is any possibility for ambiguity, the partition scheme will require you to specify the "Next Used" filegroup (Figures 7.9 - 7.10).

```
ALTER PARTITION SCHEME ps_OrderDate
NEXT USED fg2011
```

Messages

Command(s) completed successfully.

Figure 7.9 We must use "Next Used" whenever we write an ALTER PARTITION SCHEME.

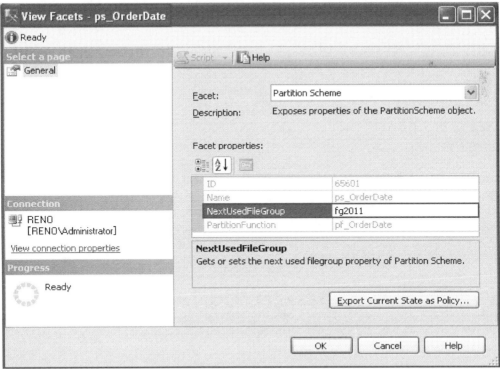

Figure 7.10 The filegroup fg2011 now shows as the NextUsedFileGroup for ps_OrderDate.

Step 3. *Add a new boundary (1/1/2011) to the partition function.*

We must add an additional boundary value "cut" in order to add partitions for the year 2011 to our SalesInvoiceHorizontal partitioned table. Let's first observe that the partition function, pf_OrderDate( ), contains five partitions. We saw this in our test data pull (refer back to Figure 7.2), and here we will see five partitions displayed by the View Facets page (see Figure 7.11). Object explorer > Databases > JProCo > Storage > Partition Function > right-click pf_OrderDate > Facets

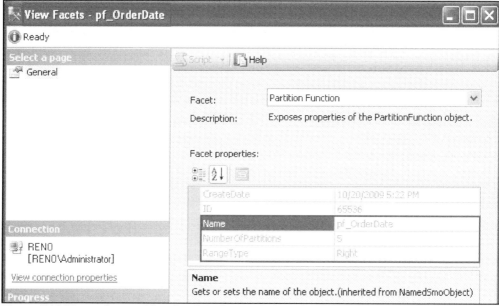

Figure 7.11 We see five partitions in pf_OrderDate before we add the additional "cuts."

The ALTER PARTITION FUNCTION command in Figure 7.12 changes the partition function and also reorganizes the records. After you see the "Command(s) completed successfully" confirmation, the properties of the pf_OrderDate partition function in Figure 7.11 will show a NumberOfPartitions value of 6.

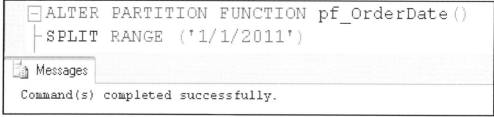

Figure 7.12 To separate 2010 and 2011, add another boundary value "cut" at 1/1/2011.

Now that fg2011 is in use and contains data, the NextUsed property of the partition function will be blank (Figure 7.8). We do the same for the year 2012 by associating filegroup fg2012 (which we created in Figure 7.5) with the NextUsed property, as can be seen in Figure 7.13.

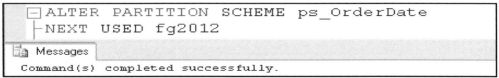

Figure 7.13 Next we will add the filegroup fg2012 to the partition scheme.

The ALTER PARTITION FUNCTION command in Figure 7.14 will consume the NextUsed fg2012 filegroup. At this point we should be up to 7 partitions.

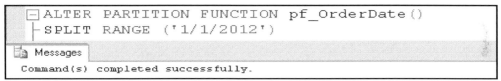

Figure 7.14 Add one additional boundary value "cut" at 1/1/2012.

These steps will help you verify the result in Object Explorer:
Object Explorer>Databases>JProCo>Storage>Partition Functions > right-click pf_OrderDate>Facets
We now see all seven partitions showing for pf_OrderDate (see Figure 7.15).

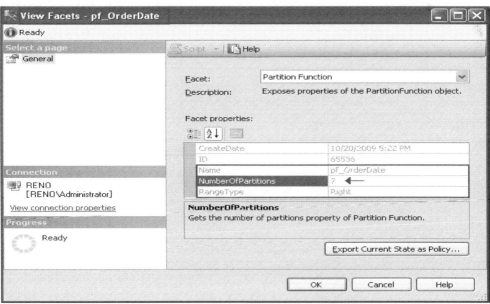

Figure 7.15 We now see all seven partitions showing for pf_OrderDate.

Based on the OrderDate each test record now lands in the correct partition. The query in Figure 7.16 shows 2011 data in Partition 6 and 2012 data in Partition 7. Please note the NextUsedFileGroup facet is empty for partition schema ps_OrderDate, meaning that they all have been used.

```
    SELECT $Partition.Pf_OrderDate(OrderDate)
    AS PartitionNum, *
    FROM dbo.SalesInvoiceHorizontal
```

	PartitionNum	InvoiceID	OrderDate	PaidDate	CustomerID	Comment
1879	5	1871	2010-02-19 ...	2010-04-02 ...	627	NULL
1880	5	1872	2010-02-20 ...	2010-03-12 ...	49	NULL
1881	5	1873	2010-02-20 ...	2010-02-22 ...	534	NULL
1882	5	1874	2010-02-21 ...	2010-02-27 ...	707	NULL
1883	5	1875	2010-02-21 ...	2010-02-28 ...	155	NULL
1884	5	1876	2010-02-23 ...	2010-03-29 ...	584	NULL
1885	5	1877	2010-02-24 ...	2010-03-29 ...	530	NULL
1886	6 ←	1886	2011-02-01 ...	2011-02-18 ...	15	This is a test record
1887	7 ←	1887	2012-04-07 ...	2012-04-30 ...	703	This is a test record

Query e...   JProCo   00:00:00   1887 rows

Figure 7.16 Our test records now land in Partitions 6 and 7.

Retiring (Switching Out) Partitions

When 2012 comes along, you might decide you no longer need the 2006 data. Perhaps the last 5 or 6 years is adequate. How can you retire the 2006 data into its own archive table? Another operation that is often needed with partitioned tables is the ability to remove unneeded data out of the partitioned table and off to an archive table while keeping the partitioned table name intact.

Let's suppose the time has come to archive fg2006 and all of its data out of the partitioned table and into its own archive table called dbo.SalesInvoice2006.

You can take an entire partition's worth of data from a partitioned table and put it into a brand new table. The structure (same fields, fieldnames, and data types) of the archive table must match the structure of SalesInvoiceHorizontal.

Using the Object Explorer, we can have Management Studio generate the CREATE code for us:

Object Explorer > Databases > JProCo > Tables
Right-click **SalesInvoiceHorizontal**>Script Table as >**Create To**>New Query Editor Window

Before running the code, let's create the dbo.SalesInvoice2006 and place it on the fg2006 filegroup. Now run the code to create this table (see Figure 7.17).

```
CREATE TABLE dbo.SalesInvoice2006  ←
 ( InvoiceID int NOT NULL,
   OrderDate datetime NOT NULL,
   PaidDate datetime NOT NULL,
   CustomerID int NOT NULL,
   Comment ntext NULL)
 ON fg2006  ←
 GO
```

Messages

Command(s) completed successfully.

Figure 7.17 We will rename the dbo.SalesInvoice2006 table and place it on the fg2006 filegroup.

We now have 1887 records in our partitioned table and 0 records in this newly created 2006 archive table.

Let's run a query to check and see how many 2006 records are in the partition we intend to archive (see Figure 7.18).

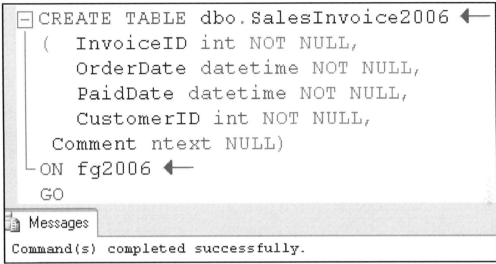

```
SELECT $Partition.pf_OrderDate (OrderDate), *
FROM SalesInvoiceHorizontal
WHERE $Partition.pf_OrderDate (OrderDate)= 1
```

Results | Messages

	[No column name]	InvoiceID	OrderDate	PaidDate	CustomerID	Comment
1	1	1	2006-01-03 00:00:00.000	2006-01-11 03:22:44.587	472	NULL
2	1	2	2006-01-04 02:22:41.473	2006-02-01 04:15:34.590	388	NULL
3	1	3	2006-01-04 05:33:01.150	2006-02-14 13:45:02.580	279	NULL
4	1	4	2006-01-04 22:06:58.657	2006-02-08 22:06:14.247	309	NULL
5	1	5	2006-01-05 11:37:45.597	2006-02-10 20:01:26.540	757	NULL
6	1	6	2006-01-06 23:53:14.320	2006-01-28 22:48:05.997	493	NULL
7	1	7	2006-01-08 08:06:33.210	2006-02-05 08:41:58.453	209	NULL
8	1	8	2006-01-08 13:04:13.613	2006-02-17 06:43:18.010	649	NULL
9	1	9	2006-01-08 21:46:03.093	2006-01-27 04:05:01.967	597	NULL

Query executed succe... | JProCo | 00:00:00 | 438 rows

Figure 7.18 There are 438 records in Partition 1, which contains OrderDate values thru 12/31/2006.

The code in Figure 7.19 moves data from Partition 1 in the SalesInvoiceHorizontal table to the archive table, SalesInvoice2006.

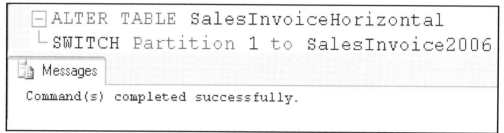

```
ALTER TABLE SalesInvoiceHorizontal
  SWITCH Partition 1 to SalesInvoice2006
```

Messages

Command(s) completed successfully.

Figure 7.19 This code removes the Partition 1 records and sends them to an archive table.

```
SELECT * FROM SalesInvoice2006
```

Results | Messages

	InvoiceID	OrderDate	PaidDate	CustomerID	Comment
1	1	2006-01-03 00:00:00.000	2006-01-11 03:22:44.587	472	NULL
2	2	2006-01-04 02:22:41.473	2006-02-01 04:15:34.590	388	NULL
3	3	2006-01-04 05:33:01.150	2006-02-14 13:45:02.580	279	NULL
4	4	2006-01-04 22:06:58.657	2006-02-08 22:06:14.247	309	NULL
5	5	2006-01-05 11:37:45.597	2006-02-10 20:01:26.540	757	NULL
6	6	2006-01-06 23:53:14.320	2006-01-28 22:48:05.997	493	NULL
7	7	2006-01-08 08:06:33.210	2006-02-05 08:41:58.453	209	NULL
8	8	2006-01-08 13:04:13.613	2006-02-17 06:43:18.010	649	NULL
9	9	2006-01-08 21:46:03.093	2006-01-27 04:05:01.967	597	NULL
10	10	2006-01-09 20:33:07.380	2006-02-20 15:50:04.133	736	NULL
11	11	2006-01-10 22:30:44.333	2006-01-18 16:58:10.810	329	NULL
12	12	2006-01-11 07:07:04.857	2006-01-22 06:35:09.463	52	NULL
13	13	2006-01-12 08:26:56.003	2006-02-14 08:29:13.357	234	NULL

Q... JProCo 00:00:00 438 rows

Figure 7.20 We now see the 438 Partition 1 records in the archive table, SalesInvoice2006.

We now have 438 records in our 2006 archive table (see Figure 7.20). So once we move these records to their own table, should we expect to see 438 fewer records in our partitioned table? Yes, and let's run some queries to prove that. A repeat of our query filtering just on Partition 1 (refer back to Figure 7.18) now shows zero records for Partition 1, as seen in Figure 7.21.

```
SELECT $Partition.pf_OrderDate (OrderDate), *
  FROM SalesInvoiceHorizontal
  WHERE $Partition.pf_OrderDate (OrderDate)= 1
```

Results | Messages

(No column name)	InvoiceID	OrderDate	PaidDate	CustomerID	Comment

Figure 7.21 Our query filtering on Partition 1 now returns 0 records (versus 438 in Figure 7.18).

With the 438 Partition 1 records removed, there are 1449 records remaining in the SalesInvoiceHorizontal table (see Figure 7.22).
(1887 total records – 438 Partition 1 records = 1449 records)

```
SELECT $Partition.pf_OrderDate (OrderDate)
AS PartitionNum , *
  FROM SalesInvoiceHorizontal
```

Results | Messages

	PartitionNum	InvoiceID	OrderDate	PaidDate	CustomerID	Comment
1	2	439	2007-01-01 01:17:46.263	2007-02-01 23:29:27.853	46	NULL
2	2	440	2007-01-01 15:07:20.493	2007-02-05 05:52:44.900	64	NULL
3	2	441	2007-01-02 07:38:42.810	2007-02-16 11:11:43.750	576	NULL
4	2	442	2007-01-03 12:20:22.500	2007-01-11 05:49:40.703	542	NULL
5	2	443	2007-01-03 21:06:28.120	2007-01-08 15:09:36.970	3	NULL
6	2	444	2007-01-05 09:24:24.817	2007-02-15 00:21:30.433	330	NULL
7	2	445	2007-01-05 18:02:53.730	2007-02-17 05:16:10.120	588	NULL
8	2	446	2007-01-05 21:25:01.140	2007-01-23 23:48:16.313	375	NULL
9	2	447	2007-01-06 16:20:03.627	2007-01-26 05:08:28.263	583	NULL

Query executed...   JProCo   00:00:00   1449 rows

Figure 7.22 1887 total records – 438 Partition 1 records = 1449 records remaining.

There is no 2006 data showing in the partitioned table, SalesInvoiceHorizontal (see Figure 7.23). The SWITCH PARTITION command neatly moved all records from Partition 1 (that is to say, all records with an OrderDate prior to 1/1/2007) into the archive table.

```
SELECT $Partition.pf_OrderDate (OrderDate)
  AS PartitionNum , *
  FROM SalesInvoiceHorizontal
  WHERE OrderDate LIKE '%2006%'
```

Results | Messages

PartitionNum	InvoiceID	OrderDate	PaidDate	CustomerID	Comment

Figure 7.23 There is no 2006 data showing in the partitioned table, SalesInvoiceHorizontal.

243

Lab 7.1: Altering Partitioned Tables

Lab Prep: Before you can begin the lab, you must have SQL Server installed and run the SQLArchChapter7.1Setup.sql script.

Skill Check 1: This skill check assumes you have created the storage folders C:\D_SQL, C:\E_SQL, C:\F_SQL, C:\G_SQL, C:\H_SQL, and C:\I_SQL (i.e., in place of available D:\ E:\ F:\ G:\ H:\ and I:\ drives). Achieve the following tasks.

1. Take the [CurrentProductsHorizontal] partitioned table which you created in Lab 6.1 and split it at 1/1/2010 to make a third partition.

2. All the data on the third partition should be stored on the C:\F_SQL drive to an NDF file called ProdThru2015.ndf.

3. Create a new filegroup fgProdThru2015.

When you've completed these requirements, your database properties dialog will resemble the figure below (see Figure 7.24).

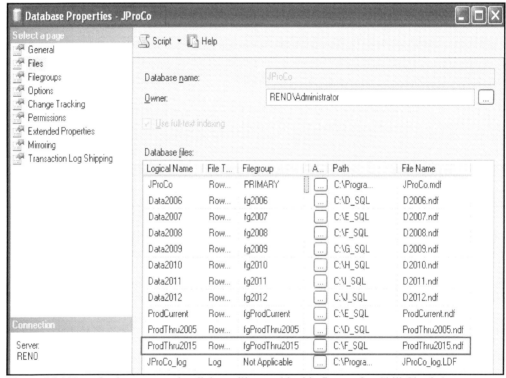

Figure 7.24 Your database properties dialog will resemble this figure after Skill Check 1.

Skill Check 2: Switch out all the 2001 to 2005 data from the partitioned table, CurrentProductsHorizontal, to a new table of identical structure called dbo.CurrentProductsTo2005. Afterwards, the CurrentProductsHorizontal table will contain 246 rows (see Figure 7.25) and the CurrentProductsTo2005 table will contain 239 rows (see Figure 7.26).

	PartitionNum	ProductID	ProductName	RetailPrice	OriginationDate	ToBeDel...	Category	SupplierID	OriginationO...
1	2	476	Wine Tasting To...	73.0152	2007-11-05 ...	0	Overnigh...	1	2007-11-05...
2	2	481	Yoga Mtn Getaw...	875.00	2009-10-19 ...	0	Medium-...	1	2009-10-19...
3	2	482	Yoga Mtn Getaw...	995.00	2009-10-19 ...	0	LongTer...	1	2009-10-19...
4	2	483	Yoga Mtn Getaw...	1695.00	2009-10-19 ...	1	LongTer...	1	2009-10-19...
5	2	484	Baja 3 Day	595.00	2009-10-19 ...	0	Medium-...	0	2009-10-19...
6	2	485	Baja 5 Day	795.00	2009-10-19 ...	0	Medium-...	0	2009-10-19...
7	2	471	Wine Tasting To...	132.795	2008-12-09 ...	0	Medium-...	2	2008-12-09...
8	2	469	Wine Tasting To...	44.265	2008-04-18 ...	0	No-Stay	2	2008-04-18...
9	2	466	Wine Tasting To...	309.232	2006-04-15 ...	0	Medium-...	3	2006-04-15...
10	2	464	Wine Tasting To...	139.1544	2008-01-14 ...	0	Overnigh...	3	2008-01-14...

Query executed successfully.   JProCo   00:00:00   246 rows

Figure 7.25 The CurrentProductsHorizontal table will resemble this figure following Skill Check 2.

	PartitionNum	ProductID	ProductName	RetailPrice	OriginationDate	ToBeDele...	Category	Supplier...	OriginationOf...
1	1	8	Underwater Tour 2 ...	145.5462	2005-06-11 ...	0	Overnig...	1	2005-06-11 ...
2	1	9	Underwater Tour 3 ...	242.577	2003-04-01 ...	0	Medium-...	1	2003-04-01 ...
3	1	10	Underwater Tour 5 ...	323.436	2005-04-13 ...	0	Medium-...	1	2005-04-13 ...
4	1	11	Underwater Tour 1 ...	404.295	2004-09-09 ...	0	LongTer...	1	2004-09-09 ...
5	1	5	Underwater Tour 1 ...	307.415	2001-07-18 ...	0	LongTer...	0	2001-07-18 ...
6	1	13	Underwater Tour 1 ...	105.059	2002-03-03 ...	0	No-Stay	3	2002-03-03 ...
7	1	15	Underwater Tour 3 ...	315.177	2004-07-10 ...	0	Medium-...	3	2004-07-10 ...
8	1	16	Underwater Tour 5 ...	420.236	2004-09-12 ...	0	Medium-...	3	2004-09-12 ...
9	1	18	Underwater Tour 2 ...	945.531	2002-03-26 ...	1	LongTer...	3	2002-03-26 ...
10	1	19	Underwater Tour 1 ...	85.585	2004-04-18 ...	0	No-Stay	2	2004-04-18 ...
11	1	21	Underwater Tour 3 ...	256.755	2005-10-14 ...	0	Medium-...	2	2005-10-14 ...
12	1	22	Underwater Tour 5 ...	342.34	2001-08-16 ...	0	Medium-...	2	2001-08-16 ...

Query executed successfully.   JProCo   00:00:00   239 rows

Figure 7.26 The CurrentProductsTo2005 table will resemble this figure following Skill Check 2.

Answer Code: The T-SQL code to this lab can be found in the downloadable files in a file named Lab7.1_AlteringPartionedTables.sql.

Altering Partitioned Tables - Points to Ponder

1. Table partitioning by rows is sometimes called horizontal partitioning.

2. A table is considered "large" if performance is severely degraded or if the table is inaccessible during maintenance.

3. Horizontal partitioning divides a table into multiple tables. Each table then contains the same number of columns, but fewer rows. You can add a new boundary by using the SPLIT RANGE clause of the ALTER PARTITION function.

4. Partitioned tables allow you to manage different sets of data within the same table. This gives you many advantages with large data.

5. Advantage: Older data might never change while the current year's data might be very active. You can back up the newest partition more frequently without having to back up the entire table.

6. Advantage: You can put the most frequently accessed data on a fast RAID data storage with no need to place the entire table there.

7. Advantage: Searches on smaller B-trees are faster than searches on larger B-trees.

8. Advantage: Fragmentation of frequently updated data (like the current year) will require re-indexing maintenance only on this part of the table (instead of the whole table).

9. Advantage: A user looking at older data at the same time as one looking at newer data now has a lower risk of dead-locking another user(s). With unpartitioned data, the likelihood of conflict is greater. However, with partitioned data, a user looking at historical data will not conflict or lock-out a user working on current data.

10. If you have data in your partitioned table that needs to be removed from partition 3 and archived, you can reassign or retire all the data in that partition to an existing table with the following code.

    ALTER TABLE dbo.SalesInvoice SWITCH PARTITION 3 TO dbo.SalesInvoiceArchive

11. You can only use the Switch Partition option if the destination table is empty and the partition filegroup and archive table's filegroup are the same.

Removing Partitioned Tables

Tables ultimately store their data on drives. You cannot specify which drive to store a table on, but you can specify the filegroup. When it is a partitioned table, you can't pick just one filegroup so you send the table to the partition scheme which selects the filegroups and then sends the data to the drives. If someone removes the filegroup, then your table would not have a way of getting directed to the physical storage. For this reason, SQL Server will not let you delete a filegroup that is being depended upon for database operations. This means that SQL Server protects your dependent objects and only allows database objects to be deleted once all dependencies have been removed.

Dependencies

This term refers to objects that are supporting other objects. For example you can't delete a datafile if a filegroup is using it. The datafile is the dependency. You also can't delete a partition function if a partition scheme is using it as its dependency. The concept of dependency means we need to utilize a specific sequence when creating or deleting objects which have dependencies.

Steps to Remove Partitions From Objects

When you have a partitioned table like SalesInvoiceHorizontal, you have a number of things at work: the partition scheme (which indicates which filegroup(s) data should go into), the partition function (which defines the borders between the partitions), and the partition table.

So if you want to get rid of all of these objects, you need to give some thought to which one(s) you need to remove first. The database will not allow you to remove an object (table, partition scheme, etc.) while another object within the database is reliant upon it. Recall we saw a similar pattern in Chapter 2, where we were unable to remove a scheme upon which a table within the databases was dependent. We first needed to locate the dependency (e.g., the table), remove or delete it, and then the database would allow us to delete the scheme. Let's see what happens when we try to get rid of the function pf_OrderDate.

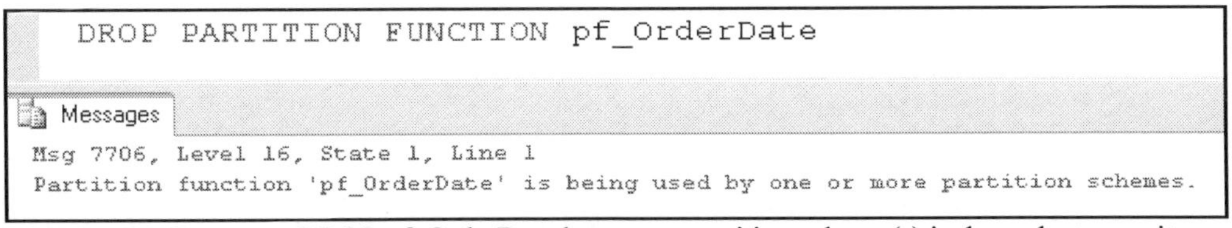

```
DROP PARTITION FUNCTION pf_OrderDate
```

Messages

Msg 7706, Level 16, State 1, Line 1
Partition function 'pf_OrderDate' is being used by one or more partition schemes.

Figure 7.27 We cannot DROP pf_OrderDate because a partition scheme(s) is dependent upon it.

The error message indicates we can't drop this partition function because it is being used by one or more partition schemes in the (JProCo) database. Thus, we need to locate and remove the scheme before we can remove the function.

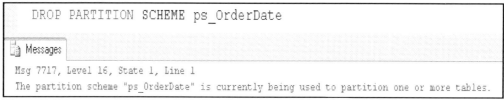

Figure 7.28 We cannot DROP ps_OrderDate because a partitioned table(s) is dependent upon it.

This error says you can't drop this partition scheme because it is being used to partition one or more tables. So let's check the dependencies for the table. Navigate to the SalesInvoiceHorizontal table in Object Explorer, right-click on it, and select View Dependencies. First we see an empty Object Dependencies dialog, because the "Objects that depend on [SalesInvoiceHorizontal]" radio button is active. Select the other radio button "Objects on which [SalesInvoiceHorizontal] depends" and expand the items (see Figure 7.29). This identifies all of the dependencies, and we can use this to properly order our DROP statements.

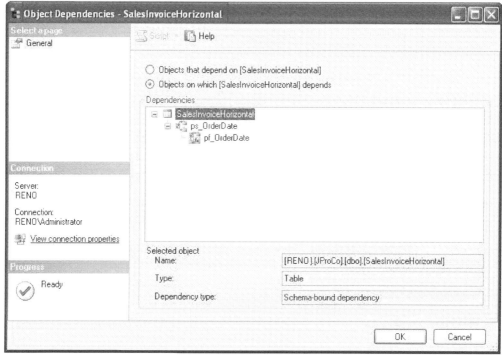

Figure 7.29 SalesInvoiceHorizontal is dependent upon two objects, so we cannot drop them.

Since SalesInvoiceHorizontal is dependent upon the partition scheme, it is blocking our ability to drop the partition scheme (as seen previously in Figure 7.28). Figure 7.29 also shows us that the partition scheme is dependent upon the partition function, which will block us from dropping pf_OrderDate.

Since no JProCo objects are dependent upon SalesInvoiceHorizontal, nothing will block us from dropping the table. So let's attempt to get rid of the partitioned table, SalesInvoiceHorizontal, then the partition scheme, and lastly the partition function.

Success! We are allowed to DROP the SalesInvoiceHorizontal table, since no other database objects are dependent upon this table (see Figure 7.30).

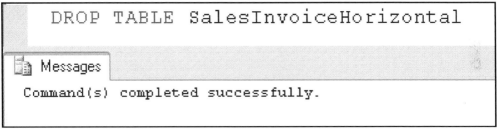

Figure 7.30 The JProCo database allows us to successfully DROP this partitioned table.

And now JProCo permits us to DROP the partition scheme (see Figure 7.31).

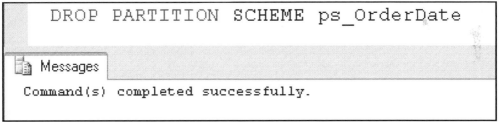

Figure 7.31 The JProCo database allows us to successfully DROP this partition scheme.

And finally the database allows us to DROP the partition function (see Figure 7.31).

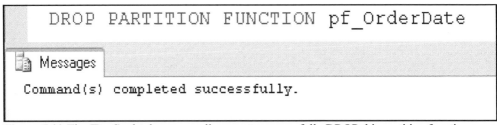

Figure 7.32 The JProCo database now allows us to successfully DROP this partition function.

Optionally, you may also want to get rid of the file(s) and the filegroup(s) unless other objects(s) are dependent upon them. The next few screens show error messages to drive home some helpful points.

- A filegroup cannot be removed unless it is empty (see Figure 7.33).
- You must use the logical name when removing a datafile – you cannot use its physical name (see Figure 7.34).

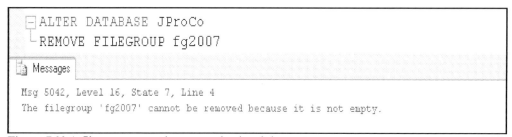

Figure 7.33 A filegroup cannot be removed unless it is empty.

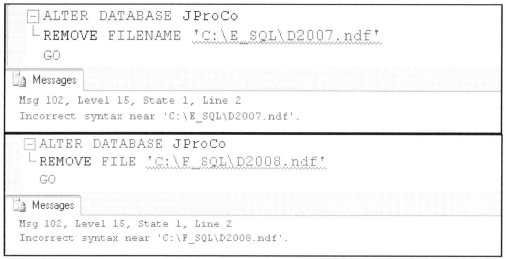

Figure 7.34 You cannot remove a datafile using its physical name. You must use its logical name.

In Figure 7.35 (next page) we successfully remove the file by its logical name (Data2007). With the only file in the fg2007 filegroup removed, we are then able to successfully remove the filegroup. Each DDL statement is followed by a GO statement to ensure each one completes before the next statement runs.

Figure 7.35 Once you remove the file, the filegroup is empty. You can then remove the filegroup.

Lab 7.2: Removing Partitioned Tables

Lab Prep: Before you can begin the lab, you must have SQL Server installed and run the SQLArchChapter7.2Setup.sql script.

Skill Check 1: Delete the partition function, partition scheme, and partitioned table relating to the CurrentProductsHorizontal data.

If you encounter any error message(s), then re-check the sequencing and T-SQL code as shown in the chapter. *Remember that viewing the object dependencies can help with the sequencing.*

If you've written the code properly and run these statements in the proper sequence, then you will receive a confirmation message "Command(s) completed successfully."

To confirm the table removal, check Object Explorer and confirm the partitioned table for CurrentProductsHorizontal is no longer there.
(Object Explorer > Databases > JProCo > Tables)

To confirm the removal of the partition function and the partition scheme, check the Storage folder of JProCo. (Object Explorer > Databases > JProCo > Storage > Partition Schemes (empty), Partition Functions (empty))

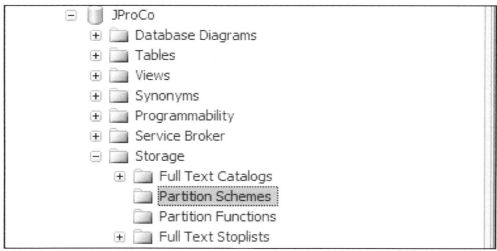

Figure 7.36 Skill Check 1

Answer Code: The T-SQL code to this lab can be found in the downloadable files in a file named Lab7.2_RemovingPartionedTables.sql.

Removing Partitioned Tables - Points to Ponder

1.   Partitioned tables allow you to manage different sets of data within the same table. This gives you many advantages with large data.

2.   By separating data across multiple drives you gain the ability to use many drives at once which can result in a performance gain.

3.   SQL Server has a safety measure where objects can't be dropped so long as there are other objects depending on them.

4.   If you want to drop a partition scheme, you must first make sure there are no tables using the partition scheme.

Chapter Glossary

Alter Partition Function: This function changes the partition function and also reorganizes the records.

Dependencies: This term refers to objects that are supporting other objects.

NextUsedFileGroup: A property of the partition scheme object. A value is required to be setg prior to adding a new filegroup to the partition scheme.

SPLIT RANGE: When used with Alter Partition, this tells where to split the data for a new or changed partition.

SWITCH PARTITION: When used with Alter Partition this moves data to an archived partition.

Chapter Seven - Review Quiz

1.) You have four partitions in a partitioned table named Orders. Partitions 2-4 contain historical data. Partition 1 contains current data. You want the data from Partition 3 to be removed and reassigned to the OrdersArchive table? What code would you use?

   O a. ALTER TABLE Orders Switch Partition 3 To OrdersArchive
   O b. ALTER TABLE Orders Merge Partition 3 To OrdersArchive
   O c. ALTER TABLE Orders Split Partition 3 To OrdersArchive

2.) You have three partitions in a partition table named Orders. Partitions 1 and 2 contain historical data. Partition 3 contains current data. You want to have four partitions by adding a new partition to handle next year's order data. What method would you use?

   O a. Switch
   O b. Merge
   O c. Split

3.) You have three partitions in a partition table named Orders. Partitions 2 and 3 contain historical data. Partition 1 contains current data. You want to archive Partition 3 data and remove it from the table. What method would you use?

   O a. Switch
   O b. Merge
   O c. Split

Answer Key

1.) a   2.) c 3.) a

Bug Catcher Game

To play the Bug Catcher game run the BugCatcher_Chapter07AlteringPartitionedTables.pps from the BugCatcher folder of the companion files. You can obtain these files from www.Joes2Pros.com or by ordering the Companion CD.

Chapter 8.   Creating Indexes

If you were to walk into a giant mall you'd never been to and wanted to find a store called Tech-Shirts, what would you do? Would you walk by every store until you see the name, or would you head straight to the mall directory map? Either system you use will result in success. By using the directory at the mall, you can save many steps in reaching your location quickly. The mall has to devote a little extra space to directory kiosks in the middle of a few walkways, but the payoff is huge. Like many things in life which grow large in size, the mall has indexed all its units for your convenience.

That is just one example of how indexes work, and the same principle applies to SQL Server. By creating an index based on what you search for most, you can get big performance gains for a nominal amount of additional storage space.

The reason we employ indexes in our tables and queries is to clear the way for SQL Server to most efficiently locate and retrieve the data we request. In previous chapters, we've looked at the organization of datafiles and data pages. We know that the ideal placement of data is one that maximizes the amount of data read and returned per disk I/O (input/output) cycle. In other words, one that allows SQL Server to work with the most data in the fewest number of steps.

This is the first of six chapters we will spend on the topic of indexing in SQL Server. Yet, despite devoting roughly half of this book to indexes, it won't be adequate to cover indexes in an exhaustive or deeply technical fashion. The SQL Server Database Engine is a complex, highly organized, and highly powerful system. Our goal will be to engage all readers – from beginners to advanced developers – and impart an understanding of how indexing works, rules of thumb for applying the right types of indexes to achieve your goals, and indexing pitfalls you want to avoid in the design of your tables and queries.

READER NOTE: *In order to follow along with the examples in the first section of Chapter 8, please run the setup script SQLArchChapter8.0Setup.sql. The setup scripts for this book are posted at Joes2Pros.com.*

The Clustered Index

The store names in a shopping mall are not lined up in alphabetical order. In other words, Zales could be right next to Benetton. These two stores might occupy Units 410 and 411. Thus, the stores in a mall are *clustered* by unit number. The **clustered index** represents the actual physical order of your data. A book is ordered by page numbers. If you locate page 99, then you know exactly where page 100 is. Thus, you could say the pages in a book represent a *clustered index* and they are *clustered* by page number.

Data Storage Terms

Think of a memory page as a carton of eggs and think of each egg as a row of data. If you only had two eggs to store, then you would just need one carton. Put in the two eggs and now you have 10 available slots for when you get more eggs. Eventually, you could acquire more eggs than could fit into one carton. What would you do then? You would fill up your first carton and get another one. Similarly, only so many records will fit into one memory page. If more records come in, then SQL Server will use multiple memory pages for that table.

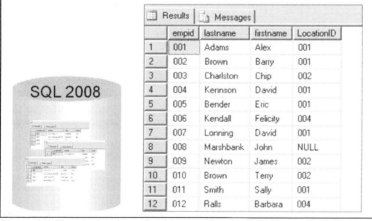

Figure 8.1 How is data in each table stored and referenced by SQL Server?

Records

While a table can have a maximum of just 1024 columns, or fields, it can have trillions of records. What makes a table take up space is the number of records in that table. If a table had no records, then it would take up very little space.

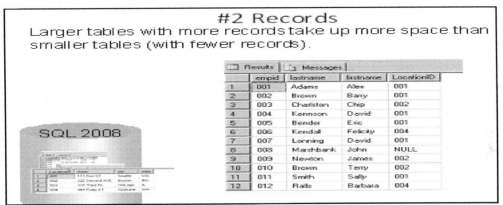

Figure 8.2 Small tables with fewer records take up less space than larger tables.

Memory Pages

A page can hold up to 8K of data. If each record takes up 2K of data, then 4 records would fit in each datapage. If such a table had 12 records, then it would use 3 memory pages (see Figures 8.3 through 8.5).

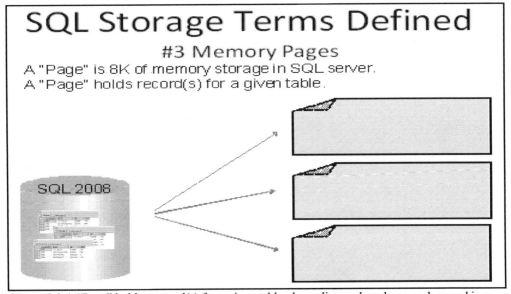

Figure 8.3 A "Page" holds a record(s) for a given table, depending on how large each record is.

SQL Storage Terms Defined

#3 Memory Pages cont...

How big each record is determines how many records can fit into one page of memory.

1	001	Adams	Alex	001
2	002	Brown	Barry	001
3	003	Charlston	Chip	002
4	004	Kennson	David	001
5	005	Bender	Eric	001
6	006	Kendall	Felicity	004
7	007	Lonning	David	001
8	008	Marshbank	John	NULL
9	009	Newton	James	002
10	010	Brown	Terry	002
11	011	Smith	Sally	001
12	012	Ralls	Barbara	004

Figure 8.4 Most tables have numerous records and thus require multiple memory pages.

SQL Storage Terms Defined

#3 Memory Pages (cont'd)

Example: Suppose that four records from the table below would fill one memory page.

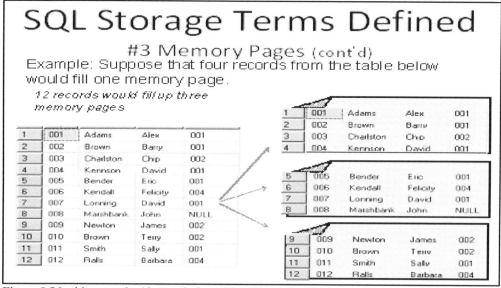

Figure 8.5 In this example, 12 records from this table would fill up three memory pages.

Since the physical storage of data impacts the speed and efficiency of our queries, this chapter explores how indexes can impact the physical location of data and the way SQL Server retrieves query data.

Clustered Index Data in Memory

In Volume 2 (*SQL Queries Joes 2 Pros*), you learned that with the use of an ORDER BY clause you can view a table's records in any order you like. This is true regardless of the order in which the table has its rows stored. If you don't use an ORDER BY clause, then you get the table's natural sort order. What is a natural sort order? It is the sequence, from beginning to end, in which each row is stored in the table. You can tell a table how it should store its data or let the table just store data in order as it is entered.

Absent a clustered index or constraints (e.g., a primary key, a foreign key, etc.), the default order of records is the order in which they were entered into the table. As we read at the opening of the chapter, the clustered index represents your selection of the actual physical order of your data.

If we decide to add a clustered index to this table based on the SSN field, then regardless of the order in which you insert these records, each record will be stored in order of SSN. If you insert SSN 888-88-8888 first and then later add 222-22-2222, SQL Server would physically reorder the records in storage so they line up by SSN.

SQL Storage Terms Defined
#4 Clustered Index

Clustered Indexes: This table is sorted in the system by SSN. The clustered index is the placement order of a table's records in memory pages.

Page1

222-22-2222	Jonny	Dirt
565-66-6767	Sally	Smith
888-88-8888	Irene	Intern
Empty	Empty	Empty

Page2

Empty	Empty	Empty
Empty	Empty	Empty
Empty	Empty	Empty

Figure 8.6 The clustered index is the placement order of a table's records in memory pages.

The **clustered index** is the placement order of a table's records in memory pages. When you insert new records, then each record will be inserted into the memory page in the order it belongs.

Rick Morelan's SSN (555-55-5555) belongs with the 5's, (see Figure 8.7) so his record will be physically inserted in memory here (between Jonny Dirt and Sally Smith). Is there enough room in this page to accommodate his record without having to move other record(s) to a new page? Yes there is, and afterwards the first memory page is full.

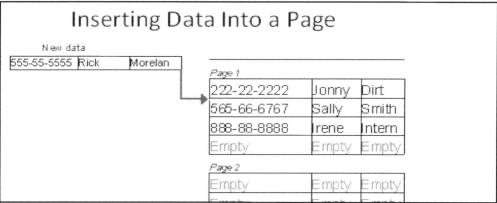

Figure 8.7 If you insert a new record(s), it is inserted into the memory page in the order it belongs.

Next, we have another new record coming in, Vince Verhoff (see Figure 8.8). His record belongs in sequence after Irene Intern, so he will begin occupying the next page of memory.

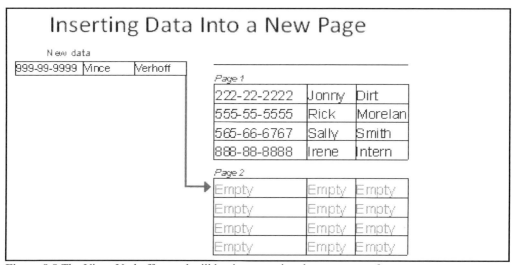

Figure 8.8 The Vince Verhoff record will begin occupying the next page of memory.

Page Splits

Page splits arise when records from one memory page are moved to another page during changes to your table. Here we see another new record (Major Disarray) being inserted, in sequence, between Jonny and Rick (Figure 8.9). Since there's no room in this memory page, some records will need to shift around. The page split occurs when Irene's record moves to the second page.

Page splits are considered very bad for performance, and there are a number of techniques to reduce, or even eliminate, the risk of page splits.

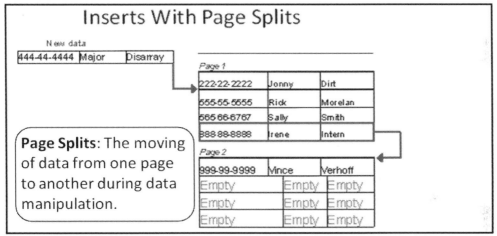

Figure 8.9 Since there's no room in the first memory page, some records will need to shift around. The page split occurs when Irene's record moves to the second page.

Next we'll see this data entered into the HumanResources.Contractor table, which contains a clustered index on the SSN field (see Figure 8.10 and 8.11).

```
IF EXISTS(SELECT * FROM Sys.tables
          WHERE [name] = 'Contractor')
DROP TABLE JProCo.HumanResources.Contractor
GO
CREATE TABLE JProCo.HumanResources.Contractor
(SSN CHAR(11) PRIMARY KEY,
FirstName varchar(25) NOT NULL,
LastName varchar(35) NOT NULL,
EMail varchar(50) NOT NULL,
Pay money NULL)
GO
```

Figure 8.10 The code which created the JProCo.HumanResources.Contractor table.

Notice SSN is set as a primary key. (A primary key is a constraint which ensures non-nullability and uniqueness (i.e., no duplicate values) in a field. Book 4 covers primary keys and constraints in depth.) Only one primary key per table is allowed. When you create a primary key, SQL Server creates two objects: the primary key and an index (which by default is clustered). The data in this table will be physically ordered by SSN (see previous Figure 8.10). Now insert the first three records into the table (see Figure 8.11).

```
--This code inserts 3 records into the HumanResources.Contractor table.
INSERT INTO JProCo.HumanResources.Contractor
  VALUES ('222-22-2222','Jonny','Dirt','Jdirt@JProCo.com',35000),
         ('656-66-6767','Sally','Smith','SallyS@JProCo.com',45000),
         ('888-88-8888','Irene','Intern','I-IreneI@JProCo.com',null)
--SQL Server 2005 users can refer to p.122 (Figure 4.2) to write this
--INSERT statement without row constructors.
```

Figure 8.11 INSERT three records in the JProCo.HumanResources.Contractor table.

Let's use our same assumption that four records fit into a page of memory. These three records (see Figure 8.12) would all occupy the same memory page.

SELECT * FROM JProCo.HumanResources.Contractor

Results | Messages

	SSN	FirstName	LastName	EMail	Pay
1	222-22-2222	Jonny	Dirt	Jdirt@JProCo.com	35000.00
2	656-66-6767	Sally	Smith	SallyS@JProCo.com	45000.00
3	888-88-8888	Irene	Intern	I-IreneI@JProCo.com	NULL

Figure 8.12 These three records reside in the first memory page of HumanResources.Contractor.

So that means there is room in the same memory page for an INSERT to add one additional record to this table, for a total of four records (see Figure 8.13).

INSERT INTO JProCo.HumanResources.Contractor
VALUES ('555-55-5555','Rick','Morelan','rmorelan@JProCo.com',25000)

page-1

222-22-2222	Jonny	Dirt	Jdirt@JProCo.com	35000
555-55-5555	Rick	Morelan	rmorelan@JProCo.com	25000
656-66-6767	Sally	Smith	SallyS@JProCo.com	45000
888-88-8888	Irene	Intern	I-IreneI@JProCo.com	NULL

page-2

empty	empty	empty	empty	empty
empty	empty	empty	empty	empty
empty	empty	empty	empty	empty
empty	empty	empty	empty	empty

Figure 8.13 The layout of the memory page with the fourth record inserted.

In our example, the first memory page is now full, since it contains four records. The second memory page is empty. The layout in the memory page is depicted (see Figure 8.13) with the fourth record (highlighted) added between Jonny Dirt and Sally Smith. The two bottom records (Sally Smith and Irene Intern) shifted down to make room for the Rick Morelan record to be inserted in proper sequence, according to the value of the clustered field (SSN).

The next insert (for Vince Verhoff - see Figure 8.14) goes straight into the second memory page and does not cause a page split. Now look at the SSN values in the table. Vince's SSN is the last possible SSN, since 999-99-9999 is the highest possible nine-digit SSN. Now the SSN value of the next record to be added will tell us whether there will be a page split. Any subsequent INSERT with an SSN value within the range 888-88-8889 through 999-99-9998 would go into one of the three available rows in the second memory page.

```
INSERT INTO JProCo.HumanResources.Contractor
VALUES ('999-99-9999','Vince','Verhoff','Viv@JProCo.com',65000)
```

page-1				
222-22-2222	Jonny	Dirt	Jdirt@JProCo.com	35000
555-55-5555	Rick	Morelan	rmorelan@JProCo.com	25000
656-66-6767	Sally	Smith	SallyS@JProCo.com	45000
888-88-8888	Irene	Intern	I-Irenel@JProCo.com	NULL
page-2				
999-99-9999	Vince	Verhoff	Viv@JProCo.com	65000
empty	empty	empty	empty	empty
empty	empty	empty	empty	empty
empty	empty	empty	empty	empty

Figure 8.14 The insert of Vince's record goes into the 2nd memory page and causes no page split.

Any SSN value below 888-88-8888 will cause a page split (see Figure 8.15). Since 444-44-4444 Major Disarray must be inserted in Page 1 between Jonny and Rick, a page split is caused and Irene Intern's record must move to Page 2. *Notice that it won't take long before almost every insert causes a page split.*

```
INSERT INTO JProCo.HumanResources.Contractor
VALUES ('444-44-4444','Major','Disarray', 'Majord@JProCo.com',20000)
```

page-1				
222-22-2222	Jonny	Dirt	Jdirt@JProCo.com	35000
444-44-4444	Major	Disarray	Majord@JProCo.com	20000
555-55-5555	Rick	Morelan	rmorelan@JProCo.com	25000
656-66-6767	Sally	Smith	SallyS@JProCo.com	45000

page-2				
888-88-8888	Irene	Intern	I-Irenel@JProCo.com	NULL
999-99-9999	Vince	Verhoff	Viv@JProCo.com	65000
empty	empty	empty	empty	empty
empty	empty	empty	empty	empty

> The first page split occurs when Irene's record must shift down into the second memory page.

Figure 8.15 The insert of Major's record causes the first page split.

Fill Factor

While we won't go into all the behind-the-scenes details of the impact of a page split, we know they are bad for performance and want to be aware of techniques to reduce or eliminate the likelihood of page splits.

The fill factor setting was introduced in SQL Server 2000 and helps prevent the need for pages to split. We can tell SQL Server not to fill up every section of every page on the first sweep of data. Recall a clustered index requires the records to be physically stored in order.

We can instruct it to leave some empty space for later inserts, so we don't have to move around the other existing pieces of data. This tool is the *fill factor* setting.

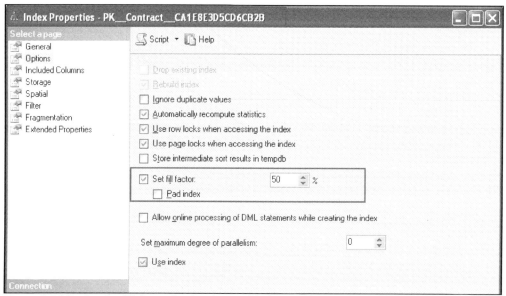

Figure 8.16 Setting the fill factor for the clustered index on SSN to 50%.

How to locate the Options page (Figure 8.16) to check or adjust the fill factor:
   Object Explorer > Databases > JProCo > Tables > HumanResources.Contractor > Indexes (folder) > right-click on the index > Properties > Options (page)

A fill factor of 50% would leave every other record empty on the initial insert of data into the HumanResources.Contractor table (see Figure 8.17).

Setting a fill factor uses more space, but it reduces or eliminates the likelihood of page splits.

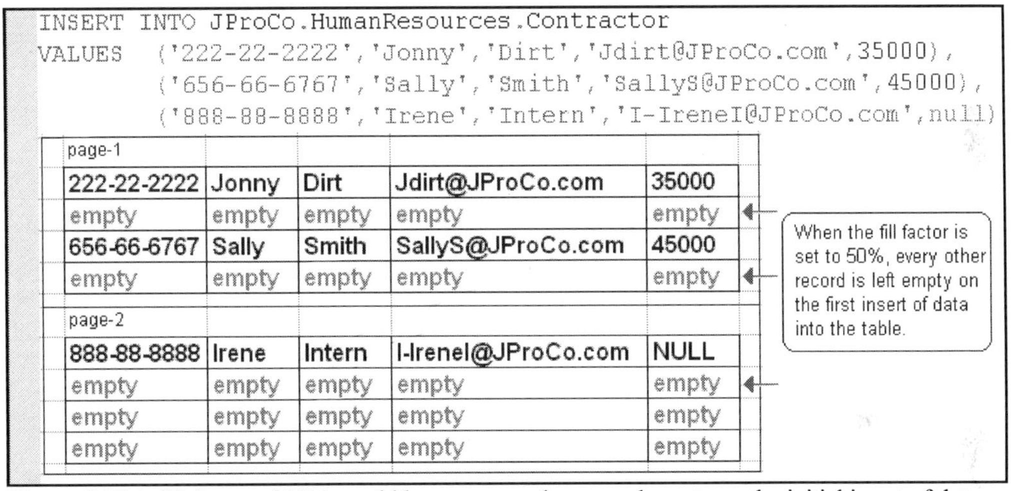

```
INSERT INTO JProCo.HumanResources.Contractor
VALUES  ('222-22-2222','Jonny','Dirt','Jdirt@JProCo.com',35000),
        ('656-66-6767','Sally','Smith','SallyS@JProCo.com',45000),
        ('888-88-8888','Irene','Intern','I-IreneI@JProCo.com',null)
```

page-1				
222-22-2222	Jonny	Dirt	Jdirt@JProCo.com	35000
empty	empty	empty	empty	empty
656-66-6767	Sally	Smith	SallyS@JProCo.com	45000
empty	empty	empty	empty	empty
page-2				
888-88-8888	Irene	Intern	I-Irenel@JProCo.com	NULL
empty	empty	empty	empty	empty
empty	empty	empty	empty	empty
empty	empty	empty	empty	empty

When the fill factor is set to 50%, every other record is left empty on the first insert of data into the table.

Figure 8.17 A fill factor of 50% would leave every other record empty on the initial insert of data.

With a fill factor of 75%, the initial insert would immediately fill 75% of the records in the table and leave 25% of the records empty. In other words, every fourth record would be empty. A fill factor of 90% would leave every tenth record empty.

You can set the fill factor in the UI (as we saw earlier in Figure 8.16) or by using T-SQL code. This Alter Index statement will rebuild all indexes with a fill factor of 75:

ALTER INDEX ALL
ON [HumanResources].[Contractor]
REBUILD WITH (FILLFACTOR = 75)
GO

Identity Fields

We've learned that fill factors use up a little extra space and they help reduce page splits. In our next example, we will examine an approach to eliminate page splits, yet it wastes no space and allows us to have 100% fill factor.

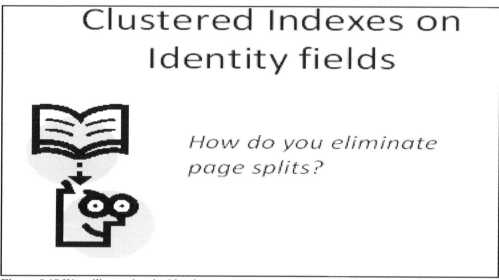

Figure 8.18 We will examine the identity property as a strategy to eliminate page splits.

Let's take the example of the JProCo.HumanResources.Contractor table, and suppose we add an extra identity field to keep track of the inserts. We will build the clustered index based on the identity field (see Figure 8.19).

Physical Sort of Data

Clustered Index located on Counter Field.

Page 1

1	222-22-2222	Jonny	Dirt
2	565-66-6767	Sally	Smith
3	888-88-8888	Irene	Intern
	Empty	Empty	Empty

Page 2

Empty	Empty	Empty
Empty	Empty	Empty
Empty	Empty	Empty
Empty	Empty	Empty

Figure 8.19 We've created a clustered index on the identity (counter) field.

If we were to drop the table (JProCo.HumanResources.Contractor), rebuild it with an identity field, and add a clustered index based on the identity (counter) field, then the table would not have to readjust itself with each insert to physically order the records by SSN.

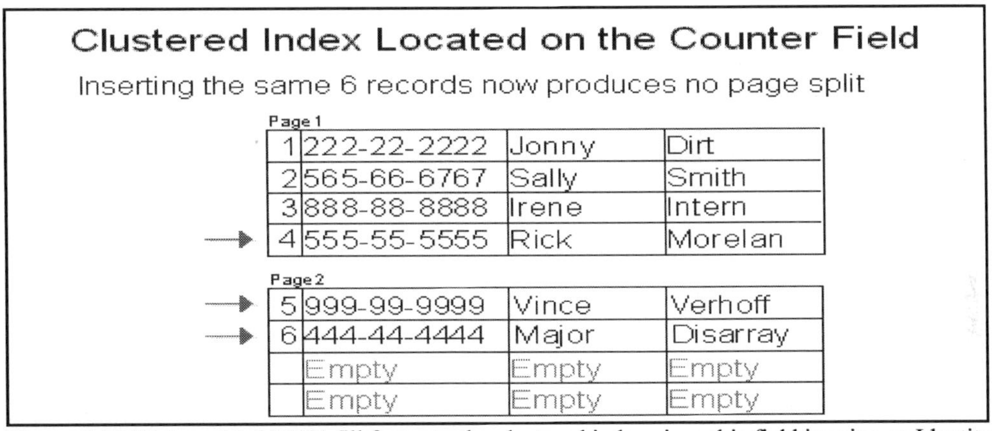
Clustered Index Located on the Counter Field
Inserting the same 6 records now produces no page split
Page 1
1 222-22-2222 Jonny Dirt
2 565-66-6767 Sally Smith
3 888-88-8888 Irene Intern
4 555-55-5555 Rick Morelan
Page 2
5 999-99-9999 Vince Verhoff
6 444-44-4444 Major Disarray
Empty Empty Empty
Empty Empty Empty

Figure 8.20 We've added 100% fill factor to the clustered index since this field is using an Identity property which counts sequentially.

What would this do for us? When Rick Morelan's record is inserted, he would receive the counter field of 4. The next one (Vince Verhoff) would be added to the second page, and Major Disarray would come right after him because his ContractorID field would get the value of 6. In this way inserts are sequential – you can have a 100% fill factor, and no page splits.

Lab 8.1: Clustered Indexes

Lab Prep: Before you can begin the lab, you must have SQL Server installed and run the SQLArchChapter8.1Setup.sql script.

Skill Check 1: In the prior section, we learned about the fill factor setting in clustered indexes. Set the fill factor in the JProCo.dbo.Supplier table's index to 70%.

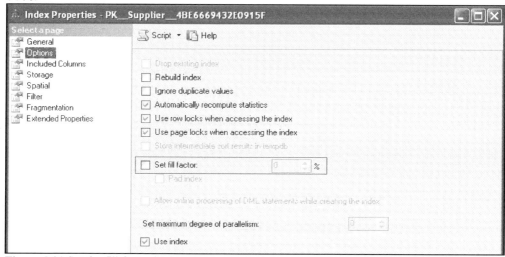

Figure 8.21 Set the fill factor in the JProCo.dbo.Supplier table's index to 70%.

Skill Check 2: Drop and re-create the JProCo.HumanResources.Contractor table with the same fields and records as shown in this section. Include an identity field called ContractorID that is also the primary key. When you are finished, your table should resemble the figure below (Figure 8.22).

```
SELECT * FROM JProCo.HumanResources.Contractor
```

	ContractorID	SSN	FirstName	LastName	EMail	Pay
1	1	222-22-2222	Jonny	Dirt	Jdirt@JProCo.com	35000.00
2	2	656-66-6767	Sally	Smith	SallyS@JProCo.com	45000.00
3	3	888-88-8888	Irene	Intern	I-Irenel@JProCo.com	NULL
4	4	555-55-5555	Rick	Morelan	rmorelan@JProCo.com	25000.00
5	5	999-99-9999	Vince	Verhoff	Viv@JProCo.com	65000.00
6	6	444-44-4444	Major	Disarray	Majord@JProCo.com	20000.00

Figure 8.22 Re-create the Contractor table with an identity field which is also the primary key.

Answer Code: The T-SQL code to this lab can be found in the downloadable files in a file named Lab8.1_ClusteredIndexes.sql.

Clustered Indexes - Points to Ponder

1. An index is an ordered list of values from a table.

2. An index is used by an RDBMS (like SQL Server) to organize data for frequent searches to improve performance and data access.

3. Indexes can be created when you create the table, or they can be added after the table is created.

4. Columns that change frequently OR are too wide don't make good clustered indexes.

5. Properly designed indexes improve query performance.

6. When you create a primary key on a table, a clustered index is created for you by default.

7. A clustered index determines the physical organization of data in the table.

8. Each table can have only one clustered index.

9. A heap is a table without a clustered index.

10. If you create a primary key or unique constraint then SQL Server automatically creates a unique index during the CREATE TABLE or ALTER TABLE statements.

11. If a frequently changed field is contained in a clustered index, then the entire row of data might be moved so the physical sort can remain intact.

12. The adjustment of memory pages is known as a "page split."

13. The FILLFACTOR option lets you allocate a percentage of free space on the leaf level pages to reduce splitting.

14. Leaf level is a term that represents the actual storage location of your data.

15. The FILLFACTOR option's main purpose is to postpone and reduce page splitting.

16. The lower the FILLFACTOR percentage, the fewer page splits you get.

17. The lower the FILLFACTOR percentage, the more unused space you have.

18. If your primary key is on an IDENTITY field, then there are no page splits even with a 100% FILLFACTOR.

19. Think of the FILLFACTOR setting as a one-time allocation event. In other words, the FILLFACTOR percentage is applied at the time you create or

rebuild an index. It does not include ongoing monitoring to make sure you always have x% of empty rows in your table.

20. Tables that are clustered based on an IDENTITY column are not subject to page splitting and therefore do not benefit from a FILLFACTOR.

21. A field with an Identity property produces system-generated, sequential values that identify each row in the table.

22. An IDENTITY column must use one of the following data types: decimal, int, numeric, smallint, bigint, or tinyint.

23. Each table can have only one column with an Identity property, and the column cannot allow NULL values or contain a DEFAULT.

24. There are four main ways to obtain information on existing indexes.
    a. SQL Management Studio
    b. System Stored Procedures
    c. Catalog Views
    d. System Functions

25. Sometimes heaps are better than clustered indexes.

26. Heaps make better sense for a table when:
    a. The data which the index is based upon is volatile (changes often)
    OR
    b. The table data is very compact (i.e., small)
    OR
    c. The table contains mostly duplicated rows

27. "Predicating" is geek-speak term which essentially describes filtering a query with criteria (most often with a WHERE or HAVING clause). To say a query is *predicating* on the InvoiceID field means the query is filtering based upon the criteria specified for the InvoiceID (e.g., WHERE InvoiceID = 3). The condition WHERE Invoice=3 is the *predicate* of the following query:

    ```
    SELECT * FROM SalesInvoiceDetail
    WHERE InvoiceID = 3
    ```

Nonclustered Indexes

Sometimes we look at everything before deciding and sometimes we have our likely options narrowed down conveniently for us. This can be true of our search patterns when shopping, when looking at a restaurant menu, and when looking at available options for our reports and data.

At a very high level, these are helpful ways to think about the two distinct approaches SQL Server takes toward retrieving query data. Sometimes SQL Server must scan all available data in a database object(s) in order to provide the data we've requested. At other times, SQL Server is able to use indexes to more quickly navigate and zero in on the requested data.

Before we tackle our main topic of nonclustered indexes, we should find out exactly what indexes are doing for us.

Index Scan

A **scan** is the scenario we described where you look at every item before selecting. This is not always bad, especially with small lists you intend to really analyze thoroughly. When you go to a new restaurant, you want to look over all the items before deciding. This will take longer as the list you must scan gets bigger. However, in a large list where you know what you are looking for, a scan of every item becomes a big waste of time and you probably wish the list had been better organized.

For example, when visiting my favorite restaurant with a vegetarian colleague, I noticed he immediately went to the lower left corner and picked one of their three vegetarian options. This restaurant chose to *index* the menu to make this easier. However, another restaurant we visited did not do this but simply placed an asterisk next to each vegetarian item. With the vegetarian options interspersed throughout the menu, my guest had no choice but to scan the entire menu to locate the items which met his criteria.

Index Seek

A **seek** is when your indexes are set up to make searching done with fewer steps. Quickly finding exactly what you need is a wonderful thing. Everyday life is filled with examples of orderly systems to help us navigate quickly.

For example, suppose I handed you the 400 page *Joes 2 Pros* Programming Book and told you to turn to page 210. Since pages are in order, it's easy to eliminate a lot of unneeded searches and scans. There's no need to begin at page 1 when you can go straight to the middle of the book and then turn a few pages to the right until you locate page 210. *Going straight to the page you want in very few hops is known as a **seek***.

On the other hand, suppose you had been asked to find the page in the *Joes 2 Pros* Programming Book which contains a word with the letter O appearing 4 times. It will likely take you a very long time to find that page, since you would have to scan each page in the entire book in order to find that data. Similarly, some queries cause SQL Server to scan ALL of your data to find your requested information.

Let's imagine the request had been a little more specific and you were asked to find the word "onomatopoeia" in a book. Knowing that most books have an index, you would probably flip to the back of the book, check the index, and find the number of the page which contains the term "onomatopoeia." Since you know the precise page number, you could ***seek*** directly to the page. So the fact that the index kept track of the data you needed and quickly pointed you right to the data sped up your query time considerably.

Clustered Indexes Recap

In the first section of this chapter, we learned that *clustered indexes* arrange your records physically according to the column where you place the clustered index.

Our last example showed that a book is essentially *clustered* in order by page numbers, and it is indexed by words. In geek speak, we would say a book has a *clustered index* by pages, and it has a *nonclustered index* pointing directly to the pages where specific words are located.

Thus, the purpose of indexes is much like that of the index found at the back of a book: it takes up a little extra space, but it speeds up the way you search for data. *Indexes reduce query processing time.*

In looking at the design of our CurrentProducts table, we see it has one index. Let's look at the properties of this index and see which field the index is based on (see Figures 8.23 and 8.24, next page).

  Object Explorer > Databases > JProCo > Tables > dbo.CurrentProducts >
  Indexes (folder) > right-click on the index > Properties > General (page)

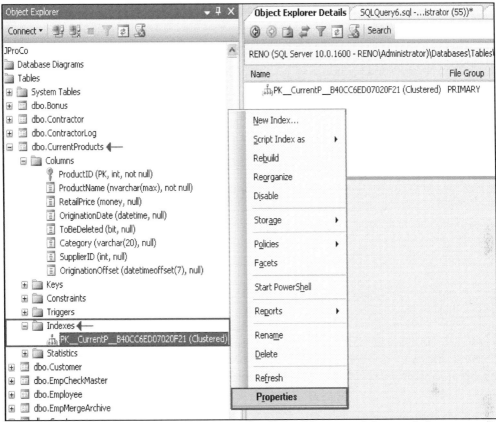

Figure 8.23 Looking at the design of the CurrentProducts table, we see it has one index.

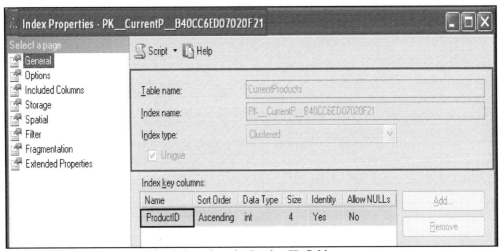

Figure 8.24 This clustered index is based on the ProductID field.

Since this clustered index is based on the ProductID field, any query predicating on the ProductID field should run very quickly. For that reason, the first query shown here (in the top of Figure 8.25) should run a lot faster than the second query looking for all the Supplier 1 records (shown in the bottom of Figure 8.25).

```
--Since this query will be covered by the Clustered Index,
--it will run faster than a query not covered by an index.
SELECT *
FROM JProCo.dbo.CurrentProducts
WHERE ProductID = 5

--This query will not be covered (no index is on SupplierID).
SELECT *
FROM JProCo.dbo.CurrentProducts
WHERE SupplierID = 1
```

Figure 8.25 Queries covered by an index run faster than queries not covered by an index.

Let's look at the execution plan of the faster query. As shown below (Figure 8.26), highlight the query for which you want to see the execution plan and then hit the toolbar icon ("Display Estimated Execution Plan"). Alternatively, you can highlight the query and hit Ctrl+L to see your estimated execution plan. For our faster query, SQL Server shows it will do a seek on the clustered index.

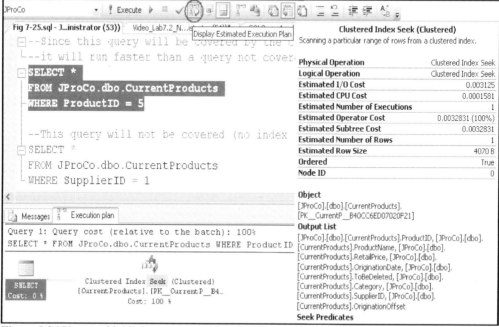

Figure 8.26 You can highlight a query and hit Ctrl+L to see its estimated execution plan.

If you hover the mouse over the execution plan 'Clustered Index Seek', you can see more detail as shown on the right side of Figure 8.26 (see previous page). The highest amount shown here is the "Estimated Subtree Cost", which is how long the operation takes. Next we'll look at the execution plan for the SupplierID query, which will not be covered by the index (see Figure 8.27). SQL Server will need to scan the table in order to find the SupplierID.

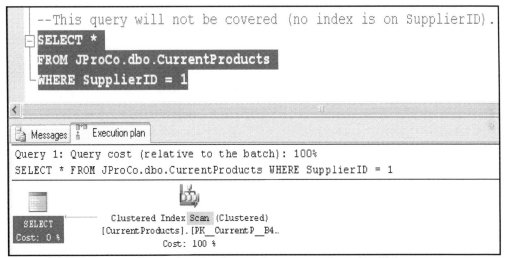

Figure 8.27 The estimated execution plan for our slower query shows it will do a scan.

The two queries below return the same record. If you run these queries separately, you'll see the second one takes a little longer to find the same record.

```
SELECT *
  FROM JProCo.HumanResources.Contractor
  WHERE ContractorID = 1
SELECT *
  FROM JProCo.HumanResources.Contractor
  WHERE SSN = '222-22-2222'
```

	ContractorID	SSN	FirstName	LastName	EMail	Pay
1	1	222-22-2222	Jonny	Dirt	Jdirt@JProCo.com	35000.00

	ContractorID	SSN	FirstName	LastName	EMail	Pay
1	1	222-22-2222	Jonny	Dirt	Jdirt@JProCo.com	35000.00

Figure 8.28 Two queries that give identical results, but the first uses indexes and will run faster.

Let's look at the estimated execution plan for the first query. That one will do a seek (Figure 8.29).

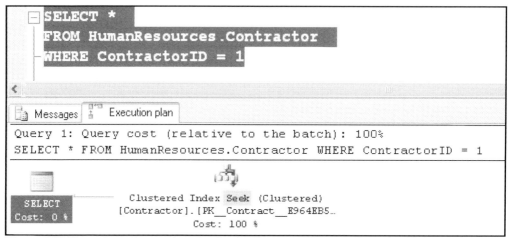

Figure 8.29 The estimated execution plan for the ContractorID query shows it will do a seek.

The execution plan for the second query shows it will do a scan (Figure 8.30).

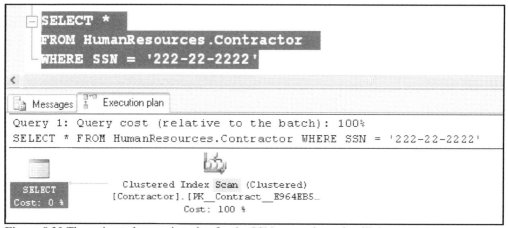

Figure 8.30 The estimated execution plan for the SSN query shows it will do a scan.

Why can the ContractorID query use a seek while the SSN query is only able to do a scan? If we look at the design for the JProCo.HumanResources.Contractor table, we see that the table's only index is the clustered index based on ContractorID (see next page - Figure 8.31).

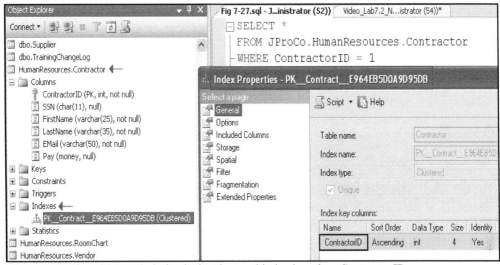

Figure 8.31 The table's only index is the clustered index based on ContractorID.

Could we create a clustered index based on SSN in order to speed up our SSN query? No, because the clustered index determines the physical ordering of the records. Since there can be just one physical ordering of records in a table, you can only have one clustered index per table. However, a table can have many **nonclustered indexes**.

Creating Nonclustered Indexes

So what are **nonclustered indexes** and how do we use them?

Nonclustered indexes allow us to look at our data from many perspectives. If a clustered index physically orders a table's records, then a **nonclustered index** is a way of organizing information in a non-physical manner.

Let's think back to our book example. We know the sequential ordering of the pages is analogous to a clustered index. It's extremely helpful to have the pages in order, but can the page numbers themselves actually tell us anything about the nature of the book? When you picked up this book and wanted to learn about the new Spatial data types in SQL Server 2008, you looked in the index and found over a dozen pages listed which include a reference to Spatial data types. Do the three digit numbers 159, 164, or 168 tell you anything about the topic? No, but they do allow you to rapidly find the information you want. This is similar to the way nonclustered indexes can be used in conjunction with clustered indexes in our queries.

Let's think back to our two queries on the JProCo.HumanResources.Contractor table (Figure 8.28). The records in this table are physically arranged in order of ContractorID. But other queries we will perform on this table will involve themes more important to us, such as pay data and name data. As long as the table contains just a handful of records, it won't matter much that a scan query takes an additional few seconds to run. However, we know this table will grow to contain many thousands of records and include contractors working at locations all over the world.

So if you are only allowed one clustered index per table, how do you use many perspectives? Our shopping mall directory illustrates how we can have many nonclustered indexes in a table, despite having just one clustered index.

The mall has chosen to number the units (which follows the physical ordering of the stores like a clustered index), but the customer is more concerned with the store name than the store number. The list which keeps track of the store names in alphabetical order is one possible nonclustered index. Another nonclustered index would be the list which keeps track of the store categories (e.g., Childrens, Cosmetics, Electronics, Kitchenware, Men's Apparel, Toys, Women's Shoes, etc.). Yet another nonclustered index would be the list keeping track of all the restaurants in the mall. Before the December holidays, some stores remain open an additional two hours for holiday shoppers. The list keeping track of the stores open late would be another nonclustered index.

A nonclustered index is ordered and points you to the location you need. The mall directory allows customers to quickly locate the store(s) they want by referencing the physical location (i.e., unit number). Similarly, a nonclustered index will order its items and point to their positions in the clustered index.

Unique Nonclustered Indexes

Nonclustered indexes may be used with fields that have either unique or nonunique values.

At the Tacoma mall there are two T-Mobile stores. One is really a center mall kiosk. There is no requirement for two stores to have different names. Therefore, the directory at the mall is a **nonunique nonclustered index**.

Let's return to the JProCo.HumanResources.Contractor table and think about which nonclustered indexes may be unique versus nonunique.

How about the workplace e-mail address of each contractor? We often search an employee by e-mail address, and each employee's e-mail address is unique. We can create a nonclustered index based on the Email field and specify an option to make it unique. We can also make a unique nonclustered index on SSN because each employee's SSN is a unique value which we query frequently.

Let's add a unique nonclustered index to the HumanResources.Contractor table.

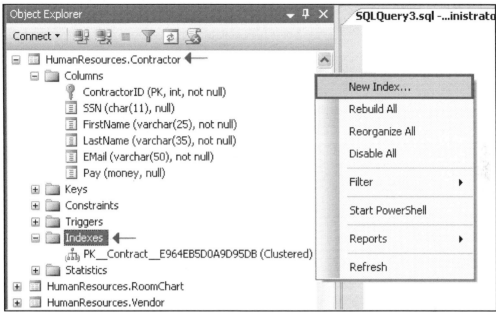

Figure 8.32 HumanResources.Contractor > right-click on the Indexes folder > New Index.

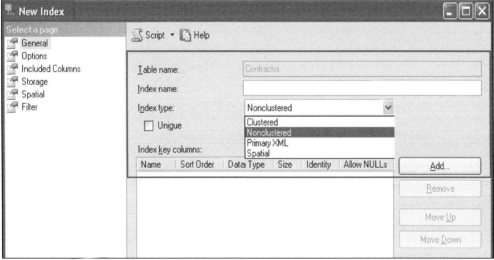

Figure 8.33 The dialog to create a New Index in the HumanResources.Contractor table.

We know this new index will be nonclustered, but for illustrative purposes we have momentarily digressed and selected the "Clustered" option in order to show readers this message box (see Figure 8.34). Since you can only have one clustered index per table, SQL Server will ask you to reconfirm before allowing you to drop the existing clustered index and create a new one.

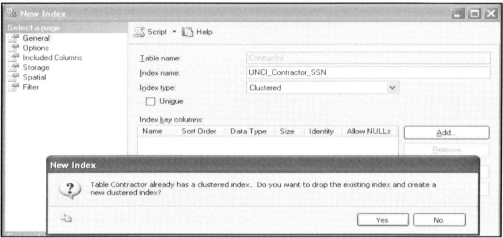

Figure 8.34 You can only have one clustered index per table.

However, we can add a nonclustered index, which we'll give the UNCI prefix (to help remind us it's a **U**nique **N**on**c**lustered **I**ndex), name the index (UNCI_Contractor_SSN), check the "Unique" box, click Add to select the SSN column, OK, then OK again (Figure 8.35).

Figure 8.35 Pick the column to be indexed.

280

We can now see the new index showing in Object Explorer (see Figure 8.36).
Object Explorer > Databases > JProCo > HumanResources.Contractor > Indexes

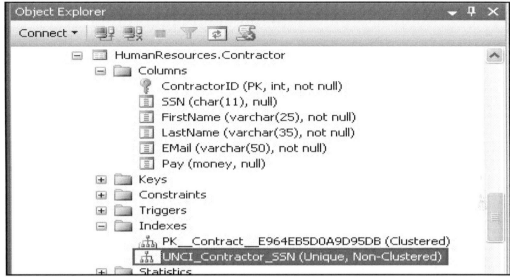

Figure 8.36 Verify that the UNCI_Contractor_SSN index has been created.

Now let's re-check the execution plan for the SSN query we attempted earlier (refer back to Figures 8.28 through 8.30). Notice the query is now more efficient, since we've added a nonclustered index to the field. The execution plan now shows a seek for the SSN query, instead of a scan (see Figure 8.37).

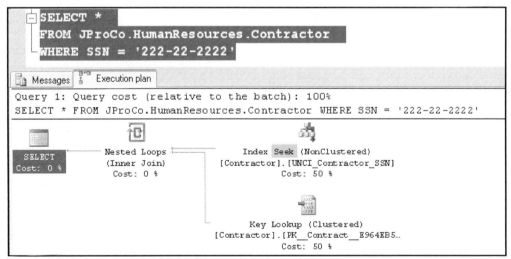

Figure 8.37 The query on the SSN column now does a seek.

Lab 8.2: Nonclustered Indexes

Lab Prep: Before you can begin the lab, you must have SQL Server installed and run the SQLArchChapter8.2Setup.sql script.

Skill Check 1: Create a nonclustered index called UNCI_Contractor_Email that is a unique nonclustered index on the HumanResources.Contractor table.

Once you've successfully created this index, it will appear in your Object Explorer (see Figure 8.38).

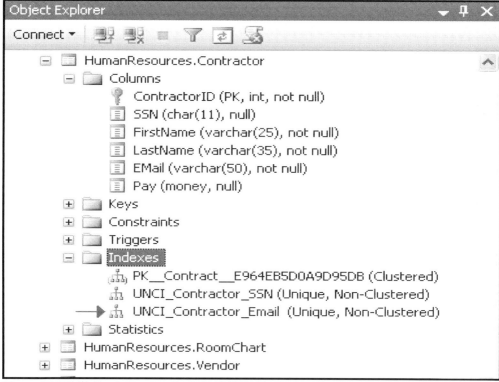

Figure 8.38 Skill Check 1 creates the index UNCI_Contractor_Email.

Answer Code: The answer to this lab can be found in the downloadable files in a file named Lab8.2_NonClusteredIndexes.sql.

Nonclustered Indexes - Points to Ponder

1. A table that does not have a clustered index is referred to as a "heap" and a table that has a clustered index is referred to as a "clustered table."

2. You can put a nonclustered index on a heap or on a clustered table.

3. In SQL Server 2005, each table was allowed up to 249 nonclustered indexes and 1 clustered index. In SQL Server 2008, each table may have up to 999 nonclustered indexes (including indexes which SQL Server generates to support constraints, such as a primary key, unique constraint, etc.) and 1 clustered index.

4. Nonclustered indexes are useful when users require multiple ways to search for data.

5. The term "coverage" refers to the number of columns predicated on in a query which are supported by an index.

6. Covered queries reduce disk I/O and improve query performance.

7. Nonclustered indexes work best when the data selectivity ranges from highly selective to unique.

8. Nonclustered indexes do not affect the physical location of data. Rather, nonclustered indexes create a list of pointers to the rows where the data resides.

9. It's best to create the clustered index before you create nonclustered indexes in a table.

10. Nonclustered indexes are automatically rebuilt when:
    a. An existing clustered index on the table is dropped.
    b. A clustered index on the table is created.
    c. A column covered by the nonclustered index changes.

11. You can create indexes by using SQL Server Management Studio or T-SQL code.

12. A unique index is an index which ensures all data in a column is unique and has no duplicates.

13. Columns that are used with a unique index should be set to NOT NULL. You cannot add a unique index to a column containing multiple null values, because these are considered duplicates when a unique index is created. A unique index will allow at most one NULL value.

Chapter Glossary

Clustered Index: The clustered index represents the actual physical order of your data.

Clustered table: A table that has a clustered index is referred to as a clustered table.

Coverage: This refers to the number of columns, predicated on in a query, that are supported by an index.

Execution plan: An execution plan allows you to see how the query is executed.

Fill Factor: The fill factor setting was introduced in SQL Server 2000 and helps prevent the need for pages to split.

Heap: A table that does not have a clustered index is referred to as a "Heap".

Identity Fields: A field with an Identity property produces system-generated sequential values that identify each row in the table.

Index Scan: An index scan is when you look at every item before selecting.

Index Seek: A seek is when your indexes are set up to make searching done with fewer steps.

Natural sort order: The sequence, from beginning to end, in which each row is stored in the table.

Nonclustered index: This type of index allows us to look at our data from many perspectives; a nonclustered index is a way of organizing information in a non-physical manner.

Nonunique nonclustered index: An index with nonunique, or duplicate values.

Page splits: Page splits arise when records from one memory page are moved to another page during changes to your table.

Primary key: A primary key rule is a constraint which ensures non-nullability and uniqueness (i.e., no duplicate values) in a field.

Chapter Eight - Review Quiz

1.) A heap has:

   O a. No clustered indexes.
   O b. One clustered index.
   O c. Many clustered indexes.

2.) You want to reserve your table to have 25% free pages and use 75% of the available pages. What should you do?

   O a. Use the default fill factor.
   O b. Use a fill factor of 25.
   O c. Use a fill factor of 75.
   O d. Disable the fill factor.

3.) What is true about clustered and nonclustered indexes? (Choose two)

   □ a. You can have only one clustered index per table.
   □ b. You can have up to 999 clustered indexes per table.
   □ c. You can have only one nonclustered index per table.
   □ d. You can have up to 999 nonclustered indexes per table.

4.) You have a table with one clustered index and one nonclustered index. Later research shows you have another field called "date" which is often queried and would benefit from some type of index. What can you do?

   O a. Create another clustered index.
   O b. Create another nonclustered index.

5.) Your SQL Server 2008 database stores all employees in a table. New employees are added every day. The table has a clustered index based on the EmployeeID column. You often query by SSN but the query is too slow. How can you support an efficient reporting solution by SSN?

   O a. Create another clustered index.
   O b. Create another nonclustered index.

Answer Key

1.) a   2.) c   3.) a, d 4.) b 5.) b

Bug Catcher Game

To play the Bug Catcher game run the BugCatcher_Chapter08CreatingIndexes.pps from the BugCatcher folder of the companion files. You can obtain these files from www.Joes2Pros.com or by ordering the Companion CD.

Chapter 9.   Creating Indexes with Code

Suppose you know how to create indexes that really make a database and its queries purr like a kitten. You have just optimized the indexes for your branch office, and management now wants you to tune the same databases which sit at the sister office in Toledo. It would be risky to give a bunch of point and click instructions to the Toledo DBA, as one missed step could make or break the system's performance. If you could set up all your indexes with T-SQL code, then you would just need to send over a script for the Toledo team to run.

While indexes can be created by clicking through the SQL Server Management Studio interface, a best practice is to create them by running reusable code. The Toledo scenario highlights the usefulness of being able to leverage code which has been validated.

This chapter will set up the same types of indexes as we saw in the last chapter and do so using T-SQL code. Writing code for indexes and index options is what this chapter is all about.

READER NOTE: In order to follow along with the examples in the first section of Chapter 9, please run the setup script SQLArchChapter9.0Setup.sql. The setup scripts for this book are posted at Joes2Pros.com.

Coding Indexes

In the last chapter, we used the JProCo.HumanResources.Contractor table, which contained just a clustered index before we created two nonclustered indexes on it.

We also have a similar table called JProCo HumanResources.Vendor, which has nearly the same fields as the JProCo HumanResources.Contractor table. The Vendor table also has a clustered index (which was generated by the primary key constraint).

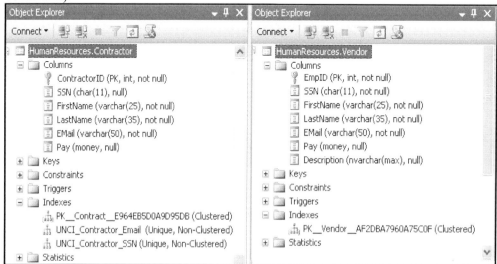

Figure 9.1 The HumanResources.Vendor table is similar to the HumanResources.Contractor table.

```
CREATE TABLE JProCo.HumanResources.Vendor
( EmpID int IDENTITY PRIMARY KEY,
SSN CHAR(11) NOT NULL,
FirstName varchar(25) NOT NULL,
LastName varchar(35) NOT NULL,
EMail varchar(50) NOT NULL,
Pay money NULL,
Description nvarchar(max) NULL )
GO

INSERT INTO JProCo.HumanResources.Vendor VALUES
('123-22-2222','Lewis','Apple','LA@JPROCO.com',35000,'Just the Boss')
INSERT INTO JProCo.HumanResources.Vendor VALUES
('321-22-2222','Steve','Cheery','SC@JPROCO.com',35000,'Sweet Guy')
```

Figure 9.2 The code used to create and populate the JProCo.HumanResources.Vendor table.

Nonunique Option

We will create a nonclustered index on SSN and a nonclustered index on the Email field, except this time we'll create our indexes using T-SQL code.

Let's start off by creating another index on the HumanResources.Vendor table. We're going to create the NCI_Vendor_SSN nonclustered index.

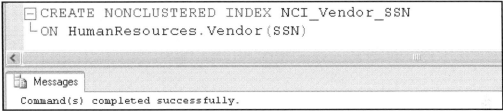

```
CREATE NONCLUSTERED INDEX NCI_Vendor_SSN
ON HumanResources.Vendor(SSN)
```

Messages

Command(s) completed successfully.

Figure 9.3 The code to create a nonclustered index on SSN.

Check the properties for this index in Object Explorer (right side of Figure 9.4).

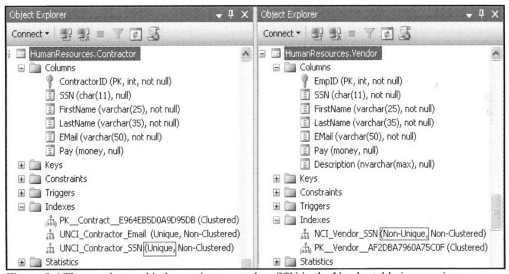

Figure 9.4 The nonclustered index we just created on SSN in the Vendor table is nonunique.

After you execute the code and refresh the indexes folder in your Object Explorer, you will see the newly created index NCI_Vendor_SSN. But there's a subtle difference between the nonclustered index for Social Security Number on the Contractor table (left hand side of Figure 9.4) and the Social Security Number nonclustered index on the Vendor table. Notice that the index on the Vendor table is *nonunique*, whereas the index on the Contractor table is unique. The UNCI_Contractor_SSN index is a unique nonclustered index, and the NCI_Vendor_ SSN index is a nonunique, nonclustered index.

Unique Option

We will drop the index we just created, in order to re-create it as a **unique** index.

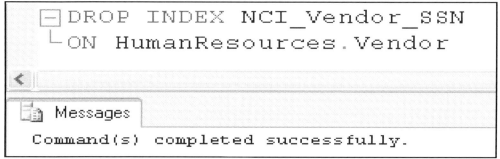

Figure 9.5 Drop the nonclustered index on SSN so we can re-create it as a unique index.

In order to create the **NCI_Vendor_SSN** as a unique index we would have to create it using the UNIQUE keyword. Specifying the keyword UNIQUE right after the Create command will create an index as unique. *If you leave out this keyword, then you would allow duplicate values in your table.*

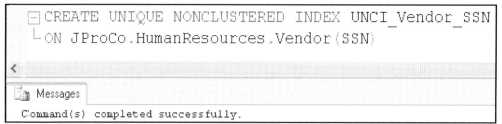

Figure 9.6 Re-create the nonclustered index on SSN as a unique index.

After running this code (see Figure 9.6), refresh your Object Explorer and you will see UNCI_Vendor_SSN as a unique nonclustered index (see next page, Figure 9.7).

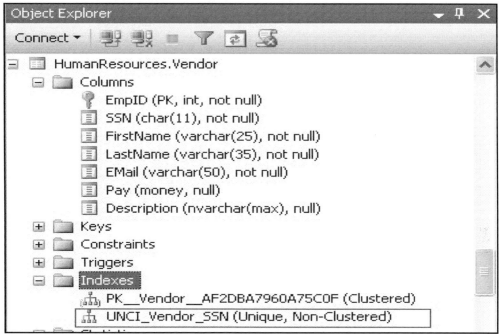

Figure 9.7 UNCI_Vendor_SSN now shows as a unique, nonclustered index.

Lab 9.1: Coding Indexes

Lab Prep: Before you can begin the lab, you must have SQL Server installed and run the SQLArchChapter9.1Setup.sql script.

Skill Check 1: Create the UNCI_Vendor_Email unique nonclustered index on the JProCo.HumanResource.Vendor table. Once you've successfully created this index, it will appear in your Object Explorer (see Figure 9.8).

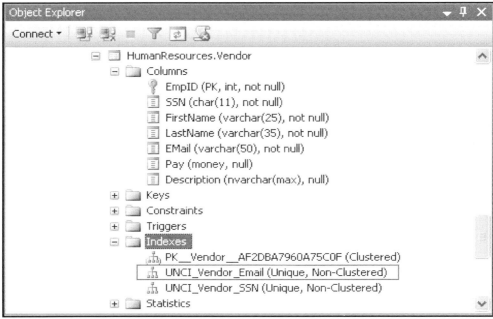

Figure 9.8 UNCI_Vendor_Email now shows as a unique, nonclustered index.

Answer Code: The T-SQL code to this lab can be found in the downloadable files in a file named Lab9.1_CodingIndexes.sql.

Coding Indexes - Points to Ponder

1. There are three indexing options in SQL Server:
    a. Clustered indexes
    b. Nonclustered indexes
    c. No indexes

2. You can implement nonclustered indexes on heaps.

3. Bonus Feature: When you create a primary key on a table, a clustered index is created by default unless you use the NONCLUSTERED argument.

4. Larger numbers of nonclustered indexes in an OLTP (**On**Line **T**ransaction **P**rocessing) application affect INSERT, UPDATE, and DELETE statements because all indexes must update as the table changes.

5. You can create indexes by using SQL Server Management Studio or T-SQL code.

6. The T-SQL command for creating an index is CREATE INDEX.

7. Once indexes are generated, SQL Server keeps them updated. When the data changes, the corresponding indexes are updated, as well.

Index Options

In the last section we saw that the same index, on the same table, could have been specified as unique or non-unique. Either way, you created a nonclustered index on your table. There are many more options for building indexes, like using multiple fields in one index as well as setting the speed and size of the indexes. This section will explore the common index options you can specify.

In an employee table, it is quite clear that a SSN belongs to a specific employee. For example, if 555-55-5555 belongs to Rick Morelan and he later leaves the company, then no other employee can use that number because it deterministically belongs to Rick. In fact, if Rick also works part time at the local college teaching night classes, then 555-55-5555 would have the same significance in the college's database. How about Territory #6? What does Territory #6 mean? In one company that might mean Central Canada and in another that could be the Midwestern United States.

Suppose two companies merge, and each company has its own "Territory 6." That means there could be a danger of duplication, where we could have the following same two IDs with different names:

TerritoryID	TerritoryName
6	Central Canada
6	Midwestern United States

Composite Indexes

Observe that in Figure 9.9, there are six distinct cities listed. Yet you see the name "Springfield" twice, "Des Moines" twice, and "Toledo" twice. This is because Springfield, Oregon and Springfield, Michigan are two different cities. The same is true with the two Toledo records and the two Des Moines records.

Suppose we want to take an extra step to ensure data integrity and make certain we never have a duplicate city. If you were to base a unique clustered index on the City field, the database wouldn't allow these situations where multiple cities actually do have the same name. However, a composite index – an index composed of more than one field – would help data integrity while also allowing both "Des Moines, Iowa" and "Des Moines, Washington" to appear in the database.

```
SELECT *
FROM Sales.Localities
```

	GeoID	State	City	Population
1	1	Oregon	Springfield	35000
2	2	Michigan	Springfield	68000
3	3	Washington	Des Moines	24000
4	4	Iowa	Des Moines	212000
5	5	Oregon	Toledo	6500
6	6	Ohio	Toledo	413000

Figure 9.9 Six distinct cities are listed here, despite some city names appearing twice but in different states.

The Sales.Localities table has a unique clustered index on the GeoID field. That means we can't have two Location 6's. But that doesn't help enforce allowing only one combination of city and state in the table. Look at this insert statement where we insert Toledo, Ohio with a population of 45,000 (Figure 9.10). We already have a GeoID of 6 for Toledo, Ohio. Running a select statement on our table, we see we just added a GeoID of 7, which is also Toledo, Ohio.

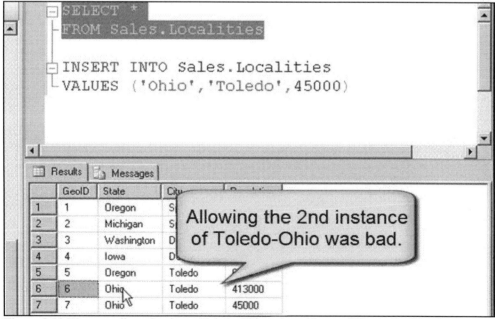

Figure 9.10 We were allowed to insert Toledo-Ohio twice with two different GeoID values.

This duplicate record will cause problems. To undo the last insert action, we will run **SQLArchExtraResetLocalities.sql** script so the Sales.Localities table will again contain just the original six records. Once that's done, we will have our table reset and once again the existing data complies with the requirement that records cannot be contain duplicate City-State combinations. But since our table is still vulnerable to future City-State duplicates, we must take steps to ensure that such duplications are prevented (Figure 9.11).

State	City	Population
Oregon	Springfield	35,000
Michigan	Springfield	68,000
Washington	**Des Moines**	24,000
Iowa	**Des Moines**	212,000
Oregon	Toledo	6,500
Ohio	Toledo	413,000

How do we restrict duplicate City-State Combinations?

Figure 9.11 The goal is to make the composite of City-State unique for all records in the Localities table.

Since city names in the U.S. are unique within a state but can be duplicated in other states (e.g., Toledo, OH and Toledo, OR), we know a city name could legitimately appear as many as 50 times in our table. Springfield, Oregon and Springfield, Michigan are two different cities. In other words, we cannot achieve our goal by simply locking down the City field. If we were to create a unique nonclustered index based on City, it would not allow us to enter the second Springfield for Michigan.

The same is true for the State field. We can't simply constrain the State field (e.g., with a unique nonclustered index based on State), because we clearly need to be able to list a State multiple times (as shown by our data in Figure 9.11).

In order to formulate an indexing plan, we need to first understand the combination of fields in our data which constitute uniqueness. So what is unique about cities in the United States?

Well, a city name may exist only once per state – that is to say, two cities in one state are not permitted to have the same name. It is legal to have a Springfield, OR and a Springfield, MI, but it is not possible to have two cities named "Springfield" within a single state.

A **composite index** includes multiple fields as part of one index. The fields combined together in one index create a constraint where only one combination of the fields is allowed in the table. Subsequent attempts to add duplicate instances of the same combination into the table will be disallowed by the index.

Coding Unique Composite Indexes

We want to lock down the Localities table to ensure we never have a duplicate city-state combination. So we will create a unique **composite index** to enforce that *each combination of city and state* cannot be repeated in our table (Figure 9.12).

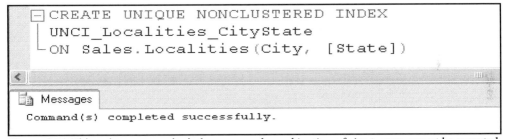

```
CREATE UNIQUE NONCLUSTERED INDEX
  UNCI_Localities_CityState
ON Sales.Localities(City, [State])
```

Messages

Command(s) completed successfully.

Figure 9.12 This unique composite index says *each combination of city + state* cannot be repeated.

We have successfully created our composite index.

In Object Explorer, we can see the new unique non-clustered index, UNCI_Localities_CityState (see Figure 9.13).

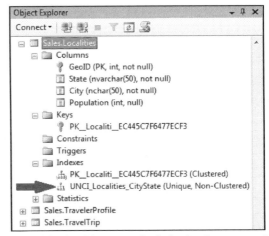

Figure 9.13 This composite index has been created.

Let's test our new index by attempting to insert a duplicate record for Toledo, OH (see Figure 9.14).

```
--Intentionally trying to generate an error by entering
--a duplicate city-state combination into the table.
INSERT INTO JProCo.Sales.Localities
VALUES ('Ohio', 'Toledo', 45000)
```

Messages
Msg 2601, Level 14, State 1, Line 3
Cannot insert duplicate key row in object 'Sales.Localities'
 with unique index 'UNCI_Localities_CityState'.
The statement has been terminated.

Figure 9.14 We are testing our new composite index by attempting to insert a duplicate record.

A composite index uses two or more fields added together as one larger field. Concatenating fields makes the composite index larger than one index on a single field, but it has some performance benefits. For example, the following query will run faster thanks to our newly created composite index, UNCI_Localities_CityState:

SELECT City, [State]
FROM Sales.Localities
WHERE City = 'Toledo'

The index helps the WHERE clause run much faster. This query must display data from the City and State fields, *which it now can pull directly from the composite index.* Since all the needed data is already contained in the index, then there is no need for the SELECT statement to pull more data from the table. If our query contained one more field, additional I/O would likely be needed to access the table.

Indexes With Included Columns

We've learned that the index will aid the efficiency of the WHERE clause, and that the SELECT statement often pulls directly from the index location. Suppose one more field were added to the above SELECT statement. We could re-create the index to include the additional field. However, this can become problematic, because the index creation will require more time, as each combination of fields must be maintained. The **INCLUDE option** can help our dilemma. It will allow us to effectively add more fields (i.e., nonkey columns) to a nonclustered index while only requiring one of the fields to be part of the actual index key calculation.

This strategy works particularly well if your query contains an ID field to use in the nonclustered index and your WHERE clause predicates on the ID. In our example, we will see the INCLUDE option extend the functionality of the index and bring along the other fields named in our SELECT query.

Recall that we added a unique nonclustered index on the SSN field of the
Contractor table (added in Figure 8.35 and shown in Figures 9.1 and 9.4). We've
learned that creating nonclustered indexes can aid us in the querying of data and
that they can also enforce uniqueness of certain fields. In the case of SSN, it can do
both.

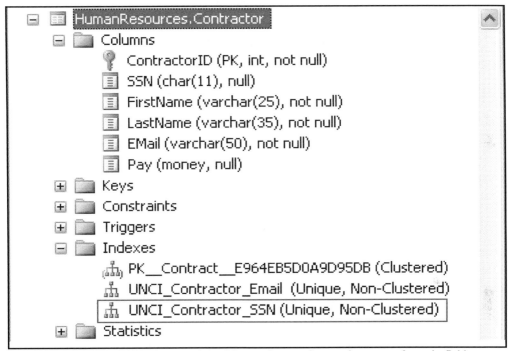

Figure 9.15 NCIs can aid in the querying of data and can enforce uniqueness of certain fields.

So if you predicate on SSN, you're going to get a performance gain. As a matter of
fact, this query will run very rapidly because we're not just predicating on SSN, but
it's also currently the only field in our SELECT list (Figure 9.16).

Figure 9.16 This query runs rapidly, since we're only selecting SSN and also predicating on SSN.

In this query the WHERE clause found the SSN value in the index and since the SELECT list wants just that value, there is no need to lookup the corresponding values in the clustered index. If all the fields you want are already in the index, just one Index Seek will be performed, as shown in the "Execution Plan" (see Figure 9.17). Execution Plans will be covered in depth in Chapter 10.

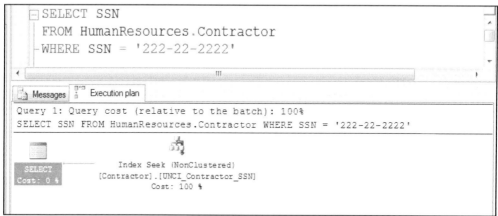

Figure 9.17 The execution plan shows an Index Seek without needing a Key Lookup, since all the fields in the SELECT list are included in the index.

The query below (see Figure 9.18) will not run as quickly, because we're retrieving data in the SELECT list that is not a part of the index (i.e., from the FirstName and LastName fields). However, since the additional data is being pulled from the same row (i.e., the FirstName and LastName values are in contained in the same row of the table because they belong to the same contractor), it impacts performance less.

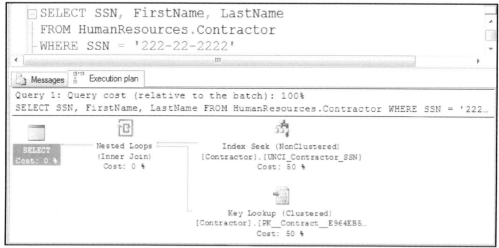

Figure 9.18 This query won't run quite as fast, because the SELECT list is getting data which is not part of the index and thus requires a Key Lookup to the clustered index.

If this (see Figure 9.18) is the main query you run frequently, then you would see a performance gain by putting all three of these fields in a composite index, even though FirstName and LastName don't add anything more to the uniqueness of SSN.

However, our example will show that the INCLUDE option offers an even better approach which keeps your indexes small while still having the non-indexed fields perform very rapidly when retrieved by your SELECT statement.

We'll now drop this nonclustered index and re-create it with the INCLUDE syntax (see Figures 9.19-9.20).

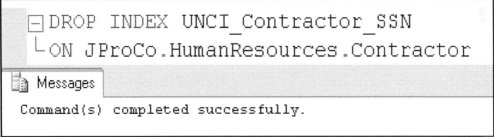

Figure 9.19 We will drop this index in order to re-create it in a way that optimizes our main query.

The statement below creates the nonclustered index and includes other nonkey columns along with the index in order to improve performance (see Figure 9.20).

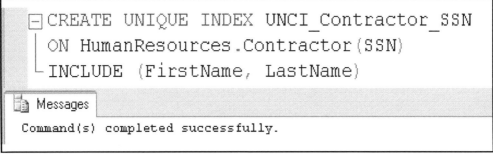

Figure 9.20 This index optimizes the query we run most (SELECT SSN, FirstName, LastName).

If we check Object Explorer, we see the index re-created and appearing as it did previously (see Figure 9.15). However, if we check the index properties, we see that the included columns (FirstName and LastName) appear also (Figure 9.21).

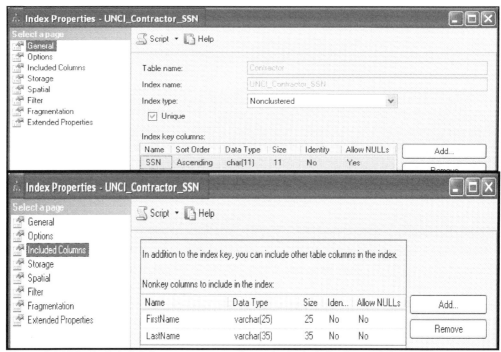

Figure 9.21 The Included Columns page now shows the included columns (Firstname, LastName).

ONLINE Option with Indexes

How long it takes to create a new index depends on how much data is in the table at the time you create it. It could take a fraction of a second or sometimes even several hours. During that time, the table is offline and not able to handle any requests. At least, that was true in SQL Server 2000 and earlier versions. Is it OK for your business to have your table offline while you create an index? If so, then that's great, because the creation of that index will run much faster. With SQL Server (versions 2005 and later), you now have the option to keep a table online and available to your users during index creation. The creation step takes a bit longer, but it's a worthwhile tradeoff because the table will have zero downtime.

Creating an index on a table normally brings the table offline while the index is created. In this chapter, the indexes we've built/dropped/re-created have all been on small tables. Thus, these tables were down for only a fraction of a second, which really didn't cause any disruption.

Suppose the HumanResources.Contractor table had a million, or more, records. We're planning some index maintenance or creations, which would bring the table down for a few minutes (if not longer). Suppose this is a table you cannot afford to have made unavailable to your customers, even for a second. The ONLINE = ON option can help you keep the table online while you create the index.

We will now drop the current index, and then re-create it with absolutely zero downtime (see Figures 9.22-9.23).

Figure 9.22 We've dropped this index in order to re-create it using the ONLINE option.

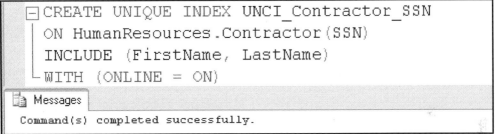

Figure 9.23 This index is being re-created using the ONLINE option – zero table downtime.

We can see the index re-created in Object Explorer and in the Index Properties interface. Everything appears identical to our previous creation of this index when we introduced the included columns (Figure 9.21). The ONLINE option helped to re-create everything and kept the table available, just as we expected.

Covered Query vs. Covering Index

Sometimes you use the term 'covered query' to indicate a query that has a 'covering index'. 'Covered queries' and 'covering indexes' are closely related concepts but aren't the same thing. A 'covered query' occurs when every column used in your query are covered by one or more indexes. (This includes every column in your SELECT list, as well as every column in your WHERE clause.) A 'covering index' is where the needed data is found more quickly through pointers from the nonclustered index to the data in the cluster.

Filtered Indexes

This is a new SQL Server 2008 feature and it is great if a large number of nulls appear, yet you only want to index the actual data (i.e., the non-null data).

We know that indexes perform at their best when they're on a field which contains highly selective data. Selectivity is one of the measures SQL Server uses to determine which index to use, or whether it should ignore an index(es).

Let's look at the CompanyName field in the JProCo.dbo.Customer table (see Figure 9.24). Do these records seem highly selective?

	CustomerID	CustomerType	FirstName	LastName	CompanyName
1	1	Consumer	Mark	Williams	NULL
2	2	Consumer	Lee	Young	NULL
3	3	Consumer	Patricia	Martin	NULL
4	4	Consumer	Mary	Lopez	NULL
5	5	Business	NULL	NULL	MoreTechnology.com
6	6	Consumer	Ruth	Clark	NULL
7	7	Consumer	Tessa	Wright	NULL
8	8	Consumer	Jennifer	Garcia	NULL
9	9	Consumer	Linda	Adams	NULL
10	10	Consumer	Robert	Wilson	NULL
11	11	Consumer	Kimberly	Taylor	NULL

`SELECT * FROM JProCo.dbo.Customer`

JProCo 00:00:00 775 rows

Figure 9.24 CompanyName is highly selective on values that are not null.

In the CompanyName field, 773 of 775 records are the same – that is to say they are nulls. So as a whole, having only three different values out of 775 records (i.e., null, MoreTechnology.com, and Puma Consulting) is *not selective*.

The data in the CustomerType field relates to the data in CompanyName and thus also has low selectivity (i.e., 773 of 775 records have a value of "Consumer").

If it weren't for the null values, you could make an argument that the remaining CompanyName values are actually unique and thus highly selective. Since most of the column's values are nulls, we don't tend to predicate on CompanyName – certainly not filtering for nulls. The only time we predicate on CompanyName is when we query the JProCo.dbo.Customer table looking for a specific company.

Figure 9.25 shows a query predicating on CompanyName. And we'll look for the company MoreTechnology.com (i.e., one of the two non-null values).

```
SELECT *
  FROM JProCo.dbo.Customer
  WHERE CompanyName = 'MoreTechnology.com'
```

	CustomerID	CustomerType	FirstName	LastName	CompanyName
1	5	Business	NULL	NULL	MoreTechnology.com

Figure 9.25 A query that filters on CompanyName looking for 'MoreTechnology.com'.

If you enable the execution plan and run the query again, you will notice that the query performs an index scan to locate the row. What we would ideally like to do is add a nonclustered index based on the CompanyName field, except we would like to instruct it to only index the populated portions of the field. In other words, we would like the index to ignore the null values. With filtered indexes, you can now add criteria to your index creation.

Even though our query predicates on CompanyName alone (Figure 9.25), we will include the CustomerType field because it will appear in the SELECT list.

How do we turn a non-selective field like CompanyName into a selective one? We're going to think outside of the box and say that the data is actually selective if we just look for the CompanyName to not be null (Figures 9.26-9.28). Then every record will be unique, which is extremely selective!

```
CREATE NONCLUSTERED INDEX NCI_Customer_CompanyName
  ON dbo.Customer(CompanyName)
  INCLUDE(CustomerType)
  WHERE CompanyName IS NOT NULL
```

Command(s) completed successfully.

Figure 9.26 Filtered Indexes are a new SQL Server 2008 feature.

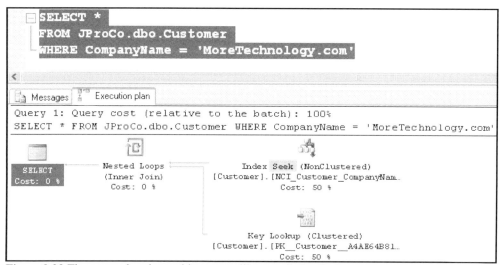

Figure 9.27 The Index Properties dialog shows the newly created index for CompanyName.

Figure 9.28 On the **Filter** page of the Index Properties dialog, we see the filter criteria we specified.

Figure 9.29 shows the query execution plan for the query that predicates on CompanyName. Notice the query is ready to perform a seek, instead of a scan.

```
SELECT *
FROM JProCo.dbo.Customer
WHERE CompanyName = 'MoreTechnology.com'
```

Messages   Execution plan

Query 1: Query cost (relative to the batch): 100%
SELECT * FROM JProCo.dbo.Customer WHERE CompanyName = 'MoreTechnology.com'

SELECT   Nested Loops   Index Seek (NonClustered)
Cost: 0 %   (Inner Join)   [Customer].[NCI_Customer_CompanyNam...
                Cost: 0 %   Cost: 50 %

                                          Key Lookup (Clustered)
                                          [Customer].[PK__Customer__A4AE64B81...
                                          Cost: 50 %

Figure 9.29 The query plan shows this query will use an Index Seek.

Lab 9.2: Index Options

Lab Prep: Before you can begin the lab, you must have SQL Server installed and run the SQLArchChapter9.2Setup.sql script.

Skill Check 1: Create a unique nonclustered composite index called UNCI_Employee_FirstNameLastName on the dbo.Employee table that enforces the rule that two employees cannot have the same first and last names.

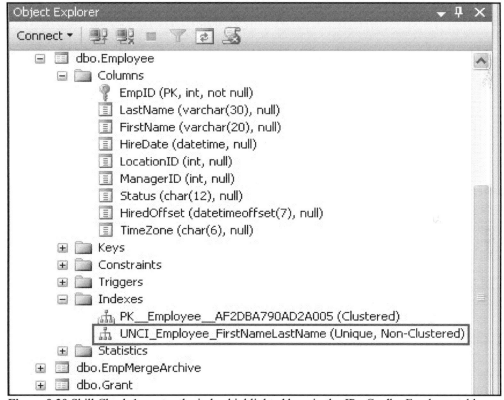

Figure 9.30 Skill Check 1 creates the index highlighted here in the JProCo.dbo.Employee table.

Skill Check 2: Create a unique nonclustered index called UNCI_Vendor_SSN on the HumanResources.Vendor table. Make sure that the Vendor table is optimized for the following type of query (see Figure 9.31) so that all the data is already contained within the index. Make sure the table remains online while the index is being created. *Note:* since this already exists from an earlier demo, you may need to drop this index before you can re-create it.

```
SELECT FirstName, LastName
FROM HumanResources.Vendor
WHERE SSN = '222-22-2222'
```

Figure 9.31 Skill Check 2 will increase the performance of this query.

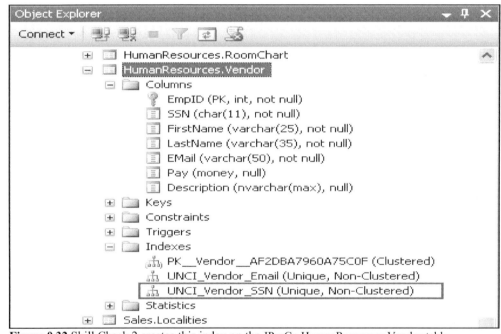

Figure 9.32 Skill Check 2 creates this index on the JProCo.HumanResources.Vendor table.

Skill Check 3: Create a nonclustered index on the SalesInvoiceDetail table based on the UnitDiscount field for all values that are not equal to zero. Call the index NCI_SalesInvoiceDetail_UnitDiscount.

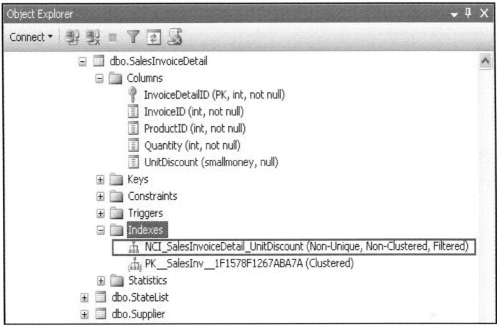

Figure 9.33 Skill Check 3 creates the index shown here in the JProCo.dbo.SalesInvoiceDetail table.

Answer Code: The T-SQL code to this lab can be found in the downloadable files in a file named Lab9.2_IndexOptions.sql.

Index Options - Points to Ponder

1. A composite index specifies more than one column as the key value combination.

2. Composite key limitations are:
    a. Maximum 16 columns.
    b. Maximum 900 bytes.
    c. Columns must be in the same table or view.

3. The order in which you create the composite key matters. For example, if you did your searches on City most often, then a City-State index would help your performance whereas a State-City index would not.

4. When creating a composite index, the first column defined should be the most unique.

5. If you have an INSERT operation on many rows at once, and any of them violates the unique constraint, then all are rolled back and no inserts are made.

6. If you want just the violating inserts to fail and the remaining inserts to succeed, then set the IGNORE_DUP_KEY to ON in the CREATE INDEX statement.

7. IGNORE_DUP_KEY causes only the violating rows to fail.

8. The syntax for IGNORE_DUP_KEY places it in the options, or WITH, section of the statement
    WITH (IGNORE_DUP_KEY = ON)

9. If you create a unique index on a table that already contains data, SQL Server first validates that there are no existing duplicate values.

10. WITH (ONLINE = ON) is an option of the CREATE INDEX command, which was introduced in SQL Server 2005 and works only in the Enterprise edition. If you use that option, then queries and other indexes can still access the underlying table while the index creation operation is in progress.

11. The sp_helpIndex stored proc returns details of the indexes created on a specified table.
    EXEC sp_helpIndex [HumanResources.Vendor]

12. With the new SQL Server 2008 feature, Filtered Indexes, you can add criteria to your index creation.

Chapter Glossary

Coding Index (es): Using code to create an index.

Composite Index: A composite index is where multiple fields are included as part of one index.

Covering index: A 'covering index' is where the needed data is found more quickly through pointers from the nonclustered index to the data in the cluster.

Filtered index (es): This is a new SQL Server 2008 feature and it is great if a large number of nulls appear, yet you only want to index the real data.

IGNORE_DUP_KEY: When WITH (IGNORE_DUP_KEY = ON) this causes only the violating rows to fail.

INCLUDE: To add more fields added to your index while only requiring one of the fields to be part of the index calculation you can use the INCLUDE option.

Included Columns: The additional nonkey fields added to your nonclustered index through use of the INCLUDE option. Because SQL Server doesn't include these fields in the calculation of the index, included columns can help you bypass the limitation on size and number of columns permitted in an index (900 bytes, 16 columns).

Index Options: The various options available to enhance performance and functionality of your index, such as using multiple fields in one index as well as setting the speed and size of your indexes.

ONLINE Option: WITH (ONLINE = ON) is an option of the CREATE INDEX command new to SQL2005 and works only in the Enterprise edition. If you use that option, then queries and other indexes can still access the underlying table while the index creation operation is in progress.

OLAP: Online **A**nalytical **P**rocessing. Refers to a system which is geared toward reporting reliable data. The system is not updated in real-time (i.e., as is the case with OLTP) and instead emphasizes efficiency and speed of data retrieval and report building.

OLTP: Online **T**ransaction **P**rocessing. Refers to a system which continuously performs numerous transactions. The design and performance of such systems are geared toward accommodating many transactions per second.

Chapter Nine - Review Quiz

1.) You work with a SQL Server 2008 database named FASTDB. You discover that a table scan on Table1 in the FASTDB causes a query to run slowly. Table1 is a very large table that is used frequently. The query contains the following statement:

SELECT Col1, Col2
FROM Table1
WHERE Col3 = <value>

You need to provide maximum query performance. Table1 must remain available to connections at all times. What should you do?

- O a. Implement horizontal partitioning.
- O b. Update all statistics on Table1 in FASTDB.
- O c. Use the CREATE STATISTICS statement in FASTDB to create missing statistics on Col3 of Table1.
- O d. Set the priority boost server option to 1.
- O e. Execute the following statement: CREATE INDEX Index1 ON Table1(Col3) INCLUDE (Col1,Col2) WITH (ONLINE=ON) GO
- O f. Execute the following statement: CREATE INDEX Index1 ON Table1(Col3,Col2,Col1)

2.) You work with a database named JProCo on a SQL Server 2008 machine. You discover poor query performance on the Employee table for a selective query that uses the SSN field. A clustered index already exists based on the EmployeeID field. You need to provide maximum query performance and keep the table available to users at all times. What should you do?

- O a. Update all statistics on the Employee table.
- O b. Use the CREATE STATISTICS statement in your JProCo database.
- O c. Set the priority boost server option to 1.
- O d. Execute the following statement. CREATE INDEX IX_1 ON Employee(SSN)
- O e. Execute the following statement. CREATE INDEX IX_1 ON Employee (SSN) WITH (ONLINE = ON)

3.) You have a database with a 15GB table named dbo.SaleInvoice. This dbo.SaleInvoice table gets a lot of updates and inserts. You discover that excessive fragmentation is caused by frequent page splits. You have plenty of extra space in your datafiles if you need it. What code should you run to reduce the page splits?

O a. ALTER TABLE dbo.SaleInvoice Add PageComment VARCHAR(50) NULL

O b. EXEC sp_helptext dbo.SaleInvoice

O c. ALTER INDEX ALL ON dbo.SaleInvoice
      REBUILD WITH (FILLFACTOR = 50)

O d. UPDATE TABLE dbo.SalesInvoice SET FillFactor = 50
      WHERE FillFactor =100

4.) You have a field in your Employee table named Gender which is either M or F. You have over 1000 records in your employee table. The clustered index is based on EmpID. You often query the Employee table with the following criteria: WHERE Gender = 'M'. What should your index scheme be for the Gender Field?

O a. There should be no index based on this field.

O b. There should be a clustered index based on this field.

O c. There should be a nonclustered index based on this field.

O d. There should be a default index based on this field.

O e. There should be a Geometry data type in this field.

5.) You have a field in your Employee table named HireDate which is not null. You have over 1000 records in your Employee table and 995 distinct hire dates. The clustered index is based on EmpID. You often query the Employee table with specific criteria like the following:
      WHERE HireDate = '1/1/2005'

What should your index scheme be for the HireDate field?

O a. There should be no index based on this field.

O b. There should be a clustered index based on this field.

O c. There should be a nonclustered index based on this field.

O d. There should be a default index based on this field.

O e. There should be a Geometry data type in this field.

6.) You have a field in your Employee table named Hiredate which is not null and highly selective, as almost everyone has their own HireDate different from other employees. You have a field called Gender which is not very selective. Your primary key is a composite of FirstName and LastName. You want to optimize the index of the following query:

SELECT FirstName, LastName, HireDate, Gender
FROM Employee WHERE Hiredate = '1/1/2005'

Currently the only index is a clustered index. What index strategy would optimize this query?

O a. Create a nonclustered index based on HireDate and INCLUDE (Gender).

O b. Create a nonclustered index based on Gender and INCLUDE (HireDate).

7.) Your employee table has 10,000 records. The EmpID field is the field the clustered index is based on. There are no other indexes. The SSN field has no index but all the values for each employee are different. The FirstName and LastName fields have many repeating names. The following query is run very often:

SELECT EmpID, SSN, FirstName, LastName
FROM Employee WHERE SSN = '555-55-5555'

Create a nonclustered index to optimize this query.

O a. Create a nonclustered index based on FirstName and Include (LastName, SSN)

O b. Create a nonclustered index based on LastName and Include (FirstName, SSN)

O c. Create a nonclustered index based on SSN and Include (FirstName, LastName).

O d. Create a composite nonclustered index based on (FirstName, LastName) and Include (SSN)

8.) You work with a database named JPRO1, which is located on a machine running SQL Server 2008. You discover that a table scan on CustPurchase in JPRO1 causes a slow query. CustPurchase is a very large table that is used frequently. The query contains the following statement: SELECT RepID, CouponCode FROM CustPurchase WHERE ShoppingCartID = <value>. You need to provide maximum query performance. CustPurchase must remain available to users at all times. What should you do?

O a. Update all statistics on CustPurchase in JPRO1.

O b. Use the CREATE statistics statement in JPRO1 to create missing statistics on ShoppingCartID of CustPurchase.

O c. Set the priority boost server option to 1.

O d. Execute the following statement. CREATE INDEX Index1 ON CustPurchase(ShoppingCartID) INCLUDE (RepID, CouponCode) WITH (ONLINE=ON) GO.

O e. Execute the following statement. CREATE INDEX Index1 ON CustPurchase(ShoppingCartID ,CouponCode, RepID) .

9.) You have an employee table with over 100,000 records. The employee table has the following definition:

CREATE TABLE Employee
(EmpID int primary key CLUSTERED,
LastName varchar(30) null,
FirstName varchar(20) null,
Hiredate datetime null,
LocationID int null,
Gender char(1) NULL)
GO

The following query really needs to be optimized:

SELECT EmpID, LocationID, HireDate, Gender
FROM Employee
WHERE HireDate IS NOT NULL
AND LocationID IS NOT NULL

What nonclustered index scheme will optimize this query while taking a minimum amount of disk space?

O a. CREATE NONCLUSTERED INDEX NCI_Emp
ON dbo.Employee (Gender) INCLUDE (HireDate, LocationID)

O b. CREATE NONCLUSTERED INDEX NCI_Emp
ON dbo.Employee (HireDate, LocationID, Gender)

O c. CREATE NONCLUSTERED INDEX NCI_Emp
ON dbo.Employee (HireDate) INCLUDE (LocationID)

O d. CREATE NONCLUSTERED INDEX NCI_Emp
ON dbo.Employee (HireDate, LocationID) INCLUDE (Gender)

10.) You have a SalesInvoice table with the following structure:

CREATE TABLE [dbo].[SalesInvoice](
[InvoiceID] [int] NOT NULL PRIMARY KEY CLUSTERED,
[OrderDate] [datetime] NOT NULL,
[PaidDate] [datetime] NOT NULL,
[FeedbackDate] [datetime] NULL,
[RepID] [int] NULL,
[CustomerID] [int] NOT NULL)

There are over 100 million records in this table. Most people don't bother to leave feedback, so over 99% of the records have null for the FeedBackDate. Orders are done online with the assistance of a representative less than 5% of the time, so 95% of the records have a NULL value for RepID. You want to create a nonclustered index to optimize the following query:

SELECT InvoiceID, FeedBackDate, RepID
FROM dbo.SalesInvoice
WHERE FeedBackDate IS NOT NULL
AND RepID IS NOT NULL

How do you set up the nonclustered index?

O a. Update all statistics on Table1.

O b. CREATE NONCLUSTERED INDEX NCI_1
ON dbo.SalesInvoice(FeedBackDate, RepID)
INCLUDE(InvoiceID)

O c. CREATE NONCLUSTERED INDEX NCI_1
ON dbo.SalesInvoice(InvoiceID)
INCLUDE(FeedBackDate, RepID)
WHERE RepID IS NOT NULL

O d. CREATE NONCLUSTERED INDEX NCI_1
ON dbo.SalesInvoice(FeedBackDate, RepID)
INCLUDE(InvoiceID)
WHERE RepID IS NOT NULL

Answer Key

1.) e   2.) e   3.) c   4.) a   5.) c   6.) a   7.) c   8.) d   9.) d   10.) c

Bug Catcher Game

To play the Bug Catcher game, run the
BugCatcher_Chapter09CreatingIndexesWithCode.pps from the BugCatcher folder
of the companion files. You can obtain these files from www.Joes2Pros.com or by
ordering the Companion CD.

Chapter 10. Index Analysis

Implementing a good database is a lot like other things in life which we plan and build. We put a lot of planning, care, and effort into building a database much the same way a family would design and build a new home. The Design and Build phases of any project are exciting and important for the success of the project.

Also important to the success of a new structure or system is analysis to confirm that new systems and processes are working as expected. In the Implementation phase of delivering a project, the team often needs to measure actual results versus expected and make any necessary adjustments.

The same is true when implementing indexes for database tables. Just seeing a database's design is only part of the picture. How the indexes are actually being utilized is the other part. By putting indexes where they will get the most use, you get the most benefit.

This chapter is all about examining the past, current, and future uses of your database in order to ensure you're utilizing the best indexing scheme.

READER NOTE: In order to follow along with the examples in the first section of Chapter 10, please run the SQLArchChapter10.0Setup.sql setup script. The setup scripts for this book are posted at Joes2Pros.com.

Query Execution Plans

Just today, as I was coming to my office to work with my technical editor, Joel, something happened that caused me to make a decision much the same way SQL Server Query Optimizer makes a decision. To achieve a productive day, we needed a printer and two laptops, each with a double monitor. Normally I do not store this much gear in my office, so it all travels in a big moving box in the back of my vehicle.

As I removed the box from the vehicle, I looked around and noticed my folding dolly wasn't there. With the dolly, I'm normally able to wheel the large box into the building and upstairs to the office. This box is heavy and difficult to carry. But in the absence of the dolly, my next best choice was to use a little extra brute force, so the goal of getting all this stuff upstairs could be achieved.

Much like the decision process of SQL Server's Query Optimizer, when I realized my trusted dolly wasn't available I made the decision to complete my task inefficiently rather than not working at all. If my dolly had been in the back of my truck, my decision would have been to use it and make the job easier.

When we add an index where it will really count, the Query Optimizer has the freedom to make a decision which gets the job done without excessive heavy lifting on the part of the SQL Server service.

Covering Indexes

The query from the SalesInvoiceDetail table of the JProCo database (see Figure 10.1) is predicating on the InvoiceID field. What would we have to know in order to predict whether the query will be covered or not? *Remember, if a query is not covered then SQL Server will perform a scan.*

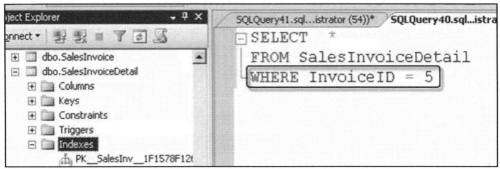

Figure 10.1 A selective query on the SalesInvoiceDetail table.

The first thing we need to do is review the table's indexes. Looking at the same figure (Figure 10.1), we see it has just one index. That may be all we need if the index is keying on the same field which appears in the WHERE clause of the query. The properties of this index will tell us which field has been indexed. The PK_SalesInv_*nnnnn* index shows us that this is a clustered index, which is covering the InvoiceDetailID field and not the InvoiceID field (Figure 10.2).

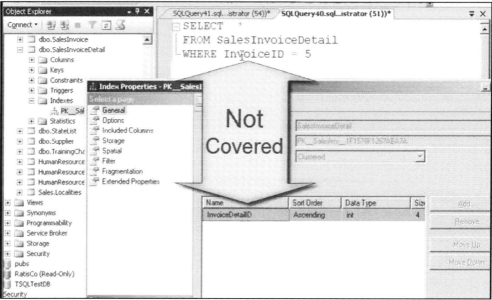

Figure 10.2 The only index on the SalesInvoiceDetail table is not going to cover a predicate on the InvoiceID field.

From this configuration, our query is predicating on a field which doesn't have an index covering it. The Query Optimizer will choose to do a scan, irrespective of whether or not this query is selective. In running this query and getting the execution plan, we can see it indeed used a "Clustered Index Scan" (see Figure 10.3) to return the mere six records in the result.

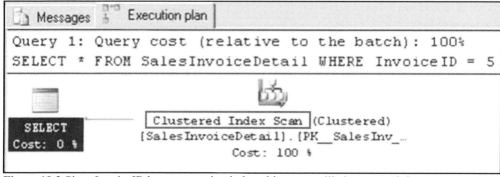

Figure 10.3 Since InvoiceID has no covering index, this query will always result in a scan.

Our goal is to run this query in a way so that the Query Optimizer will perform a seek. To do this, we will create a nonclustered index covering the InvoiceID field in the WHERE clause. Use the following code to create an index named **NCI_SalesInvoiceDetail_InvoiceID** based on the InvoiceID field of the SalesInvoiceDetail table:

> **CREATE NONCLUSTERED INDEX**
> **NCI_SalesInvoiceDetail_InvoiceID**
> **ON SalesInvoiceDetail(InvoiceID)**

You can confirm the creation of the index in the Object Explorer by refreshing the Indexes folder under the dbo.SalesInvoiceDetail table. To verify the index has been created correctly, we simply right-click to see the "Index Properties" dialog (see Figure 10.4), which shows that this index is based on the InvoiceID field of the SalesInvoiceDetail table.

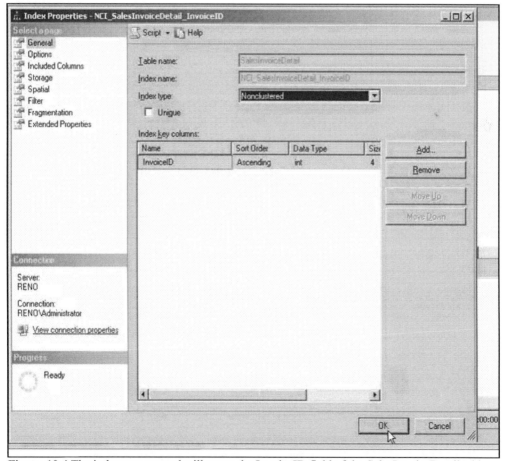

Figure 10.4 The index you created will cover the InvoiceID field of the SalesInvoiceDetail table.

The purpose for creating this index is to optimize our query. Let's examine the query execution plan for the same query that did a scan the last time we ran our query. The Query Optimizer will now do a seek based on the nonclustered index (see Figure 10.5). The nonclustered index piggybacks off the clustered index and our query's performance shows a big improvement.

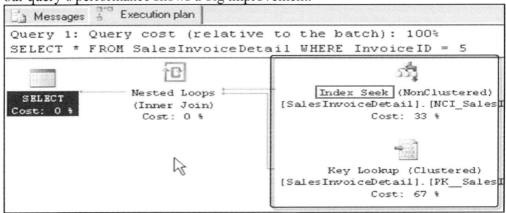

Figure 10.5 With the InvoiceID field covered by the index, Query Optimizer performs a seek.

How Nonclustered Indexes Work

If you turn to the index at the back of any textbook, you will get an idea of how SQL Server thinks when it encounters a nonclustered index. For example: let's take an index at the back of the first Joes 2 Pros book, *Beginning SQL Joes 2 Pros* (Figure 10.6). Suppose you heard there would be a quiz in class tomorrow, on the REVOKE keyword. You could simply turn to the book's index to find (i.e., *to seek*) the precise location of the pages which include REVOKE. If your copy of the book had the index torn out, then you might have to *scan* every page of the book just to find the two pages which include the word "Revoke."

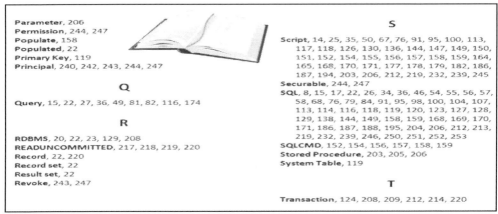

Figure 10.6 An index example from the back of a book.

Your textbook has an index at the back, so how much work will it be to find the pages about REVOKE? You simply look down the list until you reach the R section and find the word REVOKE. There it tells you pages 243 and 247 have what you need to know about the REVOKE keyword. This saves a tremendous amount of time versus scanning through page by page until you find the word you need. That's the difference between running a query which is covered by an index (i.e., similar to the book index pointing you directly to the page(s) you need) versus a query not covered by an index (i.e., the page-by-page scan of every word).

The index does not hold the data you need to read but it does point to the exact data location. With that reliable lead in hand, you no longer need to scan the whole book. Rather, you get to read only pages 243 and 247, a much faster way to find your information.

Your index lists topics from A to Z. If your book were 300 pages, do you think that the word Revoke, should be around page 200, since R occurs roughly 2/3 into the alphabet? No, that's silly. Only reference materials, like dictionaries and encyclopedias, store their items in alphabetical order. Revoke could easily be on Page 1. Most non-reference books aren't ordered alphabetically, they are ordered by page number.

The main part of the book is ordered *by page number*. The index is ordered *alphabetically by keyword* and the index points to the page numbers. Your book is clustered (i.e., physically ordered) by page number, which makes things easy to find once you know what page you are looking for. The index in the back of the book pointing to the needed page number is similar to a nonclustered index in SQL Server. Nonclustered indexes normally do not contain the data you want, but they know exactly where it is stored. A nonclustered index points to the exact position within a clustered index, so SQL Server can retrieve your data quickly.

When a Query Needs a Covering Index

We've learned quite a bit about the usefulness and how they help our queries. But at this point, should we just slap an index over every single field of every query's WHERE clause? One memorable December 26th, I met a number of developers who believed so. A system I was testing had its performance crippled. After a day of analysis, I recommended removing one such index. Once the offending index was removed, the system benchmarks showed a 77,000% increase in performance. *Yes, Seventy Seven Thousand percent!* A very important, yet lesser understood, process is how indexes work according to the selectivity level of your data.

What was happening? Think about a time you may have paid for something but never used it. Since you pay money in exchange for the items and supplies you use, you want to be conscientious and avoid wasting money. Often these occasions may have only a small impact (e.g., you wasted 90 cents because you forgot to eat the banana you bought at lunchtime), or they can have more substantial consequences (e.g., if you pay $100 for a monthly gym membership you never use).

The same is true in the SQL Server environment. SQL Server needs to spend processing time on anything you tell it to maintain. Indexes come at a cost, so you should only create them if they will be used for your benefit. This section will help to identify what types of nonclustered indexes are likely to be used by SQL Server.

If you know you will need to frequently filter on a particular field, then the field is a good candidate for an index. The system I tested that memorable December day had an index on a binary field (e.g., having values 0/1, Y/N, M/F). This binary field was indeed being queried many times per minute all day long. The problem was this field, being binary, was not very selective. There were about 100,000 records. About 50,000 records had the number 1 and 50,000 were 0. Our WHERE clause was searching for all records with a 1 in the field. Well, it's faster to scan 100,000 records and filter for what you want than it is to individually put 50,000 records through an index. Hence, the Query Optimizer said "no thanks" to using the index and instead performed a scan. To put it metaphorically, SQL Server was paying for the upkeep of an index it had no intention of using in the query.

For this query, the scan was the best option it had and was indeed the fastest way to query. The real problem was the 90 times per second the table was receiving inserts. Every insert to the table caused another insert to the nonclustered index. This meant the index was being recalculated 90 times per second. The result was the index was being maintained at a heavy processing cost but was never used by the query.

Selectivity

If you have 900 employees, how many different Social Security Numbers (SSNs) do you expect you will have? You should expect 900 distinct SSN values. How many different birthdays (including year)? Some will have the same birthday and year, so let's estimate 850 distinct birthdays exist for your 900 employees. How many different genders? Two genders: male and female. The most selective attribute of this table will be the SSN, where each record has its own value and rarely do two people share one. The least selective characteristic is gender where you have 900 employees but only 2 distinct gender values. *The higher the selectivity level, the better the benefit you will gain from the index.*

Data selectivity (like SSN being unique) is one thing. How you write your query is just as important. For example, if you queried to find the employee with the SSN of 555-55-5555 you would find one employee:

WHERE SSN = '555-55-5555' – Highly selective query

If you wanted to see every employee who didn't have a specific SSN, then that would have very low selectivity:

WHERE SSN != '555-55-5555' – Very low selective query

In the back of *Beginning SQL Joes 2 Pros*, there is an index that shows the word REVOKE is very selective. In other words, it didn't appear many times in that book. As a matter of fact, there were only two pages where the word REVOKE appeared. The term "SQL" appeared many more times (as we saw in Figure 10.4); therefore, you'd have to do a lot more seeks just to fulfill the retrieval of the data. So finding the word SQL in *Beginning SQL Joes 2 Pros* wasn't as selective a query as finding the word REVOKE. By definition, the less selective the value, the more times it appears. The workload of SQL Server's query engine increases along with the number of times a value appears.

How about finding the word "the"? Well, that's not a selective query at all. If you were told to find the word "the", and assuming "the" was in the index, would you be saving any work? In this case, both you and the SQL Server Query Optimizer would say it's faster to scan the whole book from beginning to end rather than using the index. In other words, looking for all pages containing the word "the" is an example of extremely low selectivity.

A highly selective query is one where your result set will show a small percentage of the records from your table. When the covering index has a query that is selective enough, then the query optimizer chooses a seek rather than a scan. What if I were to tell you to find all of the pages in *Beginning SQL Joes 2 Pros* that don't have the word REVOKE? If there are 260 pages in this book and 2 contain the word Revoke, then 258 pages do not. That search has very low selectivity, since you get so many records. Sometimes, your predicate will actually be on an indexed field but the query you're running will actually ignore the covering index and perform a scan. Doing a scan is more efficient that doing so many individual seeks.

Here are the rules of thumb for Scans vs. Seeks:

- Covered Indexes on queries with a Highly Selective column = Seek
- Covered Indexes on queries with a Poorly Selective column = Scan
- Queries without Covered Indexes = Scan

Selective Predicate Operations

Our query predicates (i.e., the criteria of our WHERE or HAVING clauses) can make use of operators such as =, >, <, IN, NOT IN and many others. Thanks to our growing understanding of how indexes behave, we can predict which conditions will likely cause a query to seek rather than scan. In running a query from our SalesInvoiceDetail table without any criteria, we see it has nearly 7,000 records.

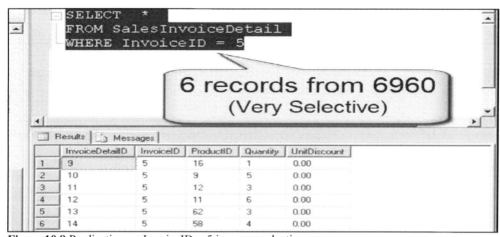

Figure 10.7 Querying the SalesInvoiceDetail table without a WHERE clause returns ~7000 rows.

How selective is the following query (Figure 10.8)? Just 6 of the 6960 records relate to InvoiceID 5. Well that's a very selective query. It is likely to seek if covered by the index.

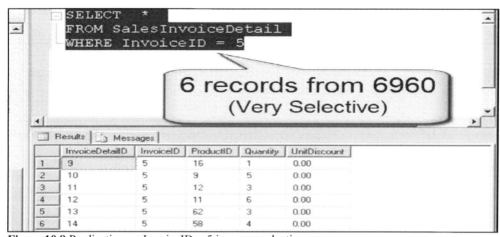

Figure 10.8 Predicating on InvoiceID = 5 is a very selective query.

Look at this next query which searches for all records which do not have an InvoiceID of 5. This is not a very selective query, since it fetches over 99% of all records (see Figure 10.9). To see the execution plan, choose the "Display Estimated Execution Plan" option from the Query menu (results in Figure 10.10).

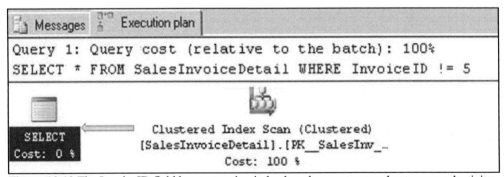

Figure 10.9 Predicating on InvoiceID not equal to 5 is not selective.

You can probably guess what kind of plan this "Not Equal" query in Figure 10.9 uses. It scans despite the fact that this query has a covering index. This is like our example where flipping through pages of a book (scanning) for the word "the" was more efficient than using an index (seeking). When selectivity gets too low, then there are too many records to seek and an index becomes less beneficial. In these instances, SQL Server knows we are better off scanning all the records.

```
Messages    Execution plan
Query 1: Query cost (relative to the batch): 100%
SELECT * FROM SalesInvoiceDetail WHERE InvoiceID != 5

                            Clustered Index Scan (Clustered)
SELECT                      [SalesInvoiceDetail].[PK_SalesInv_...
Cost: 0 %                              Cost: 100 %
```

Figure 10.10 The InvoiceID field has a covering index but chooses to scan due to poor selectivity.

Optimization Hints

There are two types of hints that will affect whether or not your optimizer decides to use an index in its execution plan. One is truly a hint that allows SQL Server to decide whether to seek or scan, and the other is really more of a mandate where you are able to force which index gets used. The **Query Hint** will suggest a way to optimize the query and let SQL Server pick the right index to use. The **Index Hint** tells SQL Server precisely which index to use.

Index Hints

We have seen SQL Server make excellent decisions about how best to pull out the data based on the selectivity of the predicated fields. However, you can tell the SQL query execution engine to seek even if the optimizer would prefer to scan.

A slight change to the query allows you control how the query runs. Right before the WHERE clause, type WITH followed by a set of parentheses containing the keyword INDEX. INDEX, too, needs its own set of parentheses which will specify the name of the index you want to force the query engine to use (Figure 10.11).

```
SELECT *
FROM SalesInvoiceDetail
WITH(INDEX(NCI_SalesInvoiceDetail_InvoiceID))
WHERE InvoiceID != 5
```
Figure 10.11 You can tell the query optimizer which index to use during a query.

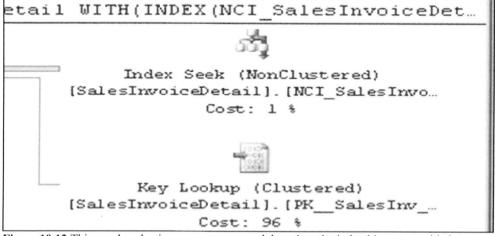

Figure 10.12 This poorly selective query usess a seek based on the index hint we provided.

Our index hint (query syntax shown in Figure 10.11) instructs the query engine to seek no matter what Query Optimizer says. The query execution plan (Figure 10.12) confirms that yes, the engine will seek through every single record, even though a scan would be faster.

Query Hints

The Query Optimizer looks at an index and the predicated value to decide whether seeking or scanning is more appropriate. Once the value is known, SQL Server figures out the field's selectivity level and determines the best plan. A highly selective query will likely scan if it's not covered by an index. Let's look at a selective query with no index. The Customer table has 775 records. Just two records have the CustomerType value of 'Business'. Predicating on those two records alone, we see the execution plan is to scan (Figure 10.13).

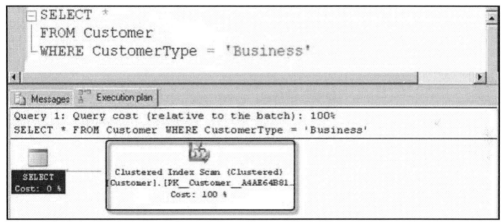

Figure 10.13 A selective query with no index will generally perform a scan.

Creating a nonclustered index will make this query covered, so that it can seek instead. Create a nonclustered index named NCI_Customer_CustomerType, which is on the Customer table keying on the CustomerType field (Figure 10.14).

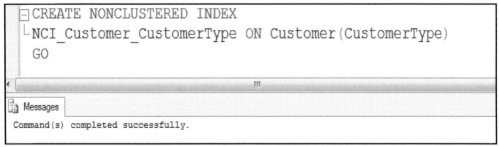

Figure 10.14 Create an index keying on the CustomerType field of the Customer table.

Our query should now be optimized to seek. Let's verify the execution plan and confirm that it indeed will perform a seek (Figure 10.15).

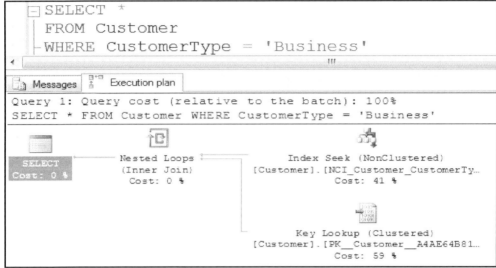

Figure 10.15 After creating the NCI_Customer_CustomerType index, this query now does a seek.

Not every query covered by this index will seek. Only queries that are selective will seek. Change the query so the predicate looks for Consumer. Remember 773 of the 775 records are of the consumer type – not a very selective query. The result is a plan that will do a scan. Thus, when you query by Business, it will seek; when you query by Consumer, it will scan (Figure 10.16).

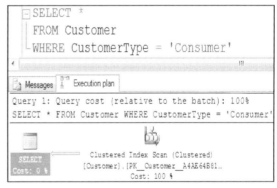

10.16 NCI_Customer_CustomerType is ignored and the query scans when selectivity is too low.

SQL Server is actually smart enough to take the exact same index and realize, through statistics, which of these criteria is selective and which is not. There is a way you can accidentally trick SQL Server into making the wrong decision. First we will add a variable to our current query to show the problem environment, and then we will see how a query hint can help us overcome the problem.

Let's declare a variable named @Type, which is a Varchar (50) and set it equal to "Business." This variable will be part of the predicate. Run the query with the variable set to "Business" and you get two records (see Figure 10.17).

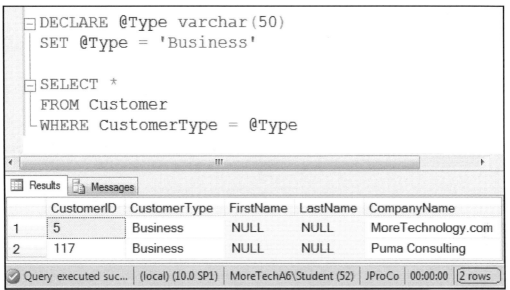

Figure 10.17 Using 'Business' for the @Type variable is a highly selective query.

Change the @Type variable to 'Consumer' and you get a nonselective query which returns 773 records (Figure 10.18).

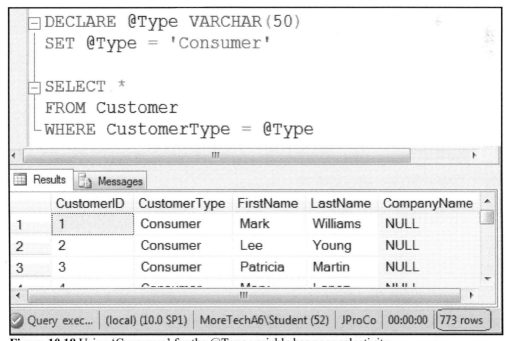

Figure 10.18 Using 'Consumer' for the @Type variable has poor selectivity.

The query that predicates on 'Consumer' is better off scanning since it's pulling almost all of the records from the entire table. The query execution plan shows that we have performed a scan to get our result set (Figure 10.19).

```
DECLARE @Type varchar(50)
 SET @Type = 'Consumer'

SELECT *
 FROM Customer
WHERE CustomerType = @Type
```

| Messages | Execution plan |

```
Query 1: Query cost (relative to the batch): 0%
DECLARE @Type varchar(50) SET @Type = 'Consumer'
```

`T-SQL`

```
Query 2: Query cost (relative to the batch): 100%
SELECT * FROM Customer WHERE CustomerType = @Type
```

```
SELECT              Clustered Index Scan (Clustered)
Cost: 0 %           [Customer].[PK__Customer__A4AE64B81...
                    Cost: 100 %
```

Figure 10.19 Using 'Consumer' for the variable causes a scan.

After changing our @Type variable back to 'Business' again, it becomes a very selective query covered by an index. Thus, you might be shocked to see that it is still scanning (see Figure 10.20). It doesn't know what value the @Type variable holds until runtime, and Optimizer doesn't check statistics for variables before a query runs. *When in doubt, the Optimizer chooses a scan.*

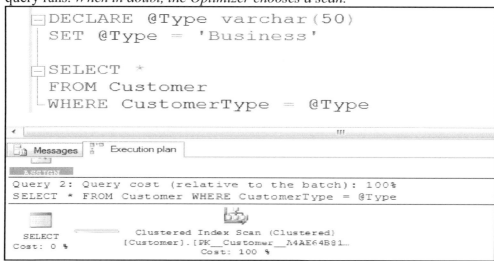

```
DECLARE @Type varchar(50)
 SET @Type = 'Business'

SELECT *
 FROM Customer
WHERE CustomerType = @Type
```

| Messages | Execution plan |

```
Query 2: Query cost (relative to the batch): 100%
SELECT * FROM Customer WHERE CustomerType = @Type
```

```
SELECT              Clustered Index Scan (Clustered)
Cost: 0 %           [Customer].[PK__Customer__A4AE64B81...
                    Cost: 100 %
```

Figure 10.20 Using 'Business' for the variable causes a scan even though the selectivity is high.

When predicating on queries values from variables you may need to give the query a hint, so the query knows the best way to run. If our @Type variable is most often set to the value of 'Business', it would be smarter to optimize this query to perform seek (Figure 10.21).

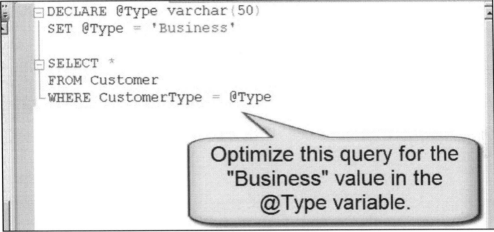

Figure 10.21 Variable values do not get used by the query optimizer.

To optimize this query based on the value being 'Business', we'll need to add some more code to our query. Use the following code (see Figure 10.22). Notice that the Query Execution Plan now indicates that it will use a seek to perform this query.

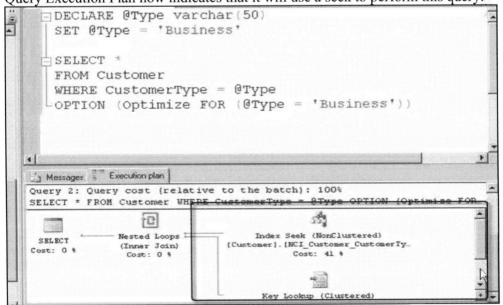

Figure 10.22 Using the Optimize for hint allows a seek on a predicated variable.

When the keyword OPTION appears after any query, it's a signal that a *query hint* is being used. In the last example we supplied a hint to the Query Optimizer to optimize the query for the value of 'Business' in the variable. There are more types of query hints you can use.

Our next example works best with a large number of records, so let's look at the SalesOrderDetail table of the AdventureWorks database. Some queries take awhile to run, particularly when the result contains a very large recordset. In many such cases, you aren't really interested in seeing all of the records. You may just need to see a sample, or you may want the ability to quickly see a representative sample of the result set while you're waiting for the rest of the large record set to return. Informally, you will see colleagues in this situation run the query and then stop it after a few seconds and look at the partial results returned by the query. Another easy step would be to write a Top 50 query which finishes in far less time. The disadvantage of both of these shortcuts is that you will never get all the records.

There is a query which will run and display the first 50 records rapidly. Once you get the first 50 records, it can then produce the next hundred thousand or million records at its own speed. Well, we've got to use another query hint with the FAST option (Figure 10.23). Notice you see many records but the row counter shows zero while the query is still running.

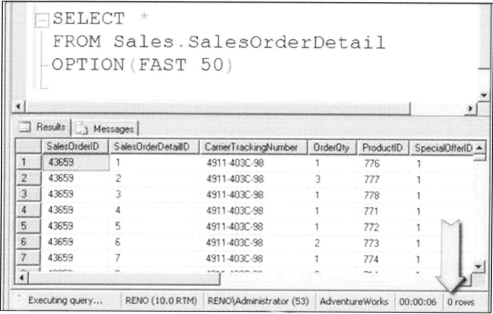

Figure 10.23 OPTION(FAST 50) displays the first 50 records right away but the status indicator shows "0 rows" unil the query is finished.

Be aware that 50 is simply the example we've chosen for this demonstration and that 50 is generally a good representative sample of records when you are evaluating a query or a very large table. You are free to choose any integer to specify the recordcount you want rapidly (e.g., OPTION(FAST 100), OPTION(FAST 25), OPTION(FAST 35), etc.).

When you run this query the first 50 records come up right away, then the rest of the records will display as soon as they can. You can tell when the query is complete because you will see the actually row count on the lower right corner of your result (see Figure 10.24).

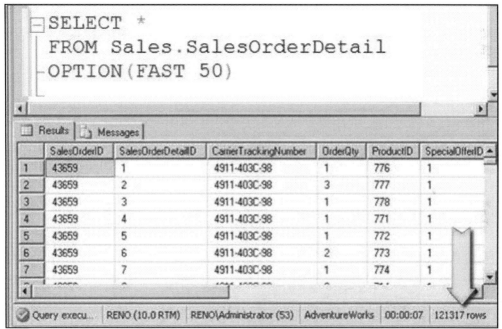

Figure 10.24 Once the query is done, you see all records and the number of rows from the query.

Lab 10.1: Query Execution Plans

Lab Prep: Before you can begin the lab, you must have SQL Server installed and run the SQLArchChapter10.1Setup.sql script.

Skill Check 1: Create a nonclustered index named NCI_SalesInvoice_CustomerID on the CustomerID field of the SalesInvoice table of the JProCo database. Notice the following query with a covering index uses a scan.

Note: CustomerID 155 has placed so many orders that this query is not selective enough to use the covering index. If you were to query for CustomerID = 1 you would see a seek on the index.

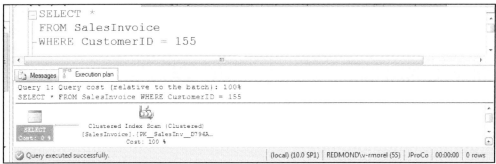

Figure 10.25 When you are through with Skill Check 1, this query still does a scan.

Skill Check 2: With the index named NCI_SalesInvoice_CustomerID from Skill Check 1, re-write the query to use an index hint forcing this query to do a seek.

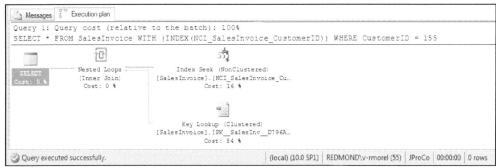

Figure 10.26 After Skill Check 2, this query does a seek.

Skill Check 3: You are mostly querying for customers by CustomerID (like CustomerID 1). You want to optimize this variable in the query for a value assuming CustomerID 1 will be predicated.

```
DECLARE @CustID INT
SET @CustID = 1


SELECT *
FROM SalesInvoice
WHERE CustomerID = @CustID
--Put "Query Hint" code here
```

Figure 10.27 Skill Check 3 needs a hint to optimize the query for the value of CustomerID 1.

Skill Check 4: The largest table in JProCo is SalesInvoiceDetail with almost 7000 records. Write a query so that the first 10 records come up right away, then the rest of the query records will come as soon as they can. Get all fields and all records.

Answer Code: The T-SQL code to this lab can be found in the downloadable files in a file named Lab10.1_ QueryExecutionPlans.sql.

Query Execution Plans - Points to Ponder

1.   An index seek is similar to:
        a. Turning to the back of this book to look at the index.
        b. Looking up the word you want.
        c. Turning directly to the page that contains that word.

2.   A index scan is similar to:
        a. Turning to the first page of this book.
        b. Searching through all the pages for a word until you reach the end
            of the book.

3.   An index scan is like scanning the entire table row by row. This is a 1 to n
        search, where n is the total number of rows in the table. Therefore the scan
        is efficient if the table is small, or most of the rows qualify for the
        predicate.

4.   The "With *Index*" hint allows you to specify which index you want to use.
        This is very useful if you want to force the query to execute using an index
        seek rather than an index scan.

5.   The index hint syntax is WITH (INDEX (*IndexName*))

6.   An execution plan allows you to see how the query is executed. This is
        useful for seeing if a scan or seek is being done and for troubleshooting
        other inefficiencies in the query.

7.   If data isn't adequately selective, Query Optimizer may surprise you by
        ignoring the index and choosing to perform a scan on a covered query.

8.   The OPTIMIZE FOR query hint allows you to override incorrect SQL
        parameter sniffing. (Parameter sniffing is the default behavior of SQL
        Server which determines the query execution plan at compile time and
        judges the selectivity of your data based on your parameter values. A
        suboptimal execution plan may be stored if your initial run of the query is
        performed with an atypical data sample).

9.   The OPTIMIZE FOR syntax is OPTION (OPTIMIZE FOR (*@Parameter = Value*))

10.   A related syntax (OPTIMIZE FOR UNKNOWN) lets you force Query
        Optimizer to look at available statistics in generating the queryplan, rather
        than looking at the parameter values:
        OPTION (OPTIMIZE FOR (*@Parameter = UNKNOWN*))

11.   OPTION (FAST n) does not make the whole query run any faster; it returns
        n rows to the client as soon as they have been found then continues with the
        remaining rows.

Analyzing Indexes

How are our current indexes benefiting us and how can we improve them? While shopping at Costco one day, an employee greeted me after my checkout was done. She said that, based on my buying pattern, the 2% pay back plan has earned me more than the cost of upgrading my membership from Gold to Executive. At first, this was not clear to me so I asked her to explain. My $50 annual membership could be upgraded to a $100 annual membership which would give me 2% back on all purchases. In fact, I had already earned $65 before the end of the year. She offered to give me $15 in pocket to upgrade my membership and consider the upgrade paid in full. The cost of an extra $50 per year for my executive level membership was a worthwhile idea because of my usage patterns at Costco.

For people who sign up for the Executive level membership then rarely shop at Costco, the opposite is true. Some might be paying an extra $50 per year and only getting $10 back. When you use something frequently, you realize a greater return on your investment. The same idea is true for indexes. If you create an index that is never used by your query optimizer then the extra cost in maintaining the index is wasted. If the index is used frequently then it is worthwhile.

How many times in the last hour, or last day, has SQL Server been able to do a seek rather than a scan for the queries you have be running? Knowing this will help tell you how well your indexes are being utilized.

Seek vs. Scan Recap

If the SalesInvoice table did not have a nonclustered index on the InvoiceID, then all of the queries below would do a scan:

SELECT * FROM SalesInvoiceDetail --Scan

**SELECT * FROM SalesInvoiceDetail
WHERE InvoiceID = 5** --Seek if covered.

**SELECT * FROM SalesInvoiceDetail
WHERE InvoiceID IN (5, 10, 60)** --Seek if covered.

**SELECT * FROM SalesInvoiceDetail
WHERE InvoiceID != 5** --Scan

By putting indexes on fields when you query them selectively, you can increase their performance by having more seeks versus scans on your table.

We know these queries are potentially using the indexes of the SalesInvoiceDetail table. The total number of seeks and scans for this table will grow each time it is queried. Let's get a report on how the SalesInvoiceDetail table's indexes are working for our queries.

Historical Index Metadata

How often is a seek being done on a covering index? That fateful Dec 26th day I alluded to in the last chapter happened when someone put an index on a field called Completed. The possible values for Completed were either a zero or a one. After doing a little research, we found out that in the last 24 hours we did 4.7 million scans and 0 seeks. Imagine paying for a Costco membership and shopping 4.7 million times at various stores but never once at Costco!

These results meant the overhead to maintain this index was wasted. That silenced all arguments about the benefit of this index. How do you show someone the metadata on index usage? It's a common question that has been addressed by Microsoft through some cool new ways to look at metadata.

Before we can begin, we need to know some items like the Database ID and the Object ID of the table we wish to analyze. The name of our database is JProCo but what is the Database ID of JProCo? In a new query window we use the DB_ID function to figure out the Database ID and an OBJECT_ID function for table ID (Figure 10.28).

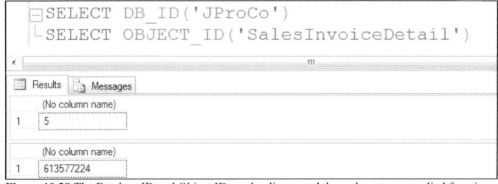

Figure 10.28 The DatabaseID and Object ID can be discovered through system-supplied functions.

For this demonstration, 5 is the Database ID of JProCo and the Object ID for the SalesInvoiceDetail table is 613577224. We want to see how many seeks and scans have been done for Database 5's 613577224 object.

Now it's time to look at exactly how we're doing as far as index usage in our queries. So far, six queries have been run on the SalesInvoiceDetail table. The query in Figure 10.29, on the sys.dm_db_index_usage_stats dynamic management view, shows we have two seeks and four scans.

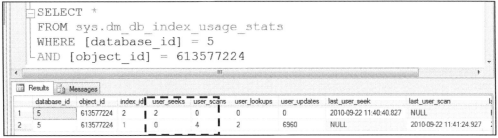

```
SELECT *
FROM sys.dm_db_index_usage_stats
WHERE [database_id] = 5
AND [object_id] = 613577224
```

	database_id	object_id	index_id	user_seeks	user_scans	user_lookups	user_updates	last_user_seek	last_user_scan	la
1	5	613577224	2	2	0	0	0	2010-09-22 11:40:40.827	NULL	
2	5	613577224	1	0	4	2	6960	NULL	2010-09-22 11:41:24.927	

Figure 10.29 Two seeks and four scans have been run on the SalesInvoiceDetail table.

The next query is seen in Figure 10.30. Since it's not very selective, we will likely go from 4 scans to 5 scans.

```
SELECT *
FROM SalesInvoiceDetail
WHERE InvoiceID != 5
```

	InvoiceDetailID	InvoiceID	ProductID	Quantity	UnitDiscount	
1	1	1	76	2	0.00	
2	2	1	77	3	0.00	

Figure 10.30 This non selective query should perform another scan.

Switch to the **sys.dm_db_index_usage_stats** query seen in Figure 10.29. Now it looks like we've done five scans (Figure 10.31).

```
SELECT *
FROM sys.dm_db_index_usage_stats
WHERE [database_id] = 5
AND [object_id] = 613577224
```

	database_id	object_id	index_id	user_seeks	user_scans	user_lookups	user_updates	last_user_seek	last_user_scan	la
1	5	613577224	2	2	0	0	0	2010-09-22 11:40:40.827	NULL	
2	5	613577224	1	0	5	2	6960	NULL	2010-09-22 11:43:16.170	

Figure 10.31 The sys.dm_db_index_usage_stats view verifies one more scan has been run.

To cause another seek to take place, we can run a highly selective query covered by the index. The dynamic management view, dm_db_index_usage_stats, keeps track of each table and its indexes and how many times seeks and scans were performed against that table.

Lab 10.2: Analyzing Indexes

Lab Prep: Before you can begin the lab, you must have SQL Server installed and run the SQLArchChapter10.2Setup.sql script.

Skill Check 1: Query the SalesInvoice table to find out how many seeks and scans have been done. *Note*: Since this table has more than one index it's possible you might see several rows like the one you see in Figure 10.32 below.

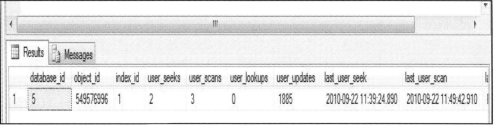

Figure 10.32 Skill Check 1 shows the number of scans and seeks against the SalesInvoice Table.

Answer Code: The T-SQL code to this lab can be found in the downloadable files in a file named Lab10.2_AnalyzingIndexes.sql.

Analyzing Indexes - Points to Ponder

1. Two of the many ways to view your metadata is to query a Catalog View (like sys.sysobject) or a Dynamic Management View (like sys.dm_db_index_usage_stats).

2. There are many different Catalog Views available and many Dynamic Management Views.

3. Catalog Views contain metadata about all the objects and their settings inside SQL Server.

4. Dynamic Management Views can view metadata about run time settings (like how many times a "seek" or "scan" was used on a table) where Catalog Views only look at settings.

5. A DDL or DCL statement will make a change to metadata that is viewed by Catalog Views.

6. Running a DML statement (like SELECT or UPDATE) will not make any setting changes to your Catalog Views.

7. Dynamic Management Views are the only type of metadata views that can change after you run a DML statement.

8. Once you reboot your server or restart the SQL service (Object Explorer > right-click the name of your SQL Server instance > Stop/Start) all your Dynamic management views are reset.

9. SQL Server accesses data in one of two ways.
   a. Index scan – If your query's "WHERE" clause is not part of an index.
   b. Index seek – If your query is covered by an index and is highly selective (better performance).

10. SQL Server determines if an index exists on your query and if so it then determines if it should be used. If the table has only two records then it might skip an index (even if one exists) since the table is small and the query runs faster with a scan.

11. For larger tables, selective queries covered by an index are much faster.

12. It's best to keep the clustered index on a unique or identity field to avoid duplicates.

13. A "Composite Index" specifies more than one column as the key value.

Database Tuning

A co-worker recently told me, after he moved to a new home, how relieved he was to live less than a mile from work. He used to live over an hour away. His trip to work (that he does 5 times a week) is now really optimized for his lifestyle. He also mentioned a small drawback. His weekly trip to the grocery store is a longer drive than before. The short work commute seems to overshadow the new 2 mile drive when shopping for food. It is an overall gain when you can save time on the most frequently performed operations that matter. Doing this means you have optimized and tuned your tasks for your lifestyle. It should be obvious what tasks in your life are daily, weekly, and monthly and how to prioritize them.

Tuning a database is like any challenge. Let's take a simple one where you are to run the 100 meter dash as fast as you can. You have your work cut out for you. Some suggestions, like "Wear shorts and sneakers rather than jeans and sandals", might be helpful. Following good optimization advice, your results will show up as a faster time in the race using the same amount of effort. The 100 meter dash is your workload. How to best perform this 100 meter dash (including what to wear) is all part of the recommendations to get the workload done in the easiest way.

Naturally, you are not trying to get SQL Server the best time in the 100 meter dash. Your server has a different workload to run. It needs to perform the most important queries in the shortest possible time. What are the most used and important queries? Over time, with sampling and testing your database using various monitoring resources, you can get a good idea of what queries are run most often. Once you have this information, you essentially have a list of queries which becomes like the 100 meter dash for your SQL Server. This list of important and frequently used queries is known as your workload file.

The core part of this section will be two main items called *Session Definitions* and *Session Results*. A Session Definition is made up of a workload file and a list of recommendations based on the workload file. The second item evaluates the recommendations' effects on the workload file to create the Session Results. These results are usually expressed as a percentage of performance SQL Server will gain when using the recommendations on the workload. Analyzing your Session Definition in DTA (Database Engine Tuning Advisor) will return your Session Results. This can be done through a Windows interface or a command line.

Workload Files

To make the biggest impact in performance, you need to know the most used queries. Let's say after tracing all the activity, we found that ninety percent of our workload is the same three queries (Figure 10.33).

```
USE JProCo
GO

--Query #1
SELECT SInd.InvoiceDetailID
    , SUM(SInd.Quantity * cp.RetailPrice) AS SubTotal
  FROM SalesInvoiceDetail AS SInd
  INNER JOIN CurrentProducts AS cp
    ON SInd.ProductID = cp.ProductID
  WHERE SInd.InvoiceDetailID = 877
  GROUP BY SInd.InvoiceDetailID
  ORDER BY SInd.InvoiceDetailID

--Query #2
SELECT SupplierID
    , SUM(RetailPrice) AS SubTotal
  FROM dbo.CurrentProducts
  GROUP BY SupplierID
  ORDER BY SupplierID

--Query #3
SELECT InvoiceID
    , OrderDate
    , PaidDate
    , CustomerID
  FROM salesinvoice
  WHERE PaidDate < '1/1/2008'
```

Figure 10.33 Many queries saved together represents our workload file.

Note: The term "Tracing" comes from running a tool known as SQL Profiler. It's the job of SQL Profiler to record activity taking place on your SQL Server. The recording is saved as a "Trace" file (.trc) that you can analyze to see what tasks are run most often on your system. SQL Profiler is a big topic with entire books around that subject matter and is beyond the scope of this book.

In Figure 10.33, the first query is an interesting one where it looks for a specific InvoiceID and it finds out exactly what the total is by multiplying the Quantity times the RetailPrice. That's our most popular query. Our second most popular query (Query #2) gets a report of our suppliers, and exactly what their subtotals are based on RetailPrice. The third most popular query (Query #3) is one that's looking for a range; this one is finding all of the PaidDate values that are less than the first of January 2008 from the SalesInvoice table.

Knowing these three queries make up most of the work, we can save this data for further analysis. Our goal is to see how well our indexing is helping these queries and what else can be done. Save the workload file as a SQL script and analyze it against the correct database. As shown below, we save this workload file called JProCo_workload.sql to the C drive in the Joes2Pros folder (Figure 10.34).

Figure 10.34 You can save the workload file as a .sql file.

Database Engine Tuning Advisor DTA

How efficiently this workload file would run against our current index structure needs to be known. If some important index is missing, or is designed poorly, then we want recommendations on indexes we should create or alter. The tool that will give us this type of analysis is called the Database Engine Tuning Advisor (usually called "Database Tuning Advisor" or DTA). To find DTA go to Start/Programs/Microsoft SQL Server/ Performance Tools and select Database Engine Tuning Advisor (Figure 10.35).

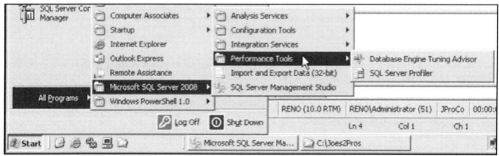

Figure 10.35 Database Engine Tuning Advisor can be found under Performance Tools.

In Figure 10.36, you choose the server you wish to connect to by clicking the connect button.

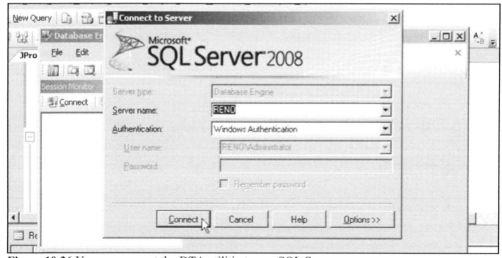

Figure 10.36 You can connect the DTA utilitiy to any SQL Server.

You might want to run several tests (Sessions) over several days on the same server. Give each one a session name that you can refer to later, if needed. In Figure 10.37, we call this session JProCoTest1. Click on the button that has the pair of binoculars and choose the workload file on the C-drive in the Joes2Pros folder.

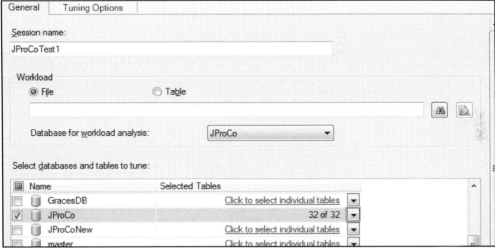

Figure 10.37 We named the session JProCoTest1 and changed "Database for workload analysis:" from "master" to "JProCo".

You could run this workload file against many databases at once, but we only want to analyze the JProCo database. Within that database, we only need to analyze 3 tables. Click the dropdown list next to the JProCo database name and make sure just three tables are selected: CurrentProducts, SalesInvoice, and the SalesInvoiceDetail tables (Figure 10.38).

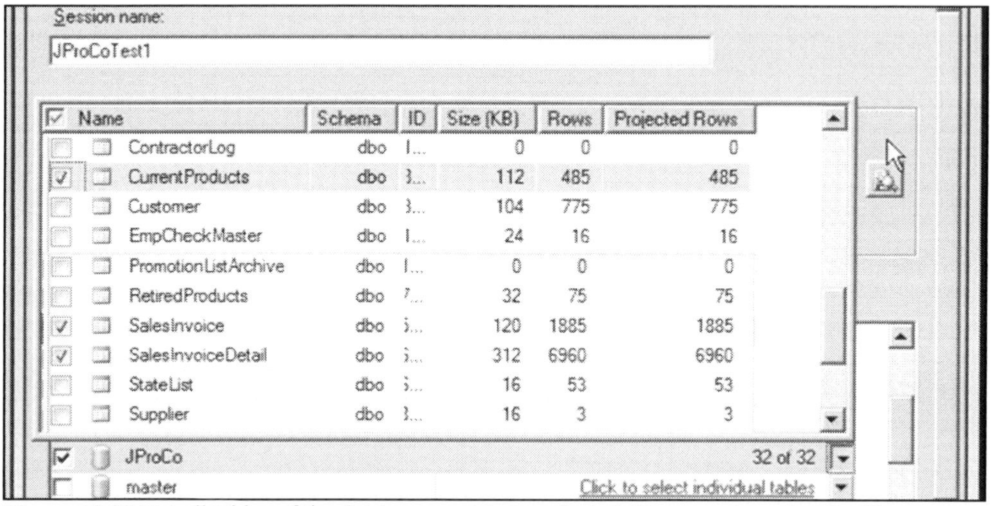

Figure 10.38 Not all tables of the database need to be selected. Here we chose just 3 tables.

The "Tuning Options" tab allows you to choose what type of advice you want to get from the Database Tuning Advisor. In this example, we will allow suggestions for making nonclustered indexes. We don't want to partition any of our tables, and we'll keep all the existing physical data structures (like MDF and NDF files) the same. In Figure 10.39, we've selected the "nonclustered indexes", "No partitioning" and "Keep all existing PDS" radio buttons.

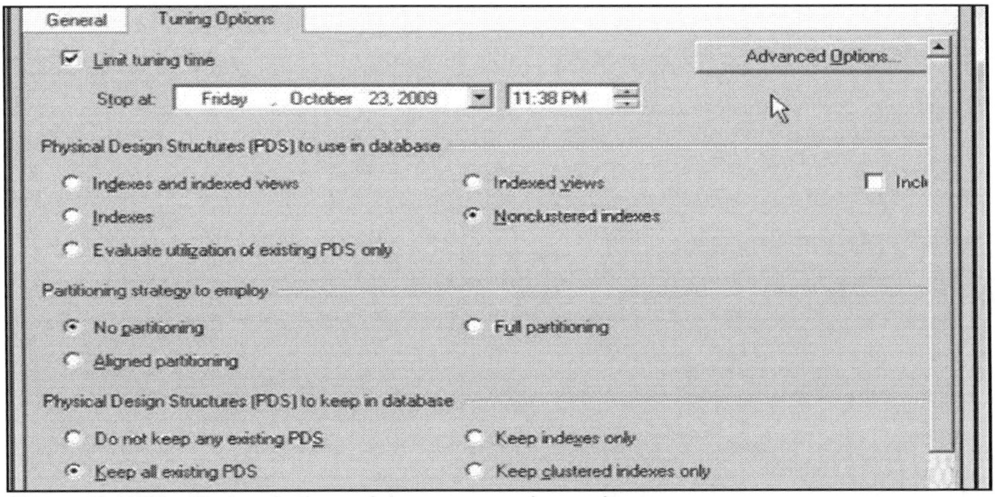

Figure 10.39 The Tuning Options tab has many session settings.

Click the "Advanced Options" button in the upper right corner (see Figure 10.39) to set some advanced limits or allowances on your session. For example, some recommendations could take up a lot of space and you may want to limit this based on how much you can afford. Check the "Define max. Space for Recommendations (MB):" check box so the text box to the right will allow you to enter a value. You also have the power to specify if any index recommendations should be generated either online or offline. When you are done with your "Advanced Options", you can click the OK button (Figure 10.40).

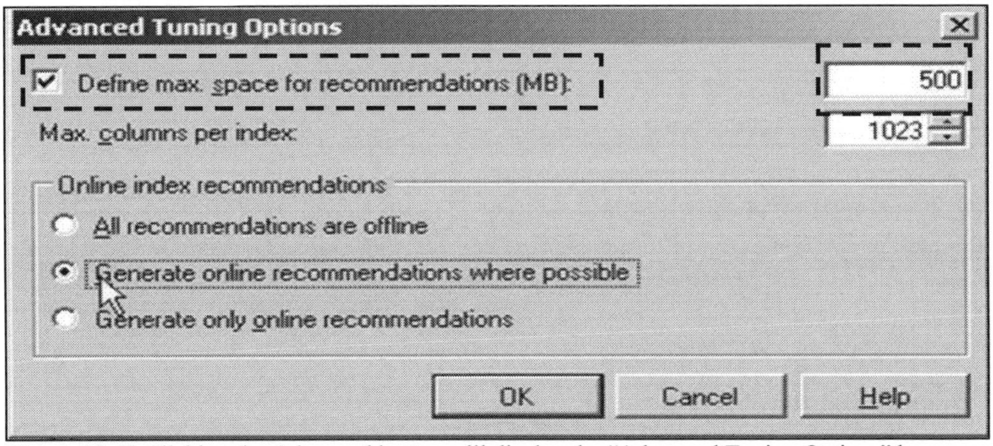

Figure 10.40 Clicking the Advanced button will display the "Advanced Tuning Options" box.

When all of your session options have been chosen, you can start an analysis and get all the recommendations. Simply click the "Start Analysis" button and the

Progress tab comes up (Figure 10.41). Please note we will use the terms "Recommendation" and "Suggestion" interchangeably in this chapter.

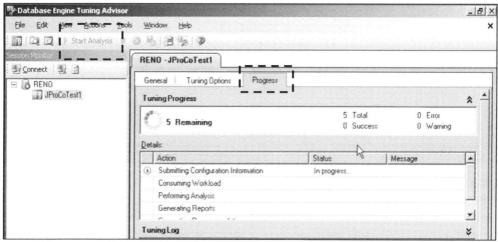

Figure 10.41 Clicking Start Analysis shows your status in the Progress tab.

After the analysis runs, you will notice five recommendations that appear listed in the "Recommendations" tab. Each line listed in this tab is a DDL statement you can run (Figure 10.42). *Note*: It's possible that your system hardware could get more or less than 5 results.

General	Tuning Options	Progress	Recommendations	Reports

Estimated improvement: 63%

Partition Recommendations

Index Recommendations

tition Scheme ▼	Size (KB)	Definition
		([SupplierID], [RetailPrice])
	16	([SupplierID] asc) include ([RetailPrice])
	88	([SupplierID] asc) include ([ProductID], [ProductName], [RetailPrice], [OriginationDate])
	48	([PaidDate] asc) include ([InvoiceID], [OrderDate], [CustomerID])
		([InvoiceDetailID], [ProductID])

Figure 10.42 The analysis shows suggestions in the Recommendations tab.

To look at a recommendation, click its definition link. Clicking the second link expands the code for the second recommendation (Figure 10.43). This second suggestion creates a nonclustered index on the CurrentProducts table covering the SupplierID field. Doing so should give your workload a performance gain.

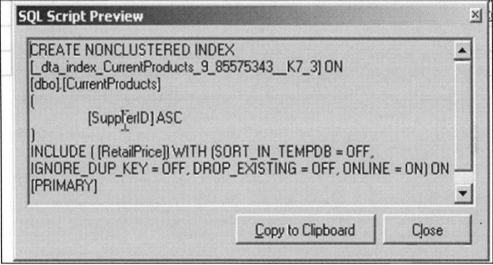

Figure 10.43 This recommendation is to create a nonclustered index on the CurrentProducts table.

You can actually run the code in this recommendation by copying it to the clipboard and pasting it into a new query window. How much of a performance gain do we get if we run all five suggestions? The "Reports" tab has these answers. Figure 10.44 shows us that if we were to do all five of these recommendations our retrieval speed of our most popular queries will increase by 63.65%.

General	Tuning Options	Progress	Recommendations	Reports

Tuning Summary

Date	10/23/2009
Time	10:40:09 PM
Server	RENO
Database(s) to tune	[JProCo]
Workload file	C:\Joes2Pros\JProCo_workload.sql
Maximum tuning time	58 Minutes
Time taken for tuning	1 Minute
Estimated percentage improvement	63.65
Maximum space for recommendation (MB)	500

Figure 10.44 The Reports table gives you your Session Results.

What if you want to know more about just the third recommendation from your session? On the Recommendations tab, simply uncheck every box but leave the check mark for the third recommendation in place. Once done, click Actions from the menu then select Evaluate Recommendations as seen in Figure 10.45.

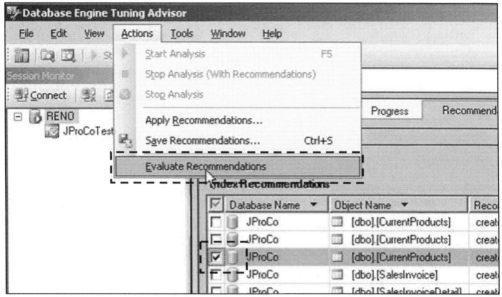

Figure 10.45 You can start a new session based on the last one by selecting "Evaluate Recomendataions".

In essence, you are really starting a new session and must, therefore, pick a new session name. In the "Session Name:" text box, type something meaningful, like "Suggestion#3PerfGain", and start the analysis (Figure 10.46).

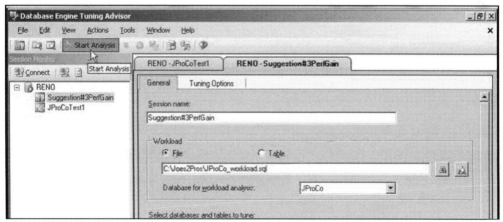

Figure 10.46 The "Start Analysis" button will run against the current session.

If we took just that third suggestion (recommendation), how much of a performance increase will we get? After your analysis finishes, the Reports tab shows a thirty-one percent increase in performance (see Figure 10.47).

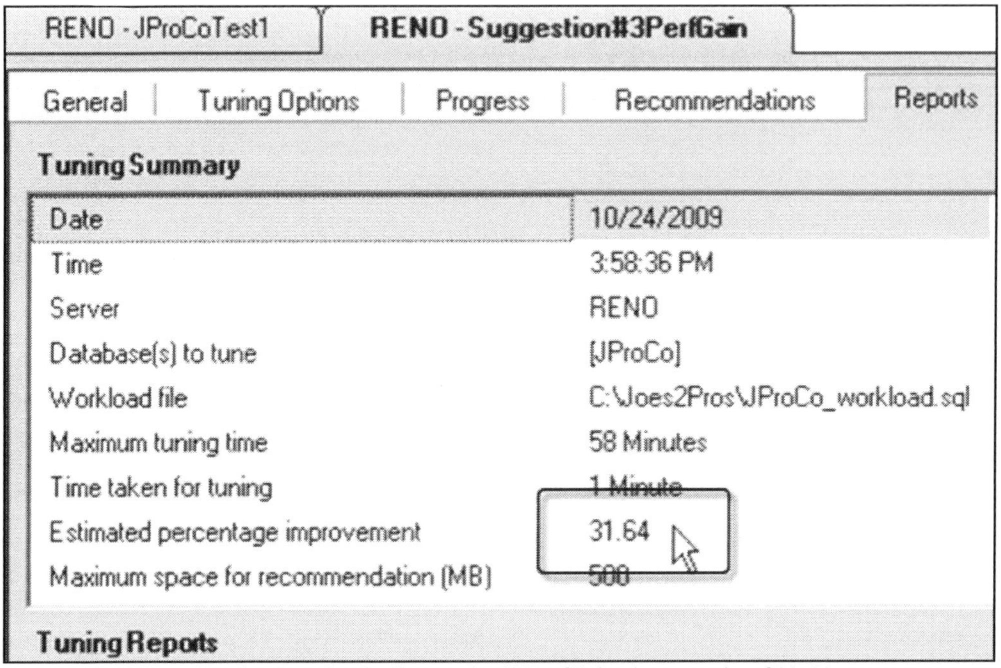

Figure 10.47 Your Session Results for Suggestion#3PerfGain show a gain of 31.64 percent.

Analyzing Session Definitions

Let's go back to the comparison of your workload to running the 100 meter dash. Both the race itself and what you plan to do, like "Wear shorts and sneakers rather than jeans and sandals", are parts of your *session definition.* At the end of the race you see your race time on the scoreboard. This is like your *session results.* Think of the queries you need to run as your workload and the indexes that will run them quickly as the recommendations. The workload and the suggested indexes make up the Session Definitions.

You can send a Session Definition to someone else so they can analyze the effects it will have on their system. Perhaps the head office knows you have sped things up in your region and wants to see if the same recommendations will help them at the main office. After they run your Session Definition on their system, they get their own Session Results. Perhaps the same Session Definition will show a 50% gain on your smaller database and a 70% gain on a similar database in the larger main office.

It might be valuable to save a session definition for later analysis. To do so you click the File menu and select Export Session Definition. It's a good idea to save the file as a meaningful name like JProCoDTADefinition.xml. You can analyze this suggestion later or even evaluate this session definition on another SQL Server.

Let's analyze JProCoDTADefinition.xml in the Command Prompt. In Figure 10.48 we type DTA (for Database Tuning Advisor) and for our command line switches we will use -E for trusted, -ix for the input (JProCoDTADefinition.xml), -s for session name and –d for the database to analyze. In this example it again tells us the Session Definition file gets a Session Result showing a 31% improvement.

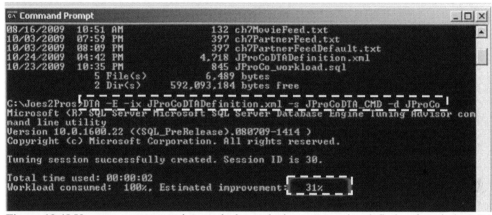

Figure 10.48 You can get your session results by analyzing your session defintion though the DTA command line interface.

What exactly is stored in the Session Definition file? Open your XML file in notepad and we see some important pieces (Figure 10.49). We can make some sense of the bottom of this file. We have a nonclustered index that has a key column of SupplierID, because the query has ProductID, ProductName, RetailPrice and OriginationDate fields it is recommended we include these columns in the Index. We didn't include any more fields because that's all the query needs.

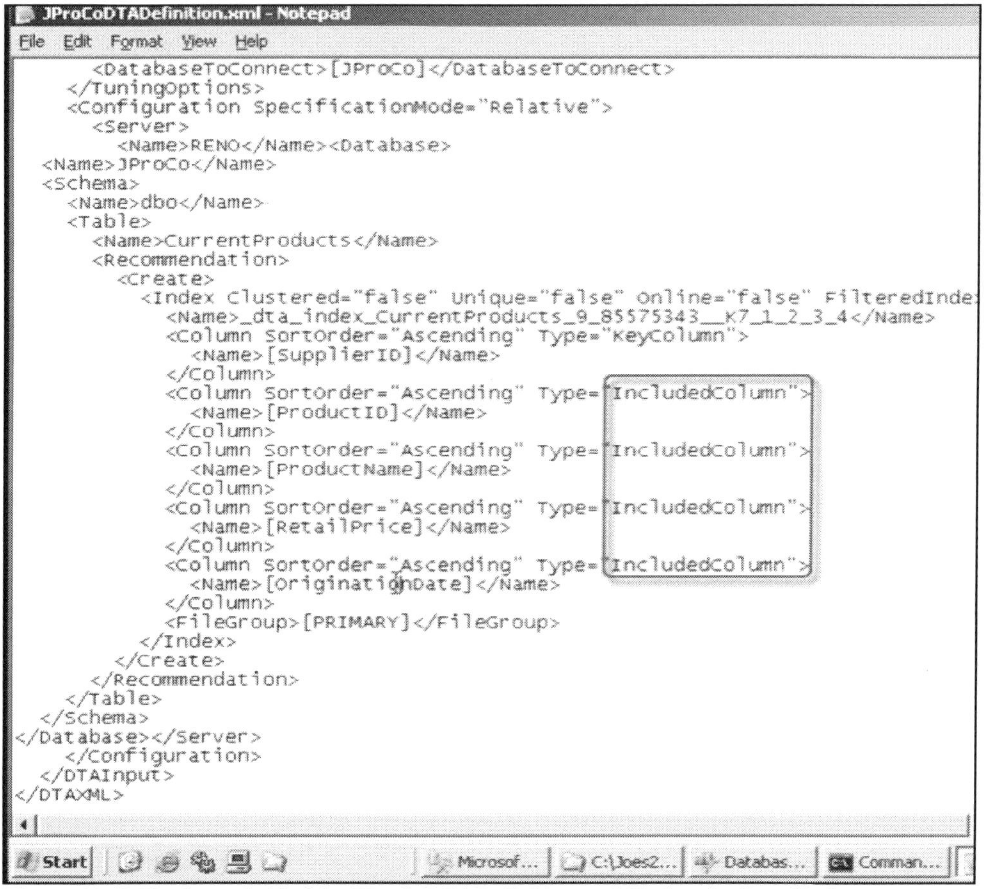
JProCoDTADefinition.xml - Notepad

```
      <DatabaseToConnect>[JProCo]</DatabaseToConnect>
    </TuningOptions>
    <Configuration SpecificationMode="Relative">
      <Server>
        <Name>RENO</Name><Database>
  <Name>JProCo</Name>
  <Schema>
    <Name>dbo</Name>
    <Table>
      <Name>CurrentProducts</Name>
      <Recommendation>
        <Create>
          <Index Clustered="false" Unique="false" Online="false" FilteredInde
            <Name>_dta_index_CurrentProducts_9_85575343__K7_1_2_3_4</Name>
            <Column SortOrder="Ascending" Type="KeyColumn">
              <Name>[SupplierID]</Name>
            </Column>
            <Column SortOrder="Ascending" Type="IncludedColumn">
              <Name>[ProductID]</Name>
            </Column>
            <Column SortOrder="Ascending" Type="IncludedColumn">
              <Name>[ProductName]</Name>
            </Column>
            <Column SortOrder="Ascending" Type="IncludedColumn">
              <Name>[RetailPrice]</Name>
            </Column>
            <Column SortOrder="Ascending" Type="IncludedColumn">
              <Name>[OriginationDate]</Name>
            </Column>
            <FileGroup>[PRIMARY]</FileGroup>
          </Index>
        </Create>
      </Recommendation>
    </Table>
  </Schema>
</Database></Server>
    </Configuration>
  </DTAInput>
</DTAXML>
```

Figure 10.49 The lower half of the JProCoDTADefinition.xml file has the list of indexes to create.

Analyzing and Saving Session Results

If you had two taxis waiting to take you exactly where you wanted to go, that is a performance benefit compared to walking. Both taxis travel at 31 Miles Per Hour, normally, but today the second taxi will also be carrying a ski rack that you don't have any use for. With this rack on top, it now only goes 25 m.p.h. (miles per hour). By choosing the first taxi, you'd receive a 6 m.p.h. benefit.

A change to the Session Definition file means your Session Results may be different. For example, the more columns an index covers, the less efficient it will be. Leaving some necessary columns off will hurt performance just as adding unused columns will cost you some performance.

The example in Figure 10.50 will add the Category column to the index. The workload file does not contain a query that uses Category. This index will be

slightly larger and run slightly slower while offering the same information as before.

```
        <Name>[RetailPrice]</Name>
    </Column>
    <Column SortOrder="Ascending" Type="IncludedColumn">
        <Name>[OriginationDate]</Name>
    </Column>

    <Column SortOrder="Ascending" Type="IncludedColumn">
        <Name>[Category]</Name>
    </Column>

    <FileGroup>[PRIMARY]</FileGroup>
    </Index>
    </Create>
</Recommendation>
Table>
```

Figure 10.50 A new "IncludedColumn" has been added to the Session Definition.

Our performance gain from the Session Definition before this change was 31%. Odds are we put a small dent in that number. Run a new session from the command prompt called JProCoDTA_CMD2 against the newly saved JProCoDTADefinition.xml definition file. In the example in Figure 10.51 our performance gain has been reduced to 30% from 31% earlier.

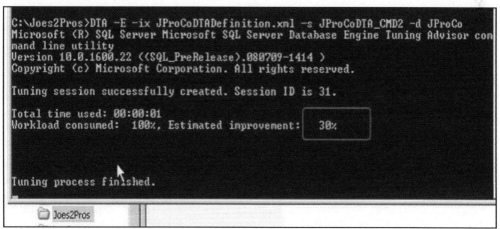

Figure 10.51 This Session definition has a slightly lower performance gain in the session result.

Your Session Definition gave you the Session Result of 30%. You might be told to report your findings officially. Don't close this command window so you can point to the screen and prove the results. Better yet, you can save the Session Results and send them to someone. The Session Results can be exported to an Output XML file. Let's repeat our same command and specify an Output XML file (-ox option) called DTAExportedSessionResultsForSuggestion3.xml.

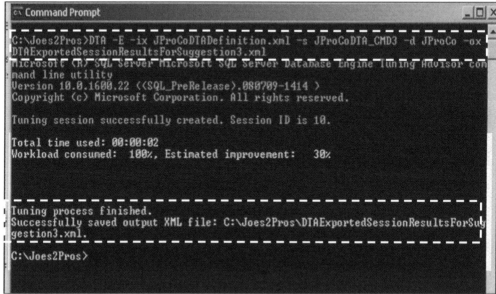

Figure 10.52 The Session Results are run and saved to an XML file for analysis.

Your file is now saved to the path location as an XML file. We can see inside the XML file the performance gain is 30.04%.

```
    <Value>1 Minute</Value>
  </ReportEntry>
  <ReportEntry>
    <Name>Estimated percentage improvement</Name>
    <Value>30.04</Value>
  </ReportEntry>
  <ReportEntry>
    <Name>Maximum space for recommendation (MB)</N
    <Value>500</Value>
  </ReportEntry>
```

Figure 10.53 Analysis of the Session Result XML file shows a gain of 30.04 percent.

Lab 10.3: Data Tuning Advisor

Lab Prep: Before you can begin the lab, you must have SQL Server installed and run the SQLArchChapter10.3Setup.sql script.

Skill Check 1: Copy the Ch10_AW_Workload.sql file to the C:\Joes2Pros folder from the resources folder and analyze it via the DTA in the AdventureWorks database on just the SalesOrderHeader and SalesOrderDetail tables. Call the session AW_CH10. Look for nonclustered indexes with no partitioning and keep all existing PDS. Specify up to 500MB for recommendations and generate online recommendations where possible. Keep the DTA window open to complete the next skill check.

Figure 10.54 Skill Check 1 shows a 74% performance imporvement.

Skill Check 2: Take the second suggestion from the session definition in Skill Check 1, paste the code into a query window and run it.

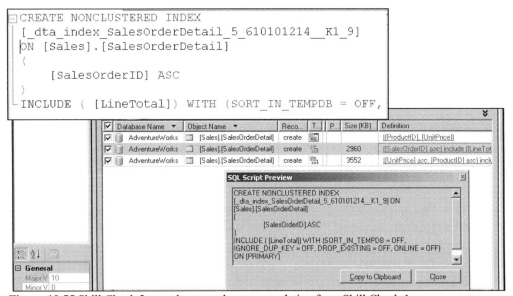

Figure 10.55 Skill Check 2 runs the second recommendation from Skill Check 1.

Skill Check 3: Evaluate the third suggestion in a session named AW_Suggestion3 to see the performance gain. (This should be 69%).

General	Tuning Options	Progress	Recommendations	Reports

Tuning Summary

Date	10/24/2009
Time	5:13:26 PM
Server	RENO
Database(s) to tune	[AdventureWorks]
Workload file	C:\Joes2Pros\CH10_AW_Workload.sql
Maximum tuning time	55 Minutes
Time taken for tuning	1 Minute
Estimated percentage improvement	69.19
Maximum space for recommendation (MB)	500

Figure 10.56 The 3rd suggestion from Skill Check 1 shows a 69% performance gain.

Export the session definition into the C:\Joes2Pros\AWSuggestion3.xml location.

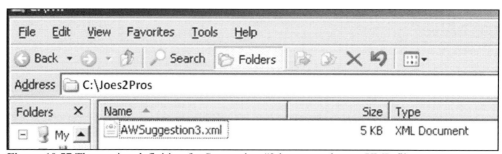

Figure 10.57 The session definition for Suggestion #3 is exported as an XML file.

Skill Check 4: In the C:\Joes2Pros\AWSuggestion3.xml file add an included field called RowGUID. Use the DTA command line utility to test the performance gain with the newly included field.

```
<Column SortOrder="Ascending" Type="IncludedColumn">
    <Name>[UnitPriceDiscount]</Name>
</Column>

<Column SortOrder="Ascending" Type="IncludedColumn">
    <Name>[RowGUID]</Name>
</Column>

<FileGroup>[PRIMARY]</FileGroup>
</Index>
```

Figure 10.58 Add a new "IncludedColumn" to the session definition.

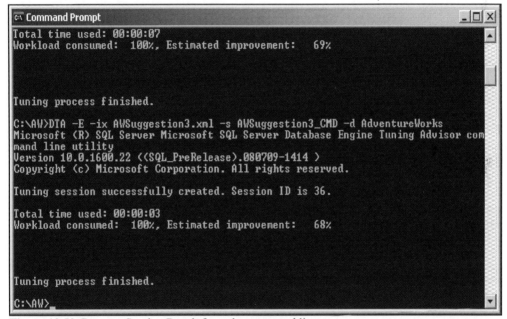

Figure 10.59 Get your Session Result from the command line.

Answer Code: The T-SQL code to this lab can be found in the downloadable files in a file named Lab10.3_DatabaseTuningAdvisor.sql.

Database Tuning - Points to Ponder

1. The key consideration in creating an index is to identify those columns that are used frequently in queries and to create the index using those columns. However, in most cases, it may not be obvious which columns are the best to include in an index. For this reason, the optimal way to identify the indexes you need to create is to use the Database Engine Tuning Advisor.

2. Database Engine Tuning Advisor was a new tool introduced SQL Server 2005 which goes beyond the older Index Tuning Wizard.

3. The Database Engine Tuning Advisor can analyze the performance effects of workload files.

4. The Database Engine Tuning Advisor provides two interfaces:
    a. Stand alone GUI 2.
    b. Command line utility dta.exe.

5. The Database Engine Tuning Advisor allows two different types of exploratory analysis. Evaluate mode and tune mode. Evaluate mode (discussed above) allows you to evaluate potential new design structures. Tune mode allows you to "tune" your database with a custom user design structure through xml.

6. A workload is a set of T-SQL statements that executes against databases you want to tune.

7. The workload can be a script or a trace file generated by SQL profiler.

8. You can create workload files in the following formats:
    a. XML File
    b. T-SQL File
    c. SQL Trace file (from SQL Profiler)

Chapter Glossary

Catalog View: Catalog Views contain metadata about all the objects and their settings inside SQL Server.

Composite Index: A composite index is where multiple fields are included as part of one index.

Database Engine Tuning Advisor (DTA): The Database Engine Tuning Advisor allows two different types of exploratory analysis. Evaluate mode and tune mode.

Dynamic Management View: Dynamic Management Views can view metadata about run time settings.

Index Hint: The "With *Index*" hint allows you to specify which index you want to use.

OPTION FOR: When the word OPTION appears after any query, it means you're using a query hint

Optimize for: The Optimize for hint allows a seek on a predicated variable.

Query execution plan: An execution plan allows you to see how the query is executed.

Query Hint: The Query Hint will suggest a way to optimize the query and let SQL Server pick the right index to use.

Query optimizer: The SQL Server Query Optimizer determines the best way to run a query (using a seek or a scan).

Selectivity: A highly selective query is one where your result set will show a small percentage of the records from your table.

Session Definitions: The workload and the suggested indexes make up the Session Definitions.

Session Results: Running the session definitions will yield session results.

Tracing: The term "Tracing" comes from running a tool known as SQL Profiler. It's the job of SQL Profiler to record activity taking place on your SQL Server. The recording is saved as a "Trace" file (.trc) that you can analyze to see what tasks are run most often on your system.

Chapter Ten - Review Quiz

1.) You have the following query

> SELECT SalesInvoiceDetailID, SalesInvoiceID, Amount
> FROM SalesInvoiceDetail
> WHERE SaleInvoiceID = 1500

You have a Clustered index on SalesInvoiceDetailID called PK_SIDetail_SalesInvDetID and a nonclustered index on SalesInvoiceID called IX_SIDetail_SalesInvID. You want to force the query to use a query execution plan that uses a seek rather than a scan. Which query hint should you use?

O a. HINT(1)
O b. INDEX(1)
O c. WITH(INDEX(PK_SIDetail_SalesInvDetID))
O d. WITH(INDEX(IX_SIDetail_SalesInvID))
O e. WITH(INDEX(PK_SIDetail_SalesInvDetID, IX_SIDetail_SalesInvID))

2.) You have the following query:

> **SELECT ***
> **FROM CurrentProducts**
> **WHERE ShortName = 'Yoga Trip'**

You have a nonclustered index on the ShortName field and the query runs an efficient index seek. You change your query to use a variable for ShortName and now you are using a slow index scan.

What query hint can you use to get the same execution time as before?

O a. NOLOCK
O b. LOCK
O c. FAST
O d. OPTIMIZE FOR
O e. MAXDOP
O f. READONLY

3.) Which two types of queries are most likely to perform an Index Scan?

☐ a. Uncovered query
☐ b. Covered query with high selectivity
☐ c. Covered query with low selectivity

4.) You manage a SQL Server 2008 database that contains a table with many indexes. You suspect that some of the indexes are unused. You need to identify which indexes were not used by any queries since the last time SQL Server 2008 started. Which dynamic view should you use?

O a. sys.db_fts_index_population
O b. sys.dm_exec_query_stats
O c. sys.dm_db_index_usage_stats
O d. sys.dm_db_index_physical_stats

5.) You want to analyze your existing index scheme against a known workload file and get recommendations for only nonclustered indexes. In which portion of the DTA would you specify these options?

O a. Sessions
O b. Tuning Options
O c. Recommendations
O d. Reports

6.) You have three stored procedures that use many DML statements. You need to create a list of suggested index changes to the database. What is the best way to accomplish this task?

O a. Use Index DMVs
O b. Use Non-Indexed DMVs
O c. Use Performance Monitor
O d. Use Database Tuning Advisor (DTA)
O e. Use a SQL Trace
O f. Export Database Wizard

7.) You want to use the Database Engine Tuning Advisor (DTA) and need to get a workload file. What format of workload files can DTA accept?

□ a. SQL MDF File
□ b. T-SQL Script File
□ c. SQL Event log file
□ d. SQL Trace file
□ e. Excel Spreadsheet file .xls or .xlsx
□ f. XML File
□ g. Performance counter log

367

8.) You use the DTA to analyze a workload from a T-SQL script. You want to use this to do exploratory analysis for what-if analysis. Which should you use?

O a. Export Session Results
O b. Import Session Results
O c. Export Session Definition
O d. Import Session Definition

9.) You use the DTA to analyze a workload from a T-SQL script. You want to save the recommendations generated by the DTA. Which command should you use?

O a. Export Session Definition
O b. Persist Session Results
O c. Import Session Results

10.) You have 15 million rows returned in one query of your SalesInvoiceDetail table and wish to run the entire query. It takes awhile to run. You want to return the first 40 records right away. What code will achieve this result?

O a. SELECT * FROM SalesInvoiceDetail
      OPTION (FAST 40)

O b. SELECT TOP 40 * FROM SalesInvoiceDetail

O c. SELECT * FROM SalesInvoiceDetail
      OPTION (OPTIMIZE TOP = 40)

O d. SELECT * FROM SalesInvoiceDetail
      OPTION (FIRST 40 ONLY)

11.) What is the difference between Export Session Definition and Export Session Results?

O a. Export Session Definition will show the performance gain while Export Session Results will not.
O b. Export Session Results will show the performance gain while Export Session Definition will not.

Answer Key

1.) d   2.) d   3.) a, c   4.) c   5.) b   6.) d   7.) b, d, f   8.) c   9.) a   10.) a
11.) b

Bug Catcher Game

To play the Bug Catcher game, run the BugCatcher_Chapter10IndexAnalysis.pps from the BugCatcher folder of the companion files. You can obtain these files from www.Joes2Pros.com or by ordering the Companion CD.

Chapter 11. Index Maintenance

If you are raising a child, what steps to you do you need to take when your son or daughter becomes two years old? How does your job as parent/guardian/mentor change as he or she progresses and becomes 10, 16, and then 18 years old?

Indexes keep track of data, but the data itself keeps changing. Indexes must keep pace with changes in the underlying data.

This chapter is all about setting indexes up correctly so they are useful, support the needs of the table, and can be maintained with little or no effort over time.

READER NOTE: *In order to follow along with the examples in the first section of Chapter 11, please run the SQLArchChapter11.0Setup.sql setup script. The setup scripts for this book are posted at Joes2Pros.com.*

Fragmentation Basics

So what exactly is fragmentation and what causes it? One time I threw a birthday party and expected 14 people based on the confirmed list. I made sure the restaurant had 14 seats ready by putting several dining tables together. Everyone arrived, was seated, and given menus. Minutes later, my friend, Dr. Dave, got paged and had to quickly leave. With him, his wife and 7 year old son also left the party and promised to make it up with a dinner next week. Our party was still taking up room in the restaurant as though 14 people were present, but only 11 people were now sitting with us. When data is removed from a database table, the table contains empty spaces just like those empty seats at my restaurant table.

Let's begin with a small example using the HumanResources.Contractor table. We will start populating this table with more data. Pretend we can fit exactly three records in every memory page and have a total of fourteen records. This means we filled four memory pages, and partially filled a fifth memory page. Adding more records would start claiming more memory pages.

But what would happen if we were to remove about half of these records after we already set aside the memory pages for them? If we were to remove the six dotted records you see in Figure 11.1 that would leave eight records remaining. The end result is we have gaps.

Page1		
419-27-7057	Irene	Intern
160-74-8643	David	Daves
185-31-9202	Dick	Jones
Page2		
281-70-5339	Bill	Loewen
439-31-3069	Lilly	Bannister
546-49-2179	Sally	Sears
Page3		
551-40-5302	Major	Dissary
591-91-1309	Jonny	Dirt
598-13-5818	Sara	James
Page4		
667-52-5923	Tina	Fisher
816-81-6243	Phil	Jaffe
829-91-4207	Rick	Morelan
Page5		
906-23-5462	Tom	Smith
931-55-9948	Harry	McCallister
Empty	Empty	Empty

11.1 Deletions of existing data can leave scatter gaps in your memory storage.

With only 8 records remaining, our data could fit into just three memory pages. But in reality we are still using five memory pages.

Looking at Figure 11.2, we see the records in the table on the left represent our table before we do any deletions and the records in the table on the right represent our data after we've deleted the records from the previous figure. We no longer have the same density of data in our memory pages. The data was removed but SQL Server did not re-align the way they are stored.

Page1

119-27-7057	Irene	Intern
160-74-8643	David	Daves
185-31-9202	Dick	Jones

Page2

281-70-5339	Bill	Loewen
439-31-3069	Lilly	Bannister
546-49-2179	Sally	Sears

Page3

551-40-5302	Major	Dissary
591-91-1309	Jonny	Dirt
598-13-5818	Sara	James

Page4

667-52-5923	Tina	Fisher
816-81-6243	Phil	Jaffe
829-91-4207	Rick	Morelan

Page5

906-23-5462	Tom	Smith
931-55-9948	Harry	McCallister
Empty	Empty	Empty

Page1

Empty	Empty	Empty
160-74-8643	David	Daves
185-31-9202	Dick	Jones

Page2

Empty	Empty	Empty
Empty	Empty	Empty
Empty	Empty	Empty

Page3

551-40-5302	Major	Dissary
591-91-1309	Jonny	Dirt
598-13-5818	Sara	James

Page4

667-52-5923	Tina	Fisher
Empty	Empty	Empty
829-91-4207	Rick	Morelan

Page5

Empty	Empty	Empty
931-55-9948	Harry	McCallister
Empty	Empty	Empty

Figure 11.2 Deletions have caused your data storage to become fragmented.

Future inserts will take up more memory pages. When you get more deletions then there will be more gaps in memory. This phenomenon is known as **Fragmentation**. Fragmentation is the inefficient use of pages within a table caused by gaps formed during data manipulation.

Detecting Fragmentation

The quickest way to create fragmentation is to fill a table up with many records then delete some of the records scattered throughout the clustered index. Looking at our HumanResources.Contractor table we have 565 rows.

```
SELECT * FROM HumanResources.Contractor
```

This table of 565 records holds our contractors and interns. At the end of the summer it is time for the interns to go home. We will delete them from the table. The records where pay equals zero show there are 218 interns.

```
SELECT * FROM HumanResources.Contractor
WHERE Pay = 0
```

This tells us that 218 of our 565 contractors are interns. So scattered throughout the clustered index will be a number of deletions.

```
DELETE FROM HumanResources.Contractor
WHERE Pay = 0
```

If you reserved a party room for 565 guests and 218 walked out, the party room would be no smaller. Likewise, the 565 original records in our table occupied several memory pages. We want to look at the level of fragmentation in the clustered index of the HumanResources.Contractor table. Let's locate this table's clustered index in Object Explorer (see Figure 11.3).

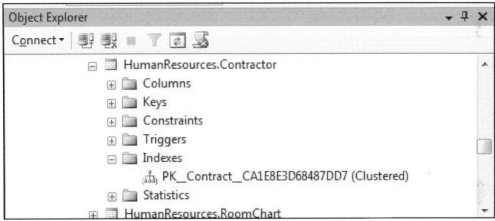

Figure 11.3 The HumanResources.Contractor table has a clustered index.

Detecting Fragmentation with Management Studio

The properties of any index will allow you to see its level of fragmentation. One page of the index properties is the "Fragmentation" page. In Figure 11.4 the total fragmentation is 87.5%. *Your system results may vary, so just remember your number for later in the lesson.*

Right-click on the index in Object Explorer > Properties > **Fragmentation** (page)

Figure 11.4 The properties of the clustered index shows its 87.5% fragmented.

Detecting Fragmentation with Dynamic Management Views

Now, we will find the level of fragmentation for the clustered index of the HumanResources.Contractor table by using code. In order to do that, we need to find out a couple of things first, like the IDs of the database we're talking about and the table that has the clustered index. The database name is JProCo and the Table is HumanResources.Contractor. In Figure 11.5 we see that the JProCo database has an ID of 5, and the HumanResources.Contractor table's ID is 1525580473. *(Please note that these numbers will likely be different on your system.)*

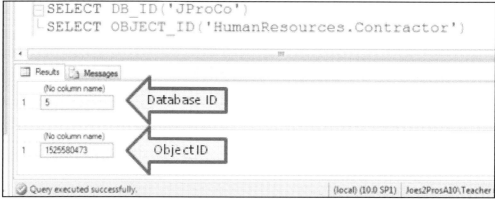

Figure 11.5 You can use system supplied functions to get your database and object IDs.

With these two IDs known, we can run a Dynamic Management View to find the level of fragmentation in our clustered index. In Figure 11.6, a value of 5 for the DatabaseID and 1525580473 for the Object ID will be passed into the sys.dm_db_index_physical_stats DMV. This DMV is expecting five parameters so we can pass in three more parameters with null values. Running this query shows us the same thing we discovered a few moments ago. We have a clustered index that has 87.5% fragmentation.

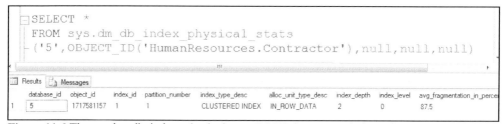

Figure 11.6 The sys.dm_db_index_physical_stats DMV shows your index's fragmentation level.

It seems like using code to find the level of fragmentation in this one index was a little bit more work than using the GUI. If you wanted to find the fragmentation for every single clustered index in your database, then a query would be much faster then clicking each index in the Object Explorer. Perhaps you want to find which index in the database has the most fragmentation. You can analyze all indexes in your database at once with the sys.dm_db_index_physical_stats DMV. You don't have to specify which object you're interested in viewing, since you want to see every one in DatabaseID 5. Put a null in the last four parameters after the DatabaseID. This will get all indexes in the database and their levels of fragmentation.

We want the most heavily fragmented indexes on top. The field to sort on is called avg_fragmentation_in_percent. Putting an ORDER BY, in descending order, on this field shows you the most fragmented index listed on the top of the results (Figure 11.7).

```
SELECT *  --Gets all index for JProCo
FROM sys.dm_db_index_physical_stats
(5,null,null,null,null)
ORDER BY avg_Fragmentation_in_percent DESC
```

Results | Messages

n	index_level	avg_fragmentation_in_percent	fragment_count	avg_fragment_size_in_pages	page_count	avg_page_space_used
1	0	91.6666666666667	12	1	12	NULL
2	0	87.5	8	1	8	NULL
3	0	66.6666666666667	3	1	3	NULL
4	0	66.6666666666667	3	1	3	NULL
5	0	50	2	1.5	3	NULL
6	0	30	4	2.5	10	NULL

Figure 11.7 You can sort your results to find the the most fragmented indexes of the JProCo database.

Lab 11.1: Detecting Fragmentation

Lab Prep: Before you can begin the lab, you must have SQL Server installed and run the SQLArchChapter11.1Setup.sql script.

Skill Check 1: Use the correct Dynamic Management View to see the level of fragmentation in the Employee table of JProCo.

Figure 11.8 Result set for Skill Check 1.

Skill Check 2: Use Management Studio to confirm the fragmentation level of the clustered index on the Employee table from Skill Check 1.

Figure 11.9 UI result for Skill Check 2.

Answer Code: The T-SQL code to this lab can be found in the downloadable files in a file named Lab11.1_DetectingFragmentation.sql.

Detecting Fragmentation - Points to Ponder

1. Index fragmentation is the inefficient use of pages within an index.

2. Although indexes can increase performance, using indexes comes with a cost. Indexes require disk space for storage as well as increased processing requirements to keep the indexes up to date.

3. With a high level of fragmentation, queries become less efficient since more pages need to be loaded to locate data pages.

4. You can use Management studio or the sys.dm_db_index_physical_stats "dynamic management view" to determine the extent to which your indexes are fragmented.

5. Some of the arguments you can pass to the sys.dm_db_index_physical_stats view are DatabaseID, ObjectID, Index, Partition number, and Mode (don't ask).

Fragmentation Reports

You can look at your Fragmented Indexes all at once by querying the sys.dm_db_index_physical_stats DMV. This way you can identify and prioritize the indexes which need the most amount of attention.

Fragmentation Recap

As a quick recap on Analyzing Fragmentation, we saw that the DB_ID function will return the DatabaseID if you pass it a valid database name. With this ID we can query the sys.dm_db_index_physical_stats Dynamic Management View. This way we can get all the index statistics for a database. If you don't pass in a database ID at all, but pass in five null parameters, then the sys.dm_db_index_physical_stats Dynamic Management View will run and show you all the indexes from all the databases on your SQL Server (Figure 11.10).

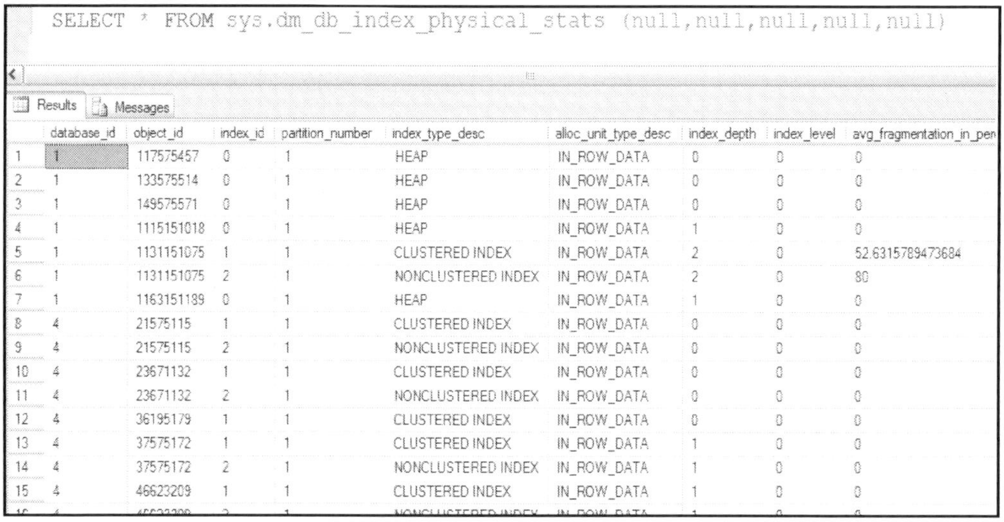

Figure 11.10 Passing all null parameters into sys.dm_db_index_physical_stats Dynamic Management View shows all indexes on your server.

Combining Fragmentation Metadata

We have learned that querying the Index Physical Stats Dynamic Management View and passing in the ID for the JProCo database shows you the physical stats of every index in the JProCo database. This is helpful, except that the sys.dm_db_index_physical_stats Dynamic Management View doesn't tell you the name of the index. It does, however, give you the Object ID of this index. In Figure 11.11 we will take the value that is returned from the DB_ID function for the first parameter instead of typing in 5.

```
SELECT *
FROM sys.dm_db_Index_Physical_Stats(DB_ID('JProCo'),null,null,null,null)
ORDER BY Avg_Fragmentation_In_Percent DESC
```

	index_id	partition_number	index_type_desc	alloc_unit_type_desc	index_depth	index_level	avg_fragmentation_in_percent	fragment_count	avg_fragment_size_in_pages
1	1	1	CLUSTERED INDEX	IN_ROW_DATA	2	0	91.6666666666667	12	1
2	1	1	CLUSTERED INDEX	IN_ROW_DATA	2	0	87.5	8	1
3	2	1	NONCLUSTERED INDEX	IN_ROW_DATA	2	0	66.6666666666667	3	1
4	3	1	NONCLUSTERED INDEX	IN_ROW_DATA	2	0	66.6666666666667	3	1
5	0	1	HEAP	IN_ROW_DATA	1	0	50	2	1.5
6	2	1	NONCLUSTERED INDEX	IN_ROW_DATA	2	0	30	4	2.5
7	1	1	CLUSTERED INDEX	IN_ROW_DATA	2	0	25	3	2.6666666666667
8	1	1	CLUSTERED INDEX	IN_ROW_DATA	2	0	16.6666666666667	2	3
9	1	1	CLUSTERED INDEX	IN_ROW_DATA	2	0	16	5	5
10	0	1	HEAP	IN_ROW_DATA	1	0	0	1	1
11	1	1	CLUSTERED INDEX	IN_ROW_DATA	1	0	0	1	1
12	1	1	CLUSTERED INDEX	IN_ROW_DATA	1	0	0	1	1
13	5	1	NONCLUSTERED INDEX	IN_ROW_DATA	2	0	0	2	1
14	1	1	CLUSTERED INDEX	IN_ROW_DATA	1	0	0	1	1

Figure 11.11 Passing just the DatabaseID parameter into the sys.dm_db_index_physical_stats Dynamic Management View.

Taking the Object ID from the first record in the figure above, we can find out which Clustered Index name was the most fragmented. In Figure 11.12 the sys.indexes table tells us the index name based on the Object ID.

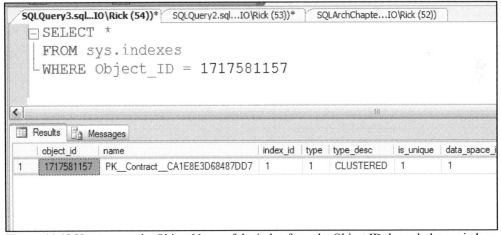

Figure 11.12 You can get the Object Name of the index from the Object ID through the sys.indexes catalog view.

In Figure 11.12 we see a long name starting with PK_Contract. We can now look at this index in the Object Explorer (Figure 11.13).

Figure 11.13 You can use Object Explorer to see the indexes of the HumanResources.Contractor table.

When it's time to find the name of the second-most heavily fragmented index you can repeat this process. Query your Dynamic Management View and look for the second record which is the second-most heavily fragmented index. Simply copy and paste the value of the object_id field into the predicate of the query on the Sys Indexes View. You could repeat this process for every index or you can combine these two views into one query (Figure 11.14).

```
SELECT * FROM
sys.dm_db_index_physical_stats
(DB_ID('JProCo'),null,null,null,null) AS ips
INNER JOIN sys.indexes AS so
ON ips.[Index_id] = so.[Index_id]
AND ips.[object_id] = so.[object_id]
ORDER BY avg_fragmentation_in_percent DESC
```

	warded_record_count	compressed_page_count	object_id	name	index_id	type	type_desc	is_
1	JLL	NULL	1653580929	PK_Contract_CA1E8E3D6477ECF3	1	1	CLUSTERED	1
2	JLL	NULL	85575343	PK_CurrentP_R40CC6ED07020F21	1	1	CLUSTERED	1
3	JLL	NULL	789577851	NULL	0	0	HEAP	0
4	JLL	NULL	549576996	PK_Salesinv_D796AAD522AA2996	1	1	CLUSTERED	1
5	JLL	NULL	357576312	PK_Customer_A4AE64B8173876EA	1	1	CLUSTERED	1
6	JLL	NULL	613577224	PK_Salesinv_1F1578F1267ABA7A	1	1	CLUSTERED	1
7	ILL	NULL	677577452	NULL	0	0	HEAP	0

Figure 11.14 Getting information from both views in one query is possible with a join.

The query from the sys.dm_db_index_physical_stats Dynamic Management View has all of our index statistics, and you can join it to the Sys.Indexes Catalog View, which has all of our index names. Since the Sys.Indexes catalog view knows all the indexes, if you have the right object_id you can join these two views. In Figure 11.15, the DMV has a shorter alias ("ips") and the Sys.Indexes Catalog View is aliased as "so." These two views are joined on the object_id field and index_id field.

```
SELECT * FROM
sys.dm_db_index_physical_stats
(DB_ID('JProCo'),null,null,null,null) AS ips
INNER JOIN sys.indexes AS so
ON ips.[Index_id] = so.[Index_id]
AND ips.[object_id] = so.[object_id]
WHERE index_type_desc = 'CLUSTERED INDEX'
ORDER BY avg_fragmentation_in_percent DESC
```

	page_count	object_id	name	index_id	type	type_desc	is_unique	data_space_id	ignore_du
1		1653580929	PK__Contract__CA1E8E3D6477ECF3	1	1	CLUSTERED	1	1	0
2		85575343	PK__CurrentP__B40CC9ED07020F21	1	1	CLUSTERED	1	1	0
3		549576996	PK__SalesInv__D796AAD522AA2996	1	1	CLUSTERED	1	1	0
4		357576312	PK__Cuhomer__A4AE64B8173876EA	1	1	CLUSTERED	1	1	0
5		613577224	PK__SalesInv__1F1578F1267ABA7A	1	1	CLUSTERED	1	1	0
6		821577965	PK__Supplier__4BE6689432E0915F	1	1	CLUSTERED	1	1	0
7		835578193	PK__Contract__3736C5EE36B12243	1	1	CLUSTERED	1	1	0

Figure 11.15 You can limit your search of indexes to just clustered indexes.

It looks like there are many types of indexes. To narrow your search down to just look for the clustered indexes, you can predicate on the index_type_desc field and specify the value of 'CLUSTERED INDEX'. Our third most heavily fragmented clustered index is called PK_SalesInv_*nnnnn* (Figure 11.15).

Index Defragmentation

Knowing the names of the fragmented indexes is valuable information towards actually doing some index maintenance and clean up steps. The fragmentation can often be fixed by performing a defragmentation operation.

Rebuilding Indexes

Our most heavily fragmented index in JProCo is just over 87% fragmented and is named PK_Contract_*nnnn*. You can alter the index on the table and specify you want it rebuilt. Specify the index name and the table the index is on, then use the REBUILD keyword (Figure 11.16).

The hope here is that the 87% fragmented index has improved through the index rebuilding process. Rebuilding an index is the preferred choice for indexes with high levels of fragmentation. One disadvantage of using REBUILD is that the table is offline for the duration of time that the index is being rebuilt.

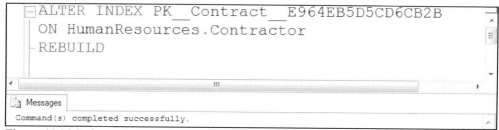

```
ALTER INDEX PK__Contract__E964EB5D5CD6CB2B
ON HumanResources.Contractor
REBUILD
```

Messages

Command(s) completed successfully.

Figure 11.16 Code to rebuild the clustered index on the HumanResources.Contractor table.

Reorganizing Indexes

A slightly less aggressive option (i.e., versus choosing REBUILD) is the REORGANIZE keyword. Doing this would leave the data accessible but does not work as well on heavily fragmented indexes. Here's a kind of a rule of thumb: You want to rebuild indexes if the fragmentation is over 30%, and you want to reorganize them if it's under 30%.

Let's look at our indexes that are below 30% fragmentation by changing our query to look for avg_fragmentation_in_percent less than or equal to 30. All our clustered indexes having below 30% fragmentation can be seen in Figure 11.17. It looks like we have a 25% fragmented index called PK_SalesInv_*nnnn*. This would be a good candidate for trying the REORGANIZE option.

```
SELECT * FROM
sys.dm_db_index_physical_stats
(DB_ID('JProCo'),null,null,null,null) AS ips
INNER JOIN sys.indexes AS so
ON ips.[Index_id] = so.[Index_id]
AND ips.[object_id] = so.[object_id]
WHERE index_type_desc = 'CLUSTERED INDEX'
AND avg_fragmentation_in_percent <= 30
ORDER BY avg_fragmentation_in_percent DESC
```

Results | Messages

	orwarded_record_count	compressed_page_count	object_id	name	index_id	type	type_desc	is
1	NULL	NULL	549576996	PK_SalesInv__D796AAD522AA2996	1	1	CLUSTERED	1
2	NULL	NULL	357576312	PK_Customer__A44a64B8173876EA	1	1	CLUSTERED	1
3	NULL	NULL	613577224	PK_SalesInv__1F1578F1267ABA7A	1	1	CLUSTERED	1
4	NULL	NULL	821577965	PK_Supplier__4BE6669432E0915F	1	1	CLUSTERED	1

Figure 11.17 Show all indexes that have less than 30% fragmentation.

In Figure 11.18 we have a code that will reorganize the index with 25% fragmentation. This will be similar to your ALTER INDEX statement from earlier. Simply use the index name, the table it's on, and then specify reorganize.

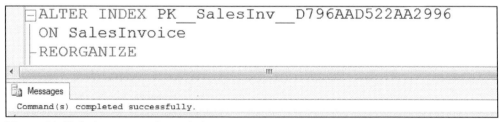

Figure 11.18 Code to reorganize an index.

After the reorganization of the SalesInvoice table's clustered index, we expect the fragmentation to be an improvement from the 25% that it was just moments ago. Our query can check this for us. In the example in Figure 11.19 we see our PK_SalesInv_*nnnn* index appears in the second row of the query. Scrolling to the right to see the avg_fragmentation_in_percent show our fragmentation level now stands at 16%. *The results and numbers you see on your system may vary.*

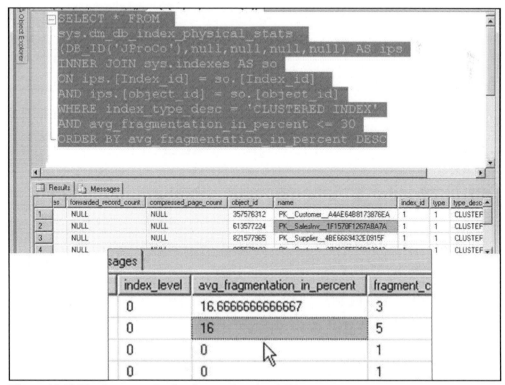

Figure 11.19 The fragmentation has been reduced to 16%.

Lab 11.2: Index Defragmentation

Lab Prep: Before you can begin the lab, you must have SQL Server installed and run the SQLArchChapter11.2Setup.sql script.

Skill Check 1: Fix the fragmentation level in the dbo.Customer table by using code to rebuild the Index.

Answer Code: The T-SQL code to this lab can be found in the downloadable files in a file named Lab11.2_IndexDefragmentation.sql.

Index Defragmentation - Points to Ponder

1. If you use management studio to look for fragmentation, you can only look at one index at a time by getting the properties of the index.

2. You can use sys.dm_db_index_physical_stats to look at a specific index, all indexes in a table, all indexes in a view, all indexes in a database, or even all indexes on SQL Server at once.

3. There are two types of fragmentation:
   a. Internal – Amount of data stored within each page is less than the data page can hold.
   b. External – The logical order of the pages is wrong.

4. If your fragmentation is lower than 30% then use the Reorganize option, if higher than 30% then use the Rebuild option.

5. The ALTER INDEX with the REORGANIZE option replaces the older DBCC INDEXDEFRAG from earlier versions of SQL.

6. The ALTER INDEX with the REBUILD option replaces the older DBCC DBREINDEX statements from older versions of SQL Server.

7. You can REORGANIZE one index or even do this on all indexes on a table. *Reorganizing* indexes leaves the table online, while *Rebuilding* takes it offline for the duration.

8. You can leave your indexes online with a rebuild by using the following option on your code:
   REBUILD WITH ONLINE = ON

9. The CREATE INDEX statement allows you to create indexes and specify index characteristics. After you have created an index, you can use the ALTER INDEX statement to change, reorganize, and rebuild the index.

Index Metadata

The movie "As Good as it Gets" contains the well-known restaurant scene where Jack Nicholson tells Helen Hunt that she makes him want to be a better man. Just minutes before, as they were entering the formal restaurant, there was some tension when the waiter stopped Jack Nicholson to let him know he can't enter without a jacket and tie. The dress code of such restaurants requires such attire before you can dine there. Sometimes you are missing a required or just a recommended object. SQL Server actually keeps an eye on your activity and the database requirements and suggests indexes that might be missing.

Actual Execution Plans

By looking at the SalesInvoiceDetail table in the Object Explorer and some of the metadata that makes up its design, we can see that we have a clustered index and a nonclustered index to help the performance of queries against this table (Figure 11.20).

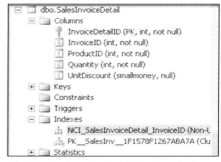

11.20 SalesInvoiceDetail has two indexes.

The NCI_SalesInvoiceDetail_InvoiceID nonclustered index is on the InvoiceID field. This means the query in figure 11.21 is covered. That being the case, it's probably going to do a seek to find its records.

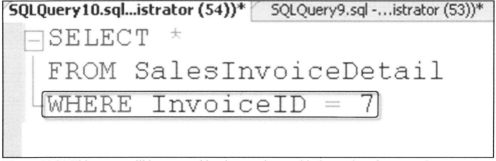

Figure 11.21 This query will be covered by the nonclustered index and perform a seek.

Even before we run this query, we can see the estimated execution plan that the query optimizer has in mind. By clicking the "Display Estimated Execution Plan" button we get an execution plan tab next to our Messages tab. In clicking on that tab it tells us this query is going to do a seek (Figure 11.22).

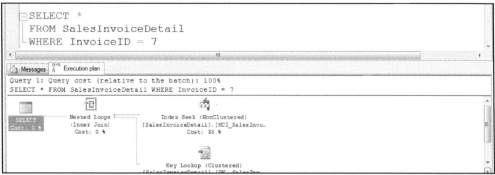

Figure 11.22 Clicking on "Display Estimated Execution Plan" shows that a seek is to be done.

After you run this query, what was the actual execution plan? Choose Query from the menu, and select "Include Actual Execution Plan" (Figure 11.23).

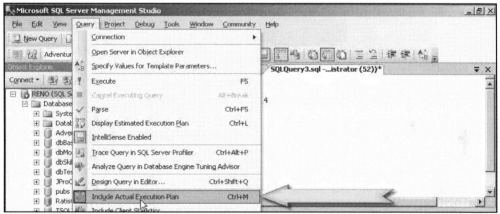

Figure 11.23 When you run a query you can specify that the actual execution plan be shown.

Run the query and, in Figure 11.24, you see a third tab called "Execution plan."

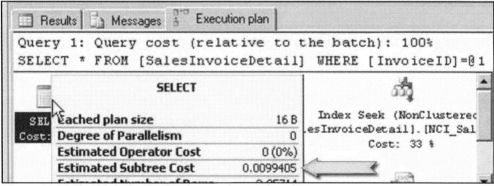

Figure 11.24 The third tab contains the actual execution plan.

Missing Indexes

In all of our examples thus far, we've seen that our predicates have included fields that have covering indexes. This means that all of our activity has been covered and query execution runs using index seeks. Based on our activity, we are not really missing any indexes. If we do run a selective query, predicating on a field that does not have an index, then you could say we are missing an index. With that in mind, here's an interesting Dynamic Management View you should know called **sys.db_missing_index_details**. This DMV will keep track of activity that indicates missing indexes. As we query this view, it doesn't look like we're missing any indexes that would have benefited our system's performance (Figure 11.25).

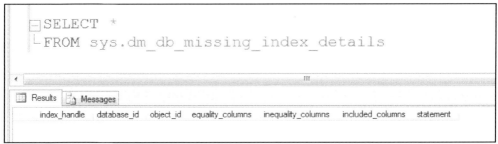

Figure 11.25 Currently there are no missing indexes observed in our database.

When do records appear in the sys.db_missing_index_details DMV? Let's use the AdventureWorks database to write a query that would have benefited from an index. Query for TerritoryID 4 from the Sales.Customer table. You will want to make sure the actual execution plan will be displayed when you run the query.

To really make this example work, we need a large table in a large database. Fortunately, AdventureWorks is big enough to afford us such an example. The query will be on the Sales.Customer table of the AdventureWorks database. We will predicate on a selective field that is not covered by an index. Let's look for all records from TerritoryID 4 (Figure 11.26).

By clicking the "Execution Plan" tab, you can see how the query actually ran and the total cost of the query.

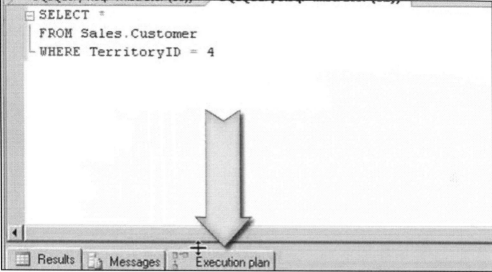

Figure 11.26 The third tab shows the actual execution plan after the query ran.

Since this query was not benefiting from a covering index, the estimated execution plan is doing a scan. When you run the actual execution plan, this is confirmed. The green text you see in Figure 11.27 shows you an index you could create.

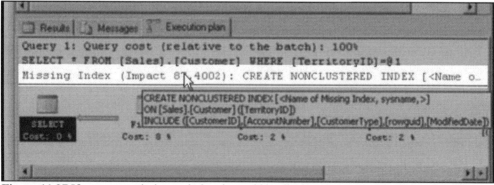

Figure 11.27 If you were missing an index, it would be displayed as part of the Execution Plan.

According to this DMV, you should create a nonclustered index on the Customer table keying on TerritoryID and include the following fields you see listed. We could jot this information down, but how do we keep track of all the suggested missing indexes as they are tallied? This suggestion came and went only as long as we ran the query. Luckily the suggestion is stored someplace. That someplace is the sys.dm_db_missing_index_details Dynamic Management View. Figure 11.28

queries this DMV and shows the list of suggestions about Missing Indexes. This view will continue to grow as SQL Server discovers missing indexes based on queries you have as they are run.

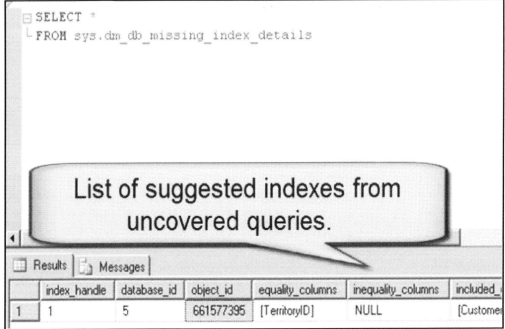

Figure 11.28 The sys.dm_db_missing_index_details DMV shows all observed missing indexes since the SQL Server service started.

Before SQL Server 2008, to get an historical list of missing indexes, you had to run a series of analysis steps. Now, SQL Server keeps a running track of suggested missing indexes. The list keeps growing as more missing indexes are found. If you want the list to start over, simply restart the SQL Server service. Restarting the SQL Server service and running this query again shows us we no longer see any missing indexes (see Figure 11.29).

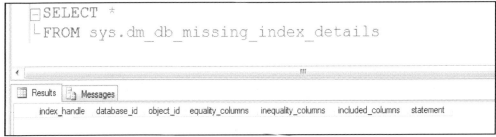

Figure 11.29 After restarting the SQL Server service, the sys.dm_db_missing_index_details view is empty.

Object Property Metadata

Back in our JProCo database, we will compare two different tables. If you expand both tables in the Object Explorer and look for the list of indexes, you see a big difference. The SalesInvoice table has a clustered index and the RetiredProducts table has no index of any kind at all (Figure 11.30).

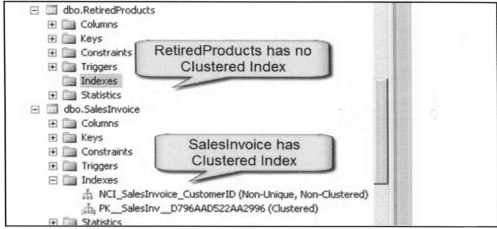

Figure 11.30 Tables can have no indexes, one index, or many indexes.

How many tables in JProCo have a clustered index and how many do not have any index at all? Tables are like any object in SQL Server and they have an Object ID associated with them. We need to find out the Object ID for these two tables. (Figure 11.31).

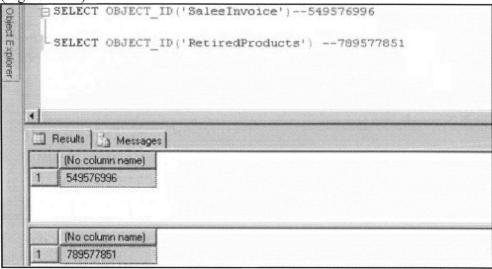

Figure 11.31 The ObjectIDs can be gathered from the Object names using the OBJECT_ID function.

Index Functions

We know the SalesInvoice table has a clustered index. By taking the Object ID of the SalesInvoice table and passing it into the OBJECTPROPERTY function we can get more detailed information about dbo.SalesInvoice. The property we are interested in is called TableHasClustIndex. Pass that in as the second parameter and you can get a result. A 1 means "Yes" (Figure 11.32) and a 0 means "No".

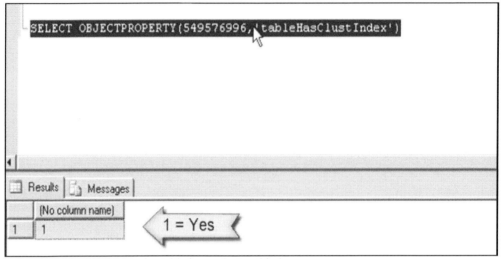

Figure 11.32 The SalesInvoice table has a clustered index.

Repeating the process for the RetiredProducts table should show us a table that does not have a clustered index on it. Putting the Object ID of the RetiredProducts table into the OBJECTPROPERTY function satisfies the first parameter. Using 'TableHasClustIndex' for the second parameter we get back a zero (Zero means "No"). With no clustered index, the RetiredProducts table is a heap. Running both queries at the same time, we see that the first table has a clustered index; the second one is a heap (Figure 11.33).

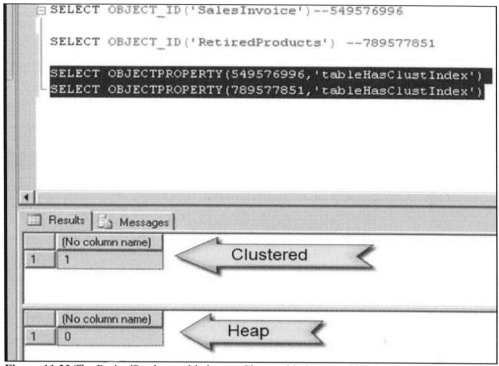

Figure 11.33 The RetiredProducts table has no Clustered indexes and is a heap.

We have confirmed two of our tables in JProCo. How many tables in JProCo have clustered indexes? *Your results may differ, so follow the steps and make note of the numbers you get.* The sys.tables catalog view will tell us how many tables are in the JProCo database. Add a predicate that uses the OBJECTPROPERTY function. For the first parameter, we pass the Object ID. We then specify the TableHasClustIndex option is equal to one (Figure 11.34).

```
SELECT *
FROM sys.tables
WHERE OBJECTPROPERTY([Object id],'TableHasClustIndex') = 1
```

	name	object_id	principal_id	schema_id	parent_object_id	type	type_desc	create_date	modify_date	is_ms_shippe
1	MgmtTraining	21575115	NULL	1	0	U	USER_TABLE	2010-09-29 18:30:12.650	2010-09-29 18:30:12.650	0
2	CurrentProducts	85575343	NULL	1	0	U	USER_TABLE	2010-09-29 18:30:12.667	2010-09-29 18:30:23.477	0
3	Employee	149575571	NULL	1	0	U	USER_TABLE	2010-09-29 18:30:13.047	2010-09-29 18:30:23.310	0
4	Customer	357576312	NULL	1	0	U	USER_TABLE	2010-09-29 18:30:16.757	2010-09-29 18:30:23.450	0
5	SalesInvoice	549576996	NULL	1	0	U	USER_TABLE	2010-09-29 18:30:17.363	2010-09-29 18:30:23.470	0
6	SalesInvoiceDetail	613577224	NULL	1	0	U	USER_TABLE	2010-09-29 18:30:18.480	2010-09-29 18:30:23.463	0
7	Supplier	821577965	NULL	1	0	U	USER_TABLE	2010-09-29 18:30:21.317	2010-09-29 18:30:21.317	0
8	Contractor	885578193	NULL	1	0	U	USER_TABLE	2010-09-29 18:30:21.350	2010-09-29 18:30:21.350	0
9	PayRatesFeed	1189579276	NULL	1	0	U	USER_TABLE	2010-09-29 18:30:21.397	2010-09-29 18:30:21.397	0
10	Vendor	1589580701	NULL	5	0	U	USER_TABLE	2010-09-29 18:30:23.420	2010-09-29 18:30:23.430	0
11	Localities	1653580929	NULL	9	0	U	USER_TABLE	2010-09-29 18:30:23.433	2010-09-29 18:30:23.447	0
12	Contractor	1717581157	NULL	5	0	U	USER_TABLE	2010-09-29 18:30:23.480	2010-09-29 18:30:23.790	0
13	PayRates	2105058535	NULL	1	0	U	USER_TABLE	2010-09-29 18:30:12.613	2010-09-29 18:30:12.613	

Query executed successfully. (local) (10.0 SP1) Joes2ProsA10\Teacher (53) JProCo 00:00:00 13 rows

Figure 11.34 There are 13 tables in JProCo with a clustered index.

We have figured out that we have thirteen tables in the JProCo database that have a clustered index. So how many of these tables have at least one nonclustered index? Just change your second parameter to TableHasNonClustIndex (Figure 11.35)

```
SELECT *
FROM sys.tables
WHERE OBJECTPROPERTY([Object_id],'TableHasNonClustIndex') = 1
```

	name	object_id	principal_id	schema_id	parent_object_id	type	type_desc	create_date	modify_date	is_ms
1	CurrentProducts	85575343	NULL	1	0	U	USER_TABLE	2010-09-27 17:33:09.557	2010-09-27 17:33:20.610	0
2	Location	213575799	NULL	1	0	U	USER_TABLE	2010-09-27 17:33:10.113	2010-09-27 17:33:20.360	0
3	Grant	277576027	NULL	1	0	U	USER_TABLE	2010-09-27 17:33:10.157	2010-09-27 17:33:10.160	0
4	Customer	357576312	NULL	1	0	U	USER_TABLE	2010-09-27 17:33:14.120	2010-09-27 17:33:20.513	0
5	SalesInvoice	549576996	NULL	1	0	U	USER_TABLE	2010-09-27 17:33:14.600	2010-09-27 17:33:20.533	0
6	SalesInvoiceDetail	613577224	NULL	1	0	U	USER_TABLE	2010-09-27 17:33:15.690	2010-09-27 17:33:20.527	0
7	GrantFeed	1045578763	NULL	1	0	U	USER_TABLE	2010-09-27 17:33:18.433	2010-09-27 17:33:18.437	0
8	GrantCheckMaster	1109578991	NULL	1	0	U	USER_TABLE	2010-09-27 17:33:18.440	2010-09-27 17:33:18.443	0
9	Vendor	1589580701	NULL	5	0	U	USER_TABLE	2010-09-27 17:33:20.467	2010-09-27 17:33:20.477	0
10	Localities	1653580929	NULL	9	0	U	USER_TABLE	2010-09-27 17:33:20.480	2010-09-27 17:33:20.493	0

Figure 11.35 There are 10 tables in JProCo with at least 1 nonclustered index.

Of our clustered indexes, we discovered that we were better off making some of them as a part of an identity field to prevent page splits. How many of our tables actually have an identity field? Change the second parameter to TableHasIdentity (Figure 11.36). In this example we see we have seven of them.

```
SELECT *
FROM sys.tables
WHERE OBJECTPROPERTY([object_id],'TableHasIdentity') = 1
```

	name	object_id	principal_id	schema_id	parent_object_id	type	type_desc	create_date	modify_date
1	Mgmt Training	21575115	NULL	1	0	U	USER_TABLE	2010-11-03 13:24:07.410	2010-11-03 13:24:
2	CurrentProducts	85575343	NULL	1	0	U	USER_TABLE	2010-11-03 13:24:07.463	2010-11-03 13:24:
3	RetiredProducts	789577851	NULL	1	0	U	USER_TABLE	2010-11-03 13:24:18.517	2010-11-03 13:24:
4	Supplier	821577965	NULL	1	0	U	USER_TABLE	2010-11-03 13:24:18.523	2010-11-03 13:24:
5	Contractor	885578193	NULL	1	0	U	USER_TABLE	2010-11-03 13:24:18.557	2010-11-03 13:24:
6	Vendor	1589580701	NULL	5	0	U	USER_TABLE	2010-11-03 13:24:20.720	2010-11-03 13:25:
7	Localities	1653580929	NULL	9	0	U	USER_TABLE	2010-11-03 13:24:20.733	2010-11-03 13:24:

Query executed successfully. | (local) (10.0 SP1) | Joes2ProsA10\Teacher (54) | JProCo | 00:00:00 | 7 rows

Figure 11.36 This will show all the tables in JProCo that have an identity field.

We want to figure out how many tables don't have identity fields? We put an "equals zero" at the end of the same function. Figure 11.37 shows we have 25 tables without an identity field.

```
SELECT *
FROM sys.tables
WHERE OBJECTPROPERTY([Object_id],'TableHasIdentity') = 0
```

	name	object_id	principal_id	schema_id	parent_object_id	type	type_desc	create_date	modify_date	is_ms_sl
1	Employee	149575571	NULL	1	0	U	USER_TABLE	2010-09-27 17:33:10.110	2010-09-27 17:33:20.317	0
2	Location	213575799	NULL	1	0	U	USER_TABLE	2010-09-27 17:33:10.113	2010-09-27 17:33:20.360	0
3	Grant	277576027	NULL	1	0	U	USER_TABLE	2010-09-27 17:33:10.157	2010-09-27 17:33:10.160	0
4	Customer	357576312	NULL	1	0	U	USER_TABLE	2010-09-27 17:33:14.120	2010-09-27 17:33:20.513	0
5	SalesInvoice	549576996	NULL	1	0	U	USER_TABLE	2010-09-27 17:33:14.600	2010-09-27 17:33:20.533	0
6	SalesInvoiceDetail	613577224	NULL	1	0	U	USER_TABLE	2010-09-27 17:33:15.690	2010-09-27 17:33:20.527	0
7	StateList	677577452	NULL	1	0	U	USER_TABLE	2010-09-27 17:33:18.293	2010-09-27 17:33:18.293	0
8	LocationChanges	1013578649	NULL	1	0	U	USER_TABLE	2010-09-27 17:33:18.420	2010-09-27 17:33:18.420	0
9	PromotionList	1029578706	NULL	1	0	U	USER_TABLE	2010-09-27 17:33:18.423	2010-09-27 17:33:18.423	0
10	GrantFeed	1045578763	NULL	1	0	U	USER_TABLE	2010-09-27 17:33:18.433	2010-09-27 17:33:18.437	0
11	GrantCheckMaster	1109578991	NULL	1	0	U	USER_TABLE	2010-09-27 17:33:18.440	2010-09-27 17:33:18.443	0

Query executed successfully. | (local) (10.0 SP1) | Joes2ProsA10\Teacher (53) | JProCo | 00:00:00 | 25 rows

Figure 11.37 There are 25 tables in JProCo that do not have identity fields.

Lab 11.3: Index Metadata

Lab Prep: Before you can begin the lab, you must have SQL Server installed and run the SQLArchChapter11.3Setup.sql script.

Skill Check 1: Find all the tables in the JProCo database that have clustered indexes on them.

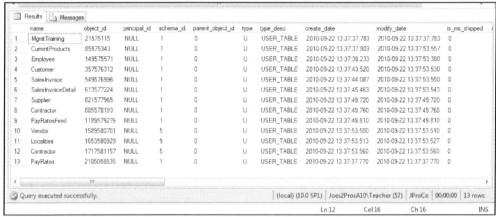

Figure 11.38 Result for Skill Check 1.

Skill Check 2: Find all the tables in the JProCo database that are Heaps (i.e., they have no clustered index).

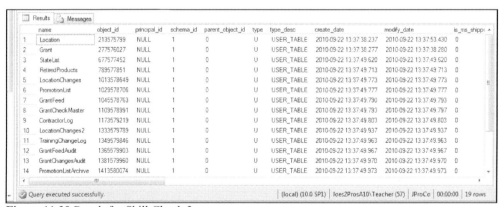

Figure 11.39 Result for Skill Check 2.

Skill Check 3: Find all the tables in the JProCo database that have no indexes at all.

	name	object_id	principal_id	schema_id	parent_object_id	type	type_desc	create_date	modify_date	is_ms_shippe ▲
1	StateList	677577452	NULL	1	0	U	USER_TABLE	2010-09-22 13:37:49.620	2010-09-22 13:37:49.620	0
2	RetiredProducts	789577851	NULL	1	0	U	USER_TABLE	2010-09-22 13:37:49.713	2010-09-22 13:37:49.713	0
3	LocationChanges	1013578649	NULL	1	0	U	USER_TABLE	2010-09-22 13:37:49.773	2010-09-22 13:37:49.773	0
4	PromotionList	1029578706	NULL	1	0	U	USER_TABLE	2010-09-22 13:37:49.777	2010-09-22 13:37:49.777	0
5	ContractorLog	1173579219	NULL	1	0	U	USER_TABLE	2010-09-22 13:37:49.803	2010-09-22 13:37:49.803	0
6	LocationChanges2	1333579789	NULL	1	0	U	USER_TABLE	2010-09-22 13:37:49.937	2010-09-22 13:37:49.937	0
7	TrainingChangeLog	1349579846	NULL	1	0	U	USER_TABLE	2010-09-22 13:37:49.963	2010-09-22 13:37:49.963	0
8	GrantFeedAudit	1365579903	NULL	1	0	U	USER_TABLE	2010-09-22 13:37:49.967	2010-09-22 13:37:49.967	0
9	GrantChangesAudit	1381579960	NULL	1	0	U	USER_TABLE	2010-09-22 13:37:49.970	2010-09-22 13:37:49.970	0
10	PromotionListArchive	1413580074	NULL	1	0	U	USER_TABLE	2010-09-22 13:37:49.973	2010-09-22 13:37:49.973	0
11	ProductPriceChange	1445580188	NULL	1	0	U	USER_TABLE	2010-09-22 13:37:49.980	2010-09-22 13:37:49.980	0
12	EmpCheckMaster	1461580245	NULL	1	0	U	USER_TABLE	2010-09-22 13:37:49.980	2010-09-22 13:37:49.980	0
13	EmpMergeArchive	1477580302	NULL	1	0	U	USER_TABLE	2010-09-22 13:37:49.997	2010-09-22 13:37:49.997	0
14	RoomChart	1493580359	NULL	5	0	U	USER_TABLE	2010-09-22 13:37:52.473	2010-09-22 13:37:53.443	0

Query executed successfully.   (local) (10.0 SP1) | Joes2ProsA10\Teacher (57) | JProCo | 00:00:00 | 15 rows

Figure 11.40 Result for Skill Check 3.

Answer Code: The T-SQL code to this lab can be found in the downloadable files in a file named Lab11.3_IndexMetadata.sql.

Index Metadata - Points to Ponder

1. The sys.dm_db_missing_index_details missing indexes feature does not return suggestions for every query. This feature only returns suggestions for complicated execution plans.

2. The missing index feature uses a simplistic model to generate cost information for queries.

3. The missing index feature only gives suggestions on what might be missing. You must still exercise caution and determine if this index suggestion is really going to improve performance.

4. The database administrator should backup the missing index information to have this information available after a reboot.

5. SQL will collect and retain up to 500 different occurrences of missing indexes. However, if the SQL database server is rebooted then these missing index suggestions will be lost.

6. For best gain, you should order equality columns by selectivity. Meaning there should be a lot of variation in the column's values. With the first index column being the most selective, the second index column being less selective, and so on.

7. Equality columns are the columns with an "=" in the WHERE clause. For instance: WHERE TerritoryID = 4

8. Inequality columns are the columns in the where clause with something like: ">", "<", "!=". Meaning anything that isn't using "=" is considered an inequality.

9. You might wonder, "Why would I use sys.dm_db_missing_index_details when the Database Tuning Advisor (DTA) also recommends indexes?" The difference is that DTA recommends indexes based on a workload you provide; whereas, sys.dm_db_missing_index_details recommends indexes based on queries that have actually run on the database. The database collects statistics for this purpose. This is an improvement because before SQL Server 2005, you would have had to do a profiler trace to get similar information.

Chapter Glossary

Fragmentation: Fragmentation is the inefficient use of pages within a table caused by gaps formed during data manipulation.

Fragmentation page: This is available in Management Studio by locating an Index in the Object Explorer, right-clicking on the index name and expanding the properties. Select "fragmentation" from the list and you will see the fragmentation page.

Index Fragmentation: Index fragmentation is the inefficient use of pages within an index.

OBJECTPROPERTY: This function helps locate object metadata, such as whether there is a clustered index on a table.

REBUILD: A keyword used to improve the function of an index.

REORGANIZE: Another keyword used to improve the function of an index; less verbose than REBUILD.

Chapter Eleven - Review Quiz

1.) What is fragmentation?

   O a. A table is partitioned into fragments across multiple filegroups.
   O b. The table with many conflicting alias names.
   O c. The inefficient use of memory storage from having discontinuous data.

2.) Which Dynamic Management View will show you how much fragmentation an index has?

   O a. sys.dm_db_index_physical_stats
   O b. sys.dm_db_index_usage_stats.

3.) You discover that all indexes of the dbo.SalesOrderDetail table in your JProCo database are heavily fragmented. You need to decrease the fragmentation of all indexes in the dbo.SalesOrderDetail table to a minimum while keeping the table available to users. What should you do?

   O a. Defragment the disk that contains the Sales table.
   O b. ALTER INDEX ALL ON dbo.SalesOrderDetail REORGANIZE
   O c. Execute the following statement
       CREATE INDEX (dbo.SalesOrderDetail)

4.) You manage a SQL Server 2008 database which contains a table with many indexes. You notice that, with data modification, performance has degraded over time. You suspect that some of the indexes are unused. You need to identify which indexes have not been used by any queries since the last time SQL Server 2008 started. Which Dynamic Management View should you use?

        O a. sys.dm_db_index_usage_stats
        O b. sys.dm_db_missing_index_details
        O c. sys.dm_db_missing_index_columns
        O d. sys.dm_db_missing_index_stats

5.) You want to generate the CREATE INDEX code for all missing indexes that SQL Server has identified. Which DMV should you use?

        O a. sys.dm_db_index_physical_stats
        O b. sys.dm_db_missing_index_details
        O c. sys.dm_db_missing_index_columns

6.) You are told to find all the tables in the JProCo database that are heaps. Which T-SQL statement should you run?

  O a. SELECT *
        FROM Sys.tables
        WHERE OBJECTPROPERTY(object_id,'TableHasIndex') = 0

  O b. SELECT *
        FROM Sys.tables
        WHERE OBJECTPROPERTY(object_id, 'TableHasClustIndex') = 0

  O c. SELECT *
        FROM Sys.tables
        WHERE OBJECTPROPERTY(object_id, 'TableHasNonClustIndex') = 0

  O d. SELECT *
        FROM Sys.tables
        WHERE OBJECTPROPERTY(object_id, 'TableHasIdentity') = 0

7.) You are told to find all the tables in the JProCo database with an identity field but no clustered index. What Transact SQL statement should you run?

  O a. SELECT *
        FROM Sys.tables
        WHERE OBJECTPROPERTY(object_id, 'TableHasIndex') = 1 AND
        OBJECTPROPERTY(object_id, 'TableHasIdentity') = 0

  O b. SELECT *
        FROM Sys.tables
        WHERE OBJECTPROPERTY(object_id, 'TableHasIndex') = 0 AND
        OBJECTPROPERTY(object_id, 'TableHasIdentity') = 1

  O c. SELECT *
        FROM Sys.tables
        WHERE OBJECTPROPERTY(object_id, 'TableHasClustIndex') = 1 AND
        OBJECTPROPERTY(object_id, 'TableHasIdentity') = 0

  O d. SELECT *
        FROM Sys.tables
        WHERE OBJECTPROPERTY(object_id, 'TableHasClustIndex') = 0 AND
        OBJECTPROPERTY(object_id, 'TableHasIdentity') = 1

Answer Key

1.) c   2.) a   3.) b   4.) a   5.) b   6.)b   7.) d

Bug Catcher Game

To play the Bug Catcher game, run the BugCatcher_Chapter11IndexMaint.pps from the BugCatcher folder of the companion files. You can obtain these files from www.Joes2Pros.com or by ordering the Companion CD.

Chapter 12. Special Index Types

We are not surprised to see warm ski jackets appearing on display shelves starting in September. It's not yet cold, but we know that winter time is a few months away based on our own recollection of the weather, which we've observed in previous seasons and prior years. Our own memory of temperature and weather patterns is a knowledge store we informally draw upon when planning for steps we will take before the cold weather arrives (e.g., pull your boots, mittens, scarves, and heavy jacket out of storage after Halloween; winterize your vehicle prior to November by flushing the car radiator and checking the condition of your snow tires; if it snows before U.S. Thanksgiving (fourth Thursday of November), then you know it likely will be a harsh winter; etc.). By sampling existing data, we can make reasonable decisions about things which have not yet happened.

This is precisely what SQL Server does when it comes to statistics. Similar to how we might look or step outdoors to sample the temperature, SQL Server observes your data to understand how selective certain values are within a field. With these statistics collected, SQL Server's query optimizer can make good seek and scan decisions on fields with covering indexes.

READER NOTE: *In order to follow along with the examples in the first section of Chapter 12, please run the SQLArchChapter12.0Setup.sql setup script. The setup scripts for this book are posted at Joes2Pros.com.*

SQL Statistics

SQL Server looks at the data in its tables long before you run your first SELECT statement. Because it's already done this, SQL Server knows how to best run a query when the time comes. Sampling of this data is stored in statistics, so the query optimizer can make the right decisions.

Sampling to save time is something we do in our daily lives. How long do you think it will take you to drive to work in the morning? You already have a good estimate, because you have done this many times. We frequently need to predict how long it will take to do some combination of errands we have never done before. Suppose, for example, you have your first appointment with a new dentist in the morning and need to pick up your dog from the poodle parlor afterwards. Based on your sampling of the general area, your knowledge of traffic patterns in the area, the weather, and the time of day, you estimate how long it will take and the best way to go. SQL Server takes data samples, as a fraction of the real data in a table, so the query optimizer can decide the best way to run a query. These small samplings of data from a table are known as *Statistics*.

Shown here are the first 12 records of the SalesInvoiceDetail table (see Figure 12.1). By visually inspecting this figure, we can sample our way to a few conclusions. The values in the InvoiceDetailID and ProductID fields are unique, which means those values are *highly selective*. The InvoiceID field looks fairly selective with just 5 distinct values. The values in Quantity appear less selective. With this very small amount of data, it's hard to tell for certain. We probably should sample more data to know which fields are selective enough to benefit from an index seek. Statistics are used by the Query Optimizer to know how selective certain query results will be based on their criteria.

Figure 12.1 The SalesInvoiceDetail table has selective and Non Selective fields.

If there were millions of records in the table and you had just five records with an InvoiceID of 1, that's highly selective. If that query has a covering index then it will benefit by doing a seek. But in order to know exactly how selective the values are within each field, SQL Server would first have to scan the entire table of millions of records. Scanning your table then generating statistics would be slower than just scanning the table when the query is run. Because of the statistics which SQL Server has gathered, the query optimizer knows how selective each value in each field is without doing an entire scan of the table at query time.

Sometimes, statistics are gathered by scanning the entire table and sometimes, statistics are gathered by scanning a sample of a table. Right now, the JProCo database reflects a retail operation with small scale customers whose invoices contain just a few products, at most. If we later shifted to a wholesale operation, where we had invoices with thousands of products on each bulk order, then you could have the same InvoiceID value repeated for each line item of a single order. Today InvoiceID is a selective field; however it could slowly become less and less selective as time goes on. Statistics need to constantly be updated to know the most recent selectivity information for an index. If a field does not have an index, then there is no pressing need to retain statistics: any query which predicates on the field will always use a scan instead of a seek.

The bigger the table, the more statistics there will be for each index on the table. To easily see how the statistics are created for a table, let's choose a small table in JProCo (Figure 12.2). The HumanResources.RoomChart table has just eight records. Looking closer at these records, we see an ID which is very selective – in fact, this ID is unique. We have a field called Code which is also unique. The field RoomName is unique. None of these first three fields contains a duplicate value: each field has 8 different values. The NULL value is duplicated several times in the RoomNotes field and RoomDescription fields.

```
SELECT * FROM HumanResources.RoomChart
```

Results | Spatial results | Messages

	ID	Code	RoomName	RoomDescription	RoomNotes	RoomLocation
1	1	RLT	Renault-Langsford-Tribute	This room is designed for Customer Previews	NULL	NULL
2	2	QTX	Quinault-Experience	Parties and Morale events get top priority	NULL	NULL
3	3	TQW	TranquilWest	misc	NULL	NULL
4	4	XW	XavierWest	NULL	NULL	NULL
5	5	YRD	Industrial Yard	Holds Lumber and Stocking Warehouse	NULL	0x00000000010405000000000000000000000000000000000...
6	6	WRS	WareHouse	Holds Supplies	NULL	0x00000000010405000000000000000000000024400000000000...
7	7	WOD	Lumber Area	NULL	NULL	0x00000000010405000000000000000000000003040000000000...
8	8	PRK	Yard Parking Lot	NULL	NULL	0x00000000010405000000000000000000000000000000000...

Query executed successfully. | (local) (10.0 SP1) | Joes2ProsA10\Teacher (53) | JProCo | 00:00:00 | 8 rows

Figure 12.2 The HumanResources.RoomChart is a small table with eight records.

Statistics Metadata

SQL Server has a handy system stored procedure ("sproc") for showing the available statistics for a table. Let's run sp_Helpstats to see some statistics for the HumanResources.RoomChart table (see Figure 12.3).

Figure 12.3 You can see the list of statistics on any given table by running the **sp_Helpstats** system stored procedure.

Notice this statistic (_WA_Sys_00000001_59063A47) is on the first field of the HumanResources.RoomChart table. As well, it is the only statistic currently being tracked for this table – SQL Server isn't tracking the other fields with statistics. None of the fields have an index on this table.

To look at the statistics details of the HumanResources.RoomChart table, use the DBCC SHOW_STATISTICS. You will need to supply the table name and the name of the statistic you found above (in Figure 12.3). Pass in each value as a parameter (Figure 12.4). Keep in mind our table has ID values 1 through 8, all of which are unique.

```
sp_Helpstats 'HumanResources.RoomChart'

DBCC SHOW_STATISTICS
('HumanResources.RoomChart',_WA_Sys_00000001_59063A47)
```

Name	Updated	Rows	Rows Sampled	Steps	Density	Average key length	String Index	Filter Expression	Ur
_WA_Sys_00000001_59063A47	Sep 23 2010 9:27AM	5	5	3	1	4	NO	NULL	5

All density	Average Length	Columns
0.2	4	ID

RANGE_HI_KEY	RANGE_ROWS	EQ_ROWS	DISTINCT_RANGE_ROWS	AVG_RANGE_ROWS
1	0	1	0	1
3	1	1	1	1
5	1	1	1	1

Figure 12.4 The histogram for the only statistic on the HumanResources.RoomChart table.

Histogram

In the second result set (see middle of Figure 12.4), we see the ID column has four bytes, because the ID field of the HumanResources.RoomChart is an integer. The bottom result set is known as a *histogram* (see Figure 12.4). This histogram shows you the spread of values for a field, and how many values are repeated for that field. For example, ID 1 appears once. ID 3 is listed once, as is ID 5. Notice it didn't list all of the IDs; we see just a sampling.

In this histogram you see records with a small number of rows for each value. In fact there is only 1 EQ_ROWS count for each value, which signifies that this data is selective. However, if you see very few values with a high EQ_ROWS count, this indicates low selectivity. Note for each ID, the count of EQ_ROWS in this histogram is 1.

Creating Statistics

Creating Statistics is usually done automatically. In fact, when you create an index, SQL Server has to sample all the values in the field in order to create the index. SQL Server preserves the data-gathering work performed at the time of index creation by loading the data histogram into the statistics. As data keeps coming into the table, the statistics need to be updated. You can do this manually, with the Update Statistics command, or you can set your database to Auto-Update Statistics=True which will be explained later in this chapter.

We have statistics on the ID field. However, no statistics were kept on the RoomName field, because there's no index using that field. Normally, there is no reason to store statistics on a field which has no index. We can force SQL Server to keep statistics on a field that has no index by running a CREATE STATISTICS statement, as you see below (Figure 12.5). Here, we are creating the RoomChart_RoomName statistic on the RoomName field of the HumanResources.RoomChart table.

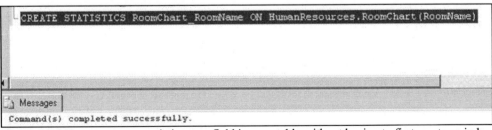

```
CREATE STATISTICS RoomChart_RoomName ON HumanResources.RoomChart(RoomName)
```

Messages

Command(s) completed successfully.

Figure 12.5 You can create statistics on a field in your table without having to first create an index.

It's considered proper to name a statistic after the table and field name combination.

A new statistic has been created. Let's see what statistics now show for the HumanResources.RoomChart table. Run the **sp_helpstats** sproc again. Notice this table now has two statistics (Figure 12.6). On the second row, we see the new staticstic called RoomChart_RoomName.

Figure 12.6 We see the HumanResources.RoomChart table now has two statistics.

Using this RoomChart_RoomName statistics name, we can again run the DBCC SHOW_STATISTICS. Just change the second parameter to the new statistic's name (Figure 12.7).

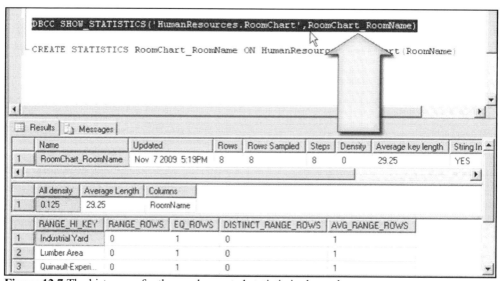

Figure 12.7 The histogram for the newly created statistic is shown here.

What do these results tell us? Look at the EQ_ROWS field in the histogram. It looks like "Industrial Yard" is a value which appears once; "Lumber Area" appears once; "Quinault Experience" appears once. This field is highly selective.

Updating Statistics

As new data gets added to a table the histogram record counts can get out of date. SQL Server already updates statistics as necessary to keep the histogram up to date with the data in the table that it represents. The auto-update statistics option is less than perfect, so you have the option of updating it at the time of your choosing. One way to get better statistics is to manually update the statistics for the table using the UPDATE STATISTICS command. The example below would update all the statistics for the Customer table:

UPDATE STATISTICS Customer

A table might have many indexes on it which would mean it would have many statistics. If the table is very large, then updating these statistics could take too much processing time. If only one of your indexes was critical for performance then it would not be necessary to update every statistic. The code example below updates the statistics on the NCI_Customer_CustomerType index of the Customer table:

UPDATE STATISTICS Customer NCI_Customer_CustomerType

Lab 12.1: Index Statistics

Lab Prep: Before you can begin the lab, you must have SQL Server installed and run the SQLArchChapter12.1Setup.sql script.

Skill Check 1: Create a statistic on the dbo.SalesInvoiceDetail table called SalesInvoiceDetail_Quantity. When you're done, show this statistic is present by running the sp_Helpstats system stored procedure.

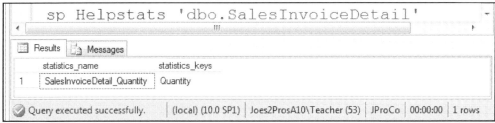

Figure 12.8 Results for Skill Check1.

Skill Check 2: Update the statistic you created in Skill Check 1.

Skill Check 3: Show the histogram for the SalesInvoiceDetail_Quantity statistic.

	Name	Updated	Rows	Rows Sampled	Steps	Density	Average key leng
1	SalesInvoiceDetail_Quantity	Sep 23 2010 10:07AM	6960	6960	6	0	4

	All density	Average Length	Columns
1	0.1666667	4	Quantity

	RANGE_HI_KEY	RANGE_ROWS	EQ_ROWS	DISTINCT_RANGE_ROWS	AVG_RANGE_ROWS
1	1	0	680	0	1
2	2	0	1363	0	1
3	3	0	1412	0	1
4	4	0	1369	0	1
5	5	0	1461	0	1
6	6	0	675	0	1

Figure 12.9 Results for Skill Check 3.

Answer Code: The T-SQL code to this lab can be found in the downloadable files in a file named Lab12.1_Index Statistics.sql.

Index Statistics - Points to Ponder

1. When you create a new clustered or nonclustered index, the Query Optimizer samples the data to see how selective it is. If the data is in a primary key or unique field, then it will be highly selective (in fact, it will be unique).

2. The query optimizer uses statistics to choose the best query execution plan by estimating the cost of using an index for a given query.

3. Statistics for indexes which are highly selective are more likely to get used for a seek (a.k.a., a table seek) during query run time.

4. If the statistics are sampling a field, like status, which is either a 0 or a 1 with many duplicated records, then the Query Optimizer will call the statistic and probably decide to ignore the index and perform a table scan instead.

5. By having statistics on hand, the query optimizer knows a lot about a field's selectivity without having to look at all the records. The data sample which the statistic saves is called a Histogram.

6. Statistics are saved for later reuse.

7. When you create a new index, the query optimizer stores statistical information about the field which you have just indexed.

8. When the AUTO_CREATE_STATISTICS database option is set to ON, the Database Engine creates statistics for columns in your WHERE clauses even if they don't have indexes on them.

9. As the data in a table is updated via INSERT, UPDATE and DELETE statements, the statistics can become obsolete and cause the query optimizer to make less informed decisions. Therefore statistics need to be updated.

10. When the AUTO_UPDATE_STATISTICS database option is ON, statistical information is periodically updated as the table changes.

11. By default, SQL Server databases automatically create and update statistics.

12. SQL Server maintains statistics on indexes and key columns of all of your tables.

13. Each query must be executed at least once in order to generate a statistic.

14. The information that gets stored includes:
    a. The number of rows and pages occupied by a table's data.
    b. The time that statistics were last updated.
    c. The average length of keys in a column.
    d. Histograms showing the distribution of data in a column.
    e. String summaries which are used when performing LIKE queries on character data.
15. You can choose the amount of data to be sampled by a statistic using the SAMPLE and FULLSCAN clauses of UPDATE STATISTICS.

Partitioned Table Indexing

Hopefully you remember partitioned tables (Chapters 6 & 7) and that it's possible to have a table spread its data across many different drives. In this section we will explore indexes that are based on fields of a *partitioned table*.

Creating Partitioned Tables Recap

The data of the CurrentProducts table could be stored in its two different locations. By "cutting" the table horizontally so that all records thru 2007 go into the first partition, and all the records after the beginning of 2008 go into the next partition (Figure 12.10), you would have a partitioned table. But what happens when you put a nonclustered index on a partitioned table? How does SQL Server organize such data for fast and efficient searching?

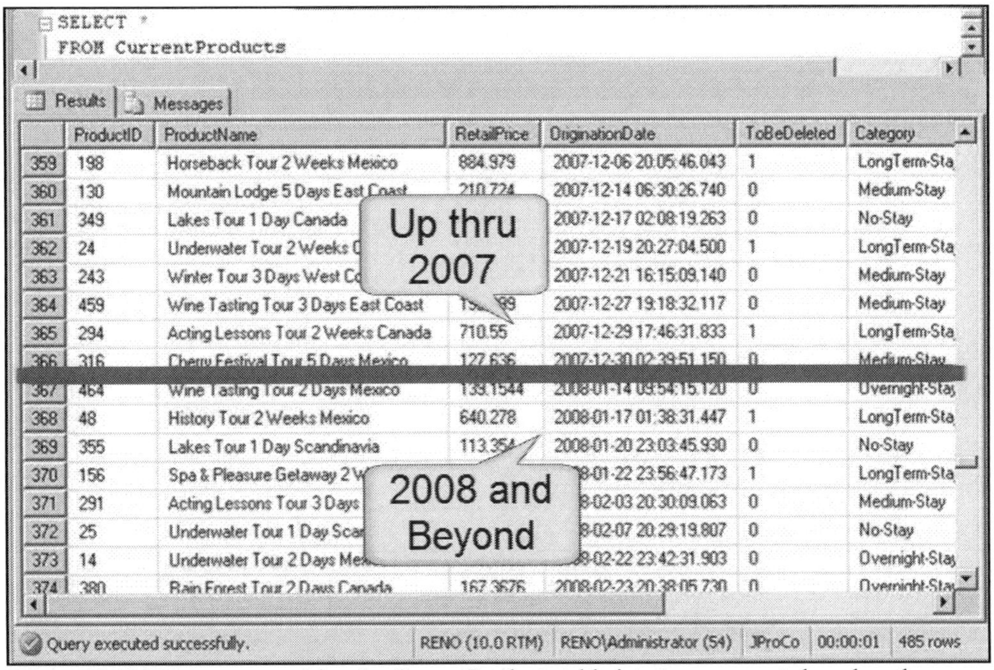

Figure 12.10 We want to partition the CurrentProducts table into two segments based on the OriginationDate field.

Another table with a datetime field we may want to partition is the SalesInvoice table. Our SalesInvoice table has many more records than the CurrentProducts table. We need to decide where to perform the *horizontal partitioning*. This table's data tells us we started taking orders in 2006, kept doing that through 2007, 2008, 2009, and even 2010. If we want this data in separate storage areas so that the 2006 and 2007 data is physically stored together in one filegroup, and all of the data from 2008 and beyond is stored in another filegroup, we'd have to create a partitioned table.

As a quick recap, let's see the code needed to create this new partitioned table. In the figure below, we see a *partition function* with one boundary value so that we get two ranges (Figure 12.11). Once the partition function is created, we need to get ready the storage areas. The first filegroup will be fgUpTo2007, and the other filegroup will be called fgBeyond2007.

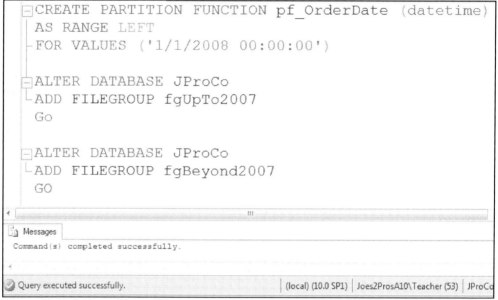

Figure 12.11 Each partition will be stored on the filegroups we create.

The storage areas fgUpTo2007 and fgBeyond2007 will not do anything on their own – we must also create datafiles. Let's put fgUpTo2007 on the D drive (C:\D_SQL) and fgBeyond2007 on the E drive (C:\E_SQL). The file names appear on the next page (see Figure 12.12).

```
ALTER DATABASE JProCo
ADD FILE (NAME = dataTo2007, FILENAME = 'C:\D_SQL\DataTo2007.ndf')
TO FILEGROUP fgUpTo2007
GO


ALTER DATABASE JProCo
ADD FILE (NAME = dataBeyond2007, FILENAME = 'C:\E_SQL\DataBeyond2007.ndf')
TO FILEGROUP fgBeyond2007
GO
```

Messages
Command(s) completed successfully.

Query executed successfully.   (local) (10.0 SP1) | Joes2ProsA10\Teacher (53) | JProCo | 00:00:00 | 0 ro

Ln 13   Col 1   Ch 1   IN

Figure 12.12 Each filegroup will need at least one datafile before it can be used.

The partition function will separate the data by time. With one boundary value, two
storage areas will be created. We need to send the first partition to the fgUpTo2007
filegroup and the second partition to the fgBeyond2007 filegroup. To do this, we
will need a partition scheme (as shown in Figure 12.13).

```
CREATE PARTITION SCHEME ps_ByDate
AS PARTITION pf_OrderDate
TO (fgUpTo2007,fgBeyond2007)
GO
```

Figure 12.13 The partition scheme directs the data into the filegroups.

We need to create a new table, SalesInvoiceHorizontal, which will hold the
SalesInvoice table data. In Figure 12.14, we see the SalesInvoice table has an
InvoiceID field, which is an INT, an OrderDate, which is a date/time, a PaidDate,
CustomerID, and Comment.

Our new table must mimic this metadata structure if we want it to hold all of the data. We can see that InvoiceID is an INT and can't be null. The OrderDate field is a datetime and is also not-null. The PaidDate field is also a datetime and is not-null. The CustomerID field is an integer and is not-null. The last field is named Comment, which is an ntext and is nullable. At the end of your CREATE TABLE statement, specify the table is ON the partition scheme which is based on the OrderDate field.

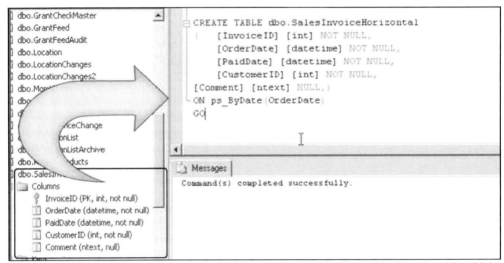

Figure 12.14 The partitioned table will have the same fields as the base table (i.e., the table which is the source of the data).

Partitioned Tables as Heaps

Our partitioned table is created, but it is empty and has no records. We can complete our task by inserting all of the data from the SalesInvoice table into the SalesInvoiceHorizontal. Simply combine a SELECT statement from the SalesInvoice table with an INSERT statement to the SalesInvoiceHorizontal table (Figure 12.15).

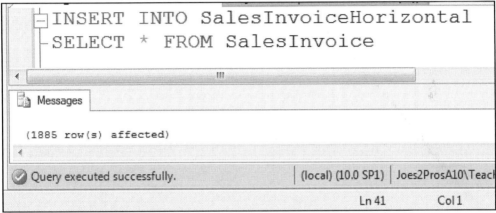

```
INSERT INTO SalesInvoiceHorizontal
SELECT * FROM SalesInvoice
```

Messages

(1885 row(s) affected)

Query executed successfully.   (local) (10.0 SP1)   Joes2ProsA10\Teach

Ln 41   Col 1

Figure 12.15 All 1885 records are inserted into the Partitioned table.

We can query all the records of this table, or we can run a very selective query. A query which would show all values from the first partition would query the OrderDate field for records having an order date prior to 1/1/2008. This query will only need to pull data from the first partition (Figure 12.16).

```
SELECT *
FROM SalesInvoiceHorizontal
WHERE OrderDate < '1/1/2008'
```

Results | Messages

	InvoiceID	OrderDate	PaidDate	CustomerID	Comment
1	1	2006-01-03 00:00:00.000	2006-01-11 03:22:44.587	472	NULL
2	2	2006-01-04 02:22:41.473	2006-02-01 04:15:34.590	388	NULL
3	3	2006-01-04 05:33:01.150	2006-02-14 13:45:02.580	279	NULL
4	4	2006-01-04 22:06:58.657	2006-02-08 22:06:14.247	309	NULL

Query executed success... (local) (10.0 SP1) Joes2ProsA10\Teacher (57) JProCo 00:00:00 893 rows

Figure 12.16 Querying for records before 2008 will pull from just the first partition and will save time.

We can find all the records before 1/1/2008 for Customer 52. Since we don't have any indexes on this table based on these fields, SQL Server will have to scan at least the entire first partition (Figure 12.17).

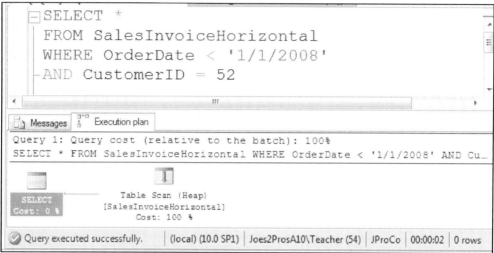

Figure 12.17 The query plan shows a scan of the first partition.

Creating Indexes on Partitioned Tables

You can create an index on a partitioned table. In the case of the SalesInvoiceHorizontal table, we want to keep our records partitioned by date (pre 1/1/2008 and post 1/1/2008). Within that, can we still create a new index based on CustomerID?

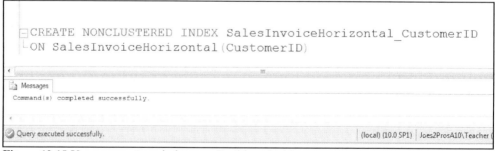

Figure 12.18 You can create an index on a Partitioned table.

Yes, Figure 12.18 shows a nonclustered index being created based on the CustomerID field. The index is named SalesInvoiceHorizontal_CustomerID.

Query Partitioned Tables

With a partitioned table partitioned on the OrderDate field and an index based on CustomerID, we get a big performance increase. The estimated execution plan indicates that the same query will do a seek within the first partition (Figure 12.19).

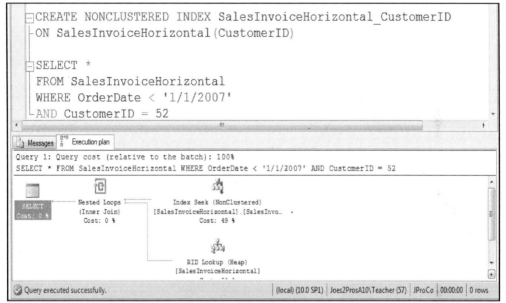

```
CREATE NONCLUSTERED INDEX SalesInvoiceHorizontal_CustomerID
ON SalesInvoiceHorizontal(CustomerID)

SELECT *
FROM SalesInvoiceHorizontal
WHERE OrderDate < '1/1/2007'
AND CustomerID = 52
```

Figure 12.19 A seek took place within the partitioned table.

Lab 12.2: Partitioned Table Indexing

Lab Prep: Before you can begin the lab, you must have SQL Server installed and run the SQLArchChapter12.2Setup.sql script.

Skill Check 1: Use the ps_ByDate partition scheme to partition the CurrentProducts table into a table named CurrentProductsHorizontal. Then create the nonclustered index NCI_CurrentProductsHorizontal_RetailPrice. Query the CurrentProductsHorizontal table for data before 2008 with a RetailPrice of $373.11. Your execution plan should resemble the figure here (see Figure 12.20).

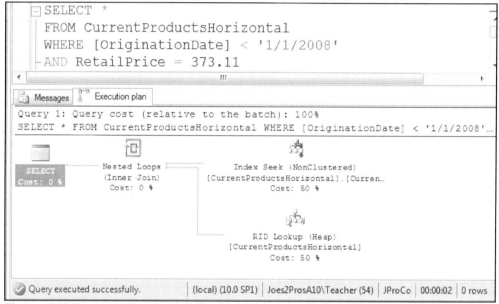

Figure 12.20 Execution plan for Skill Check1.

Answer Code: The T-SQL code to this lab can be found in the downloadable files in a file named Lab12.2_PartitionTableIndexing.sql.

Partition Table Indexing - Points to Ponder

1. When you create an index on a partitioned table, it becomes the secondary sort. In other words, if you partition on date and index on Name, then that's like a composite index (Date + Name).

Chapter Glossary

FULLSCAN: You can choose the amount of data to be sampled by a statistic using the FULLSCAN clause of UPDATE STATISTICS.

Histogram: Histograms show the distribution of data in a column.

SAMPLE: You can choose the amount of data to be sampled by a statistic using the SAMPLE clause of UPDATE STATISTICS.

SQL Statistics: SQL does sampling of the data in its tables long before a SELECT statement is run. This data sample is stored in statistics, so the query optimizer can make the right decisions.

UPDATE STATISTICS: This command allows you to update statistics on your schedule, not on an automatic schedule.

Chapter Twelve - Review Quiz

1.) What are SQL Server Statistics?

   O a. Information collected about data in columns and indexes.
   O b. The numbers about the upper limits of how many rows each table can hold.
   O c. The information about all transactions contained in the log file.

2.) What are two ways existing statistics get updated?

   □ a. Each time you restart the SQL service.
   □ b. When you issue the UPDATE STATISTICS command.
   □ c. Automatically by the database during DML changes.
   □ d. When you run a query covered by an index.
   □ e. When you create a new index.

3.) What are two ways statistics get created?

   □ a. Each time you re-start the SQL service.
   □ b. When you issue the CREATE STATISTICS command.
   □ c. Automatically by the database during DML changes.
   □ d. When you run a query covered by an index.
   □ e. When you create a new index.

4.) You work for Vandalane Inc. Users report that query execution is slow. You investigate and discover that some queries do not use optimal execution plans. You also notice that some optimizer statistics are missing and others are out of date. You need to correct the problem so that reports execute more quickly. Which two T-SQL statements should you use? (choose two)

   □ a. DBCC CHECKTABLE
   □ b. ALTER INDEX REORGANIZE
   □ c. UPDATE STATISTICS
   □ d. CREATE STATISTICS
   □ e. DBCC SHOW_STATISTICS
   □ f. DBCC UPDATE_USAGE

5.) You have a table named dbo.Wood which is a heap located in the default filegroup. The default filegroup is Primary. You just created a user defined filegroup called fg_Fast on a new dedicated drive array. You want to create a clustered index on this table at the same time you move it to the new filegroup. The field that will have the clustered index based on it is called WoodID. What code will achieve this result?

O a. CREATE CLUSTERED INDEX ci_Wood_WoodID
ON dbo.Wood (WoodID)
ON fg_Fast

O b. CREATE CLUSTERED INDEX ci_Wood_WoodID
ON dbo.Wood (WoodID)
ON [Primary]

O c. CREATE CLUSTERED INDEX ci_Wood_WoodID
ON dbo.Wood (WoodID)
ON fg_Fast(WoodID)

O d. CREATE CLUSTERED INDEX ci_Wood_WoodID
ON dbo.Wood (WoodID)
ON [Primary] (WoodID)

O e. CREATE NONCLUSTERED INDEX nci_Wood_WoodID
ON dbo.Wood (WoodID)
ON fg_Fast(WoodID)

Answer Key

1.) a   2.) b, c 3.) b,e 4.) c, d 5.) a

Bug Catcher Game

To play the Bug Catcher game, run BugCatcher_Chapter12SpecialIndexTypes.pps from the BugCatcher folder of the companion files. You can obtain these files from www.Joes2Pros.com or by ordering the Companion CD.

Chapter 13. Full Text Indexing

Ever wonder how Bing or Google seemingly search the entire World Wide Web based on a few keywords in a fraction of a second? This is because they have already crawled all the pages and stored them in some sort of index. They indexed billions of web pages and you would expect searches like "Hero of Canada" and "Canadian Hero" to pull up similar results.

Searching large quantities of data for relevant patterns is precisely what SQL Server's Full Text Indexing capability allows you to accomplish.

READER NOTE: *In order to follow along with the examples in the first section of Chapter 13, please run the SQLArchChapter13.0Setup.sql setup script. The setup scripts for this book are posted at Joes2Pros.com.*

Full Text Indexing

Back in book 1, *Beginning SQL Joes 2 Pros*, we learned the value of finding patterns using wildcards. For example if you want to find the rows where the description is "Champion Runner" or "Champion Running" you could use %Champ%Run% after your LIKE operator. This query may overlook some data you do want to see. The other records you do not find might be listed as "Runner with Champion status." In the last example the %Run% pattern was matched before the %Champ% pattern. Your favorite search engine has solved this dilemma that goes a bit beyond the SQL wildcard. Finding the word "Runner" near any instance of the word "Champion" is what you want to do. For this type of search, you can set up what is known as **Full Text Indexing**.

We learned about searching for a keyword like "ISO" using a wildcard. We can use LIKE with %ISO% to find that pattern anywhere in the field value. Now, pretend you want to search for "ISO" and "expert" in a large XML field. You want to see the results, even if the words appear in reverse order. As long as both words are present somewhere in the data, the row should be returned to your result set. A barrage of fancy wildcards could logically do the trick. However, you will find you still can't query some data types using the LIKE operator.

Suppose the AdventureWorks Company needs to hire somebody and they have a JobCandidate table which will show all the current applicants. A SELECT query, with no criteria, shows 13 records, which means there are 13 applicants. We have a very focused and specialized job for someone with ISO experience. A simple wildcard search should be able to find someone with those skills as attempted in Figure 13.1, below. The only problem is that wildcards don't work with some LOB types like XML.

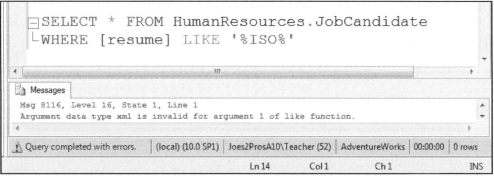

Figure 13.1 The LIKE operator does not work on the resume field, since the data type is XML.

The good news is there are pattern matches you can do with XML data types. In this situation, you can use the CONTAINS keyword. We will put the field name, Resume, as the first parameter and 'ISO', in single quotes, for the second parameter (Figure 13.2). That's a good idea, but we can do that only if we set up indexing on that particular XML field, ahead of time, with what's known as Full Text Indexing.

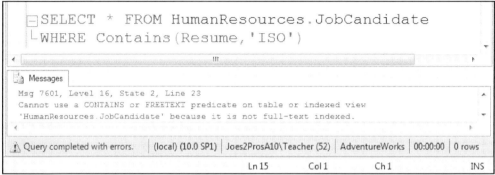

Figure 13.2 The CONTAINS keyword can search your XML field, only if you set up Full Text Indexing first.

Full Text Catalogs

We have learned that indexing speeds up retrieval of data, if we've set it up ahead of time. Your indexes need to be stored somewhere. These Full Text Indexes must be stored in a full text catalog. If you don't have a full text catalog in your database then you must create one. To create the Full Text Catalog, use the code you see below (in Figure 13.3).

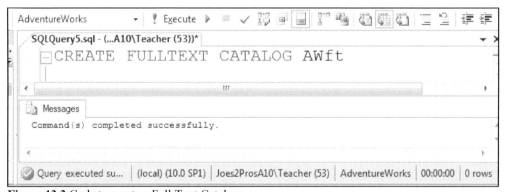

Figure 13.3 Code to create a Full Text Catalog.

Notice the code in Figure 13.3 does not specify which database we are using. Since we are in the context of the AdventureWorks database that is where the Full Text Index will be created.

To verify the creation of the AWft Full Text Catalog, in your Object Explorer, refresh and expand the database you created it in.

In our case, this would be AdventureWorks. Within AdventureWorks, expand Storage. You will notice a folder called Full Text Catalog. When you expand the Full Text Catalog folder, it will list the AWft object you just created.

Thanks to this catalog, we now have a place to store full text indexes. You can now start creating full text indexes for fields in tables within your database.

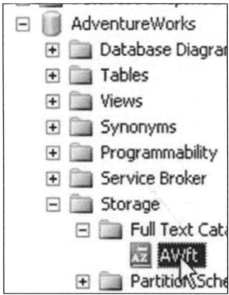

Figure 13.4 The AWft can be seen in your Object Explorer.

Full Text Indexes

We are going to create a Full Text Index on the HumanResources.JobCandidate Resume field. The first line of this code is seen below (in Figure 13.5). You can only create a Full Text Index if that table has a primary key. If your code errors out, then make sure the table has a primary key.

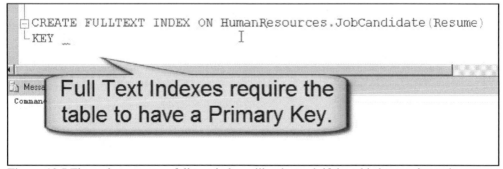

```
CREATE FULLTEXT INDEX ON HumanResources.JobCandidate(Resume)
KEY
```

Full Text Indexes require the table to have a Primary Key.

Figure 13.5 The code to create a full text index will only work if the table has a primary key.

What is the name of the primary key on the HumanResources.JobCandidate table? If you were to open Object Explorer to the AdventureWorks database, you would find the HumanResources.JobCandidate table has its primary key named PK_JobCandidate_JobCandidateID. We need this name to finish writing our CREATE statement for our FullText Index. We also need to specify this index will use the AWft Full Text Catalog (Figure 13.6).

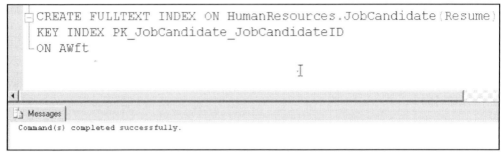

```
CREATE FULLTEXT INDEX ON HumanResources.JobCandidate(Resume)
KEY INDEX PK_JobCandidate_JobCandidateID
ON AWft
```

Messages

Command(s) completed successfully.

Figure 13.6 The Full Text Index will need to refer to the Full Text Catalog.

The query that uses the "WHERE contains" clause should now be supported by this index. Specify the Resume field is looking for the value of ISO (Figure 13.7). This query narrows down the four candidates who have some ISO experience.

```
SELECT * FROM HumanResources.JobCandidate
WHERE Contains(Resume,'ISO')
```

Results | Messages

	JobCandidateID	EmployeeID	Resume	ModifiedDate
1	2	NULL	<ns:Resume xmlns:ns="http://schemas.microsoft.co...	1997-07-24 00:00:00.000
2	6	NULL	<ns:Resume xmlns:ns="http://schemas.microsoft.co...	1997-07-24 00:00:00.000
3	9	NULL	<ns:Resume xmlns:ns="http://schemas.microsoft.co...	1997-07-24 00:00:00.000
4	12	NULL	<ns:Resume xmlns:ns="http://schemas.microsoft.co...	1997-07-24 00:00:00.000

Figure 13.7 The four records that contain the word ISO appear in your result set.

Let's run a query using the Contains clause to find out who has some management experience. When you run the query, you see there are three such candidates (Figure 13.8).

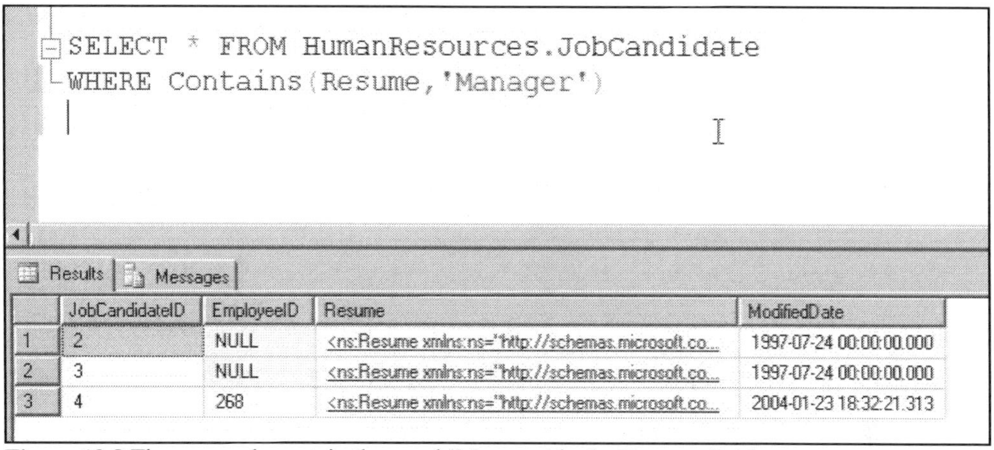

```
SELECT * FROM HumanResources.JobCandidate
WHERE Contains(Resume,'Manager')
```

	JobCandidateID	EmployeeID	Resume	ModifiedDate
1	2	NULL	<ns:Resume xmlns:ns="http://schemas.microsoft.co...	1997-07-24 00:00:00.000
2	3	NULL	<ns:Resume xmlns:ns="http://schemas.microsoft.co...	1997-07-24 00:00:00.000
3	4	268	<ns:Resume xmlns:ns="http://schemas.microsoft.co...	2004-01-23 18:32:21.313

Figure 13.8 Three records contain the word 'Manager' in the Resume field.

This Full Text Index offers even more choices. We can find out how many people have Manager or ISO experience. Put single quotes around your second parameter but put the word ISO in double quotes and the word Manager in double quotes. Separate these words with the word OR (Figure 13.9). You result set shows we have a total of six people with ISO or Manager listed in their resume.

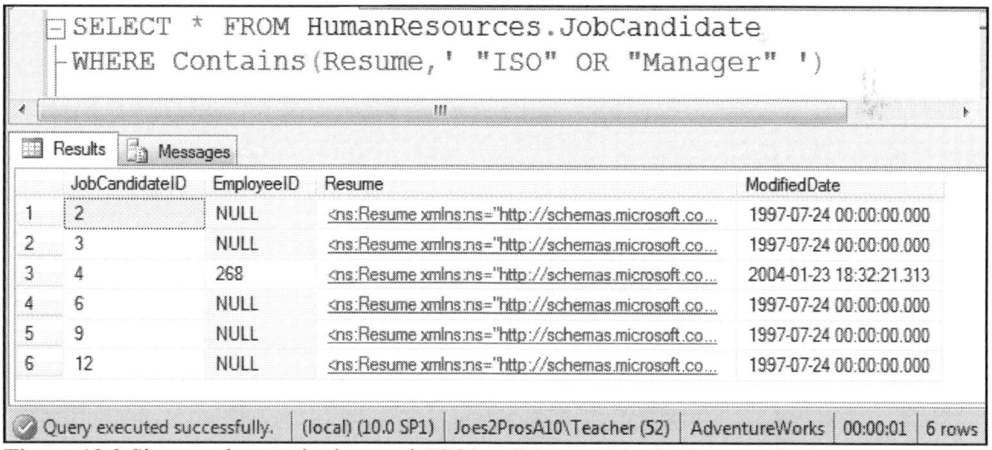

```
SELECT * FROM HumanResources.JobCandidate
WHERE Contains(Resume,' "ISO" OR "Manager" ')
```

	JobCandidateID	EmployeeID	Resume	ModifiedDate
1	2	NULL	<ns:Resume xmlns:ns="http://schemas.microsoft.co...	1997-07-24 00:00:00.000
2	3	NULL	<ns:Resume xmlns:ns="http://schemas.microsoft.co...	1997-07-24 00:00:00.000
3	4	268	<ns:Resume xmlns:ns="http://schemas.microsoft.co...	2004-01-23 18:32:21.313
4	6	NULL	<ns:Resume xmlns:ns="http://schemas.microsoft.co...	1997-07-24 00:00:00.000
5	9	NULL	<ns:Resume xmlns:ns="http://schemas.microsoft.co...	1997-07-24 00:00:00.000
6	12	NULL	<ns:Resume xmlns:ns="http://schemas.microsoft.co...	1997-07-24 00:00:00.000

Query executed successfully. | (local) (10.0 SP1) | Joes2ProsA10\Teacher (52) | AdventureWorks | 00:00:01 | 6 rows

Figure 13.9 Six records contain the word 'ISO' or 'Manager' in the Resume field.

Change the OR to an AND, and you will find all the applicants who have "ISO" and "Manager" in their resume. In fact, if you do this you would see only one record returned.

Lab 13.1: Full Text Indexing

Lab Prep: Before you can begin the lab, you must have SQL Server installed and run the SQLArchChapter13.1Setup.sql script.

Skill Check 1: The table JProCoBook1 of the JProCo database has all the words of each of the first 20 pages of the Beginning SQL Joes 2 Pros book. You want to find all pages containing both the words "Database" and "Table" by using a full text index.

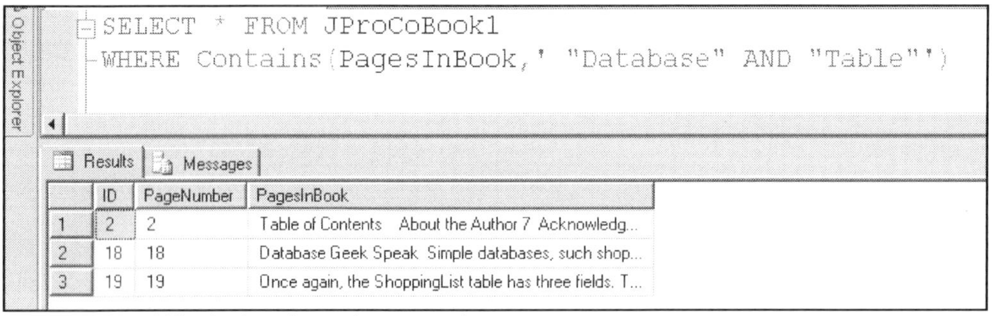

```
SELECT * FROM JProCoBook1
WHERE Contains(PagesInBook,' "Database" AND "Table"')
```

	ID	PageNumber	PagesInBook
1	2	2	Table of Contents About the Author 7 Acknowledg...
2	18	18	Database Geek Speak Simple databases, such shop...
3	19	19	Once again, the ShoppingList table has three fields. T...

Figure 13.10 Skill Check 1 shows three records.

Answer Code: The T-SQL code for this lab can be found in the downloadable files in a file named Lab13.1_FullTextIndexing.sql.

Full Text Indexing - Points to Ponder

1. Full Text catalogs allow you to perform powerful and flexible searches against large text column objects.

2. Large text column objects include XML, Ntext, and text data types.

3. To view your full text indexes use SELECT * FROM sys.fulltext_indexes

4. In order to perform full text searching on a table you need to:
   a. Ensure that the table has a unique, not null column (i.e., a primary key or unique index).
   b. Create a full text catalog in which to store full text indexes for a given table.
   c. Create a full text index on the text column of interest.

5. You can view your full-text catalogs in both UI and code:
   a. View the Object Browser in SQL Management Studio.
   b. Run a query SELECT * FROM sys.FullText_Catalogs.

Stop Words

If you were to surf the web and type in a search engine "World's largest Dog Biscuit", your search results would be about the same as if you typed in "The World's largest Dog Biscuit." The word "The" is not really important in most searches. By adding "The" to the list of "Stop Words" it will be ignored by the Full Text Index. Sometimes you will want to add new words to the Stop Words list to remove them from the Full Text Index. Sometimes the reverse is true. You may want to take some words out of the "Stop List" if you want to make sure those words get added to the FullText Index.

Figure 13.11 shows page 18 of the *Beginning SQL Joes 2 Pros* book. Page 18 contains the terms "null", "as", and "sugar" near each other in the same paragraph. So you can follow along, every page of this book has been turned into a record in a table called JProCoBook1 in the JProCo database. This table has the written words of each page put into the PagesInBook field.

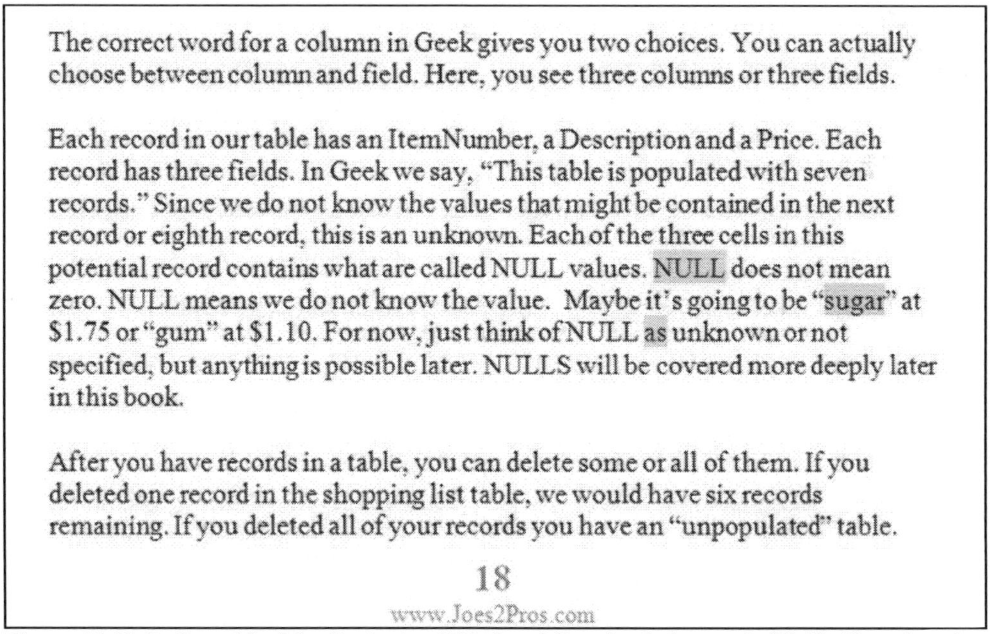

The correct word for a column in Geek gives you two choices. You can actually choose between column and field. Here, you see three columns or three fields.

Each record in our table has an ItemNumber, a Description and a Price. Each record has three fields. In Geek we say, "This table is populated with seven records." Since we do not know the values that might be contained in the next record or eighth record, this is an unknown. Each of the three cells in this potential record contains what are called NULL values. NULL does not mean zero. NULL means we do not know the value. Maybe it's going to be "sugar" at $1.75 or "gum" at $1.10. For now, just think of NULL as unknown or not specified, but anything is possible later. NULLS will be covered more deeply later in this book.

After you have records in a table, you can delete some or all of them. If you deleted one record in the shopping list table, we would have six records remaining. If you deleted all of your records you have an "unpopulated" table.

18

www.Joes2Pros.com

Figure 13.11 On Page 18 of the *Beginning SQL Joes 2 Pros* book the words 'Null', 'Sugar', and 'as' all appear near each other in the same paragraph.

Let's look for the PagesInBook field to have the words "null" near the word "sugar". When running the query in Figure 13.12 we see page 18 in our result set.

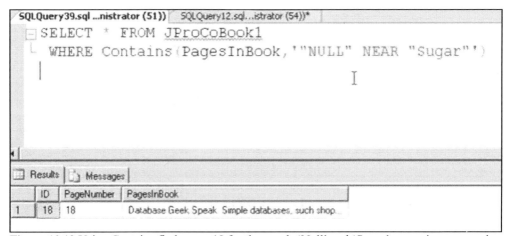

Figure 13.12 Using Contains finds page 18 for the words 'Null' and 'Sugar' appearing near each other.

Now, let's do a search we know returns many records. We want our query to find all the records from the book where the PagesInBook field has the words "the" or the word "as". That should be about every page in the book. When you run the query you see in Figure 13.13, you get no records. The reason is the words "the" and "as" are considered Noise Words (now called Stop words). Almost every literary work has an abundance of these words, so these are not included as part of the index. Now that might cause some confusion, since "as" is a critical keyword in SQL Server.

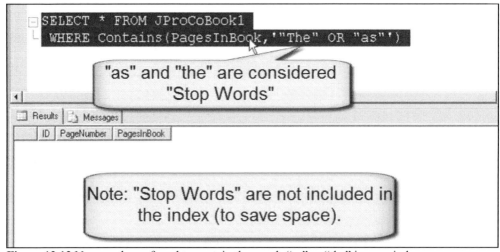

Figure 13.13 No records are found to contain the words "as" or "the" in your index.

Remember how we searched for a page with the words "Null" and "Sugar"? Let's go back to that query and use the three words which we know are near each other. We know "null" is near the word "as" which is near the word "sugar". We've seen that they're together on page 18, but this query indicates no such page exists.

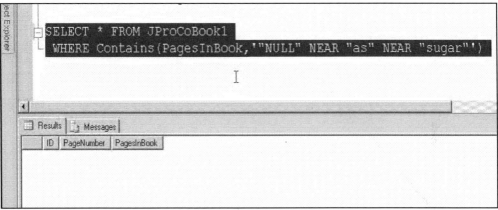

Figure 13.14 No pages appear to be indexed for the words 'Null', 'sugar', and 'as' in your table.

How do you manually control what are considered noise words, which are to be stopped and not be included in the index? What you can do is gain visibility to the stop list. The stop list contains all your Noise keywords for each language. Currently the Stop List is using the System Stoplist. We want to create our own Stoplist from this and make a few changes. Create the StopList_JProCoBook1 stoplist using the code you see here (Figure 13.15).

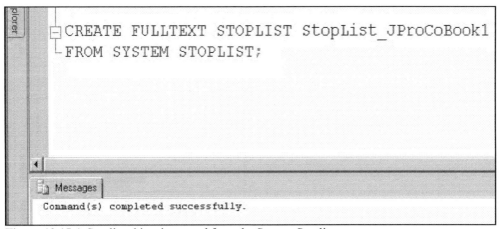

Figure 13.15 A Stoplist object is created from the System Stoplist.

With this new Stop List created, we can use it for our JProCoBook1 Full Text Index. You need to alter JProCoBook1 and set it to use StopList_JProCoBook1 (Figure 13.16).

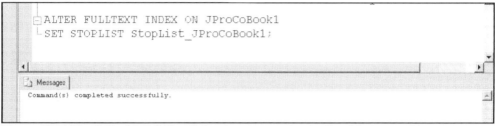

```
ALTER FULLTEXT INDEX ON JProCoBook1
SET STOPLIST StopList_JProCoBook1;
```

Messages

Command(s) completed successfully.

Figure 13.16 JProCoBook1 Full Text Index is set to use the stoplist object created just moments ago.

To see the list of stop words of StopList_JProCoBook1, query the sys.FullText_Stopwords catalog view. To narrow down to just the English words, add a WHERE clause and predicate for English, as you see below (in Figure 13.17.

```
SELECT * FROM sys.fulltext_stopwords
WHERE language = 'English'
```

Results | Messages

	stoplist_id	stopword	language	language_id
1	5	$	English	1033
2	5	0	English	1033
3	5	1	English	1033
4	5	2	English	1033
5	5	3	English	1033
6	5	4	English	1033
7	5	5	English	1033
8	5	6	English	1033
9	5	7	English	1033

Query executed successfully.   RENO (10.0 RTM)

Figure 13.17 You can query the Stoplist to see how many English words have been added.

We can see quite a few common English words listed here. Figure 13.18 shows row number 47 contains the word "as". The word "as" is not included in our Full Text Index because it's in this list of words to be stopped.

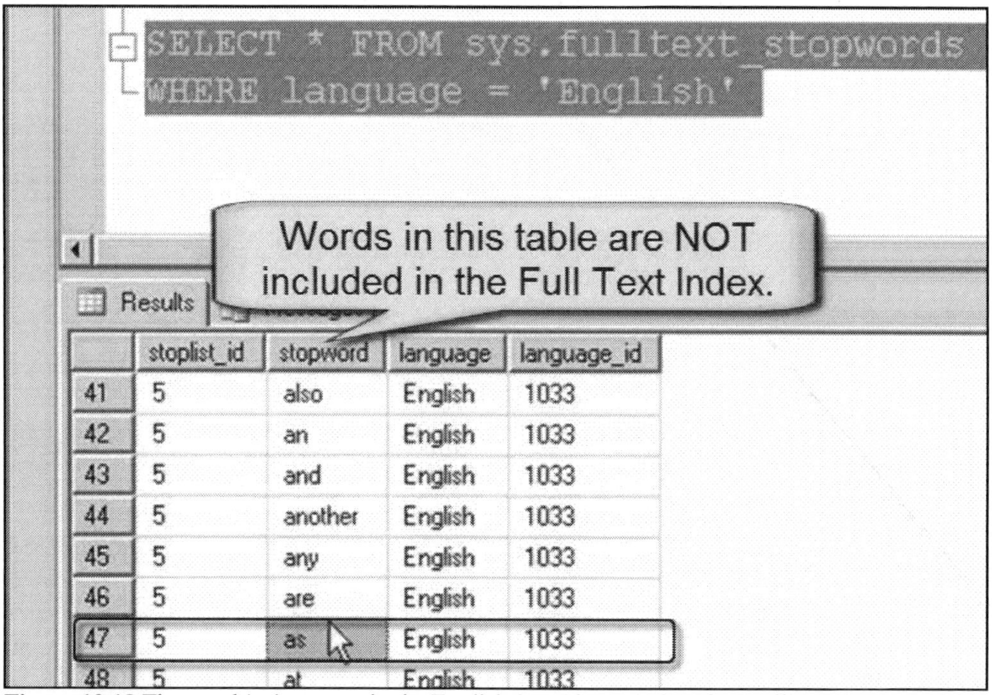

```
SELECT * FROM sys.fulltext_stopwords
WHERE language = 'English'
```

Words in this table are NOT included in the Full Text Index.

	stoplist_id	stopword	language	language_id
41	5	also	English	1033
42	5	an	English	1033
43	5	and	English	1033
44	5	another	English	1033
45	5	any	English	1033
46	5	are	English	1033
47	5	as	English	1033
48	5	at	English	1033

Figure 13.18 The word 'as' appears in the English StopList and, therefore, will not be part of the Full Text Index.

Dropping Stop Words

How do we change it so that "as" is actually included in the index? We need to remove it from the list of stop words. To remove a word from the Stoplist, you must alter the index Stoplist and drop the word 'as' from the English language list, as seen in Figure 13.19.

```
ALTER FULLTEXT STOPLIST StopList_JProCoBook1
DROP 'as' LANGUAGE English;
```

Messages
Command(s) completed successfully.

Figure 13.19 Code to drop the word 'as' from the Stoplist for JProCo.

If this really worked, then Row 47 would no longer contains the word 'as'. Figure 13.20 shows us that "as" is no longer listed as a stop word. Remember you need to query the sys.Fulltext_Stopwords catalog view for your English words. The word "as" is now free to appear in the Full Text index.

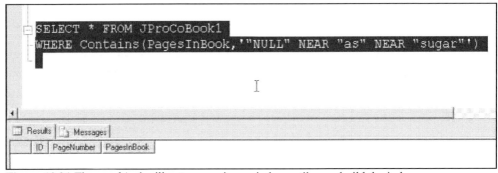

13.20 The word 'As' no longer appears in your Stoplist for English.

You would probably expect that we can see record 18 from the query looking for 'sugar', 'as', and 'null'. Upon running the query, seen in Figure 13.21, we still don't see page 18 in our result set.

```
SELECT * FROM JProCoBook1
WHERE Contains(PagesInBook,'"NULL" NEAR "as" NEAR "sugar"')
```

Figure 13.21 The word 'as' will not appear in our index until we rebuild the index.

The index you are using was created before the stop words were changed. We need to have the index rebuild itself with the new metadata from the stop word list. A quick way to do this is in your Object Explorer. Under JProCo is a folder called Storage, within the Storage folder there is another folder called Full Text Catalogs. In there you see the ft_JProCo full text catalog created in Lab 13.1 of Skill Check 1. You can right-click and choose Rebuild

13.22 To rebuild the index, right-click it in Object Explorer and choose Rebuild.

(Figure 13.22). You will have to confirm this action by clicking the OK button.

Now, when you run the query in Figure 13.23 on the JProCoBook1 table you get one record in your result set. We see [PageNumber] 18 shows up as a record from this query.

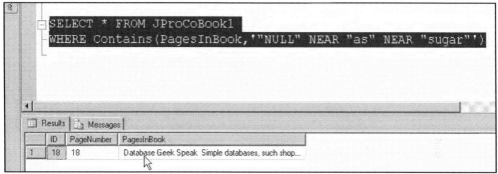

Figure 13.23 Using 'as' in your search now produces results.

Adding Stop Words

You can also customize in the reverse direction by adding stop words. You would do this for any word that you don't want to be part of the Full Text Index. For example, it looks like every single page in the *Beginning SQL Joes 2 Pros* book contains the word SQL.   That seem like a Noise Word because it's everywhere on every page of the book. There is no reason to include that word, since it's so abundant and easy to find. As seen in Figure 13.24, you can Alter the Full Text Stoplist and add a word, such as "SQL".

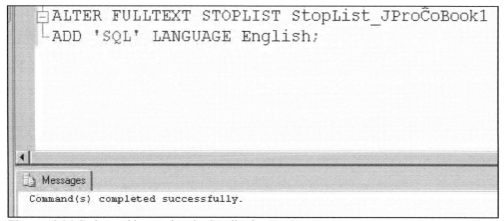

Figure 13.24 Code to add a word to the Stoplist for JProCo.

Rebuild your index to get the updated list of stop words. In Figure 13.25, the query is looking for the word "SQL" and gives us no results.

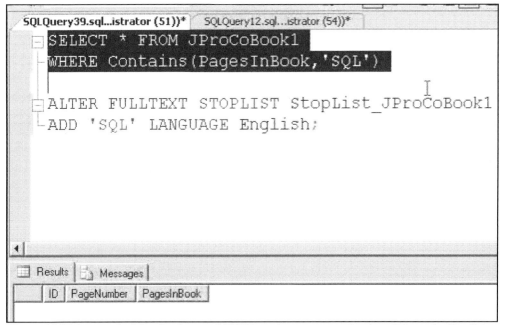

Figure 13.25 A query looking for the word 'SQL' produces no records, since it is on the Stoplist.

Lab 13.2: Stop Words

Lab Prep: Before you can begin the lab, you must have SQL Server installed and run the SQLArchChapter13.2Setup.sql script.

Skill Check 1: Currently 4 of your 20 records in the JProCoBook1 table have the word "Figure" somewhere in the PagesInBook field. Add the word "Figure" to the list of words to ignore in the JProCo database. Rebuild the index and verify that no records are found containing the value "Figure".

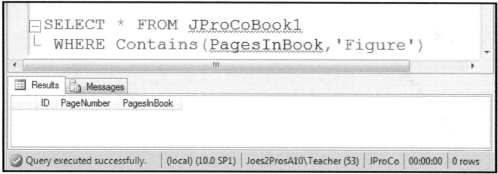

Figure 13.26 Skill Check 1 shows no records indexed for the word 'Figure' for your full text index.

Skill Check 2: In JProCo, remove the word "betweenn" from the Stoplist for English.

Answer Code: The T-SQL code for this lab can be found in the downloadable files in a file named Lab13.2_FullTextStopWords.sql.

Stop Words - Points to Ponder

1. The stop list feature is a performance improvement for full text search because it allows the full text index to skip over common words like "as", "the", and "a".

2. For full text searches, commonly used words can be ignored by using a stop list.

3. For convenience, SQL Server has a system Stoplist with common words for many languages.

4. You can access the current Stoplist words by typing SELECT * FROM sys.fulltext_stopwords.

5. In SQL Server 2005 the Stoplist Words were called noise-words.

6. "Noise Words" are sometimes refered to in other applications as "Stop Words".

7. There are other advanced features of Full Text searches like Word breakers and stemmers that are beyond the scope of this book.

Chapter Glossary

FULLTEXT Index: These are created to query unusual data combinations more easily, such as finding any combination of two words in the data, whatever order.
FULLTEXT Catalog: Full Text catalogs allow you to perform powerful and flexible searches against large text column objects.
FULLTEXT STOPLIST: The stop list contains all your Noise keywords for each language.
Noise Words: Now called "Stop Words"; these are words commonly used, such as "the" or "as".
Stop Words: Previously called "Stop Words"; these are words commonly used, such as "the" or "as" that can be ignored by using STOPLIST.

Chapter Thirteen - Review Quiz

1.) Your company website includes a page that customers use to send feedback about the company and its products. You use a SQL Server 2008 database to store notes in the Comments column of a table named CustFeedback. You need to implement full-text searching so you can run a report on the comments. Assuming you already have a primary key set up, which two actions should you perform next?

 ☐ a. Create a NonClustered index on the Comments column.
 ☐ b. Execute the USE Master T-SQL statement.
 ☐ c. Create a full text catalog.
 ☐ d. Create a full text index on the Comments column.

2.) You have set up full text indexing on your Book1 table. The comments fields have all the text for you to search. You notice that when you run a query that looks for the word "Sugar" near the word "Null" you get three records. You decide to see how many times the word "Sugar" appears next to the word "As". You get no results. You look and see the words "as" and "sugar" in the same line of the comment fields. What should you do next, to solve this problem?

 O a. Create a second Full Text Index on the same table
 O b. Drop and re-create the Full Text index
 O c. Drop "as" from the StopList
 O d. Add "as" to the StopList

3.) You want to configure a full-text search to ignore the words "level" and "Expert". Which full text component should you use?

 O a. Filter
 O b. Stoplist
 O c. Word breakers
 O d. Near

4.) You want to create a Full Text Index on your dbo.Applications table in the JProCo database. What two things must be done first? (Choose 2)

 ☐ a. You must have a primary key or Unique Constraint on the dbo.Applications table.
 ☐ b. You must have a clustered Index on the abo.Applications table.
 ☐ c. Database advanced options in JProCo must be set to 1.
 ☐ d. You must have a Full Text Catalog created in JProCo.

5.) Stop Words in SQL Server 2008 are sometime known as what?

O a. Noise Words
O b. Stealth Words
O c. Halt Word
O d. Common Words

6.) You have updated your Full Text Index to remove the "as" keyword from the StopList of your Book1 table. You still get no results from your CONTAINS predicate that is looking for "as". You verify several records should be produced. *What should you try next?*

O a. Rebuild the Full Text Catalog.
O b. Refresh the sys.fulltext_stopwords catalog view.
O c. Drop and Re-create the Full Text Index.
O d. Re-index the primary key of the Book1 table.

Answer Key

1.) c, d 2.) c   3.) b   4.) a, d 5.) a   6.) a

Bug Catcher Game

To play the Bug Catcher game, run BugCatcher_Chapter13FullTextIndexing.pps from the BugCatcher folder of the companion files. You can obtain these files from www.Joes2Pros.com or by ordering the Companion CD.

Index

H

Heap, 268-269, 282-284, **286,** 292, 391-395, 416
Histogram, 405-411, **420**

I

Identity Fields, 220, 224, 265-269, 283, 343, 394
IGNORE_DUP_KEY, 309, **310**
INCLUDE, 310
Included Columns 297-301
Index Defragmentation, 380-384, 398-399
Index Fragmentation, 38, **245,** 372-377, 380-384, 398-399
Index Options, 286-**310**
Index Scan, 270-**283**, 304, 319, 337, 343
Index Seek, 270-**283**, **337, 343**

L

Large Object Type (LOB), 108, 110, 124
Large Value Data Types, 108-126, 130
Large Value Types Out of Row, 114, 117, 123-124
Logfile, 18-43, 53

M

MAX Data Types, 100-115, 123, 124
Memory page, 108-112, 123, **124,** 130-131, 163, 255-262, 268, 283, 370-372
Metadata, 26, **53,** 75-76, 151, 219, 339, 343, 364, 377, 385, 390, 395-398, 405, 415, 435
Multiple Datafiles Placement, 29-31, **53**

N

Naming convention, 24, 40-41, 56-64, 87, 186, 200
Natural sort order, 258, **283**
NextUsedFileGroup, 235, 238-239, **252**
Nonclustered Index, 254-422
Nonunique Nonclustered Index, 277, **283**
NULL Bitmap, 101, 107, **124,** 129, 134
NULL Block, 101-104, 106, 107, 109-119, **124,** 129-135

O

OBJECTPROPERTY, 391, 392, 398
Objects, 14, 28-29, 32, 50, 53, 61, 64, **66**, 78, 82, **86,** 246-252, 343, 364, 429, 439
OGC, 186, 200, **201**
OLAP, 42, **310**
OLTP, 42, 292, **310**
ONLINE Option, 301, 302, **310**
Optimize For, 333, 337, **364**
Optimize For Unkown, 337
OPTION FOR, 332-333, 337, **364**

P

$Partition, 221, 222, 227, 228
Page Splits, 260-269, **283,** 394
Parameter sniffing 337
Partially qualified names, 66, 87
Partition function, 209-219, 224-252, 413-414
Partition scheme, 210-213, 219-228, 231 238, 246-252, 414-415, 419
Partition table, 204-252, 412-420
Partitioned view, 208, **228**
Point-static function, 171, 183, **201**
Polygon, 167, 175-181, 186, 188-191, 200-201
Primary filegroup, 32-42, 52, 221-252, 413-414
Primary key, 258, 261, 267-268, 282-**283**, 287, 292, 313, 410, 426-429, 440

Q

Qualified query, 64, 87
Query execution plan, 273-280, **283**, 299, 304-305, 318-337, 364, 385-388, 397, 410, 418-419, 421
Query hint, 327-329, 333, 337, **364**-365
Query Optimizer, 318-324, 327- 333, 337-338, **364,** 385, 402-410, 420-421

R

REBUILD, 264, 266, 269, 380-384, **398**, 435-438
REORGANIZE, 380-384, **398**
Row header, 91, 100-101, 107, 109, 113, 118, **124,** 129, 134

14775372R00237

Made in the USA
Charleston, SC
30 September 2012